Assassin's Gift

Karlene Tura Clark

Cover Artist: Raimey Launore

ISBN: 9781081526078

DEDICATION

Romona Crowell, mom, this was the only manuscript you ever saw me complete. You were the first to believe in me, the first to push me to “do something” with my writing, and to always be creative. I miss you.

ACKNOWLEDGMENTS

Jolene Wee, Aern was the last of the family when we "invented" the Bradleys over 30 years ago. Thank you for encouraging me to add "just one more" to the storytelling. I hope you like where I took the family!

Norman Clark, thank you for editing the final draft and for being a part of my family. I'm lucky to have you in my life.

Terry Clark. Can I keep you? I want you to keep me. Love you forever and always.

Kami Jo (Baxter) Myles, I know. You've been waiting ten years for me to get around to this. Thank you for pushing me (and pushing me, aaaand pushing me!) to get around to publishing this story. Your belief in my writing has kept me inspired.

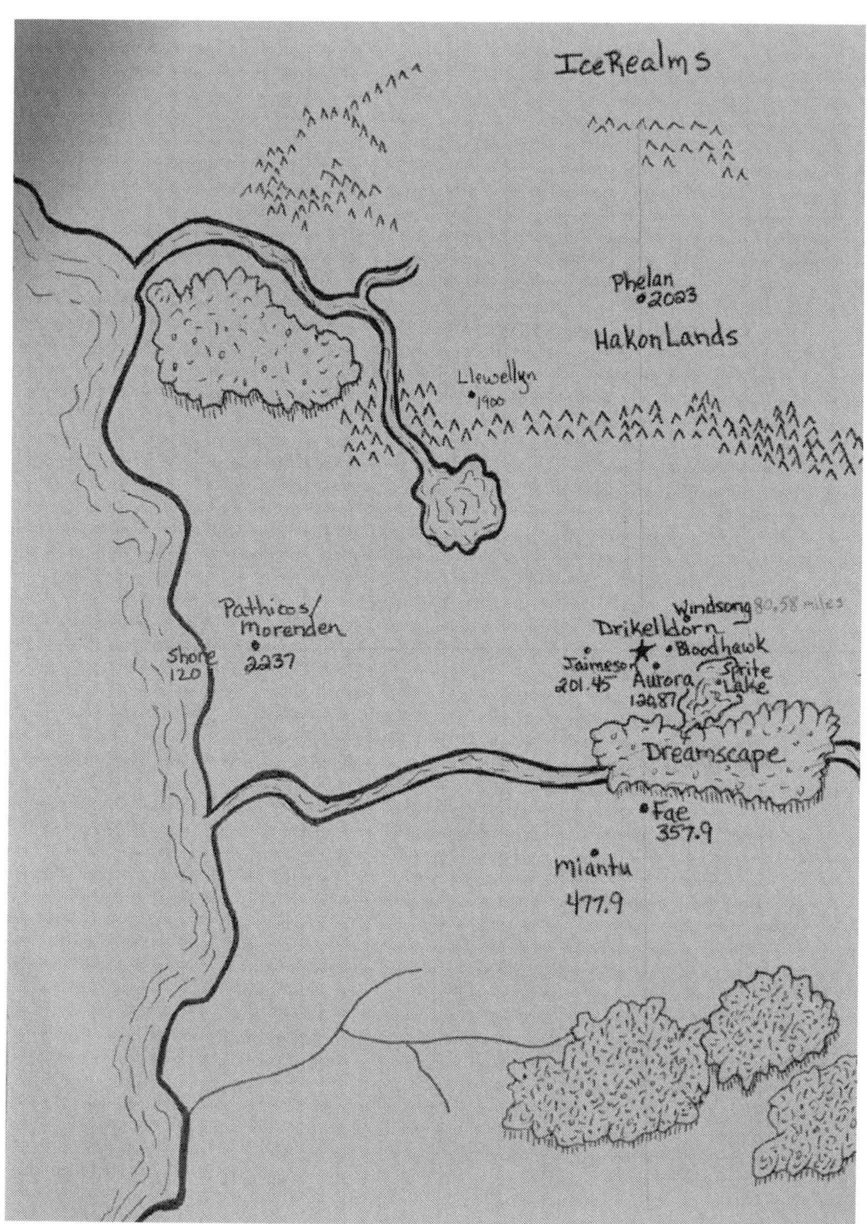
IceRealms
Phelan
2023
HakonLands
Llewellyn
1900
Pathicos/
morenden
2237
Shore
120
Windsong 80.58 miles
Drikelldorn
Bloodhawk
Jaimeso
201.45
Aurora
12087
Sprite
Lake
Dreamscape
Fae
357.9
miantu
477.9

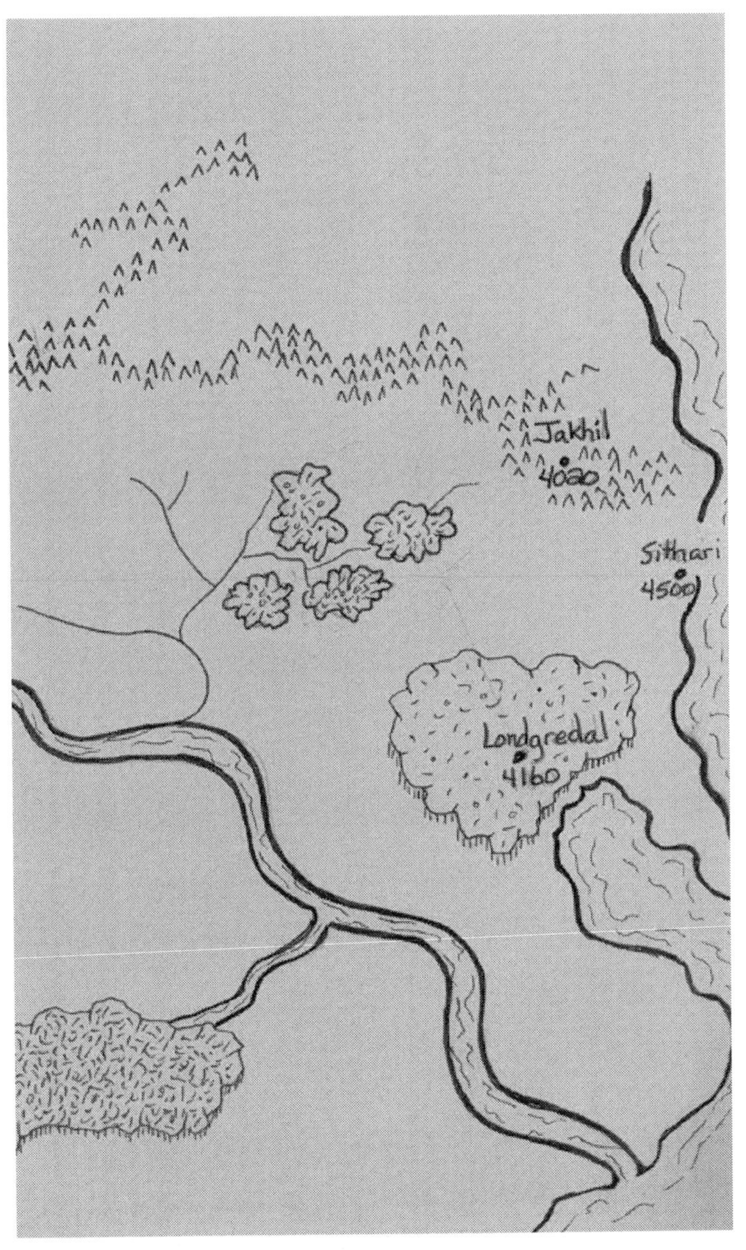
Jakhil
4020
Sithari
4500
Londgredal
4160

PROLOGUE

On a dare, much like any typical eight year old might, Aern took the proffered sweet. The older boys were sniggering as they handed it to him, making him wonder what was wrong with it. It looked okay. The flavor was much like a fresh berry; almost, but not quite. The flavor soon changed, carrying a subtle undertone of bitterness and dirt. *Odd*, Aern thought, *dirt*?

His chest constricted, his heart beating faster. Short of breath, he felt as if he were doing strenuous training rather than standing perfectly still. He looked to the older boy in fear as his throat started to constrict, as if a large hand were strangling him. Everything started to blur, his vision faded and went to black as he lost consciousness.

At some point, he was aware that he shivered, that he felt ice cold. A warm body, covered in fur and feathers, settled closer to him. He drifted back into oblivion. When next he woke, it was to the shifting of the cat-like body around him. A large beak pushed at his shoulder, a soft chirring sound coming from the animal. Blinking, trying to clear his blurred vision, he saw the large visage of a bird cock its head, beak parting slowly as if it smiled at him, voicing a happy chirrup. His eyes rolled back in his head as darkness again swam into place. It was a dream; nothing but a very odd dream.

He heard voices. It sounded like they were leagues away.

They slowly got louder, but the words were still garbled, senseless to him; something about someone being lucky. Who? Why? He tried to open his eyes but he couldn't. He couldn't move, talk…there was nothing. It was as if his body was dead.

A large meaty hand cradled the back of his head, lifting it slightly off the ground. Dizziness swirled around him, making him squeeze his eyes more tightly shut. It didn't help. Whoever was with him put their other hand around his mouth, a thumb and finger pushing into each side of his jaw, forcing his mouth open. Something bitter was poured in. Aern could taste it on his tongue, but couldn't quite remember what he was supposed to do about it. The hand moved to his throat, massaging and urging him to swallow. The liquid slid down his parched throat, cool as the morning dew. The bitter taste faded from his mouth, as did the taste of dirt.

"At least he's not dead, milord." The voice was familiar, coming from someone sitting next to him.

"Bless the Lights for that, you idiot." A man's gruff voice barked. "What were you thinking, leaving your mixtures about?" From the tone of the lord's voice, the other had made a grave error in his judgment. "Remedial lessons, boy: he dies, and your life will be forfeit as well. You know the rules. Any errors are your sole responsibility."

A violent tremor shook Aern as a coughing jag swept the entire frame of his eight year old body. He was turned to his side, just barely in time as everything in his stomach rushed out. He could barely catch a breath as wave after wave of retching emptied everything back out. It gurgled from his throat, bubbling as it left him to spray outward, running down his cheek, into his black hair.

Pulling his knees up, Aern tried to relieve the intense cramping in his stomach. As the fit finally passed, Aern opened his pale blue eyes and looked around. His vision was still hazy, but he could see the boy that had given him the treat.

Tylel was a few years older than Aern and had the honor of being in "special" training of some kind. Aern didn't know what it was, but he knew Tylel was one of the squires that received privileges set aside only for those in the same studies. Too bad the attitude came with it. Aern looked up at the twelve year old standing with his arms crossed, shifting his weight constantly back and forth. His eyes darted to the man in charge, but kept coming back to glare at Aern, warning him to keep his mouth shut. Fear prickled down the back of Aern's neck.

That would have been bad enough, but Lord Morenden, the most feared of the task-masters at the keep, now sat at his side. The man was bigger than most of the adults and was built like a bull. No one crossed him.

Aern forgot about how sick he'd just been, not even thinking about the vomit covering him. Even though he'd never met him in person before, Aern was terrified of him. All of the squires spoke about how this man was involved in secret work for the lord of the manor. There were even whispers that Lord Morenden had killed people for fun. Looking at the anger on his face now, Aern figured that he could be excused, considering even the trained fighters feared him, for being so afraid he was ready to wet himself before the man. He didn't realize he'd already let loose in that way.

"Congratulations on surviving your first poisoning, my prince." Morenden smiled coolly down at him, his voice equally cool. "And pray tell," he asked in too polite of a tone, "what possessed you to be so foolish? The dose you ingested has killed many a man. By rights, boy, you should have died as well."

Looking to the other boy, receiving a warning shake of the head and narrowed eyes, Aern considered his options. He had thought the older boy was going to be nice to him by giving him a treat. But it seemed now that the boy knew what he had been doing. Aern had heard Lord Morenden make some comment about potions left lying around, but that wasn't the truth. The boy had lied. Now Aern had to decide whether to play along with that. Were he to tattle, he'd surely pay at the hands of Tylel. If he didn't say anything, it left him free to do it again. The boy's shoulders came up and his hands balling into fists behind Lord Morenden. One corner of his mouth came up in a challenging sneer.

"Well," Morenden's voice penetrated his thoughts. "I'm waiting for an answer."

He only had one year of martial training. Tylel had five. "I was curious." The flat tone of his voice belied his words. He hated; for the first time in his young life he felt that emotion stir; felt anger at what the other was getting away with. It wasn't fair; and worse: there was nothing he could do about it.

"Curious???" Exasperation tinged Morenden's voice. "You need to be punished for this, but honestly," he sighed heavily, thoroughly vexed with the young charges, "I'm at a loss. You've barely escaped death." He looked to Aern with calculating assessment. "Perhaps, being you think poisons such fun, I should put you in training for it," he threatened. "It would soon get those fanciful notions out of your head."

Poisons! His heart leapt in excitement as thoughts of his future suddenly loomed before him. He wouldn't be a common warrior. He wouldn't be a worthless extra to the throne, instead having a daring role to fill. He would be a lone assassin, moving through the shadows, doing away with cruel villainy…

"What say you, boy?" Morenden's voice was impatient. He frowned behind his carefully manicured beard. "Is your mind still addled?"

Aern slowly sat up. "I would be honored if you would allow me the privilege."

Lord Morenden snorted in humor. "Don't know if you'll keep that mind-set once we start." He gave Aern a curt nod. "Daylight tomorrow, enter the restricted area. We'll see what you're truly made of then." With a swift turn, both Lord Morenden and his apprentice departed, leaving Aern alone in the gardens.

Aern carefully rose to his feet, waiting for the dizziness to pass again. He focused on the different things around him as he thought. Who would have imagined that he, third in line to the throne, would ever train as an assassin? A rare smile touched his mouth.

He looked to the dark leaves of the plum trees, the bright pink of the cherry blossoms and the deep navy blue of the trees that held his favorite tart fruit. The camel colored grasses around him were stained a strange black with the mess that had come back up from him. He wasn't in the least wanting to even think about eating a riitziah. The thought of any food right now made his stomach roll again. All he wanted was to go clean up.

As he got to his feet, a low sound, part chirring, part growl, came from behind as something butted softly against him. He turned to see the face from his dreams: a bright yellow-gold beak, dark skin below tufted white feathers, amber eyes in a head that cocked to one side in jerking motions, taking in Aern's appearance. "Chrrt."

He put a hand out, slowly moving towards the head. "Oh, hello."

The beautiful head pulled back, beak opening slightly, a low hiss coming from it; an instinctive warning. The wings mantled as the feathers on its head rose.

"Heyo." Aern put his hands up in supplication as it shook the large head feathers, making them swish and flow around the elegant face. "It's fine." He took a step back, only then noticing that this was no bird. The long, soft feathers went from white near the eyes into a soft butter yellow as they went up over the head and down its neck into wings. They went no further back than the front shoulders and partially down the front-taloned legs of a great bird. They faded into a honey-colored pelt covering a large cat's haunches. "Oh!" The admiration of the sigh carried across the distance between them.

The beautiful creature seemed to understand as its head came up in pride. "Rrrt," sounded as a low rumble from its throat, almost carrying a question to it. When he didn't respond, it dropped down, lying on its side, bumping its head under his hand.

He dropped to his knees, forgetting that he was covered in vomit and that his pants were wet as he sat back on his heels, tentatively reaching again to touch the white feathers at her neck. She swiveled her head, watching for signs of danger, but was no longer displaying that she would bite him. Surely, a single snap of that beak would easily take his arm off. Carefully, he allowed his fingers to curl into the softness. "You're beautiful," he spoke quietly, almost reverently to her.

It was hard to leave her, but he had to get cleaned up. "Sorry," he muttered, "I smell."

Something akin to a laugh sounded from her as she butt her head against his side, seeming to push him in the direction of the keep. He left the gardens, looking back several times at her as if she were a dream he had imagined while he was sick.

Back in the room he shared with seven other squires, he was almost convinced she had been a dream. The stark reality of his training rolled over him as he looked at the sparse room. Simple wooden beds held fresh straw mattresses and a warm quilt lay folded at the bottom of each. A chest of weathered wood rested at the end of each, holding all their personal clothing. The stone walls were bare, not even holding tapestries to keep the cold out.

Not that it was ever truly cold. The lands Aern was born to and now trained in were temperate; warm during the day and cool at night. The grass stayed a honeyed camel color year round and trees and flowers bloomed throughout. But none of that color was in this room. This room was like every other room that squires lived in: practical. And gray.

When he took his turn serving in the great hall, he could see bright tapestries, fine linens and tableware in high quality. He knew that he was supposed to be learning humility and an attitude of service by being a squire, but all he felt he was learning was how to be lonely. He didn't have any friends here because they knew his true rank in society, and he didn't feel any connection to family so far away from him.

Even after a cold bath and clean clothes, he kept thinking about her. What if she had been only in his head? No one else had seen her. He had to know for sure. His stomach was still in knots and he didn't feel like going to dance lessons with it. Instead, he went back outside to find her. "Here girl!" he whispered loudly as he crept around the garden. He wrinkled his nose as he came across the area it had happened. It still smelled horrible. "Here girl!"

A soft rumble came from within the trees just before her head peered around a riitziah tree. She was real! She stepped out with more grace than a creature built like that should be able to, coming to stand eye to eye with him. "Rrrt!" She danced back and forth in excitement, almost tripping over her own feet as her long tail swished happily behind her.

Aern realized then that as big as she appeared to him, she was still a baby. She couldn't be very old, she was different, and he loved her. It felt great to know there was another loner out there like he was. Aern may be a noble like the other boys training here, but he was third in line to a throne, something that set him apart from the others. To make things harder, he wasn't the golden prince everyone imagined he should be. He was dark haired with eyes too clear of a blue and a height too short.

If he were in Drikelldorn, where he was born, he wouldn't even fit in with his brothers and sisters there. The crown princes, Aern's older twin brothers, were fair in hair and face, like their father. That he might have been able to adapt to if they had even liked him. None of them had been in touch with him in the whole past year he'd been away at training.

But it didn't matter anymore. It didn't bother him that he was missing his lessons, forgot that his stomach still twisted and his head pounded. He didn't care what she was or where she'd come from. He finally had a friend. And it seemed that the longer he spent with her, the better he felt.

With careful movements, he tested what she wouldn't tolerate. In his youthful excitement, it never crossed his mind that she could easily kill him.

Coming up behind her without making noise wasn't a good idea. She snapped at that, but was fine if he even simply clicked his tongue first. Anything near her eyes was a definite no-no. That would get her to clamp down gently on his arm while growling. Aern could feel the strength she was holding in check while she immobilized his arm. A little more pressure and his arm would have been broken.

But then there were the things she obviously enjoyed. A good scritch in her neck feathers produced the strange happy chrr he was already crazy about. She loved to run with him. They raced back and forth across the gardens, her head bobbing in time to her gait, her wings pumping with each stride she made. Aern had to laugh, seeing all that work and she never once left the ground. When they tired of running, they would weave in and out of the trees. Aern would try to hide, but it soon became apparent that she was an excellent tracker.

Sneaking into the kitchens, Aern took a chicken, several slices of venison, a rabbit, and a handful of vegetables to see what she would eat. Almost everything was snapped down quickly, but any time he presented meat (especially the rabbit!) to her, she would do that same silly little dance step, bouncing back and forth with her beak wide open, waiting to catch it whenever he was ready to toss it upwards.

"You need a name," he told her much later that day. The shadows were lengthening and both boy and beast were exhausted. They lay in the cool of the trees, Aern resting against her side. He was playing with the tuft of fur on the tip of her tail while she beaked at his hair, preening him.

"Chhrrrt?" She cocked her head, looking at him with one large eye.

He laughed, reaching to scratch deep in her neck feathers. "Sounds good to me. How does Chirrit sound to you?" She gave another rumbling sound, returning to preening his hair. He took that as agreement. "Chirrit it is then!"

Things were starting to look up for him! She was something like a pet of his very own, and soon he'd be starting a whole new adventure in his training.

The next day he bounded out of bed, excited to start his new life. Throwing back the plain cotton sheets, he pattered across the cold stone floor to his chest, dressing quickly. He would be learning something no one else in the family would! He would learn to have a life of mystery and adventure, girls and tales – all about him! He dressed in his usual attire for lessons: simple black pants of brushed suede under a silken tunic in the royal color of turquoise blue, his family's color.

With a bounce in his step, he bypassed the usual language lesson he would have been attending to move towards a door at the far end of the keep. Pressing with all the force his young body possessed, he finally made the heavy iron door slide open enough for him to slip inside. A wide hallway met him, clean and dry, but with no rugs or true decoration. His steps started to slow. Instead of tapestries, the walls were now lined with weapons of all sorts.

Crossed swords were first on either side, then a murder hole. He could see several of these arrow slits along the corridor, breaking up the pattern of weapons and wall sconces. Whips, axes and spears all filled in space between.

There were a few doors along the hall, but all were closed. The noise all came from the door at the far end, a simple wooden door with a plaque at its side bearing naught more than two small daggers, crossed in the shape of an X.

He was still waiting for the dark, mysterious, dungeon feel he had thought would go with this type of thing. Instead, he opened the door into a huge room, light and airy. Plants sat all along one wall, on tables near the windows. It would be some time before he would learn how to use the components of the plants to create poisons from them. The opposite wall housed bottles – empty bottles sparkling from shelves, throwing rainbows back at the sunlight, full bottles of many colored liquids, some dark and thick as mud, others the shade of clear jewels.

Smirks and hostility met him as all wondered at the young prince in his silken finery. He felt at odds with the others in their simple jerkins of wool and linen, so unlike the nobility he had trained with only two days past.

He was given little time to contemplate this before Lord Morenden arrived, all dark looks and frowns. The others in the room turned from Aern to start clearing things out of the middle of the room. As rugs were rolled back, stains became visible on the floor. Dried blood, for sure, and fluids of unknown sources… the seriousness of this situation suddenly hit Aern. This wasn't going to be fun and games. This was fighting, torture, murder. The stains were testimony to some amount of pain and bleeding that had – and would – take place in this very room.

Some of the pain would come from blades, as he soon saw with the other students. Some paired off to fight with daggers, seeming to know from the look Morenden gave them that this was their task for the day. Others went to the tables with the pretty bottles, working on mixing and measuring things into them. Still others went to a group of tables and opened books.

Feeling quite out of place, he simply stood there, waiting for some word or sign as to what he was supposed to do. He would be in for weeks of this; showing up only to stand apart. His clothing and speech set him apart from the others, their hostilities widening the gap.

He found that there was a second sort of language that ran as an undercurrent, directing the students with gestures and small noises. His enthusiasm waned a bit under the lack of excitement in the room. Order and discipline were everything once the doors closed behind Lord Morenden. Exacting behaviors ruled in the serious manners displayed by everyone. There was no showmanship, no trying to get others into trouble as there had been in his previous lessons. There was no friendship, no casual discussions. There was only success… or failure.

Chapter 1

Auburn hair and reddish brown eyes marked the young man as a Fire User. The most temperamental of the elemental magics to start with, this boy had yet again smarted off to the Mage training him. Bricriu MacFurgal had been nothing but trouble since starting; worse, he promised to only bring more in the coming years. The older mage sighed, wishing for about the millionth time that this boy was more like his elder brother. Doran had been such a pleasure to train. Doran had understood that it had been a privilege, considering the family's past, to be able to train his magic. It was something Bricriu just didn't seem to understand.

If it weren't for the fact that so few Fire users made it through their training, they'd have let the boy burn himself out early on. "Focus!" he snapped at the impertinent brat yet again. If he spent anymore time fooling around, MacFurgal was going to be reported to the Keltori as worthless. He had already been complained about numerous times.

Hateful eyes turned to the older mage. The only reason he stayed with the farcical training was because the man who had raised him had said it was necessary to play their game. He may have to follow some of their rules, but Bricriu wasn't going to let some impotent Air mage tell him he was doing things wrong.

There were four ranks to magic users. Apprentice was the lowest, the beginning stage. The next was Journeyman, something Bricriu had been at twice before. Twice he had been demoted back to Apprentice for assumed slights in his behavior. Attaining Mage was the level everyone wanted. It meant training had been completed and the mage could take apprentices of his own. Training meant long years of working with a mage in each of the Elements, proving capability in weaving them into the mage's own Element, or showing that they could work in tandem alongside that other Element.

The final rank was Adept. Very few ever attained this level. These were the best of the best… supposedly. Bricriu had his doubts about that though. Things weren't done in the old ways anymore and it showed in the choice of Adepts that sat on the Keltori.

Goldwin, the man training Bricriu, sat on that council. That alone proved to Bricriu that he was right. He knew he was already more powerful than Adept Goldwin; more worthy of a title greater than Apprentice.

By the abyss, his future wife had even been picked out for him already! There were plenty of farmers and stupid cows of women that populated the land, but a mage only married the daughter of a mage, or took them for mistresses. It was the only purpose of a daughter. She was to marry a mage of her father's Element, to produce more magic users of that type.

There was, at the moment, only one other Fire family. That meant that like his brother, he'd marry one of Llewellyn's get. It didn't matter which one. They were all nothing more than eye candy, anyway; a means to an end. All he had to do was manage his training with Adept Goldwin, the Air Mage, and he would be one step closer to training with the Fire Adept. Or; or he could simply do away with this damn fool and prove he was better than a lowly apprentice.

A fireball formed in his hands, causing panic from other apprentices. He watched the fear form in the mage's eyes. With a sneer at the weakness shown, he hurled the fireball at the stupid man. It roared across the intervening space, scorching the grass and training field. He waited with glee for it to reach the old one, waited for him to be consumed by an element not his own. It would only prove Bricriu's reasoning that the Adept had been given his post, not earned it.

It was to his horror that a shield of Air formed around the mage, a bubble of protection. One of the higher ranking students ran closer, the Earth rising where he stretched his hand to move in a tidal wave over the fireball, engulfing it, smothering it before it could breach the mage's shield. "No!!!" Bricriu shrieked in fury.

He wasn't more than a few steps forward when two Apprentices, stupid fools unworthy of their station, grabbed his arms. Air pressure, more than physical strength, detained him.

Bricriu would kill them both if given the chance. He fought for all he was worth to try to break free of their magic containments. By the Lights, he had been a Journeyman! Neither Raven nor Griffon had progressed beyond Apprentice. It shouldn't be so hard to get free of their pathetic spells. Fire should counter the worthless Air spells… and yet the containments only constricted him further with each attempt.

The day dragged by as he sat with the two in a holding room. His captors were brought meals, which they barely consumed, while he was given nothing. The two of them remained focused on the containment spells. Bricriu's only pleasure during that time was seeing the struggle begin in the two apprentices to keep their wardings up on him as he fought them; if it could even be called fighting. He was just periodically checking for weaknesses. That alone should prove he was more worthy. He didn't tire at all; not like they were: pale from the strain and hair matted down with sweat.

He smirked to himself, considering how superior he was that it took two apprentices to keep one like him immobilized. If he could just find the weak spot, he would be free and would make those two suffer for interfering with him.

Just before even-tide, Adept Goldwin opened the door, motioning for them to follow him. They went back outdoors, into a carriage. It was hot and stuffy; worse because all four seats were taken and the window-flaps were tied tightly down so he couldn't see their destination.

He hated carriages. They jolted and bounced you around on hard, uncomfortable seats, and you had to allow some driver, some non-magical person, to decide your course for you.

With the two apprentices still controlling their spells, Goldwin took them all to the Phelan's, leaving the young men in the front room. Phelan was the head of the Keltori, the Earth Adept that had founded this new order of doing things. He believed that might wasn't always right, that justice could be found through a trial by the Adepts that sat on the council. He had developed a "peace" in these northern lands that had never been before. By creating a council consisting of an Adept in each of the four elements, he had given them all a place to bring concerns that were fairly dealt with, or so it was said.

Bricriu disagreed. He wasn't about to believe the old fools on the Keltori were anything but selfish. Why else would anyone set themselves apart? Some day it would be Bricriu in charge, if he could only get out of this situation. He would be THE MacFurgal, a man worth fearing and respecting. The Phelan, while respected by most for bringing all the warring clans together into some sort of peace, wasn't someone Bricriu looked up to. The Phelan had allowed too many of their old ways to go by the wayside.

After his parents' death, he had been taken in by Mage Remington. Remington had assumed his own title of Mage when the council had declared him a non-focused magic user. He didn't fit any of the four Elements, yet Bricriu had seen plenty of powerful magic from the man. He had explained to Bricriu that the old ways had been that those with enough magic would destroy the others of their Element so they could control it. Remington had told Bricriu all about how the clans used to fight and how only the strongest survived. The mages had ruled with an iron fist over the lands, those that tended the land lived in fear of what the mages could do if they weren't kept appeased.

When Adept Phelan came along, he chose a small council to sit with him, joining the four elemental magicks into a cohesive group, uniting all the lands under a common banner. What, Bricriu had to wonder, was the good of that? There was nothing for the masses to strive towards now. The common folk no longer felt an obligation to appease the mages. When he was able to destroy the Phelan, he would someday put it back to the proper way, where farmers would give offerings of crops and women to keep the mages happy. That was the way it should be done.

Taken inside, he again had to wait; this time it was on the "leisure of Adept Phelan." Proof enough in Bricriu's mind that there was no fairness to this newer system. His parents had worked with an unknown other to set up a powerful leadership. They had ruled the farming folk as they should be, and they had taken as needed. They had tried to convince others to leave the Keltori's watchful eye and take back what was theirs. That had led to nothing but their deaths. Bricriu hated the Keltori. He and his brother had watched his parents destroyed by these self-proclaimed leaders of their land.

As the sun began its descent, nervousness never once entered his mind. Only anger. His powers flared, getting no further reaction than to be absorbed by the Air shield that surrounded him yet, binding his movements. At least he had the small measure of glee in seeing the two grow more and more strained and weary as he pushed the limits of their skill in holding the shield. And then it was time. He hadn't seen the Adepts enter the room; hadn't seen the Phelan call his Keltori.

But as he was forced, bound and fighting, before the Keltori, they were all present. Although Adept Llewellyn was speaking, Bricriu couldn't hear him from within the air-tight bondage he was being contained in.

"I told you," Llewellyn said, "that the boy would be trouble. But no, you wanted him trained." He folded his arms, refusing to take a seat at the council table.

"We're no better than wild animals if we destroy indiscriminately," Adept Shanahan interjected. "We formed this council to better ourselves and our lands."

"Hmph." Llewellyn dropped into his seat as Phelan gave him a pointed look. "Fruit didn't fall far from the tree," he griped.

"We've only got so many Fire potentials out there, Llewellyn." The Water Adept leaned forward in his seat. "You know as well as we do that we need every one of them if we want the Element to continue with mages."

"I'd rather," Llewellyn grumped, "let Doran take all of my other daughters as mistresses than to give one to that lump of turds."

Phelan remained quiet in his seat at the head of the table. He could speak as an Adept here at the table, if needed, but it was better that one person merely listen to the arguments, making him better able to pass judgment when the arguments ceased. Both ears on the conversation, he kept his eyes on the boy. It was like looking at the boy's older brother. Both were of plain, solid features. Broad shoulders, strength, were topped by straight brown hair. But where Doran had been as calm as a Fire Child could be, Bricriu was nothing but pure anger.

They had wanted to destroy the entire family when they had needed to destroy the father. Some had argued that there was still potential in the younglings, which this one's brother had proven. Doran had become an excellent Fire Mage, albeit not the strongest.

Bricriu on the other hand… this boy was a problem. He had been angry at what he thought was a slight on his family; had refused to see that his father had been working against what was right for these lands, had refused to see that the mother needed to go as well, being an extension of her husband's beliefs.

No one had wanted to take Bricriu. Doran on the other hand had understood that change sometimes came with a catalyst of pain; knew that for things to get better, there would be a time of loss. When it had been explained, he had realized that his parents had been trying to destroy a way of life. It was better that two died than for untold numbers of both mages and non-mages as had been done for years before. Doran had graciously moved forward, becoming the kind of mage Llewellyn had been happy to mate to one of his daughters. But Bricriu…

He sighed. The only one who had been willing to take young Bricriu had been a renegade himself. Perhaps they shouldn't have given him into Remington's care, but there had been little choice. No one wanted the untried mageling of a traitor in their homes. None but Remington.

And now that Phelan thought on it, Remington had been a little too quick to volunteer to take the boy. He stroked his chin with the back of one hand, wondering what kind of initial training had been given to Bricriu. What could have made the boy into such an angry thing?

"No, no, no!" Llewellyn was wildly motioning with both hands in a negating fashion. "He tried to kill one of us! How much more do we need to tolerate? How long until 'tried to' becomes a truth? I say we strip him of his powers. Send him down to the farms or villages. We don't need something like him in our midst. And really: Remington?" He brought up Phelan's own worries. "We don't even know what Element he commands. He lives outside our boundaries, up in the far hills. He's hiding, waiting to strike. You mark me." He pointed at Phelan, shaking the finger. "Worse than a damn snake!"

A rich laugh came from Air Adept Goldwin. "A snake, hm? Not a salamander?" Despite being the object of Bricriu's outburst, the mage was the embodiment of his Element. Air currents changed, so too did Goldwin's moods. He understood the importance of trying the boy, but he didn't hate the child for simply being a Fire Child. Fire was irrational and combustible. It did no more good to hate the boy than to hate a wild fire.

Llewellyn gave him a dark look. "I wouldn't sully a fire salamander with a comparison to that…that…pile of scat!"

"The truth is, though," the Air Adept stated calmly, "we

need him." Goldwin would have loved to be rid of the trouble that Bricriu presented, but, "Other than Doran, there are *no more* fire mages left."

The fire mage was quiet a long moment before quietly stating, "There's still my son."

He put a hand up before Llewellyn could continue. "You've done your level best, friend, but honestly… one boy and *how* many girls do you have?" He shook his head. "Passion is great, but it isn't serving our magicks. And your boy… anything could happen between now and completing his training. You know as well as the rest of us it's not just getting through the levels. What if he can't pass the test?"

"So break the rules." Llewellyn's voice was level and sincere. "Don't make him wait until then. Let him take a mistress or ten now."

Humored laughter met that, knowing that Fire would find a way, whether it was permitted or not.

"We understand your Fire," Shanahan said, "but the boys won't. They'll only see favoritism to the son of the Keltori."

Llewellyn couldn't argue with that. Looking for another out, he tried appealing to the Phelan. The Earth Adept only smiled and shook his head. There would be no help from that quarter. He looked then to Air and Water. Water alone had said little. Even now, he merely shook his head. "Goldwin…?" He appealed to his old friend.

"I don't want the boy, either," the Adept stated with a sigh.

"Honestly, he tried to kill me! He's not getting back into my house anytime soon, but I don't see that we really have a choice."

Adept Beagan now sat up. Water chose to enter the debate. "He'll eventually come back to you, Goldwin. We can't risk him in a place other than an Adept's."

The four men sat in silence, staring at each other, wanting, wishing an easy answer would come to them. Finally Phelan stood, straightening his tunic. "Beagan's right. We'll need to each take a turn with…"

"I'm not going first!" Goldwin interrupted. "I need time to clean up from this little… temper tantrum first."

Phelan nodded, graciously giving that to him. "I'll take him first."

"At his current rank?!" Llewellyn fumed. "At least drop him down. Lock his powers down until he shows some respect!"

The men shared a single look, nodding to each other only once. In the next moment, they turned to Bricriu, still held inside his sound-proof air bubble. Phelan shook his head once at the boy, then, as one, they all called their magicks, discharging them at Bricriu with a single flick of their wrists.

* * *

He saw the shake of a head and the flick of the wrists that dismissed him.

He! Bricriu MacFurgal! He fought all the harder as he was removed from the council room. Like so much trash, like something as worthless as Llewellyn had seen Bricriu's parents, he too was now removed from the asshole's presence.

Pushed and shoved, he was taken back to the training grounds. Still held in bonds, the bubble of air that had kept him in silence was removed. "MacFurgal," the fire mage declared. "You are hereby stripped of rank…" There was only one rank lower than apprentice. Bricriu hadn't even really counted it as a level of training. Initiates were little better than the farmers that sometimes showed magical skill. It meant he would be starting over again.

He fumed, not hearing the rest of the pretty little speech. How dare they! How *dare* they think to take down another MacFurgal! Llewellyn thought only to keep the Fire gift to his own family. Well, Bricriu wasn't about to let it happen! Maybe Llewellyn had gotten to the rest of Bricriu's family, but he wasn't about to go down so easily; it was time for the Fire mage to burn out. He would die; just as Bricriu's family had been tried falsely and put to death; so Bricriu would see an end to the Llewellyn line, as well.

Put him back to initiate level? They'd pay for this.

Chapter 2

Two years had passed as the slight boy had finally begun to mature. Instead of being the runt, he at ten now stood even with several of the adults; only 5'5", but tall for a ten year old. Aern's large blue eyes had lost some of their innocent wonder, slowly taking on a cold, crystal tone.

He had a better understanding of his land's history, or what had been recorded, at least. His father was known as the Chosen One of the lands they lived in. King Grey alone could open the lands of Drikelldorn, allowing the surrounding peoples to enter. Within those tales, which always earned Aern smirks, were the other tales, the darker stories.

He learned that his father had been married three times before the current queen. The first was never queen, not even a lady; she had been a water sprite. The union wasn't blessed by the Lights and the woman was destroyed… so said the tales. Sprites were known to have short attention spans, to be more playful than anything. He couldn't see the Lights destroying a simple sprite, something that beautiful. Maybe the king had only sent her away. He had no way of knowing, or politely asking his father. But Aern remembered a girl with green-tinged skin that used to hold him and sing to him in a voice that even now, thinking back on it, made him think about water dancing over rocks in a stream.

He had sisters from both that union (which maybe it had been an older sister than had held him?), and from the second woman. She had been a lady but had the added stigma of being believed to be a Jakhil. Jakhil were the elves to the southeast. They were rumored to be beyond striking, like alabaster statues, with emotions as cold as marble. It was of them bedtime tales were told, used to scare small children into behaving. They were known to be selfish and deadly. They took what they wanted, leaving destruction in their wake. For scores of years, they had been denied entrance to the lands of Drikelldorn. Miantu Cats had been the guardians, granted by the Lights, to keep evil such as Jakhil from the lands.

The Miantu were large white predatory cats with ice blue eyes, standing over four feet tall, and growing to more than nine feet in length, not counting their tails. Their intelligence was said to equal that of the elves. Other stories told tales of how they could possibly speak mind to mind with others and that they might once have been elves, choosing to become a more lethal protector until the True King came. They were native only to the center of the lands Aern had been born to, and were seen so rarely as to be called ghosts, yet they had prevented any unwelcome leaders from stepping forward. They had killed any entering their area, until Aern's father had come along.

Aern vaguely remembered one of these cats often in the palace. When he thought of times he had seen it, it had always been at his father's side. But the cat didn't sit in court with the king, so few others saw it. No one believed Aern that they weren't ghosts or that one lived in the palace.

King Grey had been handed so many things on a seemingly silver platter. There was no explanation in Aern's classes on where the castle had come from or how awareness of his father's presence had been spread through the lands. Only that one day no one knew of him; the next it seemed all the lands were aware. The lands and the peoples in them were just suddenly conscious of the interior of the continent now being "safe" to travel within.

Then (and Aern hated the looks the others gave him at this point) King Grey had invited his lady to enter his lands. Along with that invitation had been the opening for all those related to her. ALL Jakhil were granted permission… all because of lust.

What happened to her was a mystery to those that taught the small assassins. There was speculation as to her death, or to the idea that she yet lived, planning to take back what she considered hers. Aern didn't know or really care either way, so long as he wasn't labeled a traitor the way the Jakhil were.

Then there was the third woman, one of delicate beauty with gossamer wings. Tales said she had swept through the castle as ethereal as smoke, her wings folded down the length of her back like a shimmering cloak. Long blonde hair had cascaded over the top of them, ending in perfect curls that accentuated the patterns on her wings. This faery, too, disappeared after a time. There was no record but that she hadn't "fit" well at the castle.

"I just hope she's okay," he worried aloud to Chirrit, as he brushed her. But it wasn't about this faery he spoke. His mother was the current queen. His young mind understood enough that if three had already disappeared, it was likely his mother would be next. "She should be. She wouldn't have had my brothers if she wasn't the One, right?" Chirrit beaked at Aern's hair, not understanding, but sensing the worry in her "pet." She did what she could to put him at ease.

That wasn't an easy thing, considering that he wasn't like most ten year olds. He understood a great deal more than he was given credit for, and he had better skills with weapons than most. Also unlike most boys his age, he knew what a real blade felt like. He didn't "wrestle" for fun, like many others at the keep. His work was limited, instead, to those others also within the "secret" chamber. They learned more than simple hand to hand maneuvers. They were learning how to get out of situations, get loose from holds, and how to find a weapon when none were present. He knew how to best break just about any piece of furniture or glass in order to turn it into a killing weapon.

He excelled at any of the lessons presented, yet wondered how some of the others couldn't. He heard and saw how the older kids were turned from their focus. Many left the training with Lord Morenden after a certain age, returning to the regular part of the keep. He saw them at times, but what had happened to take them away from this was something never discussed. It only made him work harder to prove he was worth keeping in the training.

There were letters from home for others that got them excited or sad, visits from relations that set their studies aside, but not for Aern. Roughly once every few months, a courier would arrive to personally deliver a stipend of gold and clothing to him, but no word came. If it weren't for the gold, he could have thought he had been forgotten. The others went home for holidays, but not Aern. There were no notes to ask how he did, no special gifts, and no invitations to return for anything.

Aern learned that he didn't need them. He depended on himself, even if sometimes, in the deepest dark of the night, he would cry in loneliness for his mom. He would remind himself that the dawn would come soon, it always did; that the loneliness would leave; it always did.

But more than all those things, they were learning to ingest things that others couldn't even tolerate in small doses. Poisons: the whole reason he had wanted to see the other side of that door in the first place. Even more than being a daring assassin, he would be able to protect his family.

With two years of study and only one year of training in the art of subterfuge and he understood this. A very worldly eleven year old took his only comfort from a juvenile gryphon, depending on her warmth and comfort to get him through the worst of his pain.

He left Chirrit as he returned to his sparse rooms for his evening lessons. He didn't need to be in the training room to do this. It was a nightly ritual; sharpen your own blades, no matter how small; check the stoppers on all poison vials; work on immunizing the body to each new poison. Every night there was a concoction that he needed to know the name of, the composition of, and how to use it.

Taking a deep breath, he tried to ignore the rancid smell of the newest one, downing the small vile in one gulp. It took only a moment to affect him. Aern knelt on the floor, bent over and holding his stomach. He had never known pain like this before. It was worse than the time he had gotten a dagger in his arm. This was like a thousand daggers all being twisted in his guts.

This was a hell of a way to be trained; he was sick over half the time. Crawling to his bedside table, he grabbed the newest vial. If this was like the others, a small dose might at least counteract the pain.

He gagged as it hit the back of his tongue. This wasn't meant to be taken orally. It was meant for wounds or for the daggers. It burned on the way down; it was pure fire as it came back up. Tears stung his eyes as he stumbled to his bathing room for towels.

He wanted to go home. He still had a few years of training to go, but he wanted out. He wanted his mom to be here. He wanted her to hold his hair back, to find out how to fix this, to put him to sleep.

But he was too old to be babied. He had chosen this. He had wanted the danger and excitement that went with being a Master of Poisons. Reminding himself, once again, that it couldn't get any worse (even though it would), he repeated his nightly mantra: This was his life. This was his choice. The sun would rise; it always did. He would survive; he always did. He cleaned himself up and crawled back into bed, curling into a tight ball, praying that things would be good again come dawn.

And come daybreak, it was good enough. He could breath; that would be enough. The pain would lessen once he was with Chirrit again. He threw open his chest, rummaging for something other than the silks his parents continued to send him. Finding his favorite worn set of homespun he had traded another boy for, he then slipped outside, whistling for her. "Hey, girl," he greeted her, burying his fingers in her ruff.

Chirring softly, she butt her head into his chest, taking care to keep her sharp beak clear of him. She dropped down to rest, tucking her long tail in close to her body. She had grown even more than Aern had in the last few years, now needing to duck her head slightly to meet his own gaze.

He dropped to his knees, burying his face in her soft feathers, arms around her neck. He had no idea where Chirrit had come from, but he continued to hope she would stay. She made everything easier to deal with. Knowing that she would be waiting to play encouraged him up and out of bed after a bad training spell.

It had been over two years since she had come to him. Only recently had he read that she was a gryphon; rare, elusive, and generally fickle, he knew that her taking to a human was an atypical occurrence. He didn't have any idea where she slept or where she got her meals, but when he needed her, he could usually find her sleeping in warm sunlight in one of the back gardens.

Pulling away from her, he crossed to climb up into the soft

pink flowers of a cherry blossom tree. He had taken a raw rabbit from the kitchens and now pulled it from the small bag he had brought with him. Balancing precariously in the delicate blooms, he pulled a tidbit free. She was still learning to fly and wasn't terribly graceful yet. This was one of the few things he could do to help her.

She was already excited. As soon as he went towards the tree, she had started shifting her weight, chirring and whuffing to him. He pointed skyward. "Then get up there, girl."

Chirrit inelegantly launched herself into the air, pumping her wings furiously. Aern laughed, seeing she still hadn't figured out to push off with her back legs.

As she cleared the treetops, she gave the exultant cry of a mighty eagle, stretching her neck proudly as she found an air current to ride. A twinge of sadness struck Aern as he realized that once she was truly good at flying, she might never come back to him. In the next moment, she came back into view, calling to him with a low rumble in her throat, beak clacking. He tossed the morsel as high as he could, watching her twist and spiral to catch it. Only when there was little but bone left did Aern climb down.

"Out of bed so soon?" Lord Morenden took in the rumpled clothing, the mussed hair, of the boy before him.

"Sir!" Aern pulled himself up, military straight. He was embarrassed to be seen before a man who was always perfect, even when called from his sleep. He even managed to make the white streaks at his temples look stylish. And here Aern was, wearing the same thing he'd had on yesterday. "I didn't expect…I mean…"

He smiled, but it didn't touch his eyes. "I was just out for a walk, Prince Aern." Crossing his arms, he raised an eyebrow. "You did take your…lesson…last eve?"

"Oh, yes, sir! Went down easy enough; barely got sick at all." He winced at the lie. Why would he be so stupid? That could earn him an extra dose.

Both brows went up. "Quite the constitution you have." He actually sounded impressed.

From a nearby copse of willow trees, the call came to Aern: a soft rumble, almost of a long roll of the letter R, followed by two clacks of a beak.

Morenden looked around Aern in curiosity as Aern called out, "Here, girl." She eyed Morenden suspiciously as she came into view, but ducked her head as Aern reached a hand out to her.

"By the Lights! A gryphon?" He was astounded to see such a rare creature. He was even more astonished that the boy would reach for such a dangerous thing. Morenden took a concerned step forward.

Aern's eyes were instant concern as he turned back to his instructor. "She's still a baby, sir. You won't send her away, will you?"

Chirrit's feathers rose, much as a cat when its fur stood on end when threatened. In two jerked movements, she cocked her head, turning it to view Morenden fully in one eye, then the other.

"Where did you get her?" he asked warily.

"She came to me." Aern relaxed a little; so did the gryphon. "That first time – when I almost died – she was there. She just kept coming back after that."

As Aern's anxiety disappeared, Chirrit turned her attention from Morenden to eye the pack at the boy's waist. Using her beak to push his arm out of the way, she reached with a foreleg to pull the pack open. She happily chrred at the find, trying to get her beak into it. Aern pushed gently on her forehead as he stepped away. "She's really no problem, sir." He pushed again, side-stepping her maneuvering as he removed the pack, dumping the bones at his feet.

"She'll get bigger, you know."

"I know. She's still young, sir. She can't even fly well yet."

"Bigger means more food. You'll need to keep her out of the stables. I won't have her eating all of our horses." Horses were supposed to be a favorite food of gryphons.

Aern's eyes went wide, a smile of genuine happiness lighting his face. "I promise, sir. She won't be any trouble." She looked up at that before going back to the bones.

Lord Morenden shook his head in bemusement. This boy became more peculiar the longer he was with them. A prince that trained in poisons had now befriended a gryphon. The manor lord would be ecstatic to know a gryphon had chosen his home, even if it wasn't one of the lord's own sons. The creatures were so rare as to be thought myth, yet here a youngling sat, attentive to an eleven year old boy. There was more to this prince than he had thought on that first meeting two years past. Gryphons didn't choose lightly, if at all, to tolerate a human; not unless there was something special about them. At least, so said the tales he had once heard himself as a child. He'd have to watch Aern more closely.

* * *

Lazing about, Aern got it in his head to try more than using Chirrit as a pillow. He rose to his knees, slowly turning to face her warm, furred side. She raised a wing, glancing back at him with a slightly annoyed warble. He brushed a hand over her downy feathers. "It's okay, girl." With another annoyed sound, she let her wing droop back down again.

He waited for her to relax again, rubbing her back, her powerful thighs, and her back again, then reached over her body to rub her other side. Her head came up with an irritated grumble and a clack of her beak. Her wings buffeted him, trying to dislodge him from where his stomach rested across her back.

Aern shielded his head with his free arm, continuing to rub her far side. "C'mon girl… feels good, doesn't it?" He tried to stay calm, quiet, despite the beating he was taking from those suddenly not-so-soft wings.

She went too still, then rose to her feet, reaching back to bite the arm he had raised. It never crossed his young mind that she likely saw his actions as that of another gryphon wanting to mate.

It would be weeks of this before she would let him lay across her back. Then he moved to simply sitting astride her while she rested, scratching the feathers at the back of her neck. She became more agreeable to the touch, so long as he continued the preening. It would be weeks more before he would be allowed to simply sit on her back while he talked to her.

The next few months, he enjoyed resting against her, loving the warm comfort of her wings wrapped over him. Often he'd lay draped over her back as he studied.

Normally he would slide down when she stretched, getting to her feet. But of late, he had tried to hang on. As he spent that time sitting precariously perched on her back, he contemplated the best way to go about continuing. If he were to try to let her fly this way, he'd fall off. Not to mention that she'd likely beat him bloody with her wing strokes.

His next stop was the leatherworker. If saddles were made for horses, surely they could do something for his gryphon. He had the man follow him to the field where Chirrit spent her time, thinking it wiser than introducing her to the horses quite yet. After some doing, and getting her to realize the man wasn't there to hurt either her or Aern, a design was finally measured for and designed.

It was a simple rope rigging that would sit across her chest and under her front legs. Padding had been added to keep it from biting into her skin. There was no saddle. Nothing they could think of would stay clear of her wings. It wasn't the highest of quality, but then Aern wasn't sure he wanted to spend much gold on something that might not even work.

He would need to spend many hours working with her to

even tolerate the contraption strapped to her. The first few times he turned his back on her after assembling it, he would turn back only to find she'd managed to chew through the ropes. Replacing the ropes with cheap leather straps went better, although she still didn't like it much.

It was only a few weeks later that Aern was able to start training in earnest with his "girl." The biggest concession was finding a position in which her wings weren't hampered by him and, more importantly, weren't hitting him. Once he discovered that sitting further towards her haunches while leaning as far over her neck as possible worked, he could cling tightly to the handles in the simple leather harness and they were in business to try lifting off the ground. Which she did amazingly well. Then promptly spiraled upside down to dump him from her back.

Arms wind-milling, he fought the scream that threatened to tear from his throat. It was with some pleasure he discovered the height hadn't been quite so high, as he landed in a haystack with an inelegant spray of hay into the air above him. She landed immediately, seeking reassurance that he was fine and not angry. He was, but there was no point in it. She was just doing what was natural. He was trying to make her do something at odds with that.

As they went up, and he came down again, she landed right behind, chirring and whistling in her graceful landing. A soft sound of pleasure escaped her as he got to his feet, brushing twigs and debris away. Aern shot her a dark look, dropping her to a seated position with a sad chrr, head cast down.

Storming over to her, he pushed down on her beak. "You do it on purpose, don't you, girl?" Unable to stay angry, he smoothed the feathers across her head. "I think we can do this, Chirrit. There has to be a way."

More likely a way to break his neck, but if he could do this… if he could show Lord Morenden that Chirrit had some usefulness… To think that with her height and speed, he, as a full assassin, would be able to travel more places more quickly.

She butt her head against him in apology, offering soft clicks and chrrs. Clasping a hand to both top and bottom of her sharp beak, he gazed into her eyes; beautiful amber eagle eyes. For whatever reason, this amazing creature had come to him, had stayed with him the last couple of years. She was the closest thing he had to family or friends here. Reaching one hand deep into the feathers of her neck, his other pushed her beak down and away again. "Dumb animal."

Chirrit responded to the love in his voice with another gentle bump against him. He laughed; in one of those rare moments of joy, Aern laughed at her care for him. He certainly had his work cut out for him with this riding business.

Chapter 3

Doran MacFurgal waited as his wife greeted her father before moving forward himself to shake Llewellyn's hand. The older mage looked troubled through his smile. The younger man could only guess Llewellyn's worry had to do with Doran's brother Bricriu.

His wife excused herself to visit her sisters, as was only right. Women generally stayed at home or with family. They didn't often travel and usually didn't do more than act as something pretty on their husband's arm or, if a nanny wasn't employed, were kept busy raising their babies. Doran didn't mind his wife, but, well, it wasn't like it had been a love match. She was the daughter of a fire mage; as a fire mage himself, he had a duty to produce more males for the Fire line.

Wondering about the odd course his life had taken and the luck he'd had in making something of himself, he retired to Adept Llewellyn's study with him. It still caught him off-guard that a fire mage would have decorated a private study all in Earth tones. But then, he had to keep in mind that Adept Phelan, an earth mage, was quite often entertained in this same room.

They visited for some time about inconsequentials, all the while Doran wondering about the true reason for the call to visit. It certainly wasn't that the man wished a lengthy visit with his daughter. He had only spoken with her long enough to know she was well before sending her off to the other women.

While it was obvious the mage cared for all his children, he wasn't intimately involved in many of their lives. He didn't even do more than ask briefly if the girl Doran had married was behaving. Not "are you happy," but was she behaving. As if she were a lap dog or some other pet.

Other trivialities and banalities filled the time for more than four candlemarks. Doran could stand it no longer. "Adept, you've never been one for such social calls. Is there a problem?"

Long moments went by as Llewellyn simply stared at his desk. "Yes," he stated, much more calmly than expected of a fire mage. "Your brother's temper."

Doran smiled, and then laughed. Fire mages were notorious for their short fuses. It was the reason so few made it to full mage status. They used their magic carelessly, much like the air mages, but fire was inherently more dangerous because it would consume not only the caster, but often those nearby as well. "Isn't that expected of us Fires?"

"But," the Adept smiled with no mirth in it, "our anger gets us in trouble if we give in to it." It was widely known that Fire mages ran high in passion and anger. Llewellyn was a prime example of the first, boasting… the older mage had to think to himself a moment. How many children were there now? Fifteen? No, thirteen; one of which was married to Doran. And Doran was the only family now left to Bricriu, who was the problem at hand. "Your brother is in that trouble category." He sighed. "He seems to be under the misguided idea that your father was wrongly accused."

Doran's own smile faded. His brother hadn't believed the truth all those years ago, and didn't believe it yet. "Bricriu is just like father was," he stated after some time.

"I'm afraid of that," Llewellyn answered somewhat sadly. "It's a good thing we've kept him sheltered from Remington thus far in his training." It was bad enough the man had finished raising the boy. Whatever he'd done, it hadn't been anything to help diffuse the boy's anger. Despite the other mages keeping Bricriu from contacting that man now, the thoughts were now ingrained. They couldn't do much to change his thinking, other than expose him to those that thought rightly, keeping Remington far from the boy.

Worry and alarm shivered through Doran. Remington was known for deceitful, underhanded methods. The man didn't want a unified area, not unless it meant he was in control; not in charge, no. He wanted utter and complete control. He used people; not just mages, but those they protected, the non-magical. He lived with lies and deceit. Doran knew this firsthand. He had been old enough to hear both sides at his parent's hearing. He'd been given a second chance after his parents' execution, along with his brother.

"You think he'll go that way?" he asked about his younger brother. He couldn't imagine choosing that kind of chaos when offered a place with a ruling group of adepts and something that could be called "regular."

Llewellyn wouldn't meet his eyes.

"Has he?"

The silence stretched. Finally, "He attacked Adept Goldwin on the training field." The Adept got to his feet, crossing to the small bar he kept in the room, pouring a glass of wine for each of them. "He's been lowered back to the rank of Initiate in his studies." He resumed his seat with a weary sigh. "I wish there were more fire mages. We'd be better off stripping him of his power."

The glass of wine hung forgotten in Doran's limp fingers. He hadn't realized Bricriu had remained so angry. Unchecked, and that anger would be answered. Fires, rapes, destruction; there was no need to go back to such barbaric ways. Through the Keltori, a very tentative peace reigned in their northern lands.

He wasn't sure what he could do to help matters. He had his own family now that had to take precedence. But Adept Llewellyn wouldn't have called on him to visit if there were another choice in the matter. Looking up, Doran realized that Adept Llewellyn had been not only speaking, but was now awaiting an answer.

Chapter 4

Meeting the others in the stable, all the assassin-hopefuls whispered amongst themselves. They had all learned riding and fighting from horseback, albeit not well yet. Even Aern had trouble sitting a horse well. But if they could only see what he did with Chirrit! He had learned to handle her cat-like gait and how to sit between her wings. He could lay low over her neck, fingers burying in her feathers as they both took to the skies, rolling and diving. It was just as easy to ride upon the ground. The only problem was that he couldn't quite adapt to the change in a horse as well. Horses moved differently.

Even now, they were noisier than Chirrit. They shifted and huffed and whinnied. A good portion of the boys and girls from Aern's studies all looked around at the beasts now, wondering what Lord Morenden had planned for them.

Their whispers died down as their imposing master strode in, only a dark shadow against the bright sun in the doorway. "Look at yourselves," he commanded. "There are already fewer of you than started. There are some of your group not even ready for this."

"This" was something all of them were suddenly very interested in. "This" always tended to be something of importance or excelling that the others wouldn't be given. "This" was rarely something a boy of Aern's age saw. He often heard "this is for you," as Morenden would hand a parchment or bundle to one or another of the older squires. Never did someone his age get any kind of "this" from their mentor.

Aern watched in great curiosity as Lord Morenden unrolled a parchment, giving each of them a look full of meaning; a meaning obviously lost on several of Aern's age-mates. Somehow, he knew though. Most present were older than he was. A few were near his age. What marked them all as different was there skill. He knew that Morenden was giving them something that marked them as better than the others in their training. "Those of you here today have earned both mount and tack. You're matched as follows:" He started reading names, matching each to a horse in the stables.

He noticed that a good third of those still in training weren't present. That said a lot for the skill the present group had acquired. Proud of the fact that he was the youngest to have made it this far, he waited quietly, enjoying the excitement and thrill of each of the matches. Many of his mates would never have been able to afford a pony on their own, let alone the tack for it.

But his smile started to fade as fewer and fewer horses remained. The others were either smirking at him or giving him pitying looks. One was as bad as the other, in his mind. The pitying looks seemed to be saying, "Poor fool shouldn't have come. He must have gotten the wrong message." He was starting to wonder. He knew he wasn't the best rider with the horses, and he knew he was definitely the youngest present.

The other expression though… his anger was pricked. Those looked at him as if suddenly they were better than he was.

Not that he thought himself better, but there were still so many that held his noble birth against him yet. He had never used it for his advantage. He had even traded in some of his good things to secretly leave supplies for some of his mates that couldn't afford it. He took note now of those that had benefited from his gifts… and which of those looked gleeful or sorry for him.

The last horse went to a girl standing next to him. She looked at Aern, unable to think of anything to say. Finally she gave him a weak smile before stepping to the box stall with her new horse.

Aern looked at Lord Morenden, crushed. How could he have been asked to be here? How could he have misinterpreted? Opening the rumpled note he had held tightly in his hand, he read it yet again. He was to report to the stable, saying nothing to the others in his group. It was the same message he was sure the others had gotten. He raised his hurt gaze to Morenden again.

Lord Morenden had the gall to smile at him! It was that same cold smile he usually gave, no emotion in it, no hint in his eyes of what he'd next say. "Bradley, you don't get a horse." His voice was just as harsh as ever. Snickering came from the boys and girls around him. All noise stilled under Morenden's cold sternness as his gaze scanned the stable before settling back on Aern. "Call her in."

As Aern's heart and stomach plummeted for the floor, all he could do was blink at their master in surprise. He hadn't known that Morenden had ever seen him ride Chirrit.

"It's time they all see what you truly ride. Bring her in. She'll get special tack."

All the sniggering stopped. An expectant stillness filled the stable, broken only by the occasional shifting of one of the horses.

Not quite sure that he had heard right, he moved slowly out into the field. With another look at Morenden for approval, he then whistled loudly. In moments, an answering shriek came from the sky. The beating of massive wings left the horses forgotten as all the students ran to fill the entry. None dared to walk out to where the huge gryphon was coming to land, but excited whispering and chattering certainly got her attention. Chirrit's head canted to the side, her huge amber eyes regarding the noisy group.

Setting a hand deep in her ruff feathers, Aern clicked his tongue to get her attention back. Her shoulders were now even with the top of Aern's head. She rested the bottom of her beak on his shoulder, keeping partial awareness on the students.

Several got brave, racing out, pushing others out of the way. They were going to show they were the bravest, the strongest of the group. They seemed to think they could prove they were better than everyone else as they rushed at the gryphon.

Before Morenden saw them, before Aern could tell them to stop, Chirrit reared back on her large back paws, front eagle talons in the air as her wings mantled wide. Her beak clacked a warning once as two came up on one side of her, reaching to touch her.

A scream pierced the air as that beak snapped one of the boys' arms, leaving the limb hanging useless from mid-bicep. One claw struck at the girl next to that boy, raking deep gouges across her chest, dropping her to the ground.

Aern watched in horror, everything seeming to move in slow motion, preventing him from stopping Chirrit. He was terrified that her outburst would have her taken away from him, or worse, that she'd be destroyed.

Morenden grabbed the arm of another boy racing up, spinning him around and shoving him back towards the stable. "Did your minds all escape you?" he hollered into the chaos. "Haven't you fools learned anything?" He pointed a finger imperiously at Aern. "Get control of her. Now."

Rushing to Chirrit, he raised his arms up over his head, making himself look bigger. "C'mon girl! It's me! Down!" He didn't really expect her to listen, seeing how agitated she was, but she did. She immediately dropped to a resting position, leaving her wings mantled though. She let Aern put a hand on the top of her beak, the other in her ruff.

Lord Morenden stood with one hand on his hip, the other snapping a riding crop against his leg, anger leaving his face red. But it wasn't directed at Aern or Chirrit. He faced the others still in the entry of the stable. "I've been working with most of you for how many years now?"

Aern had been with this group for five years now, putting him at a mature thirteen – but still one of the youngest in the group.

"What in the name of the Lights would possess you to do

something as stupid as running up to a strange animal? Especially one bigger than any of you?" He turned to the two on the ground. "And you two," he glared down at them. "Get to the healers. Then get your things. I don't want to see you in my classroom again. I don't have time for rash idiocy. You can't control yourself around something like this; I can't trust you to work for the kingdom."

They helped each other up, giving the stables a longing look. Everyone else knew they had lost more than just a future career. They had lost their horses, their chance at a better life, their everything. They had been two of the many commoners that had been given a chance. They would now be sent back to their families in shame.

Aern had a moment of guilt that it was his gryphon that had done it, but then he saw the look of hatred the boy gave him. It wasn't Aern's fault that the boy's arm had been snapped. No one had made the idiot race forward and try to touch a wild thing. He straightened, standing as tall as his small frame allowed. There was no place for guilt in this work. He had done nothing wrong.

He caught Morenden watching him, then giving the princeling an almost imperceptible nod. Aern lowered his eyes, a small smile on his lips. He had gotten it, and Morenden approved. He had lowered his eyes so as not to seem prideful in the matter, but he was nearly bursting with the revelation that he was right, and that Morenden knew it.

"Your next task," Morenden addressed the group, as if nothing had just happened, "will be to go north. There are peoples you haven't seen there."

One of Morenden's servants passed out a sealed parchment to each of them. Aern noted in some pride that the meek man made a wide birth around Chirrit to give Aern his packet.

Morenden waited until over half were handed out before continuing. "You each are charged with a single strike on the far side of the mountains. There are different coordinates for each of you, different tasks, and different dangers. I will see you each on your return. Hopefully." And with that, he turned and walked away.

They each turned a shoulder to the others near them, not wanting to share their private orders. Aern rolled his eyes. Obviously none of the others had heard the "hopefully." This wasn't going to be some lark; everything they had done so far was dangerous, often one step short of life or death. This would be just as dangerous. It wouldn't do to know what the others were given anyways. Hadn't they heard the word 'different' used several times?

Confident, with an almost arrogant stance, he broke the seal on his own note, not trying to hide anything. Hiding implied either guilt or something underhanded. If he were given a note in public at some point with instructions for a hit, he'd need to be able to read it without giving anything away to others. He decided to practice that now.

He read through the note several times, not quite sure he was reading it right. There was to be no assassination attempt. No murder. It was a mission in reconnaissance. "The Hakon," the note said, "are a people of mystery. Their ways are little known or understood below the mountain range that separates us. Using your new mount and tack, you are to brave these dangerous mountains and then choose one household to spy on. Return with one item from the house you chose, proving you've been in the home. I expect a full report on what was discovered."

There was no signature, but it wasn't needed. Only one would send them. Only Morenden would know who was ready. Looking around at the others, he could see that some of them still obviously were not. For all their secrecy a few moments ago, many were now sharing the details of their own notes with each other. Aern simply had Chirrit follow him to get her new tack.

The sooner he had it, the sooner he could be off on this mission.

* * *

All the others could talk about were the upcoming missions. They lorded that, and their new horses, over the ones who had not been chosen for either. Hard feelings and resentment spilled into fights, fights became grudges, and a few turned up dead over the next few mornings.

Through it all, Aern said nothing, even though he knew he was being discussed because of Chirrit. As soon as the tanner had Chirrit's leather harness ready, he packed and left within the hour. No reason to tempt fate and risk being murdered in his own rooms.

It seemed, on the surface, a silly concern. But he had

started to worry about sleeping with the others in his shared quarters. He could hear whispering after he'd gone to bed, and worried it was about him. How long until they started practicing on each other? How long until he, as the youngest, was attacked?

Better to get this next mission underway. Chirrit's new harness was much better. Wide straps of soft leather fit around her front legs, hooked together in a metal ring between her shoulders, and a surcingle (the wide strap that ran over the back and under the belly) wrapped around her back haunches. D-shaped rings on either side of the strap acted as turrets to smaller leather straps that attached to a belt that Aern put on, holding him to her in the case of flight. To help that, there was one more strap that ran from his belt to the ring at the front, giving him three points of attachment to Chirrit while not impairing her wings.

By leaning forward against her neck, or by sitting perfectly straight, he was able to avoid her wings as they came together above her for each stroke. It worked perfectly! Even the metal ring had the added benefit of giving him something to hold onto without pulling at her ruff feathers.

He flew the first part of the journey, enjoying the quiet of the sky and the gentle noise of Chirrit's wingbeats. Their flight was low enough he could see the creatures on the land below them, but high enough that he couldn't be reached. Had a bowman seen him, he'd have been an easy target but the land was mostly wild. His flight took him from the western land of Pathicos further inland to brush over the barest edge of Drikelldorn. There was little distinction to the difference; no rivers marked the borders or strong tree-lines. The difference, when Aern watched for it, was the creatures.

Pathicos had the stories of nymphs and Miantu Cats. Drikelldorn had several of the large white cats loping along the borderland, not paying any attention to him. Water nymphs played in pools of water and dryads danced near their trees. The nymphs ranged in color from deep sapphire water to algae green and the dryads were colors from the deep wood brown to the varied leaves of their trees; some pink, others blue or burgundy. None took notice of a gryphon above them, seeming to take the beast for granted as a natural element.

There were no keeps; only simple farmer's homes and crops. A few would shield their eyes, looking up from their work as they tried to make sense of what seemed to fly over them. The rare one would call and wave, signing themselves as if he were some sign of good luck. It wasn't until they had passed several farms that Aern realized it wasn't him the farmers were noticing. It was Chirrit alone that made them put hands to foreheads, quickly pressing the sign of an L to their heads with the back of their hands before pushing the palm of that same hand out and skyward. It was a sign to the Lights, the form their god was recognized with, beautiful aurora borealis that so rarely appeared to any.

Then they were at the base of the mountains. Aern dismounted, trying to take in this first experience with a land so different. All color had seemed to bleed away the further north he went. Now he faced high peaks of ragged gray stone that were topped in clouds and snow. How the others planned to get through this with horses was beyond him. There was no clear path and there were plenty of treacherously narrow ledges he could see even from the ground.

"What do you think, girl? Can you make it over these?"

Chirrit canted her head to look upwards with one amber eye, and then went back to preening her feathers. She didn't seem bothered in the least by it.

"Alright, then." He remounted, settling his feet in the small straps that passed as stirrups. "Let's do it." He buried one hand in her ruff, the other tightly around the harness ring, hanging on tightly as her powerful back legs pushed off. Keeping his head close to her own, he avoided the mighty wing strokes that launched her skyward.

She seemed almost as curious as he was once they were airborne, drifting close enough to see what kinds of things lived and thrived in such a harsh environment. There were plenty of things similar to the flatlands: different cats and goats. But there were caves as well. Darker things seemed to peer out at them. Chirrit would make a sound of distress and loft further out away from the mountains. Combined with the cold breezes that blew down and around them, Aern didn't envy the others making their way by horseback.

And then, as the air got thinner, harder to breath, they reached the peaks. Chirrit landed lightly on one of the summits, giving Aern a chance to look down in both directions. Color ran wild on the south side. The north… was much harsher. Gray stone ran down into brown scrub and some small amount of green. Trees with prickly needled green leaves dotted the landscape. A short distance from the mountains' base he could see sparse farms, but not what kind from this height.

When Chirrit had rested, he again took to the saddle. The flight down was much quicker, as she simply jumped out and away from the rocks, before tucking her wings in tightly over and around him, diving so quickly the cold brought stinging tears to his eyes.

He looked for a safe place to land, thinking to wait for dusk. At that point, he'd be able to fly relatively unhindered and not have to worry about rogue arrows being launched at them. What he found instead surprised him. Circling out from the mountains a short way, he saw a few people working the land or moving within small villages. Gryphons seemed to be revered on some level. Those below didn't seem to see him, but would shout praises and jump in excitement at the sight of Chirrit.

Finding the whole thing a bit disconcerting, he landed in the shadow of the mountains and took her into a grove of the sharp, barbed trees, kicking up a loamy, resin scent from fallen leaf needles that littered the ground below them and waited for full night. Even then, he ordered her to stay as he crept back towards the nearest village. Seeing candlelight spilling from the windows of a simple home, he edged closer, staying low to the ground. He kept an eye out for dogs or any other animal that might attack, but nothing came. A few chickens scattered from the road, and he could hear sheep and goats nearby, but his focus was mostly on that window.

Getting close enough, he sat on his heels, resting on the balls of his feet, back pressed against the rough wood wall. He could hear them moving around, the smells of supper wafting out and the dull wooden clanking of dishware letting him know what they were doing. Soon enough they were quiet, only quiet murmurs of asking for items on the table. Someone moved outdoors, pumped water from a well, and went back indoors. Soon two men came out, dressed in warm woolen clothing. Woolen boots laced up to the knee and heavy cloaks hung down, brushing the tops of the boots. Aern couldn't help a shiver racing through him and spared a moment to wish he had something as warm to wear. He had never heard of any place so cold that he could even now see his breath fog before him.

Going to the fence where the sheep were resting, the two men leaned on it as they spoke quietly. Aern went closer to them, staying in the shadow of the house.

"...said he saw a gryphon today."

"One of the mages planning to take over our farms?"

Aern saw a small spark of light, knowing the man was lighting a smoke. "Doubt it," that man went on. "We're under the protection of Water. Don't think Air would be daring to tempt a take on our lands."

"So we just keep on keeping on? No change?" Bitterness

crept into the younger man's voice. "We're nothing because we don't have their magic? Dammit, da!" He kicked at one of the fence posts. "I'm just as good a man as them."

"I know," the father placated. "I know. And you've a shot at laird of our valley. Don't ruin it with anger, boy. Nothing wrong with being a farmer or a warrior." He clapped the younger one on the shoulder. "They'd be nothing without us, hm?"

Aern crept back to the window, daring a peek inside. A few women were finishing the dishes and scrubbing the table down. Both wore floor length gowns in a simple cut, made of more of that warm looking cloth. Their talk was easy conversation about typical farming matters. They discussed their men and the animals, the farm work for the next day and matters about the animals. Nothing interesting to Aern.

Around the other side of the small home, he was able to peer in a small window to see three small children playing on an animal fur rug. Aern liked little kids. He was happy to see that, just like anywhere else, these little ones were busy playing. The older boy was pretending to be "in charge" of the other two, demanding the younger boy to give over so many of his toys. He then told the little girl she had to go to the keep.

"I do not!" she was instantly mad.

"You do too!" the older boy said. "It's the law." He pointed towards their curtain that must lead to the common room.

"I'm telling!" she cried, running from the room.

Whatever that was all about, it seemed that kids

everywhere were the same. They could only play nicely for so long before they started to fight. He remembered being small enough to want to tattle on his older siblings at some point too. That seemed like a long time ago now.

He crept back along the edge of the home to hear more of what the men were discussing. There had been talk of air and water ruling the land; that was unusual, to say the least. Everyone knew that the Lights ruled. There was the belief that the Lights had immortal representation, but air and water?

Unfortunately, the men were now discussing sheering sheep. Aern didn't need to know about that. He waited until the men left his path, and then found his way back to the trees and Chirrit. There on the cold ground, beneath trees blocking the moon, he wrapped himself in a cloak and tried to get some rest. It was freezing, but it would pass. Morning would come; it always did.

And come morning, stiff with cold and teeth chattering, he warmed his canteen over a small fire only long enough to melt the water. He made the decision that rather than go back to that small home, and since he had time the others wouldn't, he would go on to see if he could find one of these air or water people at a keep.

That turned out to be easier than he thought. Stopping in one of the local taverns, he was able to ask about them. Taking ideas from what something he'd heard the women discussing, he used the idea of needing a "spell" done for himself. While none of the patrons of the tavern were very happy about it, they gave the answers he was looking for.

For the most part, the common folk stayed away from the mages, preferring not to draw attention to themselves. When that happened, they told Aern, their women would often be the first to suffer, being taken as mistresses to the men sitting in power. It wasn't that it was done in anger or for punishment. But the common people knew their women were beautiful. The mages seemed to think it was some kind of honor to be chosen to be taken to their homes.

He also found out that the lands were held by different mages of different skills. The lands were divided into territories of a sort, with an element ruling each area. Each focused on one of the four elements – earth, air, fire or water. The only benefit the landholders saw from it was in the land itself. Water tended to have more rivers near at hand; earth seemed to have better crops. They didn't know why and didn't really care, so long as the mages stayed away.

Where most folk lived in small timber huts or earthen mound homes, the mages had large stone keeps built around whatever element they preferred to work with. Air mages tended to the mountains and cliff tops while water mages preferred large bodies of water to be around. Once Aern knew what he was looking for, it was easy to fly across the land, spotting the different homes. He doubted he'd have been welcomed in, but did see a few places with training going on outdoors. He couldn't be sure, but it looked like they were practicing some sort of magic. There were no weapons, yet they would push out with their hands and the person facing them would be deluged with water or fire.

It took all he had to keep from slipping in his harness with the way he was staring at the different elements. He barely had time to notice that there were no women on the fields before Chirrit was screeching and forcing him to pay attention by dropping suddenly in the air.

What he took back from his trip was a sampling of information on two very disparate lifestyles. Neither was wealthy in the sense of gold, but those with power… held all the power. Those not ranking as mages rated their men and women on even footing, while those with magic held the women as something a little less, something useful and pretty, but not with a purpose. It was very different from his own lands where men and women alike could be rulers or captains or any other thing they liked.

The item he chose was not from any home. He was breaking the rules set forth in the missive, but thought his find was much more important. It was a small plant with greasy, waxy leaves that grew in the underbrush behind the farmer's house he had visited. He had watched a young goat eat several, only to fall in seizures, then death. In his studies, he hadn't yet run across it. If nothing else, it would be a fresh example to show the others, something they could then draw into their own journals before they'd test it as a true poison.

Chapter 5

Giggling came from the sunniest room in the home. Thirteen sisters of various ages sat near the large window where all their embroidery was done, all thoughts of stitching far from their minds. All daughters of the Fire Adept, very few shared a common mother.

Fire mages were supposed to be full of passion. Adept Llewellyn had married twice over the years, not particularly caring for the institution. He had married young as was expected, and had been granted numerous mistresses over the years. Three of those women sat apart from the girls where they could work their embroidery while keeping an eye on the little ones.

The youngest children were barely toddling about, but still looked the part of proper maidens in dress and manner. A woman's place was to be mild-tempered and obedient in all things, especially if they were within the household of a mage.

Not all the mistresses had come from magic homes, though. Some had been brought up from the farms and villages that served the mages. They had been told they were being given a "better life." There was no disagreeing that they were given the prettiest clothing, the best materials for sewing, or that their lives were infinitely more comfortable. But these women had come from homes where men and women shared the work together. Their opinion had mattered.

It was hard for them to adjust to being meek and agreeable

to any edict that came from the mage. This transferred to their daughters, as if it were born right into them.

The oldest girls had married off some few years back and were home visiting. Not one of them was over the age of twenty. Kelly, the daughter of one of the farm mistresses, didn't want the life these sisters had been given. No matter that they had funny stories that kept the others laughing. She just didn't want this life.

It was sad, really, that her sisters could be so content to have been bartered off to mages. Those men had only earned wives by doing well on their final tests. They gained status based on how well they could work their magical element and how easily they could blend it with other elements.

The Llewellyn home was the only Fire home at the moment, which meant that her sisters hadn't even been "given" to the right element. They had been matched to Air Mages, in the hopes that fire and air would create more fire children.

It disgusted her. She hated that they were prizes. She hated that she would be one someday soon as well.

As much as she wanted to see her sisters, she couldn't take the talk about marriage and the nonsense that went with it. She excused herself to go find her only brother. They were closest in age, born only a few months apart. He didn't seem to mind that she preferred to be outdoors and had even secretly been teaching her how to use a bow and had shown her the basic workings for his cantrip spells.

She loved mimicking him with his magic. If only he were

home more often. He was often away, staying with whatever mage was teaching him at the time. But, because the whole family was here, he had come back for the week again. Kelly was looking forward to showing Mayden that she could say the words correctly and do the hand motions perfectly for the cantrip he'd shown her last time he'd been home.

If only magic would work for her. It was infuriating to her that no matter how good she was at the verbal and somatic parts, the magic itself only presented as a quick spark of white fire off her fingertips.

It wasn't her concern now. She spotted Mayden on the training field. Out of sight, she pulled the back hem of her dress up from under her legs and tucked it into the chatelaine belt that was only supposed to be ornamental. It made make-shift pants for her that would work well enough for her purposes.

Sneaking as quietly as she could, she came up behind him and shoved him. She ducked as his hand came back trying to catch her. She squealed as he turned and made a lunge for her. Scooping a handful of dirt as she came out of her crouch, Kelly tossed it at him and took off running. As expected, Mayden came after her.

It wouldn't end well; Kelly knew this. Mayden was older, bigger, faster and always caught her. But in the mean time, she was able to run free.

When he did catch her, he pounced on her from behind, knocking her to the ground with the force he'd use if he were playing with other boys. It knocked the air out of her lungs, but she knew he wouldn't hurt her.

He flipped her onto her back, straddling over her to hold his sister in place while he commenced tickling her. He loved that Kelly didn't do the simpering polite little laugh of the other girls. He hoped someday he'd get a girl like her, someone that he could have fun with. Until then, he had Kelly to happily torment.

It was good to see color in her cheeks and happiness in her eyes. It was good to see her laugh. It was good to see her happy.

CHAPTER 6

"I'm a prince," Aern told the young lady at his side. She had been staring doe-eyed at him for the last half hour with a misty smile. It was a little unnerving for him. Heather was one of the girls learning to serve as a lady-in-waiting some day. She was almost two years older than Aern, making her near fifteen. She had always been full of mischief and often spent time in penance for it.

Aern couldn't imagine causing as much trouble as she did. He would have been removed from the special training he was getting. Morenden didn't need trouble makers… like she seemed to be.

Maybe that was part of the reason this unnerved him. Normally she was always in motion. At the moment, the only sign she was really alive was when she blinked or kept up with the infernal twisting of a strand of hair around her finger.

"Third in line for the throne," he added when she didn't answer. It amazed him how many people weren't aware of that fact anymore. He didn't dress in the fancy silks now, having traded them for the clothes most of the commoners wore. When it was discovered who he really was, the comments weren't usually about his station. Those who had met the others in his family only noticed and commented to him on his twin brothers, the heir-apparents to the throne.

Because he was younger, different looking, he seemed to get lost in the shuffle. The twins were supposed to be fair and tall.

Aern still saw himself as short and plain with dark black hair, so unlike anyone else he was related to. Not to mention he wasn't really a part of things back "home." He hadn't been invited back even once during the four years he'd been in training. So, he had gotten used to being alone or left out.

This conversation with the young lady was rare. Aern wasn't quite old enough to want to consider courting. The only girls he found worth spending time with were the ones that he trained with… and most of those he didn't trust. They were like everyone else in his studies – focused on getting ahead and proving themselves at almost any cost.

So the girls he knew wouldn't really be considered ladies. Most young ladies found other things to do or see… like his brothers. Never mind that both brothers were far from here, nearing the completion of whatever training they'd been sent out to learn.

She smiled at him to indicate that she was listening. She was enamored of him. She had been to court and seen his older brothers. He didn't look much like the other two; his raven black hair was short and stylish rather than the longer style others seemed to enjoy more, not to mention that the twins had that pale platinum blonde. Long lashes framed deep, clear blue eyes. He had more of a baby face than his brothers. Sterling and Silver had very mature, classic features. Aern's were softer, more lovable…easier to trust.

Aern didn't like the way she seemed to be lost in her

thoughts, probably about his brothers. "I'm going to drag you through the courtyard by the hair." He continued to use the same soft, gentle tone he had been taught to use around ladies, but even this failed to get a reaction. His stomach turned at the thought that she was only spending time with him because the ones she wanted to talk to weren't present. She was obviously thinking of something else, or more likely someone else. Annoyed, he did what any boy his age would do. He pushed her. "Heather?"

"Oh, yes, I agree completely," she said quickly, catching herself before she could fall off the end of the bench. She batted her lashes at him as she tucked her loose hair behind her ears. She should have been angry with him, but instead she only seemed embarrassed at almost falling.

Aern laughed at how strangely she was acting. "You agree that I should drag you through the courtyard?"

A rosy blush crept into her cheeks. Aern supposed she was a pretty girl, but not for him. She had beautiful fawn-colored hair, honey-gold eyes and a smile that somehow got most boys to do anything she wanted. She was a looker, all right. But Aern wasn't going to fall in love. He had more important things to do in life. His course had been set five years back, when he had been such a childish eight year old.

He didn't want to play the game that he knew went with love. He had seen it happen to some of the older boys: always running after their sweethearts, buying them things, sitting with them while they did their embroidery. No, sir. He wasn't going to waste time on nonsense like that. Besides, it was silly. Kissing girls was hardly something he was interested in. He intended to follow the course Lord Morenden had set for him. That took valuable time and work. He couldn't waste it on girls. Besides, how many of his fellow trainees had been tossed out of the specialized training in the last year? It seemed that as they discovered the fairer sex, fewer and fewer had the desire to go through the nightly ritual of sickness. They would rather sneak about the gardens, getting beneath a woman's skirts. Maybe he was just too young yet to understand that obsession.

"I've been to your court, you know." She coyly smoothed her skirts, trying not to let him notice her peeking at him.

"Mm. Met my brothers, have you?" He tried to keep the sarcasm from his voice. He hardly remembered the twins, yet he was always compared to them. Sterling had been busy with their father and Silver had left for training when Aern was only three. "And which would you like me to give a good word to on your behalf?" Like he ever spoke to either of them. Yet girls seemed to think that he would, only wanting to talk to him in an attempt to get in good with the older boys.

"None, sir. I would know you better." She looked up at him through lowered lashes, trying to be demure.

His brows went up in surprise. That was a new one. He took her hand, dutifully raising it to his lips, hoping to cover his astonishment.

None of the others had tried to make friends with him

without some sort of purpose behind it. It was hard to think she might be any different. "Perhaps in time." With a sad smile, he bowed, taking his leave.

Morenden had told those that remained that their biggest battle would be against the women. What they trained for was not a profession for those wishing for a wife and babes. They had been asked to leave at that moment if they felt that their life would lean that direction. Morenden had pointedly looked to Aern. Several others chose to turn in blades and poisons, returning to basic weapons work. Aern had held his gaze steady, choosing to let his brothers carry on the family line, choosing to forsake any title he may have acquired at his majority. He would be an assassin, not a husband for one such as Heather.

There were days he wondered at his choice, wondered if perhaps he was too young to commit to something such as this. By the Lights, he wasn't even twelve yet!

That day wouldn't come for another two months, and that day was to be a blade testing.

Already his arms and torso held the marks and scars of hundreds of bites of a blade; each one making his skill cleaner, less noticeable to a victim. Only when he effectively slid a dagger as quickly and painlessly as a paper cut would he be ready to move on to another level, a level that was only two months from testing.

And then the day was upon him. *Happy fourteenth birthday*, he thought. The only kiss of the day would come from a poisoned blade. His only treat would be to live. Only one more year until he'd be a "man"… if he could survive that long.

It had only been one year since they had first been told to draw blood on themselves; only twelve short months since they had first felt the cold kiss of a blade. Their scars had just been fading when they had been told to partner off and deliberately knick each other. Training had been to get used to the feel of steel melding and passing through them. Different angles, different pressure…his body was becoming covered with a fine lace-work of scars.

He stared into the eyes of Tylel, willing himself to calm, to a place of no fear. Tylel's hand shook; that didn't help Aern focus. Tylel's shaking hands would not leave a clean mark. Today there was more at stake than just another scar. Today they tested their resistance. He could pass this, but not with Tylel as his partner. Too many mistakes had been left unpunished. Aern was not about to be the next mistake.

He rose gracefully and bowed before their lord. "I would have another partner, milord." He had never, not once, asked for special treatment for being a prince.

A measured glare met him. "And what makes you think you have a right to ask this, young prince?"

"Something is amiss. You've told us to watch for the behaviors that would give others away to us. He shakes as if he knows he would do me harm." Truthfully, Tylel had been one of the gutter-brats that should have been honored to be raised to this level. He should have worked twice as hard as anyone else. But too often he had used his newfound rise in stature to have fun. He had skipped lessons, blamed others for his own faults, and now… now Aern was being asked to rat him out. He couldn't do that. He had seen this sort of thing happen before. The one who tattled would be beaten by the others in the group later. *Honor among thieves*, Aern thought with sarcasm. He could face the group later for telling the truth or…

He raised his chin, squared his shoulders. "Your own blade is much stronger than ours." He pulled his left sleeve up and raised his arm, holding it level and steady. "I would have you test me."

The others murmured and whispered behind him. Death was preferable to further damning himself in the eyes of his mates. He had learned the unspoken lessons from a harsh taskmaster. Morenden guided, Morenden taught, but the true lessons came from the others. All that narrowed down to one rule: there was only ever one. You could be in a group, as he was now, and still be the only one. You could be in a crowd of nobles, looking and acting the part, and still you'd be alone. He was one. He was alone. He would survive. He willed his focus into the center of his body. Ignore the noise, ignore his left arm…The blade flashed in the light, white hot pain seared and subsided. He raised his eyes to meet his lord's. Morenden nodded to Aern in pride, and then Aern's world went dark.

He awoke in his chambers, his arm bandaged.

"Don't rise."

He froze. Lord Morenden was here in his rooms. He

lounged comfortably in a side chair, his head resting on the knuckles of one hand. "That took balls, boy."

"I…" his throat felt tight, his tongue too large for his mouth. "He…"

"He had to put his blade to his own arm. Your instincts were right. He's been sent home." Lord Morenden sat silently, staring at Aern. His tone indicated that Tylel didn't ride home, but instead went by wagon. Tylel hadn't survived the bite of his own poisons on his own blade. "By rights, you should have been on your way home, too. My blade isn't meant for those of your age. I tested your blade for you," he added, shifting the conversation. "Did you do it yourself?"

He had loved the chemistry in learning how to mix the poisons, how to get the right consistencies. Now he worried that he himself had screwed up. "Was it wrong?"

His lord's eyebrows went up as a strange smile crossed his features. "On the contrary." He rose, crossing to the door. "It was perfect. See me when you're well enough. You won't be working with that group any longer."

It turned out that he wouldn't be working at the holding anymore. He was deemed ready to face a real world trial. He didn't have the experience, necessarily, but he had proven his fortitude and would continue to build his resistances through practices that would go with him.

His first assignment was to the south, infiltrating a keep while remaining unseen, to leave a poison-lined chalice for the lord's table. All the training of the last six years was coming to a head. He knew nothing of the politics surrounding the assassination, didn't really have time to contemplate it. At fourteen, he was taking the job of a full man, carrying a poison of his own making into an adversary's keep. Nervous as never before, he knew this was a job for a man of nineteen, at least; not for the boy he still felt he was at only fourteen. He didn't feel ready for this honor, but knew that his mentor would never have chosen him without good reason.

As the sun painted the horizon in beautiful colors, Lord Morenden brought him his new clothing. No longer would he wear the soft silks and satins that marked him as a noble's son. Donning skin-tight hose of the deepest black, he pulled knee-high boots of black suede over them, sliding daggers into the hidden pockets in the tops of the boots. Lord Morenden held out the tunic as Aern tucked his arms into the close-fitting sleeves. It wrapped across his chest, tying low inside at his hip on his right side. The outer piece crossed low to his left hip, fitted with pewter clasps down the left side to hold it closed.

Morenden stayed his hand before Aern could fasten the pewter clasps down that side. "Note the pockets." Lining the inside were dozens of small pockets, each big enough for exactly one vial of poison or one packet of herbs. Aern exchanged a meaningful gaze with his Lord before going to his personal chest, the one that stored all of the different concoctions he had learned to make and use. He chose only packets of herbs and a few small bladders of poisoned liquid and placed them in the specially-designed pockets. He then fastened the clasps, shrugging to settle the tunic into place. It fit snugly, the hem even with his hips. Lightly padded, it would deflect some assault against his person.

Next the leather bracers, fitted securely against his forearms, laced tightly. Baldric next, over the right shoulder, fastened under his left arm. Morenden presented a short sword to Aern. "She was my first blade," he said as he removed it from an oil cloth. "You've earned this, boy. Guard her well."

As he slid it over his shoulder, Morenden unrolled a cloth of black velvet. Within lay two daggers, the short handled, longer-bladed ones that Aern had loved best while training. "These fit within the braces. Do your job well tonight and they'll be yours to keep."

The supper bells tolled as Morenden and Aern met upon the road leading away from the keep. He rode proudly astride Chirrit, though she growled slightly at the indignity of being land-bound for this. Her wings lay comfortably back, resting over his legs, keeping him warm in the cool night air.

Morenden kept his horse at a trot nearby, looking to the boy with some pride. He'd not had a prodigy like this in some time. To see him so studious now indicated the boy knew this wasn't a lark. Aern was getting the mind-set of an assassin, even now quietly going over his plans in his mind, considering what actions he would need to take. And to see the boy with such a noble creature, as comfortable with it as if it were a horse! He was awed and very,

very proud. "I'll wait here," Morenden whispered as the fortress loomed into view. Several gestures were made, giving him his final instructions in a language cant, one without any words, that was known only to a very few.

With an intake of breath, Aern straightened somewhat, nodding almost imperceptibly. He reached forward, tapping Chirrit lightly along the side of her wicked beak, pointing to a turret along her line of sight. "There, girl."

Full darkness enveloped them as they took to the air, hiding them from Morenden's land-locked view. There wasn't even much of a moon out to illumine things this night. Too quickly, they reached the turret, Chirrit landing quietly on her back legs, and the slight clack of talons on stone with the front. From long practice, she lifted a wing gracefully away and up for Aern to dismount. With a "stay" command from his hand gesture alone, she settled down to rest as he quietly made his way inside.

Few candles lit the passages here. In his dark clothing, he blended easily with the shadows. With even fewer people, his movements were easier. He quickly found the servants' passages, noting the emptiness. They were all below, serving in the great hall. He let out a breath he hadn't known he was holding and moved swiftly down to the main level from within the passageways.

This was it; his big chance to prove himself. At twelve years and one month, he was being tried as a full adult. He could do this, he told himself. He could. He was ready.

Yeah, right, he thought. He glanced out the passageway, trying to decide his next move. There could be no mistakes, not if he wanted to keep the respect he had earned from Morenden.

A noisy kitchen was just beyond his hiding place, full of servants and bustling activity. None seemed very happy, none seemed to enjoy what they did; not like the servants in the castle he was from. These men and women seemed more concerned that the "masters" would be upset or angry with any small infraction, right down to the matter of a spot on the chalices.

It would be easy to grab one of them and trade places for the time. He waited for a boy about his age to come near enough and then slipped a hand over his mouth as he jerked the servant backwards into the passage. A quick knock to the back of the head with a dagger hilt stilled the attempts at escape. Aern quickly donned the overtunic, covering his own clothing. Shaking his fingers through his hair, he left it mussed, hoping to add to the illusion of being nothing more than a harried servant.

He had barely stepped into the commotion before he was cuffed along the back of the head. "Git yerself in there with the wine, ye dolt!" A tray was shoved at him with several bottles on it. Aern moved ahead of the heavy set woman as she chased after him in a shrill voice, landing blows along his back and arms. He knew that any kind of party for a noble home involved days of preparation and the day of the event would be extremely busy, but that didn't excuse the woman hitting him. It didn't excuse her hitting any one, man or child, that worked under her.

Tripping over his feet, he struggled not to drop the tray as he entered a hall. It wasn't that it was even that heavy. It was just the press of people and the uneven straw strewn about with animal bones hidden within that made for a rather treacherous walk. The room was well supplied with candles, but they were a lesser quality that gave off a lot of smoke that inhibited what could be seen clearly. The room was also quite a bit noisier than the kitchens had been. Men in the center of the room were shouting at cocks and hounds that were being set to fight in different pens. Others argued or fought at the tables. He paused only a moment as he took in the chaos. The few women present were chattering or laughing in high voices, seemingly oblivious to the rest of the noise. Everyone was imbibing in large quantities of ale and wine. He shook his head at the disorder, wondering how or why anyone would want to live like this.

He found the man matching the description he had been given sitting at the head table. Sour and rather unfriendly looking, he barked orders at those near him, not above pushing, pulling, or shoving to get his way.

Making his way toward the table, he had his hands full trying not to get jostled or stepped on in the process. Placing glasses or refilling empty mugs was much easier, as they all seemed to look forward to the wine.

Two or three passes, and Aern stepped into the shadows to withdraw his chosen poison from his tunic. Shaky fingers opened the tiny bag, pouring the powder into the newest bottle. He wasn't sure how much he was supposed to use within the wine. Would it be any different than in a glass of water? For surety, he took a second amount and added it as well. From there, it was easy to refill the mugs as the men continued to down enormous quantities of the different alcohols. Some of the lighter weight ones started falling face-first to the table, seeming to only be asleep, much to the humor of the others. As two, then three more bottles were consumed, the others started to show signs as well. Those that had only had a mug or two were asleep at the tables, but many had downed much, much more. They started foaming at the mouth, eyes rolling back and going into convulsions. People started to panic, running around and screaming.

Finally, as the "master" convulsed, green ickor running from his mouth, Aern slipped back to the kitchen, up through the passageways and burst to the rooftop at a run. Chirrit was on her feet in a moment, seconds later they were up and away. Aern gave an exultant cry at having done it, ignoring the small part of himself that wanted to throw up at the disgusting deaths he had just caused and witnessed.

It was the first time he'd actually watched a death by the poisons he used, rather than just observing near-death experiences. He was pleased to know his mixtures worked, but seeing it work was a lot different than hearing that one of his mates had died from their own mixture. He had never seen the bodies before. The cool rush of air around him helped settle his stomach and Chirrit's comforting chirs and growls helped settle his nerves a little before he landed.

Lord Morenden watched the gryphon approach from the distance. His horse danced a bit, nervous at the approach of the winged beast. The gelding had been fine when the gryphon had walked alongside it earlier. It must be the rush of the creature coming at them from above that spooked the horse. Morenden scowled, reigning the horse in, even as he kept an eye on the sky.

Chirrit landed as Aern slipped the belts loose and slid to the ground on shaky legs. Morenden noted the sallow color to Aern's face. "So? Is he dead?"

"Yes, sir. A total of five others, as well. At least that I saw by the time I left. And several that'll be really sick when they finally wake up."

Lord Morenden watched as the boy slipped down the side of the gryphon. She folded down to a resting position as well, nuzzling his hair as she protectively put a wing over him. He couldn't help a smile at how the creature treated him as one of her young. In the next moment, he frowned, considering the same issue. She might become too over-protective if given half a chance. It was something he'd have to mention to the boy. But for now, he had other matters he needed to know.

He drilled the boy on what he had done, how he had accomplished his goal, anything that could have gone better… Until Morenden was done, Aern was curled against the gryphon's side, fingers absently running through her fur and feathers. It seemed to be a habitual thing the boy had taken to over the years, perhaps even using it as a way to get through some of the more difficult training Morenden had put the younglings through. "All right, prince, mount up. Let's return home." No reason to tell him he was proud of the job he'd done. The boy should know it; he was letting him keep the blades.

CHAPTER 7

"There's no need to act yet." The gentle voice belied the speaker. He was a tall whip-thin man with dark whirls of hair dancing around his shoulders in a wild mane. It framed cold eyes and a cruel smile that perpetually sat at the corners of his mouth. Long, knobby fingers poured hot tea, passing a cup to his young charge.

Remington's voice was a soothing balm to Bricriu. He sank back into the sueded chair, inhaling the strong scent of the tea. Somehow the furniture here at Remington's was softer than anywhere else he'd been. The room was dark, as always. The only light came from small murder holes near the ceiling of each room. Remington seemed to like keeping the place in a state of twilight. Candles were used sparingly.

Bricriu had learned early in his time with this man that obedience to Remington made life simple. He had lit candles to light an entire room, rather than the single one he'd needed to read by, and had been beaten with a cane for it. He had heard bones break. White pain lanced through him as the blows had come again and again until Bricriu had stopped trying to get up and away.

Afterwards, Bricriu had forced swollen eyes open to see Remington still standing over him, arms folded and disapproval emanating in every fiber of the man. "Have you learned?"

He had only managed the barest of nods. It was enough. Remington had picked him up, moving him to a couch. Sitting beside the broken boy, he had held him as a parent might, close to his side, lightly running a hand from the top of Bricriu's head down over his arm, over his thigh. Over and over, then down Bricriu's back. The pain had lessened with each pass until only a dull throbbing ache remained to remind the boy what had happened. "Never act beyond what is yours," Remington had said smoothly. "Take only what you can control."

His voice had rolled like honeyed water over Bricriu. Ever since that time, Bricriu had worked hard to please Remington. He had done everything that had been asked of him. He had listened to everything, taken all of it to heart, about how he was worthy and how his parents had been wronged.

Now he sat on the same couch where his broken body had been healed. He still didn't know how Remington had been able to repair the damage, or if it had truly been real. Remington never spoke of it.

Healing wasn't under any of the Elements the mages used. But if Remington hadn't used magic to heal Bricriu, there was no explanation for the quick recovery. He knew that mages could live very long lives, if they were strong enough and no one removed them. He knew that Remington was older even than the Phelan or any of the others on the Keltori.

"You'll return to your training." Remington's voice seemed far away as Bricriu grew sleepy. "You'll work harder. I expect you to rise through the ranks in the next few years."

He shifted, caught somewhere in a dreamlike state, not

quite awake or asleep. "They made me an initiate again." Bricriu winced. Even in his state, he heard the petulant whine in his voice. Remington wouldn't like it. He didn't like weakness of any kind.

And Remington didn't like it. He hated the sniveling brat he'd taken in. But he saw a means to an end. He had lost his place among the mages because they said he hadn't mastered any of their elements. He didn't need them. He was stronger than any of them. His magic, whatever it was, pulled from another source entirely. With a thought, he could heal a body or break a mind.

That was something he needed to be very careful with if he wanted to get his vengeance on the precious Keltori. Bricriu had been a gift from the Sources of Magic, a perfect pawn he could shape into the tool he needed to work from inside the ranks of order the Keltori had decided upon. "You know you're better than initiate," he soothingly pushed the confirmation into Bricriu, using the boy's already inflated ego against him. "You'll take down Llewellyn soon enough."

A sleepy smile formed on Bricriu. He wanted to take the place of that Adept. He wanted to see Llewellyn dead for what he'd done in the past.

"Now then," Remington's voice returned to a tone of business.

Bricriu stirred, sitting up as he blinked. He didn't remember fading off to sleep.

"You need to return to your training." Remington offered a smile that was as close to warm as he could give the boy while keeping his tone to a sharp bite. "I don't expect to find this happening again soon. You need to complete your training." He paused a heartbeat, then gave Bricriu a piercing look while his voice took on a note of parental disapproval. "You don't want to let me down now, do you?"

"No, mage." Bricriu lowered his eyes. It was in deference to the respect he was supposed to show the mage as well as to prevent some of the weird creepy-crawling feeling Bricriu got when Remington looked at him so intently.

"Then get back to the Phelan's. Master his earth magic and move on as quickly as you can."

The young magic user was up and out the door. Remington's tone was so cold and annoyed, he almost could have kicked the brat or loosed his magic on him with less consequence.

Bricriu didn't want to let him down. He wanted to prove his worth. He wanted Remington to appreciate what he'd done. But most importantly, Bricriu wanted to see Llewellyn dead.

CHAPTER 8

That first job had given Aern only a few nights of bad dreams. He had seen the effects of poisonings many times over his training. Other kids had died from badly mixed concoctions; some had survived their mistakes, but were worse than vegetables now, able only to sit and drool.

It was his next assignment that got to him. He had earned respect in his first job, but that had been easy compared to his next mark. Aern went alone once the sun was down. Terrified, he left the safety of the keep and the lights to enter into the dark unknown. Nervous fingers worked the harness and rigging onto Chirrit. With a slight tremor to his young frame he led her to a clearing, launching skyward on her for a keep two lands over. It would have taken at least two days by horse; it took him only a few hours by air. Too soon, to his mind.

All too soon he was back on the ground. He dismounted, standing beside Chirrit for long moments. He moved as if unaware of his actions as he absently went through a checklist of his weapons, touching each. Chirrit cocked her head, watching his odd movements. His eyes were slightly unfocused, but his body seemed to know what it was about. He rolled his shoulders, sensing the baldric holding the sword at his back. His twirled his wrists, sensing the knife sheaths there; with a slight flick of one wrist, he checked the ease of release in one of the knives, reaching unconsciously to then snap it back into place. He shifted his ankles, sensing the knives hidden in his boots. Fluttering nervously, his fingers slid over his padded jerkin, noting each pouch and vial hidden within, sliding over the garrote hanging at his hip.

With everything accounted for, there was only the job now. Taking a deep breath, he straightened his shoulders. "Wish me luck, Chir."

He left her in the dark as her soft chrr followed him. He watched the servants coming and going for several moments, which doors they used, and which type of servants they were. When one shut the windows and the candles in that room went out, he seized the opportunity. Moving as quietly as he could, thinking his breathing was even too loud, he raced to the wall, standing flat against it for long moments waiting for his heart to slow just a little.

Creeping to the window, he turned just his head, leaning ever so slightly to look around the frame. He jumped back as a shadowy figure came close, pulling shutters from each side, slamming the window shut.

He had almost been seen! He closed his eyes, swallowing hard against the fear beating in his throat. His mantra came to mind unbidden, helping to calm himself. This would pass; it always did. The sun would rise; it always did.

Damn straight. He wasn't about to fail now! He shook the nagging fears from his head, his confidence restored. Pushing away from the wall, he crept to the door, listening as he'd been taught. When no other sounds came from within, he pushed the door open a little at a time. He kept waiting for a squeak or a squeal from the hinges – maybe a dog from the other side to give him away – but silence reigned. There were only the night sounds to his back.

When it was open enough for his narrow frame to slip through, he went in, pushing it shut again with equal care. Glancing around the room showed him baskets of clothing and sheets. A wash room. He started to move away from it when he remembered to check for locks. It wouldn't do for him to make the hit and then be caught because he hadn't checked if someone would seal the door for the night.

Luckily for him, there wasn't even a bar to place over it. The keep was ill-managed if doors and windows couldn't be barred. This just made it easier for him. He crept further in, listening for the hush of movement or voices. Nothing nearby.

Exiting the wash room, he went through a servant's kitchen. Not the lord's kitchen by any means; this one had only the bare essentials for cooking and a high countered table they could stand at to eat their minimal meals.

It bothered him that anyone could treat another so low. Everyone deserved a few rights in their life. Only animals should have to stand to eat. There was no reason a few chairs couldn't have been provided.

A large door separated that kitchen from the lord's. And such a difference! The lord's kitchen had plenty of counters, cabinets, sinks, stoves, not to mention the baskets of fresh fruits and vegetables just waiting for the next day.

Aern was angry that such a line was demarcated by only a door. From there he saw the dining room with the fancy table and chairs. Artwork adorned the room and the side counters sat awaiting chafing dishes. Heavy silver candelabras sat at the center of the table, with silk placemats waiting for what would surely be fine dishware.

It only got worse as he went into the main halls. There were wasted extravagances everywhere. Seeing a shadow moving, he slipped up against a wall, watching a servant cross a doorway across the way. Her head was bowed, her hair pulled back in a ratty tail; her clothes were little better than rags. She looked like she had lost all will to fight for life, as if there was nothing for her to look forward to.

He slipped away from that sight but noticed a few others in similar shape. He had to wonder how bad the lord was that his entire home had such sadness in it. Even he had never been that horrid to another person. He had always – always! – given what extra he had to help make it easier for others. He never let others wait on him.

The last remnants of fear and nervousness faded as a cool anger settled over him. If things were this bad for those serving, how awful were the nobles in this home?

With quick, quiet steps he went up to the second floor, looking for the signs that would mark the family wing. One direction was opulence for the sake of it; that would be the wing for guests. He chose the other direction. Still overwhelmingly overdone, the furnishings here were at least designed for use.

"I told you I wouldn't wear that!" A young man's voice came from behind a closed door. "Stupid cow!" The sound of something used to strike another came through the door, making even Aern wince at the force that had to be behind something that loud. "If you can't find the silk robe, you must be blind! Is that it? You want to be blind?" Maliciousness overflowed from the anger-filled voice.

"No sir!" a servant's fearful voice answered.

Aern lost some of his careful cautiousness, needing to know what was going on. He pushed one of the double doors just open enough to see a boy a little older than himself holding a fire poker over an elderly servant who was on his knees before the boy.

His eyes narrowed in fury. People were NOT to be treated that way! Not even thinking, his hands found the small blow gun, loading a dart into it. THIS is why he was to be an assassin. He wouldn't let things like this exist in the lands he called home.

The boy got one strike in before the dart hit him. It was enough of a strike that the old man was now unconscious, toppled over on his side. More importantly, Aern watched the boy's knees give out just as he realized he'd been hit with something. He pulled it out, but too late. Seizures took him, blood coming from his mouth and nose.

Satisfied, Aern walked away from the door, knowing death

would follow in moments. Like Morenden had told them, "what the child does, reflects the parent." If the boy was this bad, he could now understand why he was here. This wasn't going to continue.

Care gone, he strode down the hallway as if he owned it. He knew from his studies the general placement of a lord's chambers within most keep designs. He wasn't disappointed.

Pushing open the opulently carved doors, he found the man being waited on by no less than five weary-worn servants, none of which even looked in his direction. Hands balled into fists, feet planted, he waited for the man to notice him. Maybe not the smartest act, but rage was coloring his actions now.

The man griped and bitched and complained incessantly, without ever specifying what he really wanted. He was worse than the boy… and his fists flew more readily. Several of the servants bore the signs of current abuse about their faces, as well as many older scars.

"What is this?" the lord demanded as he finally noticed the lanky boy standing in his doorway.

"This," Aern said calmly, "is death."

The man laughed as if it were the funniest thing he'd ever heard.

Aern gave him a small, cold smile, hating with everything in him. "Death is often unexpected. I wouldn't laugh at it."

"You… you're a child!" He continued laughing. He motioned to the servants who were now only standing, looking at

Aern curiously. "Take that away; get him out of my sight." When no one moved, his humor faded. He hit the one nearest him, his voice hardening to steel. "Now!"

There was only a moment to decide. Save the servants and lose the hit or sacrifice the innocents to defeat the problem?

His knives slipped from the wrist sheaths to cut down the two who approached him; one successfully to the throat, the other not so cleanly across the stomach. He'd have to work on that attack. It was a messy death.

Whirling around a third at a run, he was suddenly in front of the lord. With a fancy spin gaining him momentum, both daggers turned point to the left, he landed them in the man's stomach. He jerked, flexing his hands to twist the blades within the wound, then withdrew, wrenching them across the man's abdomen at the same time.

A horrible stench washed over the room as the man's guts spilled forward. Stunned surprise stared at Aern as the lord put hands over the mess at his waist. His legs gave out and he tumbled forward, face smashing to the floor with a wet thunk.

Nausea washed over Aern. All the practice against straw dummies had never prepared him for the truth of a kill like this. But he wouldn't retch. Not now, not with people staring at him.

He straightened, willing his stomach to keep its supper. Shaking his hair from his eyes, he looked once more at the dead man, then to the servants. "Never," he offered, "laugh at Death."

Sense returned, knowing he had to disappear before they

called for his own death. He had been foolish to let himself be seen. Stupid. Stupid stupid stupid.

He ran between the stunned men left standing, darting into the hallway. Rather than trying to run, knowing he would be followed, he chose another method. Using his momentum, he used a table to help shimmy himself up the wall, to balance stretched between beams near the ceiling, waiting.

Sure enough, their sense returned, bringing them to the hall. Aern was stunned when, rather than call for aid, they made a cursory look around, then made the sign of an L with their left hands, placing it to their foreheads in obeisance to the gods. "Lights be praised!" they offered, pushing their left palms skyward. "We been saved by a Shadow!"

And so he earned a name. The dark was his. He'd be more careful to use it in the future. As for them…it would be up to them what they did now… but they were free of the tyrant.

Chapter 9

Yet another embroidery sampler piece was stretched in the frame before Kelly. The youngest girls did simple alphabets and numbers in their patterns as a way to learn them. As much as she hated any sampler, she wished that was all she had to do now. Up and down the needle went through the faBricriu as it picked out the design she was creating.

She had decided to forego any words on this one, choosing instead to stitch a great creature from legend. It should probably have been a phoenix, out of respect for the Fire Magic that ruled the house, or even a fire salamander since those served the magi of that element. Instead, she imagined a gryphon. Already its majestic head had appeared in her design. Already she had ripped out thousands of stitches while trying to get the front legs right. It would help if she could have seen one in person.

Her brother had a friend named Griffon, but that didn't mean he could change into that creature. Mayden hadn't even tried yet, but each boy training with magic would learn to assume the form of some creature connected to their element before they became full mages. Fire was usually a salamander, but legend said that sometimes a phoenix would appear, the mage then able to rise from the ashes. Water could be anything from fish to water fowl to beavers and otters. Air tended towards insects, bats, and birds, but… Kelly sighed, thinking how splendid a gryphon would be.

One of her father's mistresses gave her a disapproving

look. "That isn't useful or teaching you anything."

"You aren't my mother," Kelly shot back rebelliously. "You can't tell me what to do."

The other girls all looked to them with baited breath. They weren't supposed to talk back. All the mistresses were to be treated with respect. It was something Kelly continued to have trouble with. She didn't need five women trying to be her mother.

"You're setting a bad example."

Kelly didn't care. As far as she was concerned, the women were setting the bad example. They were teaching the girls that it was okay to be a mistress, to wait on man for what meager attention he might dole out to them, to share one man between them. "My mother," she said as she got to her feet, "hated being a mistress."

"Then maybe," she crossed her arms with a smug smile, "your mother shouldn't have acted out like you do. Maybe she'd still be here."

Before she could reason the thought out, Kelly shrieked and flew at the woman with her fists flying. Mistresses could be set aside if the mage tired of them, but Kelly's mom had not been turned out. She had died giving birth to Samantha, Kelly's only full sister.

All of her father's women at the moment had come from the homes of other mages. None of them knew what it was to be equal. None of them had even considered it. They saw Kelly as a trouble maker, always stirring things up. They tried to keep peace in the women's wing, but that usually meant that Kelly suffered for it.

They didn't know how to fight or defend themselves, all being "good girls" that had been taught to be pretty and ornamental. Kelly knew how to fight. Too many hours with her brother had taught her how to swing and hit or how to weasel out of a stronghold.

She clenched her fingers together, making a club of her hands and swinging towards the woman's midsection. Screams from the adults cut the room as Kelly connected. The woman's hands let go as her air escaped her in a grunt. Several of Kelly's sisters were cheering her on.

Running for the door, she paused only long enough to stomp on the foot of another of the women. Tears ran from her eyes, fueled by the hurt she felt from the stupid comment.

Down the hall, through her brother's room and out onto his balcony she went. Hitching her skirts up, she hopped up on the railing, swinging herself up to the small niche Mayden had shown her was hidden from sight there.

She curled up in the cubby, not even able to take solace from the warm breeze blowing around her. Another year or two and she wouldn't fit here anymore. Already her legs were getting too long. Other things were starting to develop as well.

If her father noticed, he'd think she was old enough to marry and pawn her off. He'd probably want to just to have peace back in his home. Kelly could only be lucky that he rarely heard how often she had to go without supper. Like today would be again.

Since there was no reason to come down, she stayed in the spot that was getting too tight, listening to them search for her inside. She missed her mom. She missed having someone that told her stories about how men and women could be equal, how it was okay to be more than ornamental.

She loved Samantha, but sometimes… just sometimes, she was angry that Sam had cost her a mother. Without her mother, she didn't see much chance of ever getting away from what would be expected of a mage's daughter.

Chapter 10

Aern was to be assigned to a sailing vessel, a merchant ship legally under the king's employ, subversively working as a buccaneering outfit. It wasn't what Aern was expecting. He had thought a "sailing vessel" would be small. What Lord Morenden steadily rode towards was a massive ship that easily had 150 men aboard. A large squared gallery sat higher at the back of the ship – what he would later learn was the stern – and the midship area was depressed.

He dismounted from Chirrit, taking her harness off, all the while his eyes were on the ship. He absently dismissed her to the skies as he followed Morenden up the gangplank. Everywhere he looked, men and women scurried around the ship. They barely spared glances for Morenden or Aern, only letting them know they were in the way as they hurried back and forth, coming on and off the ship as some loaded supplies, others moving things around the deck.

The smell of brine made Aern wrinkle his nose. Wet oak wood lay under that. He had never been so close to the open water or any kind of boat this size. The dark weathered wood streaked in different colors from the water line, showing which had been exposed to more water than the rest. Barnacles crusted the lower area, sitting near the water line. But here on the deck, the smells of pitch, brine and wet wood overwhelmed him. The sounds of birds overhead, barrels rolling across the deck, people shouting in the rigging, and the sails being checked on three different masts snapping loudly besieged his senses.

"By the Lights!" The captain swore, surprising Aern as he seemed to suddenly appear before them. "You'd best be telling me this isn't another Bradley."

Aern took a step back in surprise, not knowing how this captain would recognize him. He looked at the lean yet muscular man. He was built more like an elf than human, yet had the bulk only a human could assume. There were chiseled features beneath the five o'clock shadow Aern suspected of being somewhat permanent. Wood-brown eyes studied Aern from below deep brown, windblown hair. He was dressed in practical clothing, something Aern liked right away. He was wearing black pants, calf-high boots, and a white shirt beneath a tanned leather jerkin.

"You are, aren't you? Gods, give 'em dark hair…Duke Gunner's son?" Shaking his head slightly, Aern wasn't given a chance to speak before the man went on. "The king's, then? Heyla!" He yelled up into the sails. "Watch the rigging! So." His gaze fixed again on Aern. "Grey's youngest. Prob'ly don't remember me, then." He wiped his hand on the back of his pants before extending it to Aern. "I'd be a foster sib of the Bradley clan. Jays Randulf."

"Aern." He took the offered hand. "Aern Bradley."

"Ah." He gave a knowing look. "The one born the year I left for training. No doubt now that you're a Bradley, eh? Whatever happened to that northern mage?"

Aern shook his head, not understanding. He had never heard of a mage involved in his life story. That might need more looking into. With all his older half-siblings and the royal twins above him, no one had ever spent much time fussing over his past. He had always marked that as having been the unwanted "extra" born to the king, not because of any secretive intrigue.

"No matter." The discussion was closed. "You'll do."

"Good enough." Lord Morenden said, giving Aern a mighty pat on the back. "The boy'll fit in right fine, I'd say. Tough as nails and quick on his feet." He handed a satchel to Aern. "Your…instructions are included. I'll be in touch."

"Well." Captain Jays watched the lord head down the gang plank before turning to the boy. He narrowed his eyes at the young man before him, not remembering this youngest Bradley. He would have been something like three or four the last time Jays had even been home. Now he stood here, needing his peculiar "talent" to be given a chance to develop. And he didn't look like any of the other royals he knew. This "boy" wasn't given to the frippery of court silks like the others his age. He dressed in close fitting, dark suede of some kind. He also had a much worldlier look than the normal eyes of a young boy. Not even at an age to be considered a man yet, Aern carried himself like one. All the same, better to make sure he knew his place out here. "Just so y'know, there's no favorites out here. The only title is mine. What I say stands." He nodded curtly as Aern had nodded agreement to all. "Let's get you settled."

Working with small groups and teams, Aern quickly settled to the pattern of this new life. At least here they were quite clear – in loud voices – about what was and was not expected. He would take a turn on duty, help with daily chores such as scrubbing or mending ropes, and he would need to learn to do basic cooking to take a turn there as well.

The first mate, a woman, was watchful those first weeks. Aern would catch her studying him, trying to figure out why the "child" was on the ship. There were times late at night that he even heard her arguing with Captain Jays about why Aern was allowed aboard. Jays never raised his voice and didn't fight back. He'd let the woman rage and complain, then simply say, "I accepted the proposal. I'm the captain. You don't like it, get off my ship."

She would stomp off, still muttering under her breath. Aern came to think the only reason she was allowed to stay was that she really was good at running things on the ship. All the other men and women listened to her commands without question, despite her own rather young age. The captain wasn't that old, from what Aern could tell, but the woman was younger than that. She was also extremely pretty. She didn't dress any different than the rest of the crew, wearing practical sea-worthy clothing, but it was her manner. Able to stand up to the captain, she could also sit quietly with a few of the crew and sing songs or inspire them to work.

He continued his "lessons" from Lord Morenden and became a force to be reckoned with on his own. Too bad many of those he felled never even saw his face. Chirrit became his own version of a carrier pigeon, going back and forth to Pathicos to receive instructions from Morenden. Sometimes those instructions were on how to make a new poison, which Aern would learn and send a sample back. Other times it was a task for when they would put into port.

He would be assigned a hit that needed to be taken out quickly and quietly. He would let the captain know where he was off to, but none of the others. With silent footfalls, he would creep through the towns and villages to the address given. The easiest hits were just concoctions added to drinks or meals, but Aern found himself enjoying the challenge that came with a single mark. It honed his skills and gave him a chance to discover what weapons he preferred and what methods served him best. He rarely failed, and those were only near misses. They would know someone was behind a death, but not who. And since servants tended to be faceless, he was always overlooked in disguise.

His favorites were still using cat-like footsteps to simply sneak up on the unsuspecting. No disguise, no need to mingle with others; just get in close enough to make the strike. It was almost too bad many of those he felled never even saw his face. No one knew it was him. He was just a shadow flitting through the night.

Aern found the crew to be colorful, boisterous, and full of life. They worked hard, and played harder. They knew that Aern had a side job, maybe even suspected what exactly it was he did, but cared only so far as he did his job on board the ship.

Jays turned out to be way more interesting than he had first thought, as well. He was more than a simple captain on a simple ship. It was a pirate ship Jays had worked his way up on. Jays was the pirate king…. sailing under Duke Gunner's decree now. He had instituted codes of conduct with the crew and held to them with an iron fist. Jays was fair, but very firm. There was no second chance for any that failed; there was no putting ashore for those that acted "wrongly." Disobedience resulted in either death or being keelhauled.

"You know," he told Jays one evening, "I thought Lord Morenden was tough." They had just entered the captain's cabin after a man had been flogged and thrown overboard. "You're kind of…" He searched for a word that wouldn't offend.

"…an asshole?" Jays supplied. He gave Aern a wry smile before lighting a smoke. "I have to be."

Aern blinked, trying to find an answer to that. "But… you're a noble's son." Jays had told him that he had been born to one of the lesser nobles at Whitewind, Aern's family castle.

"Yeah." A short bark of laughter escaped him. "Among other things. I'm not really cut out for court life."

Aern grabbed a blanket, sinking to the floor as he bunched the cloth before himself. He took several small vials out, laying them in the folds. He needed to work on mixing several of the potions he needed at the next "job" he would do; might as well work on those as he listened to Jays.

"I couldn't stand being stuck inside walls. Kind of like your sisters, Crys and Mist. Their sprite blood ties them to water. Part of me comes from a water elemental. My mother had fae blood. She moved around a lot. Couldn't stand to be in one place for very long."

"I thought water elementals were tied to a certain body of water." He studied the color, shaking the vial's mixture.

"Yeah. She was only part elemental. That's the part of me that likes the water. But my full name is Jaysonilyeren Longredal Randulf." He paused to see if that sank in with the younger man, then went on. "Get it? I'm part Longredal elf, too." He smiled as Aern looked up, almost dropping a vial.

"Longredal? I thought just the Sithari were real."

"Nope." He took a long drag on his smoke. "Sithari are the coastal elves, Longredal are the forest elves…" he crushed the smoke on the planks at his feet. "…and Jakhil are wasteland elves."

"There aren't any wastelands." His voice was slightly accusing.

"Hoo! Look who knows so much!" Jays dropped onto his bunk. "Just because you've never been there?" He shook his head, laying back and lacing his fingers behind his head. "You're what? Almost thirteen? There's no way you've seen everything."

"So tell me." He knew he sounded defensive. He didn't care. It sounded too much like Jays was making fun of him. He had worked hard to earn the right for others not to jest at his expense. And he wasn't that young; he was fifteen now.

"Later, kiddo." He rolled, showing his back to Aern. "I

need to rest now."

Later wasn't really part of his vocabulary. Aern liked to ferret out information; it was part of what he had been trained to do. If the captain wouldn't tell him…

"Okay, look," the boatswain explained after being badgered. "Sithari are good guys. Ain't never heard them take the wrong side of a fight. Longredal… it's hit or miss. Bein' on the water, we don't see 'em much. But I hear-tell that they'd as soon sneak ya with an arrow in the back as talk to you. Then you got the Jakhil." He shuddered slightly. "Them bastards'll smile as they run you through the heart. Wastelands and mountains – not even easy to tell where they'll come out of."

Chapter 11

He learned of the different races, picked up languages – at least enough to understand basic conversation – and how to get in and out of most port cities. Not just for "jobs," but also where to find or buy ingredients he needed to further his studies.

Some of the lands were extremely different from what he'd known. So many different coastal towns across distant waters ranged from clean and orderly to filthy chaos. None had color other than the brackish seaweed mildewing on the shore and the sand and dirt that all seemed to run towards sooty gray.

Even further inland, the ragged ruts that passed for wagon trails were a mess. Weeds and brambles choked the paths, indicating few travelled outside their home towns. He was thankful at times like that for Chirrit and the ease she added to his missions. Had he been stuck on a horse, he would have had the trouble of purchasing at each port, plus the headache of the passes. More and more, he found himself appreciating what his homelands were like.

All the lands he'd seen as a child had been visible and approachable from gryphon-back, and had bordered Drikelldorn lands. Riots of color met the eye no matter where one looked. There were wheat colored grasses more than waist high in the open fields. Pale yellow to light green willow trees were the tamest of the colors. Surrounding these were pink and burgundy cherry blossom trees. Purple plum trees shaded lilac bushes and his favorite, the tart blue riitziah trees. Bushes with limbs and leaves of various reds made them appear on fire. The waters were the deep blue of lapis lazuli, dotted with white water lilies or a brilliant summer green with dark brown cattails rising from them. Sprites and nymphs danced, for the most part quite carefree, in the clearings. It was also the only place Miantu Cats lived.

Drikelldorn was the home of the Lights and their immortal representatives. The Lights ruled from on high, appearing on rare occasion to dance across the sky in smudges of color. Often described as a great eye looking over them, Aern doubted the truth of that. If the Lights were sentient, then why have delegates walking the land? It was believed that these chosen were men and women that had purportedly gained immortality to affect things like earth, air, fire and water and to govern things such as time, luck and fate.

They allegedly lived on an island at the center of a lake (where it was rumored a revolving castle resided) within a day's ride of Aern's family home. Aern knew where the lake was, theoretically, but had never been there. It was common knowledge that a thick mist hung over that entire area at all times. Nothing could be seen there.

He had a hard time believing anyone would want to live in a castle that turned in circles, or that couldn't be found. Then again, he had a hard time believing in immortals. He had never seen them and therefore held little stock in them. Nothing was as tangible as what was right in front of a person. If the immortals were real, then he'd see them. Until then, he would withhold judgment, just like he did with the different types of elves and fae.

Drikelldorn's lands were near the center of the continent, with Lord Hennin's holdings (in Pathicos, where Lord Morenden lived) to the far west of this. The lands looked the same, full of color everywhere except for the cavernous dark of a forested area towards the southern borders of Drikelldorn that was deeply shaded by trees. As far as Aern knew, no one ever wandered into it. It was rumored that none could even see into it from above.

On the opposite side of the continent, to the east, the Sithari lands bordered the sea. It was considered a "safe" port to put into for provisions and messages. There was some sort of tacit agreement King Grey had with them that stayed the hand of both pirate and assassin while visiting there.

At the height of day, its white sandstone blinded most would-be attackers. Sithari seemed, on first glance, to be a barren land. There were few trees visible on approach by land or sea.

There was land between Drikelldorn and Sithari that housed a loosely formed forest, unlike the foreboding wood of the south known as the Dreamscape, that shifted from deep greens as it went west into the bright colors of Drikelldorn, and opened into dirt and sand the further east one went. Eventually, the dirt went from the deep black of forest undergrowth to sun-bleached white. Very little color broke the monotony of white in and near the Sithari lands.

Inside their homes was another matter entirely. Hidden behind the bleached stone was a bounty of colors, both in furnishings and wall art. Glyphs and words Aern couldn't read decorated doorways, window frames and some furniture.

Several of his lessons had taken him into Sithari lands to find some of his ingredients. They had all been gracious, polite, and had spoken with obvious fondness of their time with his brother Silver, who had trained with them.

They took him directly to the areas where plants grew wild. Several that were specific to the lands grew in abundance here: large white mushrooms, particular yellow flowers with purple veins, and bright yellow daisy-like flowers. Some, in small doses, would brew pain-dampening concoctions. Aern was more interested in the higher doses. Those ranged everywhere from heart attacks to paralysis to death.

Deep in those forested lands inland from Sithari were small mushrooms with bright scarlet caps spotted white. They had given him a very disapproving look when he asked about this particular one, but had told him where to find it. It was a known poison, not used for anything on the healing end of the spectrum. And it was in Longredal lands.

That was a trip he had to make alone. He was warned that Longredal didn't often welcome outsiders in their forest. A hunting party would soon find itself the prey if it went within the confines of the trees. Only Chirrit was willing to come along, and then just barely. Because Aern had housed her in orchards and other treed areas when she was young, she entered. But because she was so much larger now, she had to tuck her wings tight to her body. She kept her head tipped down and a rolling grumble prevented Aern from even trying to sneak. Hells, anything living in the forest had to be able to hear her.

"Lights, girl!" he finally snapped. "You're trained better than that!" He raised a finger to his lips. "Sh!"

She managed to look guilty.

"Yes. Exactly. You make any more noise and who knows what will find us. We don't know this part of the land."

"Then maybe you should heed your own words." An elf materialized from the shadows. He was dressed in tanned leathers of mottled browns and greens, hair pulled back more in practicality than fashion. An immense bow hung across his back and his hand rested on the hilt of a large knife hanging from his belt. He didn't wear any shoes.

It took Aern only a moment to assess the newcomer; not only his countenance, but the ease in which the man appeared. It took Aern a moment more to realize *what* was before him, and the opportunity presented to him. Longredal elves were believed to only show themselves to those they found worthy. Those not deemed worthy would never even know. They would be dead within a short time of entering those forests.

He bowed, holding his hands out away from his body. "I yield to your wisdom."

Something in the elf's posture shifted subtly. He smiled. "And what would you be doing trying to sneak through Longredal lands?"

Chirrit sighed, realizing Aern had found himself in another unique learning circumstance. She also realized this meant she'd be pinned beneath the trees much longer than she would like. While Aern wouldn't unnecessarily keep the ship in port longer than necessary, he also couldn't pass up an opportunity like this.

He spent the better part of a week with the elves. During that time, he discovered that the rumors about their silence were all based on fact. It amazed him that anyone could move through treetops as quietly as they did. They didn't attempt to move that way; it just seemed to be designed into their way of doing things. They had a complicated system of sign language to communicate with each other between trees, never letting those on the ground below know they were being watched. The other thing that helped their quiet movements in the trees was something Aern would never be able to duplicate. Their feet were bare on purpose; they were capable of some grasping ability with their toes. Not anywhere near what a hand could do, but it helped with their stability and footing while moving through the canopy. Strange, but very effective.

Their homes were all inside the hollows high up in the trees. Nothing was used that would have destroyed something growing. Instead, they used natural formations like the hollows. Aern stayed as a guest inside one, marveling at the walls worn smooth inside the living trees. Rough benches were made from fallen tree branches. The beds were vining plants that had taken root in nooks within the tree. Bridges were created the same way.

Dozens of footpaths wound through the canopy of the trees, all created by vines and tree roots that had been bent and twisted together over the years until they formed very solid walkways.

Small frogs were shown to him. Brightly colored and patterned, he had wondered aloud at why predators didn't take advantage of that. The elves explained by showing. They rubbed the tips of arrows and wooden darts along the back of the frogs, careful not to touch the tips themselves after that. Inserted into hollow tubes, they were then blown towards what they hunted – sometimes a bird, sometimes something creeping along the ground – never missing. Within a few heartbeats, the prey was paralyzed. "It is a toxin," he was told, "that affects their limbs. They cannot move. A large enough dose would be immediate death. However," the elf held up one of the darts, "this does not hold much." It was purposely kept to a low dose for their hunting. They didn't want to accidentally end up poisoning themselves when they ate the meat, choosing instead to finish the kill with wicked looking daggers.

He had learned in training how to operate a blow dart, but this was another level. He took his time learning it, earning him the right to keep one of the wooden tubes and a handful of darts. They helped him scrape enough toxin into a single small jar that he would be able to take with him. Dozens of frogs, all left uninjured, had produced enough to only fill a single jar he could easily conceal in the palm of his hand.

There was also the matter of the mushrooms he had needed. Not only did they show him where to find that particular one, they pointed out three others that could be used for good or ill, depending on how it was prepared. He was almost disappointed at week's end to leave them, feeling he hadn't learned near what they had to teach. He hoped a time would come he'd be able to return.

It was to his surprise on his return to find a small addition to the crew. A little boy, barely walking, was being coddled by every last one of the hardened sailors on the ship. Several hours passed before he had a chance to catch Jays alone at the helm, asking about the child. "I thought kids were bad luck." He had certainly heard enough complaints behind his back when he'd first joined the crew.

Jays didn't even look at him. He continued looking at the charts and the navigation equipment. "You thought wrong." He made several notations to his charts before looking up with a sigh. "You're thinking of women, and I don't see them as bad luck, either."

"But…"

"But the boy is mine." He rolled the maps up, carefully tucking the equipment back into a box. Aern followed him back to the captain's cabin. Jays said nothing the entire time.

Aern knew better than to ask; that would have been more than rude. But he had more than enough patience to wait the captain out. Luckily it wasn't that long.

"I told you before my life isn't all about being captain." A deep sadness resounded in his voice as he moved to stand at his window, the only glass viewpoint on the ship, over the water's wake trailing from the back of the ship. "I had to earn this post. And earning it wasn't easy." His right hand rested against the weathered wood frame, his head against the hand. "It was a straight-up pirate vessel when I started."

The silence stretched out as Jays seemed to be lost in his thoughts. Aern was very glad that he had been trained to wait and watch. As much as he wanted to ask questions, he held his tongue.

When Jays spoke again, it wasn't about how he became captain. It seemed he didn't really want to discuss that matter. "To stay on, proof was needed. They set the task." He glanced back at Aern, eyes haunted and almost hollow, matching the flat, unemotional tone of his words. "Kill the men, kill the children, and rape the women."

Aern went cold inside as he watched Jays turn back to look outside. Women could be more devious than any assassin, working to get what they wanted in subtle ways, but that didn't mean they needed to be tortured. Lord Morenden had even been quite clear about that matter in their training. "You're there to do one job and one job only," he had said. "Get in and get out. Leave all innocents alone." Now to hear that Jays had…

He had no right to judge. He had killed on orders, too. This just changed the way he saw things with Jays.

"There's a girl out there. A good woman." A long pause fell again. "She made me see a few things. She agrees with what I'm doing." That seemed to make up his mind. He nodded to himself once, straightened his shoulders and turned back to face the cabin. "She agrees," he stated once more, almost as if wanting to convince Aern.

Once Jays had composed himself again, wearing his aloof mask, the captain went up on deck, rolling a smoke, taking his time in lighting it, and only then finally looking at Aern. "I told you there were things you didn't know about me."

Something introspective crossed his features, rendering Jays silent for several more minutes. He watched his crew hard at work, momentarily considering which were trustworthy. Of them all, this kid at his side was one he knew wouldn't stab him in the back. Considering what the boy did, he wasn't sure why that was such a strong fact in his mind, but he suddenly wanted to tell someone what had happened over the years. "I walked into a tavern and saw him getting kicked around." He motioned to where the two year old boy played with a pile of rope. "His mother was making him suffer on my account." His eyes squinted slightly in the sun as he took a long pull on his smoke. "I don't want that to be the case. Not when I'm captain now and can say otherwise. He's mine. And he deserves better than what he had." He inhaled deeply, the orange glow of the smoke flaring. His voice was quiet when he added, "All my kids do."

Stunned, Aern watched him walk off to collect the small boy. Everything he thought he had known about the captain was turned upside down in that moment. Aern had defined him entirely as just "the captain," never thinking much about his life beyond here on the ship. Apparently, Jays was finding a way to have some sort of life outside of the containment of the ocean.

For the first time, Aern wondered about the same for himself. Maybe all women weren't looking to get close to the throne or the crown prince. Maybe someone would want him for him, faults and all. If a known pirate could do it… maybe, just maybe, an assassin could find the right woman, too. Someday. Maybe.

Chapter 12

It wasn't that Kelly was ungrateful to her father. She appreciated the fact that he spared nothing for the women in his life. He claimed to love each and every one of them, but when they all sat together in the dining hall, he often called them by the wrong names. Even his mistresses weren't free of this common mistake.

That should have been enough to say there were too many in the family. It obviously wasn't. Two of the women were swollen with child… again. One of the others had only recently delivered a son that had died within a few hours.

She could understand why her brother was so coddled, based on this. Considering how important the boys were supposed to be. At least with only one boy, Mayden never had to worry about their father mixing his name up with anyone else's.

"There are a few new boys being brought in," Adept Llewellyn informed them. "Any with fire magic will be in our home for the next few weeks. I expect they'll be welcomed," he glanced at each of the girls that were old enough to marry, Kelly now included, "within reason."

A noise of disgust escaped her, earning her looks from the mistresses nearest her. She didn't care. She was thirteen, hardly in a place to want to consider having babies of her own. If she were a farm girl, she'd be given at least until she was sixteen to choose a husband.

But there again, *she* would have gotten to choose. In this prison she called a life even that basic right would be denied her. She would have to marry whoever her father and the Keltori matched her to.

Knowing that if she tried to meet her father's gaze, all she could give him was a militant look, she excused herself and left the room. Dessert didn't even sound good now.

The few apprentices at the table watched her go. They didn't look directly at her, as her father would never have allowed that, but she could feel them looking up through lowered lashes. She paused only long enough to narrow her eyes and glare at them with a frown. Having breasts didn't make her something to stare at.

Her palm slapped against the door as she shoved it open with enough force to hit the wall and bounce back to slam shut again behind her. Her slippered feet didn't give away her footfalls as she stomped down the hall.

Two of the new initiates sat in the study talking in hushed whispers. Her steps faltered a little when she saw how scared they looked. It had to be awful to be pulled away from home and family. She wished she could do something for them, but it wasn't allowed. Daughters didn't see men alone. Ever.

With a last glance at them, she moved on more slowly. Rounding a corner, she rolled her eyes and backed up again. Bricriu. He had been to their home on different occasions over the years and usually had trouble follow him. He was several years older than her and was currently holding one of the servants against the wall. She didn't like him, and from the looks of it, the woman with him didn't either.

Fear was written on the woman's face as she kept turning, trying to avoid the kiss Bricriu was intent on giving her. Kelly was annoyed that even the servants were taught to be "good girls" and not fight, but she was more angry that this apprentice thought he could get away with something like this.

Anyone in training was not to touch women. They needed to stay focused on their magic until they passed their final tests. This particular one, she knew from spying on her father's conversations, was trouble. He tended to do what he wanted, when he wanted. At the moment, he seemed to think he wanted one of the serving girls.

Not on Kelly's time. She squared her shoulders, taking up one of the small chairs that sat in the hallway. Her stupid indoor slippers were finally good for something as they kept her footfalls silent. There was a moment's concern that when she lifted the chair overhead that the seams along her bodice would rip, but they held. She'd have to look at a bigger dress again. Stupid breasts.

With all the force she could muster, she swung the chair down to land on top of the weasel's head. "Get away from our help!"

The woman raced off down the hall in tears, obviously not wanting to be here when all hell broke loose as he spun to face her, one hand to the back of his head now. "Woman, what is the matter with you?" he yelled at her.

Kelly's eyes widened in fear as she realized how far above her this man loomed. He was tall and built like stone wall. But she wasn't going to back down. He'd been wrong. "There's nothing wrong with me. You were in the wrong."

He sneered at her. It just further proved to him that Llewellyn's get were nothing but trouble. They all needed to be removed. "You," he put as much menace to his words as he could, "are a woman." He stepped in closer to her, flexing his arms to show bulging biceps and fisted hands. "And barely that. Learn your place."

She shifted one foot back for balance, flexing a knee as Mayden had taught her, while bringing her own fists up. "Learn your own," she challenged. "Apprentices don't touch women."

A cruel sneer curled one side of his mouth up. "I do." One hand shot out, grabbing the back of her neck and spinning her around. Catching her off guard, he followed through with the momentum to push her into the wall behind him. The crack reverberated down the hall as she bounced, falling back to the ground.

It would bruise, if it hadn't already broken. Kelly put a hand to her cheek, trying to contain the pain as she stared up at him. He stared back with a smug grin before turning and sauntering off down the hall.

He knew. Kelly watched him go, realizing that he knew the rules. If she were to tell the truth about what had happened to her cheek, she would have to admit her own part in speaking to him, as well as hitting him, both of which were expressly forbidden. But if she kept her silence, it allowed for him to do this again, maybe to one of her sisters.

Then again, none of her sisters would break the rules. Only Kelly seemed to have that problem. Bitter tears stung her eyes as she came to the conclusion that she would have to live in some fear of this apprentice.

She just needed to stay out of his way for a few weeks. He would be gone in a few weeks. She hoped.

Chapter 13

Only one year out from the academy, one year of life on the sea, and he had been asked to return for the wedding of the ages. He tried not to roll his eyes at the invitation, considering the whole thing ridiculous. His older brothers were only going to be… seventeen? Eighteen? Surely the wedding was going to be nothing more than a political maneuver. Aern couldn't help blowing out a laugh at the thought; just one more reason he was glad to have walked away from being a prince.

But then, just getting the formal invitation had been enough to remind him that he'd never fully escape the life of a royal. He had needed to find a tailor to make him something other than his usual outfit of dark suede. It would give away his cover… and it wasn't exactly festive enough for a wedding.

Having donned one of several new outfits, he returned home with Jays. Chirrit had groused about being land-bound beside a "slow" horse again, but she acquiesced to it.

Jays pulled back as they entered the formal courtyard, letting Aern take the spotlight. It was only right for the young prince to be seen first… and it made a striking entrance to see the turquoise blue silk of his tunic shimmering from the back of a large gryphon. Chirrit's beak was a beautiful sunshine yellow below a white mask of tiny feathers around her amber gold eyes. Beyond this, her feathers lengthened from the white into what looked like a long, butter yellow mane that cascaded down over her chest and spilling onto powerful shoulders that changed from blonde feathers to tawny brown fur. Powerful hawk legs ending with sharp talons graced her front while the strong muscular legs of a large cat came behind. She was a regal creature and played the part. There were plenty of gasps, both in fear and delight, at the sight of one of their own sitting astride such a majestic creature. And she knew it.

Jays dismounted, lifting his small son down before he handed the reins of his horse over to a stable boy and stepped up to aid in moving Chirrit. No one else would know how to handle her. *Hells*, he thought, *she barely lets me handle her*! But he stood at her side while Aern dismounted, then carefully lured her away from the crowd that had gathered.

Only after seeing her following the promise of a rabbit Jays had, did Aern turn his attention to the throng gathered before him. Crowds stayed well back, despite cheers of welcome, so this large group could only be family. He didn't recognize any of them.

Resolving himself to this strange encounter, he stepped forward to be embraced by those claiming relation to him. He was glad he had chosen something other than his usual gambeson, if for nothing else than the continued secrecy of what he carried. Most of his weapons were in the pack with Jays at the moment. Only his punching daggers remained strapped to his wrists below the shirt, and his stilettos in his boot sheaths.

Gradually the overwhelming chatter died down a little and Aern was escorted inside. The man pushed through the throng, laughter in his voice as he called out, "That's enough. Let's get him situated first." Palm open, he motioned Aern to step through the now parted crowd. Kyle. That was the oldest brother. Half brother. Something like that. He was eleven years Aern's senior and worked as the Steward of Whitewind.

There was a calmness to the man, a lack of tension in his movements, that indicated Kyle was content with his life. Aern kept glancing at him, trying to see any resemblance between them.

Just inside the foyer, Kyle stopped a moment to greet several people that wandered past, gave instructions to what were likely servants, and crossed to start up the large marble stairway across from the door that led up to the left. He seemed aware of everything around him without being tense. Tall and muscular, his easy smile and wavy brown locks were nothing like Aern. It was hard to imagine how they could be brothers. Aern was always on guard, always watching for trouble.

"Ah, ah!" Kyle stopped just at the top of the stairs, admonishment in his voice. Giggles sounded from around the corner, followed by footsteps running. "You better run." His threat obviously meant little as he was smiling and laughing as he said it. "My kids," he explained to Aern.

Turning left, where the kids had gone right, Kyle showed him to a guest room just off the family rooms. The door faced the balcony overlooking the main floor, which Aern didn't particularly care for, and the room itself was large and spacious. He wasn't sure if he liked that or not. He had gotten used to sharing quarters as a page, and had little privacy aboard Jays' ship. This room easily could have fit another three beds as large as the one centered on one wall. The room was as overwhelming as everything else. The opulence was less pronounced than some of the castles and keeps he'd taken marks out at, but it was still richly appointed. There was so much busy-ness in the furnishings, the decorations … just like there were so many people and so many demands on his time.

Kyle's smile faded as concern took over. "Something wrong?"

The large open space was, but it wouldn't be right to complain since they were putting him on the same wing as the family quarters. He remembered as a small boy running the hallway outside his room, just as Kyle's kids had been doing. They meant well. They wanted to make him feel welcome, but he'd much rather have had a small room with just enough room for a bed. He had to force himself to smile politely that yes, it was fine, just so he could be left in peace.

Thankfully the wedding would be in just a few days and he could leave again. In the meantime, he took to sitting up on the roof with Jays. He would enjoy some quiet time with Chirrit while Jays would have a smoke. Jays would occasionally tease him about how he would be the next to marry, which Aern would easily laugh off.

Of course, at almost fourteen, it wasn't as if things like marriage were much on his mind. Girls in general were only beginning to find a place in his mind. He was too busy learning, studying, and working the shadows to worry about girls or marriage. Until now. He was glad it wasn't him, but still…

It was one thing to consider the matter of a political match, but Aern really hadn't thought it was something his family would stoop to. It wasn't what he'd been hearing the adults had done for their own relationships.

The day of the wedding dawned bright and clear – a good omen, some said, for a wedding day. He made his way to the main floor, crossing past a door to an office; his father's, if he remembered correctly. He heard the voices of his twin brothers, and, seeing the door cracked open just enough to peek in, he took the opportunity to find out more about these siblings without needing to speak to them. He was more than surprised to find the Crown Prince a nervous wreck over the unknown bride.

Sterling petulantly sank into a chair, crossing his arms. "I haven't even seen her. Not one word about her looks."

"Our seneschal says she's fairly smart," Silver answered, "she's quick to catch on to things."

Sterling gave his twin a pained look. "That's what, when you cut the shit out, says ugly."

Aern snickered, trying to cover it with a cough. He hurried on past the door, not wanting to get drawn into the discussion. But Sterling had the right of it, as far as he was concerned. He didn't want to marry at all, but if he did, it wouldn't be for a girl whose only description said she was "fairly smart."

Smoothing the turquoise tunic down and tugging at the hem

once again, Aern took his place among the other nobles assembled in the court. It was hard to think this style of clothing had once been all he'd ever known. Now it was almost as if he were calling attention to himself. Never mind the others all dressed similarly to him, he still felt like an idiot in such fancy items these days. He'd grown too accustomed to his dark, close-fitting every-day wear.

King Grey Bradley took his place before the assembly, seating himself calmly. Aern noted that his father didn't seem at all bothered by so many watching him. He had to extend the same note of pride to his brothers as the doors opened to admit Sterling and Silver. Both moved with surety but their differences were obvious to someone trained to watch.

Sterling moved with purpose, commanding the room. His color was more of a midnight blue, accented with the court color of turquoise. Silver dressed all in white but for the silver trim and the turquoise blue on the underside of his cape; he moved with a fluid grace, almost an echo of his twin.

The girl was kind of a mousy thing with wide, fearful eyes that attempted to look happy and radiant. Aern would have liked to raise at least a little pity for his brother, but all he could think was how he was extremely glad it wasn't him at the front in this situation.

Despite being slightly green, Sterling found himself a married man and went outside to hopefully receive the blessing of the Lights. Before anyone else could follow, an elf near the back rose to his feet. "Prince Silver." Dressed in clean cut lines, his fitted tunic flared slightly at the waist, ending at the midline of his hips. Form fitted pants were tucked neatly into knee-high boots. He was aware of how his movements flowed as easily as the blonde hair that fell over his shoulders. Even his clothing was designed to ensure the best presented image, being made of some soft yellow material that matched his hair.

"Gavriel," Steward Kyle announced, "Friend of Prince Silver, Emissary of the Sithari elves." He gave the elf a smile and a slight nod to approach the royals.

Silver stopped and turned in the direction of the visitor, a broad smile coming to his face. The guests stayed in their seats, although many did try to peer out the veranda doors the bridal couple had taken.

The fair-skinned and golden haired elf came forward, extending a sword and scabbard to Silver with a bow. "In honor of the prince's seventeenth birthday, a gift from our court."

It seemed that everyone in the room sat forward, forgetting the bridal couple for the moment as they wanted to see what was so special about the blade.

"I am… honored," Silver finally spoke, more than astounded. Several lesser nobles started to rise, trying to get a better view.

The elf went on to explain that the blade rarely was allowed outside Sithari lands. "Prince Silver has proven in his few years with us that he is proficient in the Ansavru and a worthy holder of a shayl-yar."

Now they had Aern's attention. Silver had seemed rather thin and lacking in muscle. He never carried a weapon. Aern was curious about this new development. Gavriel explained that the blade would sing if wielded by someone with great expertise. Wielded by the untrained, the blade would be unbalanced, becoming a deadly detriment to the user. The Ansavru was an Elven term for blade dancing. With this particularly fancy blade, Ansavru was the dance of death.

"Lord Father," Silver pulled off his dress gloves and jacket. "I would demonstrate. Gavriel is the only partner here that I'm authorized to practice with." He motioned for the elf's weapons to be brought as well, shrugging out of his jerkin.

The king frowned slightly, but nodded agreement to Silver. Aern saw his mother, the queen, gain a pinched look of worry that her son would be fighting. But surely she had to know and understand that all boys learned to wield a sword of some kind in their training.

"Full speed," Gavriel announced as he accepted his own weapon and turned to Silver.

"Called hits," Silver smiled. "Loss of use as appropriate."

"Man down, match called." Gavriel raised his blade before his face as Silver did the same. There was something a little too gleeful about the two of them doing this, as if it were more than just practice.

As rules of combat were announced, Aern slid out of his seat, going to stand along the back wall. He wanted a really good view of what was coming. He had only heard of the Ansavru, but the elves hadn't been forthcoming in telling him anything about it. To know that Silver could do it was a pleasant surprise. It seemed that his trip home was going to at least have something interesting come of it.

The blades saluted opposing figures as the men stepped into the dance. They began moving faster, the blades blurring. A soft humming started to rise and fall in time to their turns and strikes, punctuated on occasion as one or the other called an injury. The only pauses were on those moments as they called a hit, and told where. This was quickly followed by "Ansavru!" and they would regain their battle.

The bridal couple returned, Sterling carefully not touching his young bride, in time to see the very end of the display. Aern noticed that neither looked extremely happy. They took seats on the dais near the king, watching as "ansavru" was called a final time.

Aern watched, more than impressed, as Silver "lost" his sword arm, forcing him (according to the rules of the game) to drop his blade. Gasps from those assembled told they worried as well. Aern was halfway to his feet when he saw Silver roll beneath Gavriel's blade to retrieve his own, now fighting right handed. He hadn't realized Silver was left handed. Aern smiled in some small measure of pride that this brother was capable not only of fighting opposite of most, but that he could also use either arm equally well. His movements were fluid yet controlled as he spun, his blade now coming to land at the back of Gavriel's knees.

The elf, graceful as most elves were, fell back onto the cool marble, allowing Silver to lay the point of his blade at the elf's throat. "Death," Gavriel spoke into the now still assembly, "by honorable opponent." They were both up and hugging each other in the next moment, obviously quite pleased with their little performance.

After clapping politely along with the others, he then moved to exit the party and all the people. There would be dancing and dining into the early hours of the morning, something he wasn't particularly interested in. Leaving the throne room, Aern held no jealousy for either twin. He didn't want a bride (and didn't particularly care what the outcome of the outdoor excursion had been), and Silver had obviously earned that blade. That was apparent in the skill shown just moments before, but Aern had to wonder what would happen if Silver ever had to use that skill for "real" fighting?

Chapter 14

Waking from yet another nightmare, Bricriu sat breathing hard, drenched in sweat. It wasn't right. It wasn't right, and someday the Keltori would pay. His father had been slain when Bricriu was but a lad. He and his brother Doran had been there, had seen what their sire had gone through.

He raked his fingers through damp hair as he cursed the bane of his existence. Ayden Llewellyn had dealt the killing blow. Bricriu's father had been defenseless, no magic left to him, no weapons allowed. It had been bad enough to watch his father tortured as the Keltori painfully pulled every last ounce of magic from MacFurgal's body, but then to see Llewellyn bring his father's own Element against him… Bricriu would kill him. He'd kill Llewellyn and take everything for himself. He only needed to see an end to his own training first.

Few things mattered to him. Those that did he held sacred: prove he wasn't the traitor his father had been; acquire Llewellyn's Fire keep; kill Llewellyn… by any means he could.

He *would* have it all, maybe even a place on the Keltori as the Fire Mage. With a smile on his lips, he lay back in bed, drifting off to sleep with happy thoughts of murder.

Back at his remote stone keep, Remington smiled as he gazed into his crystal. The boy was going to be even better than his father had been. He let the glow fade from the faceted crystal as he went back to his own projects.

He had been lucky to have been given the boy. At least all the work he had invested in the father wouldn't go to waste. MacFurgal and his wife had both been easily manipulated into working for Remington, trying to tear apart the silly council and restore proper order. They had been more than useful, keeping Remington from being exposed as the true force behind the troubles. Until their deaths.

Their older boy was worthless; he had been in training already by that point. Doran was nothing but another pawn in the game the Keltori continued to play, rewarding its strongest and brightest by giving them pretty playthings to marry and bed. That boy had been given one of Llewellyn's girls as a reward for his perfect training. Remington hadn't been able to get at the boy's mind early enough.

But Bricriu… Remington smiled with the ease in which he had manipulated the boy. This one had been home yet when the father was turned to Remington's goals. Everything he had taught him, everything he had been told, had been geared towards fueling the boy's anger and frustration.

It helped that Remington had the unknown Gift, as well. The others knew he could do things, could manipulate situations, but they had never figured out exactly what he did. He had been dismissed from training for not completing the patterns they wished of him. He hadn't been able to make grand Elemental happenings, so had been deemed without a Gift.

And oh, how wrong they were! He could manipulate

minds, encourage madness, and hone anger to unreasonable levels. He would take them down. And Bricriu would be the sword he used against them.

Miles away, Bricriu dreamt of Llewellyn's pretty daughters. A cold smile graced his tempered features, even in sleep. One of them would be his; one of Llewellyn's get would be made his wife. He would make her suffer as he had. He'd take it out on her, one painful strike after another, until her body was as broken as his spirit had been that day.

His father had been a great man, wiser than these fools that ruled now. Marshall law had held sway in times past; those with the might would rule. There had been none of this pansy-ass "council" business. Men like those on the Keltori would have been killed in battle, leaving the truly strong to take command of the world.

To have taken a man like his father, publicly humiliate him before their entire hagiocracy, stripping him of magic, and then… and then…

An awful, angry scowl chased its way across his features; he tossed in bed as his dreams revisited that day. His father had been deemed traitor only hours previous to being dragged before an emergency assembly. The local rabble hadn't been invited, thankfully, so there were no farmers or other low-borns present. Only mages. Only those of any importance. Only every last member of the hagiocracy, including the initiates.

Fire crackled from Bricriu's fingers, setting nearby curtains aflame, racing down towards the bedding.

Bound by magic, his father and mother had been taken to a training ground at the Phelan's Keep. His father wasn't even given a chance to defend himself. He was left bound as his crimes were read aloud. He was left bound as the four council members joined forces, ganging up on the elder MacFurgal to strip his powers. Slowly. Painfully.

His father's screams of pain filled the air as he was tortured. Bit by bit, the entire assembly watched the magic pulled from the man. Any little bit of any of the elements was drawn out. He could see every person gathered stand a little straighter as the magic was redistributed to the proper elemental mages. There was nothing visible to say magic was moving, but then there rarely was. Magic wasn't always flashy. Like now. This was nothing more than quiet, concentrated torment.

When his father's voice was raw and he was on his knees gasping for a solid breath, three of the four backed up. The man tried to rise, only to have Phelan cause the earth to shake, the Air Adept fed the fire with more and more oxygen, fanning the small inferno higher. Llewellyn stepped closer, calling Fire to his hands. A fireball exploded out from his raised hands, striking MacFurgal, incinerating the now powerless man. Bricriu was aware of others nearby becoming slightly scorched, but his eyes were unable to look away from his father's burning body.

And then there was nothing; only a small pile of ash that had once been a woman and a man of strength and power. The others, even Bricriu's older brother Doran, had turned from the scene in silence. They had all turned their back on the "traitors" and walked away.

As his mattress exploded below him, he woke. Barely conscious yet, he managed to tamp out the flames. Heart still racing, he saw in each small fire his father's pyre. They would die. They would pay.

Chapter 15

A familiar face pushed her way through the crowds at the wedding dance, hugging him tightly. He had spent so much time learning how to not be touched, that he felt awkward with a girl suddenly in his arms. Carefully, politely, he extricated himself from her grasp, backing up a step.

She laughed. "Aern! Don't you recognize me?"

It took him a moment longer to finally place her. Heather. Aern hadn't thought much about her in several years. He remembered her as being mischievous and troublesome, always wanting to follow him around and bothering him about what he was doing. Now she had matured into a pretty girl. Seventeen to Aern's fourteen, she had developed beyond a child and looked the part of a lady.

He had only recently started noticing girls and the way they were nicely different from boys. He still didn't trust them and, considering what the poisons had done to his body, he'd never want to marry. But it didn't stop him from noting the curves and the softness and her willowy figure.

Because of the poisons, Aern's growth had stunted somewhat, placing him only at five foot eight. She was slightly taller than him, plus she wore heels, letting her stand above him. It made him feel awkward. But instead of letting it bother him, he went into his working mode, setting his emotions aside. He gave her a polite expression with a cool smile. He didn't really want to be stuck visiting with her, not during such a formal event. She was of marriageable age, even if he had a few more years before that happened for boys. He didn't want anyone looking at him as a potential husband here. He wasn't even finished with his formal training.

Not to mention that she was in his personal space. Men and women were supposed to stand at least the distance apart between an elbow and hand. She was right in front of him, touching his arm and batting her lashes at him. There was protocol to be observed, and she obviously didn't care.

"Yes, Heather." He answered, taking another step back, hoping she would take the hint. "It's…good to see you again." Not particularly. She made him uncomfortable with the intensity she had followed him around back at Lord Morenden's. She had that same look now… almost predatory.

"We wondered where you had gone." Her voice was just as tickled; she had missed his cool tone. Her fingers lightly, and repeatedly, touched his arm, despite him trying to lean away from it or stepping back. "Some of the girls wondered if you had fallen ill or if you had been called back home for something." Her voice was a happy chatter, reminding Aern of a songbird. "I couldn't imagine you having been called home, unless there was an emergency," she babbled, "but it was better than thinking that maybe you had died. And now here you are!"

He blinked, staring at her in stunned silence. What could he respond to all that with that would still be a truth?

She didn't give him a chance. She laughed in that flirtatious way some of the girls had shown, hugging him again, despite him stiffening and trying to back away.

"Sister, enough!" a male voice laced with humor called out. It was her twin brother, a boy Aern had known early on his first year in training. He had been kind enough to help Aern learn to live away from family those first months, although they had maintained little contact since Aern switched his training.

Giving Aern a pretty, petulant pout, she then blew him a kiss and bounced off to flirt with some other young man. Aern blew a sigh of relief that she was gone. She had been fine as a little girl, but seemed to only get more flirtatious as she got older.

"Sorry about that," her brother offered. "Dunno what's with her the last couple of years."

Aern simply smiled that he accepted the apology, not saying that Heather's "problem" was her being boy-crazy. She always had been; trying to kiss Aern or half a dozen others. She needed to be married, settled away from temptation, but she worked her wiles on the men in her family as well. They cozened her, apologizing for her behavior, never even really knowing how bad the girl could be. Well, he thought with a sigh, it wasn't his place to disabuse them of their "good girl." Besides, he'd be gone and back to sea in another day.

Chapter 16

Two more sisters married. Kelly felt like she was living in an hourglass, watching her own "end" coming. Every sister leaving home was one more pebble putting her that much closer to being married off herself. She saw her father pensively considering each of them at their evening meals. Too often she felt his eyes watching her.

Every time, she would fight a losing battle to keep her eyes demurely down. Every time, she bit the inside of her lip to keep from speaking something rude to her father. He didn't deserve her bad behavior. He made sure they were all well cared for and had the best of everything, and she knew he wanted them all to be matched compatibly, no matter how difficult it was to plan for something like that. But that didn't mean she felt any better about being nothing more than a prize cow for some mage she'd never met. She couldn't help glaring at her father for even considering her for marriage.

Then she'd feel bad. He always lowered his gaze with a weary sigh, more focused on his meal than on anyone at the table. He hardly even paid attention to his mistresses anymore. Most of his time was spent in his study now, avoiding everyone in the house. Even her brother didn't rate much attention when he was home, so at least she knew it wasn't particular to the girls of the house.

At least he kept Mayden's name straight. Kelly was one of

the few that seemed to always be in trouble, and yet he still had trouble with her name. "Katrine!" He called, peeking out of his office. Annoyance laced his voice as he caught himself. Katrine was long married. "Calda…"

She turned to look back from the front door. "Kelly, father."

"Kelly," he corrected with a tired smile. "Come here."

What little smile she'd had disappeared. Going to his study was never a good thing. All the same, there was nothing for it. With a sigh and a last glance out at the sunshine, she let the door close and went to her father's study.

It was strange, but he never looked so tired when the other adepts were around; just when he was with his family. She watched him take a seat in a leather chair near a window. This room was usually off limits to them.

"In here." He motioned to the chair opposite him when she didn't move from just inside the door. "And close the door."

This wasn't going well. With a kick backwards, her foot shoved the door shut, gaining her another disapproving look from him. A proper lady would have turned, using both hands to gently close it. Another mark against her.

She smiled in what she hoped was her most charming manner. One corner of his mouth perked up in recognition of it. When he spoke, his voice wasn't nearly as irritated either. "Come, girl."

That was a little better. With more of a bounce in her step, she carefully sidestepped the podium in the middle of the room with his spellbook and sat in the chair he indicated, tucking her feet up under her. It earned her another frown. Only children were allowed to sit like that. "Catherine…"

"Kelly."

"Right." Another frown. "You're of an age now…"

"Father, please," she reached over to take his hand, batting large innocent eyes at him. It had always gotten her out of trouble as a little girl. "Calda and Shannon just married. I'm not even next in line."

His eyes were troubled as he studied her. There was a slight tick in his left cheek that she'd never noticed before. "No," he finally said, not giving in to her attempts at sweetness. "You aren't. But you are old enough to be listed as a potential."

She huffed in irritation, flopping back in the chair. "I don't want to marry," she grumped.

He leaned towards her in equal irritation. "Calda…"

"Kelly," she shot back.

"Kelly." Orange flames flashed across his eyes.

She pushed further back into the chair, this time in concern. Flames showing anywhere on a fire mage was dangerous ground.

"I had no choice in marriage either. I accepted it. And the mistresses. And the headaches." His voice was clipped and Kelly was sure she saw sparks in his hair. "As the daughter of a mage, and more importantly, as the daughter of a Keltorin, you will do what's right."

"But…"

Sparks crackled around his fingers as he lifted a hand to stay her complaints. "The Keltori will be informed tomorrow." He took a few deep breaths with his eyes closed, regaining his composure. All flames faded away as he again looked to Kelly with warmth. "I care for all of you, and I want the best for you. I don't want to see any of you married to a farmer or taken as a mistress. This is the best I can do for you."

It wasn't good enough for Kelly. "It doesn't matter," she stated as she got to her feet. She kicked the floor length skirts out and swished them out of entanglement. "You're going to do what you want anyways."

"It's the way things work, Kelly."

At least he got her name right that time. And what was wrong with the farmers? They were good enough to take mistresses from, as her own mother was a testament to. They seemed fine enough to Kelly's way of thinking. But that was another argument, for another day. And she wasn't winning the one she was in.

"Fine." There was nothing else to say on the matter. She hiked her skirts up to mid-calf so she could properly storm from the room, getting almost to his spellbook before he called her name again. "What?" She didn't turn to look at him this time.

"The Keltori has our best interests in mind."

He only said that because he was on it. And his closest friends. It wasn't fair that they got to decide the lives of everyone else. "Hmph." Her hand shot out before she could consider the ramifications. She slammed the heavy spellbook closed and let the momentum keep the book moving, pushing it off the stand and onto the floor. She glanced over her shoulder with a smug look at her small rebellion.

It was short lived. He was on his feet in the same instant, yelling her name. He wouldn't be forgetting it again this day. Her best course of action at the moment was to get back to her room and out of his sight, which she did as quickly as she could.

Chapter 17

Three more years passed as he matured, letting the heavy seriousness of his career settle over him. He loved knowing he did something worthwhile, but at the end of the day, sometimes, it was hard to look at himself in the mirror. He was becoming nothing but a shadow, unknown to anyone off the ship and not even really known to those on the ship. They kept their distance, wary of both his skill and his gryphon. It didn't help that he'd never really taken to life at sea. He did his fair share of the work, but the time at sea was too long and too cramped for him.

Jays added another child to the ship's "family," a little girl slightly older than his son. Aern found that he liked the children. They weren't some random children he was doing his job for, but two amazing little people that he enjoyed entertaining. They put a face on the reason for his sacrifices.

He would take himself up to the crow's nest more often than not, just to get away from the steady press of people on the sleek ship, sometimes with the kids, sometimes just to toss treats to Chirrit or be alone. There were times of entertainment and music making, but mostly it was doing your work and staying out of the way of others. Being different from the sailors only grew over time. He learned the rigging, learned the jobs and details of a sailors life, but he was more than that.

Aern's favorite times were still the arrivals of new instructions from Morenden. He would receive a satchel with instructions, descriptions, and the ingredients, along with the job he was to be assigned. All poison mixtures were tested first on himself. From there, he would let the others do their own thing once on shore, slipping off to assassinate some troublemaker or other.

Of course, there was fighting on the waters; cannons and swords and hand to hand between ships that needed to be run down. They had their jobs to do, too, and Aern was happy to assist as he could. It improved his sword arm and his ability to fight in tight quarters. Every time he walked away from one of those skirmishes, he was thankful to Lord Morenden for giving him the fighting daggers. More than once, when his sword was lost or too big for the close combat, he had been able, with a quick flick of his wrists to draw them down from his wrist sheaths to his hands and lay low the one before him.

He kept only two sets of silks to his names now, needing one for the times within Keeps or Palaces; the other if he ever needed to return to Whitewind. If far at sea, he would wear his simple homespun… things he always purchased from local merchants that looked to need the gold most. That small part of his father lived on in his actions. Otherwise, he was a lethal shadow, dressed in the colors of darkness, striking only with the moon as his witness.

Prince Aern faded into a memory. Shadow Walker, or Shadow as he was more commonly known, moved with more stealth than the others, was more deadly, more dangerous. He was known to be a lethal killer, often striking when least expected. He was only sixteen.

As a rule, the others on board gave him a wide berth; only one woman seemed to have no fear of him. She had been there since Aern joined the crew, but in the past year she had become one of the mates closest to the captain. Jays didn't like or trust her though. She only stayed because of her skill. Because of that, she tended to dog the captain's steps, learning every nuance of his job. Perhaps, Aern thought, she knew that it was better to know the enemy than wait for him to attack.

This past year had seen them together as ship mates – partners on the high seas. Aern held his own importance among the crew; she was working towards being the next First Mate. He would never have considered her as anything of import until she propositioned him down in the hold. She was first and foremost a member of the crew, to be treated as such. But there was no denying her beauty, and despite Aern's best attempts, he had been finding his body reacting to her presence. At sixteen, he still hadn't "known" a woman and saw this as a conquest he could readily agree to, wanting to pass this final hurdle into "adulthood." The thought of her had begun to consume him: her scent, sultry eyes, and buxom figure.

When she had propositioned this tryst, he had been more than ready for it. He was between jobs at the moment. A slight diversion couldn't be so bad, as long as he kept his head about him, knowing this was to be a one time thing.

They lost no time as fevered kisses and hurried touches fueled their lust. The heady scent of her had burned away all thoughts of the world beyond them. She smiled knowingly, working hot kisses down his bare chest as she undressed him. His breath caught at sensations and touch he'd never experienced.

Lights, but the exquisite pleasure as they rolled together! In the next breath, she was begging a favor. He'd have promised her the world in that instant, so long as she didn't pull away. "What?" he managed to groan out as they came together.

"It's a small thing, really," her silky voice answered huskily as he began to find his rhythm. She waited for him to be overwhelmed, to be pure physicality rather than reason. At the final moment, just as he collapsed atop her, she whispered sensually, as if this were a normal endearment, "Kill the captain."

Nothing could have cooled the moment faster as his blood turned to ice. Bile rose and his stomach heaved at the betrayal. He tried to pull away, put some distance between them, but her legs hooked around his, one arm around his waist. Her other hand smoothed damp ebony waves away from his cheek.

"Maybe 'favor' is the wrong word for it, hm? Perhaps a trade – a bartering of services: my body in exchange for his." She wriggled against him. "Unless you feel this wasn't any better than other women you've been with." Her voice lowered to a sinister whisper, all the while she maintained a gentle, loving expression. "I'll make you my First Mate."

Horrified, he found the strength to pull away. His stomach

knotted as it had when it first learned of poisons. This…woman…wasn't even aware she had been his first. He had been used; his inner self traded off, his soul compromised…over one sexual encounter. All the backstabbing, murders, and assorted assassinations had never robbed him of his dignity as this had.

He blindly felt for his clothes, the blood pounding in his ears as she continued murmuring reasons, justifications…

As he stumbled into the sunlight on deck, fastening the ties on the inside of his shirt at the hip, he heard Chirrit scream from above, circling in agitation. He couldn't calm her at the moment. He couldn't calm himself. "Captain Jays!"

"At the helm, lad," one of the men called from the crow's nest.

Wincing against the pain when he pulled his bracers too tight, shirt still needing to be clasped shut, he caught up with the captain. Jays, for the first time, saw Aern's chest as the wind caught his shirt, blowing it aside to expose the scars on his chest. In all seriousness, he looked to the younger man.

Noting the direction of Jays' gaze, he shrugged, snapping the clasps shut. The scars were inconsequential. "The woman…"

…Appeared behind them. "Lies. I don't know what he's told you, captain. He's just trying to…"

Jays put a hand up, silencing both of them. Lashing the wheel in place, he motioned towards his cabin. Following, Aern didn't wait for privacy. "She wants you dead, captain. By my hand."

Not even slowing his stride, his head tilted to the side as he spun back to face them. "That so?"

She froze in place, caught off guard. Aern simply readjusted his bracers, giving her a look of darkness. "Wanted me to murder you in exchange for warming her bed. Thought she'd be next in line for the captain's seat."

With a snap of the captain's fingers, her fate was sealed. Jays had learned years ago that kindness and weakness would do him no good at sea. She would be an example to any other that thought to do him in. He saw the comfortable way Aern continued to move, showing his honesty; he also saw the stiffness she carried, trying to hide something. She would be thrown overboard.

A plank was put into place, weighted by several men on deck. The intent was to step off the weighted end, thereby dropping her into the ocean safely clear of the ship, but as she reached the end of the plank, the air was cut by the shriek of Chirrit. The gryphon dove from out of nowhere, screaming her hatred and anger at the woman awaiting death. Talons extended, she grasped up the conniving traitor, heading back into the skies. The screams of pain faded into the sunlight, only to return as the cry of a triumphant gryphon. The mangled, bloody body landed with a wet thump on the deck, almost at Aern's feet. He took a deep breath, looking up into the sails. It was messier than most of Chirrit's kills and definitely messier than any Aern had done.

And then the damn girl had the nerve to land on the end of the plank, walking onto the deck, chirring a request for approval.

The others backed away from the gryphon. It was one thing to have her fly along side them, snatching tidbits they threw to her; quite another to have her among their midst. She carefully tucked her wings at her sides, keeping her beak lowered as she came amid them. Aern didn't move from the opposite side of the ship where he rested palms against the railing, ankles crossed. Chirrit sat, tipping her head at him, small noises of question coming from her. Aern tipped his head, raising his brows. She came a few steps closer and sat again.

The men backed away, giving Aern a wide berth with the wild creature.

"Don't be expecting a 'good girl' from me on this," he warned.

"Rr. Chrrrt." She quietly clacked her beak once, moving a few steps closer. She looked to the others in appeal.

"This was the captain's battle, not ours." It wasn't easy to remain angry at her.

Her sounds indicated anxiety as she arched her back.

"I know, girl." She had felt his emotions when he was…having sex…with the woman. It had caused a fretfulness in Chirrit, one she was unused to. Hells, one he wasn't used to. "This was just a bit…extreme."

Jays came down the few steps, crossing to their circle. "Bloody hells, Aern, she did us a favor. Lighten up."

Chirrit rose to her feet, chirring in Jays' direction.

"He won't give it to you, then I will. Good girl." Jays put a hand out towards her.

She mantled her wings, bringing her head back in a hiss.

"Bad girl!" Aern admonished, crossing the remaining steps between them, clamping his hands around her beak. "What's the matter with you? He pays you a compliment and you threaten him!"

Sounding defeated, Chirrit dropped back to a seated position.

"Oh, enough." Aern was disgusted with her bad behavior. Bad enough he had gone against everything he stood for, but then for her to behave like this. She never came on board and she knew better than to threaten those Aern called friend. She had never killed on his behalf before, either. "You'd better get used to that agitation. All humans experience it at some point, me included. Start killing like that and our partnership will be over." Pushing her beak down as he let go, he motioned vaguely towards Jays. "Apologize to him and take yourself off somewhere unless you want them touching you." He stormed below deck, not wanting to deal with any further complications.

Sex was everything Lord Morenden had told them it was: complicated, messy, and nothing but trouble. His first experience had given him a decidedly bad taste for it. A death sentence was bad enough, but to know that Chirrit was so closely tuned to him and would kill for him…that was both blessing and curse.

Chapter 18

The other crew members had little to do with Aern the next while. The distance between them had been growing, but now he was given a wide berth, everyone wondering if they would be the next to have his gryphon called down on. There was no way to explain that she wasn't a random killer, so he let things be. Instead, Aern focused on his poisons, his weapons. He did his job ship-side, but stayed away from the rest of the crew.

Jays' son would follow Aern as usual, not realizing why the other adults were so upset with Aern, but Rake was only a boy of five. Although Aern enjoyed time with any child, it was hardly stimulating dialogue. Only Jays had any prolonged contact with him during those weeks and even then, there was little conversation.

He sat on the floor of the captain's cabin, his cloak lay bunched before him to allow his vials and packets a safe place to rest without rolling around the floor. A small bottle of red liquid was in his hand as he tapped a brown herb into it. Swirls of purple twisted through it as he held it up to the light, watching the reaction. Satisfied, he capped it, shaking the vial until the entire mixture had turned purple.

This was not only the solitary room on board, but the only area with a lock, making it the only place Aern trusted to work with his precious concoctions. He didn't particularly like having the captain watch over him, but saw little choice. He could understand the man's hesitancy to let an assassin have free reign over the domain Captain Jays called home. Now just so that man didn't interfere. He hadn't yet, but… it was always a possibility that Aern kept in mind, especially now, after Chirrit's little outburst.

Jays sat on his bunk, watching quietly. There were plenty of other things he could be seeing to on the ship, but it never failed to amaze him to see this *boy* know what he did, to watch him work. His eyes widened as Aern appraised his own work, raising the now-purple vial to the light again. It wasn't the way he looked at the mixture; it was the fact that he then uncorked it, tasting the liquid. Jays sat forward a bit in shocked surprise. He hadn't ever seen Aern actually mixing any of his concoctions. He had watched the boy working with dried herbs, with powders… small things. He had, on some level, simply assumed that Aern added his items to foods and drinks. He had thought Aern was learning what each looked like, what it did, in the instructions that arrived almost monthly for him. To find that he actually created… then *DRANK* it… amazed him.

With a slight grin, Aern raised the vial in a silent toast when he saw he was being watched. "Not quite right yet." He returned to adding herbs.

"What's it for?" Jays nodded towards the small bottle in Aern's hand.

Tasting it a final time, and then nodding to himself, Aern took up a dagger, giving it a carelessly graceful flip in the air. A smile quirked at the corners of his mouth before he carefully let the mixture drip from the bottle to the edge of the blade.

It bothered Jays on some level that someone so young would be so good at death and murder, never mind that he had followed a similar course with his own life. This was a prince of the realm. Aern should have been in fine silks, sitting in a throne room. Everything had been handed to him and yet here he sat, happily creating poisons.

Aern scowled when he looked up to see such a melancholy look on Jays' face. There was no reason to see that look on the captain's face, especially after Aern had turned the bitch in to Jays. Maybe he didn't have designs on becoming the next pirate captain, but he was good at what he did, damn it all! "I don't need the approval of some worthless pirate for what I do," he stated coldly.

Eyebrows rising, Jays looked to Aern in surprise. Before the younger man could react, Jays had him by the throat, feet off the floor. "Watch yourself." He gave the cocky little killer a good shake. "If I'm worthless, you've no idea what's ahead for yourself."

To the pirate's surprise, Aern didn't scratch and clutch at his throat like most would do. His eyes only went colder, more assessing. A moment or two later, a sharp metallic rope flashed in Aern's hands, winding about Jays' neck and arms. A quick jerk and Aern was free as the cord simultaneously choked Jays as it pulled his arms back and away from both of their bodies.

Aern landed deftly on his feet, hardly even stumbling. "I

know what my work entails. You kill simply to kill."

As Aern loosed the cord, Jays jerked himself free. His words were little more than a low hiss. "You have no idea what my job is." He had told Aern once how he had started out as a simple pirate, but that wasn't the case anymore. The boy had no right to make assumptions on someone else's ship. Jays worked for a greater good now; one that Aern had no idea on. "Or who I work for," he added as he turned to kick Aern's items with the side of his boot. "Get your shit out of my cabin."

Both men froze, at an impasse. Aern knew Jays was right in that matter. He also knew he wouldn't ask; not for whom Jays worked, and certainly not for forgiveness.

A formality settled between them after that. The insult had blown out of proportion, adding another level of tension to already tight quarters on board the ship. Aern was given a locked trunk to keep his poisons and weapons, but he was moved out of the captain's quarters and in with the wary crew.

It wasn't just the semi-privacy he missed. He missed being near the hammocks of Non and Rake, of telling them wild bedtime stories. He found himself missing the sound of their content breathing during the night.

* * *

They had put into port at the beginning of the week. The city was dirty, almost as if more than just the people had given up; the buildings themselves were bent and ready to crumble in on themselves.

The water lapping the boat was brackish, a strong scent of the sewers coming from them. The people working the docks huddled in on themselves, not touching each other, even in passing. It was like they knew they smelled as bad as the streets.

Sitting on the bowsprit, Aern looked out over the town. How anyone could let things get to this point was beyond him. That anyone would willingly let the people under them fall into such a state…

Jays cleared his throat, coming up behind Aern. He didn't step out onto the bowsprit; instead he rested his arms against the nearest railing, crossing one ankle over the other. "I have orders for your next hit." There was a hesitancy in his voice, a carefulness that hadn't been there before their disagreement. It was still the captain speaking, but it was as if he didn't really know Aern anymore, like he didn't fully trust him anymore.

Something more died in Aern in that moment. He was what he was; and good at it. But there were moments like this that it was driven home how alone he was in the world. He lived outside of everything and everyone.

It wasn't that he regretted his decision to become this; it was more that he just wanted one friend who could understand and accept him as he was. That used to be Jays, but even he had fallen to looking at him with disdain and pity. Aern didn't know how to fix the rift growing between them.

"There's a letter here from one of your brothers, too." Jays held both envelopes out to him in a firm grip, mindful of the winds blowing across them.

Finally rising, Aern accepted them, taking them up to the crow's nest to read in private. There was no privacy among the crew. Someone in the rigging or the next hammock always saw something.

Settling his slender frame into the bottom of the lookout, he broke the seal on the first envelope. There was the regular enclosure from Lord Morenden on what herbs and fluids he needed to find to work with, then the smaller note that looked like a blank sheet of paper.

Working flint and tinder from one of his many pockets, he heated the note from underneath, words slowly seeming to "burn" into the paper from the juice it had been written in. He read it, double checked the envelope for anything further, and reread it. All it said was that a letter would be arriving for him from the royal court of Drikelldorn.

For long moments he stared at the envelope from "home." Not knowing what he expected of it, he finally took a deep breath, breaking the seal. It was written in some sort of turquoise blue ink.

"Sir Shadow, I speak on behalf of the kingdom of Drikelldorn. We are aware of your past actions at our behest and hereby ask that said actions shall become a legal recourse within set boundaries so set forth by the current Duke of Drikelldorn. We would like to also forward further information regarding certain peoples outside of Drikelldorn." It was signed in a silver ink with a great flourish, *"Silver, 2nd Duke of Drikelldorn."*

A second sheet set forth the descriptions of all the different peoples he had heard about on his home continent. It went on to describe other peoples, other lands, and ended with his current orders.

He looked up in shock. They knew. Or at least, Silver knew. He had thought that no one in the family had been aware of his duties, but like so many other things in his life lately, this was turned upside down for him. Silver had taken up the mantle of duty as the duke, as was his rightful place, but that meant…

Their uncle, their father's twin brother, was aware of Aern's duty as well. The orders Aern had always assumed came from Lord Morenden had in fact been issued to him first by the duke of Drikelldorn. He wasn't sure if he felt better or worse about that.

There were days he had questioned who determined life and death for these jobs, but had always left it with the thought that older and wiser men were making the right decisions. Aern had seen himself how badly some of those situations had been before he had stepped in to eliminate a problem.

But now it wasn't someone older calling the shots. Silver was only two years older than Aern was. Could everything still be trusted? Was the good of the kingdom still foremost in importance? Would orders still come from Morenden?

When he finally made his way back down to the deck, Jays stood quietly waiting for him. He gave Aern an understanding look with a small smile. He turned and looked out over the horizon.

"Not so different, the two of us," he said quietly. Lighting a smoke, he inhaled deeply, blowing out slowly. "I work for him too." He turned and walked away, already calling orders to some of the others.

Aern's world shifted again. Jays wasn't just a pirate. Jays… worked for the crown as well.

He watched Jays moving confidently about the deck, easily swinging over obstacles or adjusting for the rocking from the waves. The man didn't act like a pirate. He never had around Aern. A pirate would never have taken in two small children on the waves, nor would he have continued to look for other children. Jays was anything but a base pirate.

Going up behind the man, Aern waited while he explained to Rake how to handle the helm. Once he had set the boy down again, Jays looked to Aern, brows raised in question.

"I'm sorry." It was the most difficult two words Aern had ever uttered. "I was an ass. I'm sorry."

The silence stretched between them as Jays looked deeply at him. At long last, Jays gave the barest of nods. "Move your things back in."

It was the closest Aern would get to a thank you, but he'd take it. He'd survive. He always did.

Chapter 19

Kelly had matured into a lady of beautiful fire. Her temperament never cooled and she found it hard to sit quietly by and let life happen to her. Most days her father found humor in her antics, stating that she was merely a child of Fire and her passion was to be expected. But then there were the days when she went against his wishes. He would fume and yell, often calling her by any number of her sisters names before finally calling her to task. Too often in the last few years she had found herself locked in her room without supper. It didn't help. She couldn't seem to keep from speaking her mind.

Or sneaking out. She had decided some time back to find out what it was about farmers that made them lesser in the eyes of mages. The only difference that she could see was honest work and more equality. Nothing was done with magic. And while many of their tasks seemed to be separated by duties specifically for men or women, when it came down to it, all hands pitched in to help.

There were no servants for them. It meant that everyone in a household helped with washing and cooking and farming. Women didn't get in trouble for speaking – or arguing! – with the men. She loved the idea of the equality her mother had come from.

As often as she could, she would find her way down to the nearest village. It wasn't as easy as it seemed. The people were grateful for any aid she brought to them, but she had to be able to account for a whole day of being absent. An hour there and an hour back, plus time to offer aid in between, went quickly. Luckily she had all those hours where others in her home assumed she was locked in her room.

Thanks to her brother, she could quite easily manage to get out her window yet, down the trellis and across the garden. A carefully placed bench would lend her a lift up and over the wall. The run no longer left her breathless with a stitch in her side, either. After three years of sneaking out and running, her leg muscles were well-defined. The sun had highlighted the freckles scattered across her nose, but she didn't care. It felt so good to be out in the sunshine with the wind blowing the scent of something other than smoke and fire.

The village had its own scents that intrigued her. Roasting meat over open fire-pits in the center of the homes, the smell of the animals and the crops with their myriad flavors mixed with the fresh soil. The homes were simple wood and mud structures, unlike the stone that made up the dwellings for most mages. Floors were dirt, lending to heavier shoes than what she had. Her elegant slippers weren't suited for more than the stone or wooden floors she normally walked on. It was just one more reason for her to be punished at home when she couldn't explain the wear and tear on house shoes.

Sneaking food and healing herbs to the people was returned to her tenfold in what she learned from them. She learned how to bake homemade bread, prepare different animals into wonderful meals, and she was able to see outcome of seeds she helped plant.

It was something her father would never understand.

If only there was a way to eventually marry someone better suited to all things she had come to love in village life. The only problem was that she wanted all of it. She wasn't sure she could give up her fine clothes and warm home to live in a place that leaked cold air and seemed full of smoke. There was no winning on either side. She'd have to take what her father arranged for her.

Chapter 20

The Shadow slipped into the manor home, keeping to the walls and side halls as he made his way towards the library. He didn't need to see those who lived within the walls to know where they were. Soft voices and almost imperceptible footfalls gave away those above stairs; quiet voices, and the gentle clinking of tableware told of others in the dining room. Servants moved about, minding their own tasks, never suspecting the man sliding along the supposedly deserted path to the study.

One man held his attention. All he wanted was to get to the man who always sat at his desk this time of the evening. His instructions had given the layout of the manor, indicating this minor lord spent several hours in his study after supper, sometimes with guests but usually alone.

Aern had spent several days watching the place to be sure no company would interrupt what needed to be done. The last guest had departed that afternoon and the man took his last meal with his family. It had been a quiet affair, his wife speaking just over a whisper to the two young children who were also unusually silent. They retreated to the second floor as soon as the meal ended.

Children under seven should never be so hushed. Aern had followed to see if they improved when away from their father. They didn't. While obviously well dressed, they were listless and often glanced towards the door as if expecting some kind of trouble.

Aern frowned. It bothered him, making him wish he could go in and hug the little ones, assure them that everything would be alright. But he couldn't give away his secret. No one could know he was there.

So he did the only thing he could do. He wanted to be in and done before any of the servants in the household came looking for the lord of the manor.

Pausing in a recessed doorway, Aern gently touched his various weapons. Not that he worried they wouldn't be there, but that he liked the reassurance that all was in readiness. A small smile curved the corners of his mouth. He enjoyed his job. He was good at what he did; the Shadow was highly sought, rarely found. If any wanted his services, they needed to be willing to do the work to find him.

Rumors abounded as to who the mysterious Shadow was. Some said he was the son of a noble, a royal brat looking for entertainment; others said he was from poverty, seeking revenge for the life he had endured. Neither was right, exactly. Aern had never lived in poverty. He had learned to earn what he had, that things were not supposed to be handed to him with a silver spoon…

He let the breath of a laugh escape him. Handed to him on a silver spoon! The humor would be lost on others. Aern was the son of a king, the youngest in a family of epic proportions. The brother closest to him in age, the "spare" in line to the throne…was named

Silver. Things, quite literally, could be handed to him on Silver's spoon…such as the job he was now engaged in.

Shifting his ankle, he felt the sheathed dagger in his boot rub against his calf. Doing likewise to his other leg, he continued his inventory. Stiletto strapped to his right thigh, short dagger at his belt. Where a sword should hang at his left hip, instead hung a coiled garrote. Various and sundry pouches completed the belt, all filled with odds and ends: ropes, hooks, darts and throwing stars.

He twisted the family signet on his left ring finger, the odd smile again touching his lips. Not a wedding band, not for him. He would never marry. Men in his line rarely made it long enough to age, and never to produce children. The poisons in their systems made sure of small issues such as that. While poison would easily kill most, fine assassins were virtually immune…all at the small cost of barrenness.

Aern loved children, but knew he was lucky not to have to worry about them. A wife or child would only be a hindrance to his line of work, one more thing to use against him, to hold hostage against a job that needed to be done. Or worse, to have a woman use his heart against him. It had been tried once. It wouldn't be done. Not while he lived.

Again, he touched his signet ring, touching a light kiss to the family emblem engraved atop it. Lady poison, hidden within the ring in a needle of the finest point, would easily be the only woman for him. She hadn't failed him yet. She wouldn't fail him now.

As he brought his hand down, he flexed his wrist, feeling the familiar band that held his wrist blade, subconsciously doing the same to his right arm. His right hand slid across his jerkin, noting the feel of bottles and bags in pockets beneath the clothing. All the small pockets that hid tiny amounts of powders near his person lay comfortably between the layers of materials crossed over his chest. A small tie on his right shoulder held a coiled rope in place, looped and held around his arm, tucked securely over and under.

Content that he was ready, he glanced into the dimly lit room. Perfect. As usual, as he had seen over the last few days, the lord was alone in the room. Keeping to the outer wall, keeping to the darkest of the shadows, Aern made his way ever closer.

Prince Silver, Duke of Drikelldorn, had noted that the man had been a thorn of contention, raising dissent among the lesser nobles. His own family, the Bradleys, were not known for injustice; had, in fact, been ordained the rulers by the Lights themselves. They listened fairly to all sides before making decisions. Yet men like this, men that wanted to be rulers themselves, stirred unhappiness and discontent among their fellows and those below them. He ruled with a heavy hand, resulting in fear rather than respect.

Worse, this fool lived in high splendor, taking way more than he should have from the poor wretches Aern had seen down on the docks. He had expensive rings and brocades on, while the poor lived in tattered, worn rags. Anything of value they had owned had likely been sold long ago.

The noble, seated behind a heavy, highly polished desk, popped another plump grape into his mouth, pulling out the finest vellum and ink to pen a note. Aern rolled his eyes at the redundancy of so much finery.

He watched from almost over the man's shoulder as he wrote his missive to another, a letter that was intended to cause yet more trouble for those that ruled Drikelldorn. Aern couldn't let that happen, not from a man that didn't even live in the country proper. He was on one of the island nations nearby. "It won't happen," he whispered as he let a dagger slip from his wrist sheath, cleanly slicing the man's throat.

The man reached for his throat as he slumped forward, gurgling against the blood spurting from the wound and frothing at his mouth from the poison that had edged the blade. Aern took the incomplete letter from the blotter, carefully folding and tucking it into one of his various pouches.

Aern tipped the man just enough to the side to see the wound clearly. The blood had made the desk slick, had seeped into the lord's clothing, yet Aern managed to avoid most of it, touching only the shoulder. He wiped his blade across the man's tunic before snapping it back into its sheath, wiping an already dry hand against his pants before setting his fingers to the man's throat, checking for a pulse. Content with the glassy eyes, and the sluggish pulse, he checked the room once more, looking for any other missives of import before slipping back to the hall. His father would be interested in the letter Aern carried.

The king wouldn't know his son had killed the man, however. Aern's father didn't know that the youngest of the family was an assassin. King Grey knew that Aern was an expert at gathering information, but he thought Aern was just that good with people. No reason to upset that idea. Aern would hand the information to Silver's man, letting his brother pass it on to the right hands. Aern certainly didn't want the glory for it.

* * *

Aern sat in the tavern, quietly sipping a dark ale. It was gritty and terrible, much like the table he sat at. He had chosen this tavern on purpose. He had seen how poor the area was. There was little enough in the way of coppers, let alone gold. These people worked hard; he had been watching since they put into port. There seemed to be little joy in the muddy streets; even less inside the dark, sooty taverns.

He didn't speak much and didn't sit in the open. He didn't need to, for what he was about. He was gathering information, simply listening at this point, trying to find out anything he could about the landholders in the area. He leaned back into the dark shadows, trying not to smile at the whispered mention of the mysterious Shadow. Men and women alike kept word of the man in secreted discussion.

"Don't say such," one would say, "the Shadow will hear you." Another would look around, thinking to see someone or something out of the ordinary. Aern wasn't sure what they thought they'd see or who they thought the Shadow might be, but that he was passed over repeatedly said he wasn't the terrible person they somehow knew the Shadow to be.

And he certainly knew he wasn't that terrible either. Terrible people didn't leave extra gold coins hidden for the tavern keeper. Terrible people didn't patronize shops with little worth buying. Yet this was something Aern felt responsible to do. He had the means to help improve someone else's life, and he intended to. If it was gold, fine. If it was the small cost of one person's life to better dozens of others, well, that worked out, too.

Several times over the following week he left the ship to wander dark alleys and bright manor homes. Things he heard in the taverns were looked into – not just complaints about being cold and miserable, but about how certain nobles were stirring trouble, how certain landholders were taking unfair cuts. Some of it turned out to be nothing but complaints from already worn-down people. Some needed his personal touch. Those he added to the pile of information that would be sent back to Silver.

Chapter 21

A small figure slipped into Mage Ayden Llewellyn's study. After a furtive glance around, she threw back the hood of her dark, heavy cloak. Once again, she wore nothing but a nightgown beneath her cloak. Sitting slightly cock-eyed off one shoulder, the knee-length red hair flowed freely about her slight form, long sleeves loose at her nervous hands. Her feet were bare this late hour of night, despite the cold seeping through the stone.

Carefully running her cold fingers over the smooth leather of his spell book, she drew it open to the spells of love. Tripping over the difficult words, a flash of panic went through her. She had never dared to touch the book before. Father's rune stones, yes; the crystal ball, sure; but she was no mage. She shouldn't, as a girl, even be touching the book. For any without magic, the pages should appear blank. Yet the words, strange though they were, were quite clear to her.

A swirl of sparkling stars formed into a plain looking young lady. Her brown hair hung straight to her shoulders instead of long like all the girls Kelly knew. Her dress was drab, even for the villagers she knew, faded almost to a dull gray-brown, but looked quite comfortable. The only color about her was her crystal blue eyes and a shimmering shamrock she wore as a broach. "Mage Llewellyn, I am…" Her effervescent voice fell flat as she caught sight of the girl. "Not yours to command. Who are you?"

She had called something into the room rather than casting

a spell. She had only meant to get the attention of the Immortal Love, not have one of them appear! Fear caused a slight tremor in her body. Pride and stubbornness found her voice. "I am Kelly Llewellyn, ninth daughter of Fire Mage Llewellyn."

"Ah!" The other exclaimed in delight. "Know you the one before you?" At a negative head shake, she happily threw her arms wide. "You have called Luck to you."

Kelly blushed at her mistake, looking to the floor. "I meant to call Love."

"But," Luck knelt before her. "As a Hakon daughter, you shouldn't have been able to even call me."

Kelly's eyes flashed in quick anger. "Why is that? If you ARE one of the gods, why can't you make us equal? I don't want to be just a plaything; a stupid girl kept pregnant. I want more than to just make more male fire babies. I want…"

Lady Luck held up a hand to stay the furious words. "Yet here I am." She rose, leading Kelly to a couch. "We aren't gods; we're immortals that work for the Lights. And what you did falls under my jurisdiction."

A fire child should only call to the Element Fire, Kelly knew this. But to her way of thinking, Love was passion. Passion was fire. Therefore love should fall under the Element of Fire. Nowhere in that logic did Luck factor in.

"It was luck that you were able to use that book, my girl. You shouldn't have been able to see anything, let alone say the words. That makes it my concern." She smiled then, her pale blue eyes sparkling. "To hell with Fate. And Fire. Ask of me what you will."

They were all real! She had known in her heart that the gods were watching out for them. This meant that she had a chance at what she really wanted in life. All she had to do was word it correctly. But her curiosity made her want to ask other questions as well. She wanted to know about these immortals, know if what the books said was true.

The lady laughed, tucking her feet up under herself on the couch. Mischief danced in her eyes. "I know that look," she said in humor. "Go ahead and ask, though I might not answer."

Her mind worked furiously, trying to form the questions she had always wondered about. "You're real," was the only thing that came out, making her sound like a lack-wit.

The immortal laughed again, patting Kelly's knee. "As real as you! I just fell into a wonderful job."

"Are there… how many of you are there?"

She bounced, happily resettling herself. "Oh, more than you could guess! But I can't tell you who they all are." There was no malice to her words, only truth.

"Does Fire hear us?"

The bright smile never left her face as she looked at Kelly. This poor girl felt lost in her world, hopelessly out of place. Lady Luck remembered a time long ago when she had been much the same, not fitting the role she had been born to. She gave the young Llewellyn a sympathetic smile. "Yes. She hears you." She reached over to squeeze her hand. "Tell me what you want."

A nervous smile was returned. "Only love." She turned away from Lady Luck, her red hair shining like the flames in the banked fire of the hearth. "I want a good man, and a home of my own." A sense of hopelessness slumped her shoulders. She was one of thirteen girls. Her father cared for each of them, but even Kelly could see the sigh of relief that escaped her father every time a daughter came of age and married. Her father was weary of parenthood. He had been so young when he started his family and had never been given respite from it. "I don't care if he's a mage or not. I just don't want him as old as my father." *And not so many children*, she added silently.

Lady Luck looked, almost stared at Kelly. She took the younger woman's hands as she closed her eyes, looking at the girl's fate. Luck's Gift was taking Fate's job and messing it up, something she loved doing. Fate was a man that thrived on order and knowing what was coming, trying to convince the others that life couldn't be turned from the path set for it. For good or ill, he believed that a life needed to play out as it was dealt.

She didn't agree. When someone, like Kelly, was willing to take that extra step to make things better for themselves, to challenge what had been given to her for a life, Lady Luck felt obligated to do what she could to aid that. And if what she saw in the young woman's future was what Fate wanted, she felt a duty to fight it. The way for this young woman was set to end early… and badly.

With a little help, there was one other path open before the girl. But… "Little Llewellyn, your heart will be tried by fire 'til you see your goal." If Kelly were willing to take on the challenges, Lady Luck would be willing to find ways to cope. Violence could be tempered by accidents, making them less brutal. But that was all she could offer. Luck couldn't majorly change a fate; all it could do was shift the odds a little more to someone's favor. She couldn't even begin to tell this fire-child how bad it might become. She'd need more than Luck to get through her trials. If she survived. "Will you willingly walk this?"

Worry and fear warred in the young woman's face as she studied the expression on Lady Luck. "Yes," she finally answered with a slow nod. "I want more than to have male children for a mage. I want love."

"Then prepare, child." She couldn't tell Kelly who would be her trial or her savior. All she could do was place the clues for her to work with. With a little luck, she'd work it out. "He will steal into your heart even as you burn a path to his."

Before anything more could be said, Lady Luck was consumed in a maelstrom of fire and wind, blowing things about the room, knocking things to the floor. Kelly was helpless to prevent the crashing of vases that alerted her father to someone being in his private study.

He had been on his way to visit one of his many mistresses when he heard the noise in his room. Other than his bed chamber, that study was the only sanctuary he had for calm and quiet. The idea of anyone in there without his permission was inexcusable, especially since he kept his personal grimoire of magic there.

Llewellyn came rushing into the room in time to see everything come crashing to the floor and his young daughter with a panicked look in her eyes. Anger flashed through him. She was hardly a child anymore. A tantrum of this sort was hardly fitting for a teenager of marriageable age. He couldn't even speak. All he did was point out the open door.

Her head dipped down in shame as she hurried past him. She knew better than to have been in here, but she felt trapped in this ridiculous "game" of life. She had wanted a way to find something that would make her happy. And now… now she had summoned magic to her. If only she could have told her father what had happened, how she had called an Immortal to her. She had been promised aid in improving her life, only it hadn't worked quite as she'd expected. "Some luck," she muttered as she ducked past her father.

He watched her go, willing his anger to fade. It didn't. Why couldn't the girl just accept his choices for her? It wasn't as if there were that many choices available to them. And at least she would be getting a fire mage. Most of his other daughters couldn't even boast that. He'd be lucky if he could match them with a compatible Element! And that little…

Looking to the room, his rage went up another notch. His personal study had been left in shambles! It looked like one of his apprentices had been in the room rather than a young lady. He ordered one of the maids to see to righting the disaster for him and went back to his own rooms. He didn't even want to see one of his mistresses anymore this night.

The girl needed to accept her place in society. She would be matched to a mage with strong potential. It was the only way to encourage the continuation of their magics. If they didn't, Lights only knew that in a few generations there could be nothing but farmers left! And what kind of life would that be? He couldn't imagine a life with the chaos of no proper rulers. And mages were proper rulers. Male mages. Women had a duty to produce sons that could carry on the magic. His daughter needed to learn this.

Chapter 22

Eleven years. It was hard to imagine that eleven years had come and gone. He should have visited more often over the years, he supposed. The last time he had been home had been for his brother Sterling's wedding, four years past. He had only been thirteen, still wet behind the ears at what he had been learning. But, he was going to visit home now. That should make them happy.

He could have taken a horse from the docks in Pathicos, but that would easily have made it ten times longer before he'd be off the road. Not that he wished to play the prince in any hurry, but why maintain the dread of it?

Taking to the skies on Chirrit, he was able to look down on the landscape he had been born to. Beautiful colors spread below him in trees of pink, plum, and amber. It seemed his home continent was the only one so rich in vibrant colors year round.

With a smile, he saw the keep he had called home for so long. He circled once, waiting to be noticed by those at the watchtower. At their call and wave, he brought Chirrit down to the turret top. He wouldn't be able to do this at Whitewind, the home he'd been born to, only here at Lord Morenden's home. His family had seen him with the gryphon that one time, but they wouldn't expect to have seen him come from the sky. Here they knew of his connection to the wild creature.

A few of the guards were boys he had started his training with, long before starting with poisons. All of them were lesser nobles that would follow the path of knights and guards. It seemed odd to see them now in positions of responsibility. All the same, he accepted the pats on the back and their words of welcome.

Then it was on to speak with Lord Morenden, gaining rights to spend a few nights before completing his journey.

Morenden straightened in interest at the young man entering the main hall. He knew the fine, dark features, but this couldn't be the timid, frail-looking child he had sent to sea so few years ago.

Watching the young man with him now, had he not known of Aern's beginnings, he'd never have guessed that the self-assured boy that stood on the far edge of manhood had once been frightened and overly worried about not being up to standard. He had nothing but pride for the young prince, although he didn't say it. He didn't need to. The man before him was more than aware enough of his abilities. Morenden was pleased to have the assassin-prince stay a few days for a visit.

Aern, on the other hand, was surprised at the change in his mentor. The man he had always been so scared of didn't seem quite as tall now; perhaps because he wasn't as short as he'd been all those years ago, or maybe because he knew now why the man had always been less than talkative. No one could see the things they'd seen, not and live without the images burned in their minds. It left their kind with dark memories that could never be shared with those who hadn't experienced it.

But it wasn't just the initial meeting, either. Aern noticed the way Morenden's hands shook when he was at table trying to use the silverware. He saw the paunch that had developed over the years, as well. Not much, but enough that anyone who hadn't seen him in a while would see it. His fine velvet clothing was now tighter across the stomach than it had ever been through the shoulders.

It didn't matter though. Aern saw the newest group working with him over the next few days and saw the same fear and respect he had always had for the man. His voice was still a bark and his say-so still determined who got to continue in the way of assassins.

Morenden was still an imposing man, well dressed, and built with a massive chest. It looked like he lifted horses for fun and could easily hoist a carriage over his head… at least until he went back inside with Aern. When he closed the door to his study and joined Aern beside the fire, he relaxed what others saw. He used his arms to help lower himself into his chair, stretching a pained leg closer to the fireplace with a grimace.

Aern couldn't help a smile, thinking about how his image of this man had likely been wrong all these years. Morenden was just a man; a stubborn, strong man, but still just a man. He had probably had gout or some other issue even when Aern had been a boy. It had never stopped the old lord from keeping the appearance of imperviability.

So Aern didn't comment on it. He only hoped he could look as strong when he got to be that old.

Chapter 23

Well away from the village nearest Whitewind castle, Chirrit landed. Aern removed the riding harness, folding the leather straps into a tight little ball before tucking them away in a pouch. He leaned into her soft feathers, taking a last moment of calm. The familiar scent of fur and feather dander fortified him. *This is my life*, he reminded himself. *I'll survive; I always do.*

Chirrit gave a growl of comfort while beaking his hair. She felt how unsettled he was about going back to the white place. It bothered her that she couldn't be at his side, lending him her strength. She couldn't heal his hurts if she didn't touch him.

With a sigh, Aern stepped back from her. "To the skies, girl." He couldn't hide the sadness in his voice. Even if he could have, she'd have sensed it in his body. Better to just let it be a truth between them. He depended on her comfort and stability in his life. Facing his family without her at his side didn't sit well with him.

But it was a truth. They wouldn't be expecting a gryphon to be winging into their space and it might end with her getting hurt. Best to do this like others would.

He watched her launch skyward before shouldering his pack and walking to the village. His bearing was still that of a noble, head high and back straight as he moved with purpose. His clothing was that of the night yet, all dark but for the pewter clasps. Many looked at him in curiosity but not came forward.

Which was fine with him. He located the stables and went directly there. He put forth the appearance of bargaining, despite the price being much lower than he would have expected for a steed. The man was disappointed to settle for lower than his asking price considering Aern's appearance.

Aern thanked him with a slight bow, going to saddle the horse he'd chosen. The villagers here were dressed better than many places he'd been and their welfare was much more stable, but they were still the working class, dependent on crops and livestock for their funding. Gold wasn't something often seen coming through.

Two little girls peered over the stall, giggling. Aern gave them a smile while he cinched the saddle into place. High squeals of laughter rang out as they ran off, making him smile to himself. The children in this place were happy – a testament to King Grey doing things right.

In that same light, Aern did the only thing he saw as right. When the stable master was looking elsewhere, Aern tucked a good sized bag of silver into the feed bin. He said nothing as he mounted and rode out. They could find it easily enough where he'd left it.

He sat easily in the saddle, reins held loosely. The horse had seen the castle miles back and now picked his own way towards a restful stable. Training and experience kept his eyes scanning the battlements. For all that he was "home," he was a stranger here. There was little in his appearance to claim kinship to the crown and his clothing was not the useless finery he'd seen beyond the walls.

"State your business."

He didn't see the speaker and didn't bother to look where he hid. Instead, he leaned forward and rubbed his horse's neck. "Put your bow down first." Only then did he sit up with all the royal bearing he possessed. "Prince Aern Bradley, returned home." He could easily have avoided this whole thing by coming on Chirrit. The way it was, she'd upset everyone by landing on the battlements when he called her.

He dismounted and walked into the inner bailey. The doors opened seemingly of their own accord…and he suddenly found himself in a very uncomfortable position. All these years of learning to blend into the backgrounds and go unnoticed, be as the shadows on the walls… Here he stood with what seemed to be hundreds of eyes upon him.

King Grey approached the young man standing in defiance, arms crossed, legs planted apart, and chin up. His youngest son looked little like his other two. Dark hair, dark eyes, and dark, form-fitted leather and suede clothing that seemed to have a myriad of purposes to it was in high contrast to the light silks, satins and cottons that his twin sons wore for court. "Prince Aern, I welcome you!" He gave him a stiff hug before taking his elbow and leading him to his private offices. "You'll be more comfortable away from the crowds, I'm guessing."

Aern spared his father a look from the corner of his eye before shrugging his hand away and walking ahead of him. It was one thing to call these people family, but he had been home so rarely since he left at the age of seven that these people were more stranger than family to him. Yet it was still a surprise to see so many faces inside the office that resembled his own features. He had grown accustomed to Jays as a foster sib, but had little idea what his real brothers and sisters actually looked like until this moment. Granted, he had seen them when he'd been home for Sterling's wedding, but that had been a while back and there had been so much commotion going on at that time, he hadn't even really gotten to know any of them.

First, though, was getting through a visit with his father. Even into his fifties, King Grey was a distinguished looking man. His hair was the white-blond his other two sons had inherited, still hanging well past shoulder length. It was a style more suited to the younger men, to Aern's thinking, but his father wore it well, as he did the clothing. Close-fitting pants of white were topped by knee high black boots and a tunic of turquoise. There was no crown.

Come to think of it, he didn't remember ever seeing one on his father. Perhaps that was only a trick of faulty memory, though. Sterling certainly had some sort of coronet on when he joined them a short time later.

Aern was simply relieved that anyone joined them. Speaking with his father had been strained in ways it never had been with Lord Morenden. Saying such inane things as "you look well" or "how was the journey" were things King Grey seemed to have brought up just to fill their time. Morenden had asked Aern the same things, but maybe it was that Aern had trained there, that in some ways he saw Morenden as more of a father figure, that it meant more.

Sterling, on the other hand, obviously saw the king as a father. He sat on one corner of the massive desk, on the same side as their father. He played with things on the desk, despite Grey taking them back and setting them on the desk again. Sterling was comfortable here in a way Aern didn't know how to be.

The only thing marking Sterling as the crown prince was the coronet. His dusky blue clothing was somewhat rumpled, if stylish, the sleeves pushed up to his elbows, and there was dried mud on his black-sueded boots.

Then there was Silver. He sat in a chair beside Aern, having come in when Sterling did. This brother's long hair was done in intricate braids at his temples, hanging loose and immaculate down his back. His faultless white clothing was accented only by modest silver trim. Even his white doe-skin boots didn't have a scuff mark on them. Compared to Sterling, he could have been a statue.

Even the manner of sitting was different for them. Silver's feet were slightly under the chair, resting on his toes, his arms rested relaxed on the arms of the chair. His back, where Sterling was in a relaxed slouch, was straight and proper.

Aern also noticed a silver band on Silver's ring finger. He had married over the years at some point. For some reason, Aern found he was slightly disappointed that no one had bothered to call him home for it.

"Sterling," Grey finally warned, taking yet another item from his son.

"It's not like any of this crap really matters to you. It's just junk people have given you."

"Just items that show those people," Silver answered, "that father remembers them even in their absence."

Sterling rolled his eyes, hopping off the desk. "Yeah, whatever. I'm going to go check on the wife. See you in the morning, dad." With a grin, he gave a playful bow from the doorway, "Aern, good to have you home."

Everything about Sterling was relaxed and it obviously bothered both Silver and Grey. Silence reigned in the office for long moments before Silver moved as if suddenly jolted. His feet now flat on the floor, palms on the chair, ready to lift him. "Well." Silver got to his feet. "Gaze pe nu je, father," he said in lilting Elven. "Aern." He bowed slightly to each.

"Goodnight to you too, Sil," Grey called after him as he left the room. Then looking to Aern, he seemed to struggle for something more to say. Aern simply watched him, waiting for him to find something to speak about.

The king finally sighed, sitting back in his chair. "I'll let Kyle see you to your rooms."

It was a simple dismissal, but it wasn't as cold as many Aern had been given. The man obviously loved Aern a great deal but wasn't sure what to say about anything. It had been a strained meeting. He was more than happy to follow Kyle, his eldest half-brother who had been waiting quietly by the door, out of the offices.

Kyle smiled back at Aern as he walked slightly ahead of him. "This can't be easy for you, eh?" He remembered back when Aern had been such a sweet, lovable little boy. Kyle had been so much older than the newest baby that he had been allowed to care for him on occasion. Now he cared for one of the others. He had been so happy to earn a position in the court as the Lord Steward to the crown prince. It was hard work, but he loved it. He loved being involved with the family and court politics while still able to remain outside of it. Much as this youngest brother must be feeling outside of things now. "I bet you'd rather be out on your own again."

Aern returned a slight smile. "I've never really been on my own. Chirrit goes everywhere I do." Kyle gave him a look of question. "Chirrit;" he answered. "My gryphon. She's always there for me when I need her."

Kyle wasn't sure what to say about that, so instead simply opened the doors they had come to. "Your rooms, your grace."

Flinching a little at the silly term, he stepped past Kyle. "Just Aern."

Warm laughter came from his half-brother. "Sorry, baby brother. It's the official stuff I need to say." He paused a moment. "Look, if you have questions or anything, you can always come find me, alright?" When no answer came, he quietly closed the doors, leaving Aern alone with his thoughts.

Chapter 24

His first official duty at home was to stand guard for Sterling while the crown prince worked alongside their father in the throne room. It was long, boring work, but he was impressed with the ease his father and brother had under pressure to keep the petitioners happy.

He hadn't been expected to do anything other than visit, but Kyle had put in a good word for him that he'd rather be busy. Sterling had then asked if he'd be willing to stand as his personal guard for the day since it was, for the most part, only a ceremonial position.

That wasn't exactly a truth, which Aern well knew. Any royal court had guards posted to protect those ruling. Dressing them up didn't change that, but he did as asked, playing the part of the younger son visiting, while in truth he was keeping an eye on all comers to the throne.

Petitioners seemed happy with the court, often coming with small problems that probably could have been solved on their own. Aern started to get the impression that most were using their petty concerns as reasons to have a few minutes before the throne, simply to say they had spoken with the king.

Both King Grey and Prince Sterling were amazing to watch. Neither lost their tempers nor gave a cross word throughout the day, always passed fair judgment, and graciously accepted all small gifts presented to them.

If Aern had been a commoner, this was the place he would

prefer to settle down. He was able to see why his father was so well spoken of wherever Aern had travelled. It almost made him wish he'd have known the man while he'd been growing up.

At long last a halt was called for the day. Any remaining complaints were given slips of parchment that granted them first rights to be seen the next morning before they were ushered out.

With a stretch, Sterling and King Grey found their feet. Grey's eyes slid over Aern, a sad smile was given, as if he knew there would be no knowing this child. He clapped Sterling on the shoulder and left for his office, several attendants in tow.

When Aern moved to step away from the thrones, Sterling reached to touch his arm. Aern stiffened, unused to so familiar a gesture. Sterling sighed. "Join me for a snack?"

At Aern's small nod, Sterling led him – not to an office – to the kitchen itself. With a furtive glance around for the cook, Sterling moved in an exaggerated sneak to "steal" a plate of cookies from a tray on a far counter. Aern had to smile at how terrible Sterling was at it. He'd never be able to do what Aern did. Worse, Aern had to laugh when Sterling took the tray to a counter with stools, calling out, "We're stealing the cookies, Jenni!"

Still chuckling, Aern joined him on a stool. "So why the sneaking?"

"Hold over from being little." Sterling grinned. "She never used to let us into them 'til after dinner, so we'd try to get in and take them." He shrugged. "Now she doesn't care, so long as we let her know. That way she can make sure the littles get a bedtime treat yet."

Aern smiled, shaking his head at the situation but, after finishing a cookie himself, he called out to the unseen cook, "Thanks for the cookies!"

He wasn't really expecting an answer, so was surprised when a female voice answered. "You're welcome! And there's fresh goat milk in the cooling box."

Sterling made an excited noise and jumped to get them each a glass. It was odd to see such a high-ranking person like Sterling serving himself… in the kitchen.

They ate in silence for some time before Aern was able to stretch for something to talk about. He recalled the last visit home and the wedding he had attended, figuring at least this would be a topic they could discuss. "So how's marriage working for you?"

The light-hearted look on Sterling's face disappeared. "It's okay," he answered flatly.

Aern's brows went up, he sat a little straighter. "Something wrong?"

He gave Aern a sad smile. "Nah. We're just… you remember how we were supposed to get the blessings of the Lights?"

He had almost forgotten about this. Silver's elf friend had kept everyone inside the courtroom with the blade presentation.

The Lights only showed themselves rarely, and always with great import. "…supposed to?"

"Yeah." He lowered his voice. "They didn't come. So she's

not my true partner."

"So set her aside." That seemed fairly obvious to Aern. It was certainly common enough in other lands he'd been through.

"There's a complication." Sterling's voice sounded older, more weary, than someone his age should be. "When the council started deliberations on the matter, we found out she was pregnant. I won't separate her from the kid, so I'm stuck with her." He stopped short, winced slightly as he glanced at Aern. "Sounds awful, doesn't it?"

He gave his brother a sympathetic smile. Not wanting to be with a woman was something Aern understood very well.

"On top of that, I don't know what to do with the boy. Or Meghan. I usually try to just stay away from both of them."

"At least you have a kid." He paused a long moment, debating if he should tell his brother. "I can't," he finally said after a long pause. "The poisons."

Sterling gave him a stricken look. "Man, I'm sorry. Here I've got a son I never really wanted and you… can't ever?"

Aern shook his head, getting to his feet. "Ever." He finished his milk, setting the glass aside. "Look, I'll see you later, okay?" He left his brother sitting there, unable to further sympathize. Sterling had no idea how pampered and lucky he was. Everything had been handed to him; Aern had worked hard and long for the few privileges he enjoyed.

Chapter 25

He rode out the next morning on his next assignment. It was within a day's flight, by gryphon, so he figured he could easily be home by the next evening. Landing outside of the small town, he left Chirrit in the trees, while he went in to a crowded, smoky tavern. Taking a table in the corner, as was his way, he settled in and ordered a bowl of the stew.

Surprisingly, this place actually had pretty good stew, as he'd found over the years. So between that and a few tolerably-tasting drinks, he was able to pass an enjoyable evening, keeping an eye on the hit across the room.

For a long moment, his sight of the fool across the room was distracted by a young woman. It was a girl, really, not quite at the edge of womanhood. It wasn't any thoughts of attraction that held him; it was more that she resembled someone. Then he knew. She resembled Jays in many ways. And if he was right, this was something he could help out with. He knew Jays' feelings about any children that *might* be out there. He kept one eye on his mark, the other on the girl that was serving the ale. If she'd just come closer to him, he could ask. Jays would want her back at Whitewind.

The man in the shadows set the girl's heart to trembling. He was so dark – from his clothes to his coloring – that he blended right into the corner. His focus had been on a man across the room, but every time she came near, he would shift his penetrating blue gaze to her. As she set a tankard of piss-warm ale before him, his arm shot out, grabbing her wrist in a light hold. "Your father, girl."

"I… I… don't have one," she stammered.

His brows knit in concentration as he took her features in. "He have a name?"

She shook all over in fear. "Randulf, sir. A Captain Randulf. Ain't been back since I was a babe."

"You have the look of him." He finally smiled at her. "Get your mother." He pushed the tankard back towards her. "And give this to the man at the far table. No names, please."

His hands hadn't visibly move to the ale, but he saw in her eyes that she knew what likely would meet the man she now went to. The few other times this man had been to their tavern, someone had been dead when he left. Still, she did as she'd been asked. Placing the tankard before the loud, obnoxious man, she then ran back to the kitchens. "Ma, there's someone asking for you. The scary one in the corner."

Wiping her hands on her apron, she followed her oldest child out to the common room. There were two younger than her sweet Colleen, all from a few extra coins in the common room. At least she had gotten names from all the men. All her children had the names of their fathers. Now, poor as they were, she didn't need the coins, not with Colleen helping with the serving. They made enough to get by. Hungry and threadbare, but she could proudly say they got by on honest means.

She had seen the man a few times over the years. Reclusive

and taciturn, he often frequented the corners. Death often came in his wake. She smiled at her Colleen. The scary one, indeed! At least they could say he'd always been polite and respectful to the wait staff. "Sir, you wish to speak?" She didn't want to upset this patron, not knowing his history or his purpose.

Aern knew the look in the woman's eye, the set to her features. She didn't want her daughter following the path of a tavern wench, especially at such a young age. He didn't really care about the wenches. Only two women had ever touched his heart, and neither had worked out. Heather was interested in finding a rich husband while she pursued her own entertainments – usually other men – and Jays' first mate, who had tried to use Aern.

And the idea of a girl barely out of childhood absolutely turned his stomach. It wasn't right. "About your daughter. Says her father is Jays Randulf." He tried to keep his tone disinterested. "I know the man."

"I ain't never asked nothing of 'em," she pleaded in panic. "Don't be doin' anything to m' girl!"

"I'm not looking to hurt her," he offered, hands up in front of himself to prove that. In mere moments, he had set her mind at ease with details about the man. "I've been keeping an eye out for his children. He's been wanting to know where they are."

She sighed, obviously weary-worn with the care of not only herself but her children. "Does no good to know her whereabouts if he's doing nothing about it."

"That," Aern said as he leaned forward, "I can help you

with." He gave her a small, polite smile. He explained to her how Jays was looking for them, how he wanted to take them in and give them a better chance at life.

He saw the girl peeking from the kitchen door, hiding badly, as they spoke. He never had to look directly at her, staying instead intent on the woman before him. "Her father wants them brought to him. We'll give you some small compensation for her loss of help to you." He reached over and patted her hand, smiling warmly as the woman relaxed at both statements. "If you could bring her to the next village over, I will take charge of her there on the morrow." In the next moment, he looked directly to the girl, motioning her to come out. He rose as she joined them, ruffling her hair. "I look forward to seeing you soon, little one."

He left the girl with a baffled expression and the mother with a look of relief, now holding a small purse of gold, to complete a job. He was distracted, not completely focused as he found the manor home. Hardly even thinking about it, he absently went through the routine he'd started years ago of double checking where each weapon was tucked on his person. A quick roll of the ankles, fingers flitting over bracers, pouches, garrote, and a brief touch over his shoulder to touch the pommel of his short sword and he was ready. On silent feet, he moved as a shadow, creeping into the home of a lesser noble.

This mark was a servant that had been stealing information and believed to be delivering it into the hands of the Jakhil. Aern hated the thought of taking someone out based on their status, but the evidence was stacked against this poor man. All the same, he followed the man long into the night, watching his habits, where he went and what he did. When the servant looked around outside a door, opening it the least amount he could to sneak inside, Aern was quick to follow.

Just as the door was ready to latch closed, he moved into place to push it back inward. He waited, knowing the man would have frozen, looking at the door, waiting for someone to come through. It was an easy way to get people off guard. When no one showed up, they would assume no one was there and focus on their task at hand.

Forty-eight, forty-nine, he counted to himself, *fifty*. He slipped into the room, keeping to the dark shadows on the walls. The man was rifling through the drawers of the master's desk. Too late, he realized he wasn't alone. Aern was there just to the right behind him. His garrote slipped around the man's neck, choking and gagging the servant. The man's hands flew up, pulling at the small wired rope, fingernails scraping over the back of Aern's hands. His feet scrabbled against the floor.

Aern waited for the tell-tale wheeze that came right before the mark was done. That last bit of air escaped the man before he knew he was dead. Aern helped him discover it by jerking one wrist, causing the dagger in his wrist sheath drop down, and drove the blade into the man's heart. The body bucked a few times before finally growing still.

He let the body slip to the floor, leaving the mess of papers and open drawers. He never hid his work, especially when it was about someone betraying a trust.

As dawn approached he went to the village where he was to meet the girl. Frowning to himself, he cursed himself for a stupid fool when he saw her arrive in town. He should have known to just take her from her home. She had a small cloth with some food bundled into it, a worn shawl that looked like it had belonged to her mother…and bare feet.

What in all the hells had he been thinking? He should have known from the poor state of the tavern that the mother wouldn't have been able to provide something as basic as shoes. It bothered him that he hadn't thought about the girl's welfare in that matter. It didn't matter that she didn't seem to have a problem with it, or that she seemed not to even realize she should have a warm cloak or something to protect her feet. He was angry that he hadn't considered it. He should have at least bought her the things she would need.

When the girl saw the stormy look on his face, she hesitated, obviously debating running. For all she knew he was going to kill her now. Maybe this father of hers didn't really want her. Maybe he just wanted her out of the picture.

Aern forced a smile at that, trying to look happy and non-menacing, as he approached her. "You're in for a real treat, Miss Colleen!" He kept his voice light as he turned, offering her his arm. He arranged for her to get a warmer cloak and a pair of worn boots to wear beneath her threadbare gown.

She continued to be skittish around him until he got her to Chirrit. He had hoped that the sight of something as magnificent as his gryphon would delight her, but it was quite the opposite. She screamed, trying to run at the sight of the creature, held there only because Aern caught her around the waist. "No no! She's not going to eat you! Sh! Please! Look," He extended a hand to Chirrit when she reacted to the girl's fear, trying to calm her while he smiled down at Colleen. "We're going to ride her. Like a horse."

Then it was a matter of figuring out how he was going to transport her. He had never ridden double on Chirrit before. "Okay, let's see here." He walked around Chirrit, inspecting the harness set up, trying to figure out how to best modify it. He knew what she was capable of and what kind of mischief she could pull. Colleen didn't. He needed to make sure the girl would be safe, especially from something preventable like Chirrit's playfulness.

Chirrit craned her head as far around as she could to see what he was doing, putting her beak in the way every time he pulled at a spot on the rigging. "Oh, knock it off," he said for what felt like the hundredth time, pushing her away again.

Colleen giggled. At least she was finding this funny. Her giggles became full laughter as Aern tried to sidestep Chirrit's attempts to get into the pouch at his hip. Around in circles they went before Aern stopped and gave her a stern look. "Honestly, what's wrong with you?" he asked Chirrit in exasperation.

The blasted gryphon parted her beak as if she were smiling. Aern stopped, staring at her. "You're doing this on purpose!" She was trying to be cute for Colleen's sake! He grinned. "Dumb animal." He lovingly pushed her beak away from him as he turned to adjust the rigging. "Well then, Colleen," He looked over Chirrit's back. "Are you ready?"

She hesitantly skirted around Chirrit to join Aern on the far side. He took the belt he normally wore for flying, fastening it about her waist. "We're going to fly. This will keep you from falling off her." He lifted Colleen's slight frame to Chirrit's back and tied her down to the straps that ran from the front ring and the back surcingle, pulling them tighter to adjust for her petite form. "Tuck your feet here." He set her feet just inside the leather that rested right behind Chirrit's front legs.

Next was to ease away the small bundle of food she was clinging to. "It will go in a pack. You'll need your hands. Here." He pulled at the metal ring to show her. She reluctantly relinquished the cloth to him as she set her hands to the ring.

Again, he felt horrible that he hadn't thought to provide for her. All she had in the cloth was a hard loaf of bread and a few bruised apples. He made up his mind that he would do better for her on the return trip.

"And you," he told Chirrit as he mounted behind Colleen, "no funny business. I'm not strapped in here." He could have sworn she laughed as she turned her head to look at him with one large amber eye.

Aern found on the ride home that he didn't mind the child. As she relaxed, she provided happy chatter about her life, asking endless strings of questions about the gryphon and where she was going. "How old is she? How long have you had her? What's my da like? Will he like me? What's his home like?"

"He lives on a ship, but I don't know if that's a good place for you."

"Where will I go then?"

"I'm sure something will be arranged for you at Whitewind."

"Isn't that the royal palace? What's it like there?"

He certainly wasn't able to give her much information, as he didn't know much about "home" anymore himself. "Look." He directed her attention away from the discussion for a few minutes by pointing out nymphs at a pond below.

The questions were tiring for him. He had never been around anyone that asked so many. He just kept reminding himself that she had been raised differently and that she was younger than him. She wouldn't know not to talk so much. All the same, she was enjoyable in her innocent wonder of the world.

It was almost disappointing to turn her over to Jays. Colleen looked back at him with eyes that seemed to accuse him of abandoning her. "It will be fine," he promised her as he closed the door. He just wished he could have done as much for the other kids the woman had.

At least one would be better off. He smiled at that thought. The sun would rise for the girl. She would survive. And for once, no one needed to die for a child to have a better life.

That chased away any sense of melancholy that had lingered. With a renewed bounce in his step, he went down the ornate hallway with all the balustrades, turning to go down the wide marble steps to the main floor. He had barely set foot in the foyer when Silver came around the banister from the open right side, lightly tugging on Aern's tunic to have him follow. "Busy?"

Chapter 26

This brother unnerved him a little. Sterling was the crown prince and had the attitude of a royal brat to go with it. Silver was second in line to the throne and almost a mirror image to his twin Sterling. Not exactly the most muscular, he came across as delicate and too caught up in finery, but Aern had seen Silver with a blade some time ago. It had all been for show, but with the speed Silver and the elf had used it could easily have been deadly. That side of Silver didn't fit with the image presented. Aern wasn't sure what to think, especially now when the normally gentle tone of the man was brusque and business-like. "I suppose I have some time."

Back the way Silver had come, they circled around the stairway, going under the balcony for the second floor and turned right again. The hallway here was dimly lit. There were only three doors on either side, a guard posted between each. Silver turned and pushed open the center door on the right. Light flooded in from large windows that overwhelmed the small space.

The room was tidy, immaculate in a way only Silver seemed able to pull off. A desk with very little on it took up most of the space. Two bookshelves flanked it, full of materials. Silver removed a stack of parchments from the chair opposite the desk, motioning Aern to sit as he closed the door. "It's about the Jakhil. We're worried something is up again. It's been too quiet."

Once he had taken his own seat, Silver told Aern about how they had been waiting for some months now for a Jakhil attack to come. He didn't go into much detail as to *why* he was expecting an attack; just that it was long overdue.

"Explain," Aern said. "Why would you think it's overdue," he went on when Silver narrowed one eye and slightly shook his head in confusion.

Silver sat back in surprise. "You never knew?"

There was no point in answering that when it was obvious. Aern kept a steady gaze on this brother.

"I thought all the family knew." Silver's voice was almost apologetic.

Aern didn't mention that he was hardly family. Other than the wedding some time back, he hadn't been included in family events. He had never gotten letters. But he had survived; he always did. It wasn't worth mentioning now.

"We've been attacked by the Jakhil many times over the years. We've lost too many to these attacks." He fell quiet, staring at the empty expanse of his desk, probably remembering fallen guards. When he looked up though, it wasn't that subject he spoke on. "I'm worried about dad." His voice was soft, almost a whisper. "He hasn't been himself either."

All he could do was look at his brother. What did Silver expect Aern to say? He had no idea what their father was supposed to act like! So, as he'd been trained to do, he simply remained silent, listening.

He wasn't given much in the way of information about the Jakhil, but he did get to look at a plan of Whitewind. That he took in with great interest. He knew every castle had its hidey-holes and secret passages. He had just never realized how extensively the ones in this home had been developed.

Silver outlined all the possible weak points he could think of, asking for Aern's input on ways to better defend against infiltration. He pointed out bolt-holes and areas that didn't seem as secure from the outside, informing Aern what had been done to help increase security. It amazed him that this quiet, weak-looking brother could be so quick-witted about needing to defend this way.

Trying to wrap his mind around all the information he'd been given, he retreated to his rooms, laying out his weapons for cleaning. It was a familiar ritual, one that calmed him, brought order to him when everything else around him could be chaos. *This was his life*, he reminded himself. *This was his choice. The sun would rise; it always did. He would survive; he always did.* It wasn't easy being here with people that considered him family. They didn't look like him, they didn't act like him. He took pleasure in the simple repetition of cleaning weapons and checking poisons. He hoped it would be a quiet evening he could spend alone, but it wasn't to be.

"C'mon," Kyle cajoled, having barely knocked before entering Aern's rooms. He hadn't waited to get Aern's approval to open the door. "Poker game downstairs. Let's go."

More than a little annoyed at the familiarity Kyle showed, he tucked his few weapons under a pillow on the bed. "I don't play," he said dryly.

"Doesn't matter," Kyle responded happily. "It's mostly a chance to hang out together. Just us guys."

With a sigh, Aern decided to follow. "What about the girls?" he asked, considering there were so many of them. "Don't they play?"

Kyle's step faltered on the stairs as he considered that. A laugh followed. "Y'know, we never thought about it. Sterling and I started this back when the girls had 'cooties'." He laughed again, shaking his head. "We just wanted something that the girls couldn't take over."

Glad there would at least be no females to annoy him, he smiled back at Kyle's infectious good nature. "So how often do you play?"

A shrug was his answer. "Pretty regularly."

Considering how much he liked order and methodical things, this was something he could maybe start planning around. It would be a good way to get to know the siblings anyways. But as he entered behind Kyle to a cacophony of voices, he reconsidered that thought. The men – his brothers – seemed much louder than the people with whom Aern tended to keep company.

Their happy chaos turned out to be the only thing "regular" about the game. The time ranged from him being told it was Third Day, to being First of Harvest, or that both moons would shine bright that night. Any excuse would do for them to get together.

Uncomfortable with this new group of people, he tended to stay to the outside of their circle. He was easily accepted by them, included in their random card games, although he usually sat back and watched, preferring to learn of them rather than join them.

He had been home one month, barely enough time to have become family, yet he was again in Sterling's office, quietly watching his brothers. Keno, one of his older half-brothers, spared him a glance, disapproval at the glass of alcohol in one hand. Keno didn't like seeing people "pollute" their bodies with things like brandy. Aern gave Keno a wicked smile as he took a long draught from his glass. Alcohol was the least of the pollutants in his body and didn't affect him.

Their card game ended with jests and laughter, many taking their winnings and leaving. Others claimed duties or family responsibilities as they left, cheerfully bemoaning their meager losses of gold.

Sterling came to sit beside Aern with a sigh as Jays lit up a smoke. Aern tipped his glass towards Jays. "That shit'll kill you." It had long been a joke between them, with Jays fully aware of the poisons Aern ingested.

Jays smiled in wondered amusement. "I think it's the only thing you haven't tried yet."

Draining his glass with a sigh, he rose to refill it. "I have. But if there's no antidote, why risk it?"

Sterling looked at Aern in puzzlement. These two often had strange, cryptic conversations, but were rarely forth-coming with explanations.

Slowly looking back to his older brother, Aern locked eyes

with Sterling. "What?" He smiled as he realized that most of his family still didn't know about his training and why it had taken longer than the others. He had deliberately not told his parents; he had worked with Jays, but… "You don't know what I do, do you, Sterling?" He motioned for a servant to bring his pack to him, from which he pulled a small vial. "Here, taste this."

Jays knocked it away from Sterling's reach. "Not funny, Aern."

He took a sip himself and offered it to his brother again with a wicked smile.

Again, Jays knocked it away, this time causing it to spill. A vile stench arose where it smoked and soldered on the rug.

Aern watched the realization hit his brother. "You…that's…poison?"

"For most people." He used the toe of his boot to tamp out the last of the smoking in the mat, and then dropped back onto the couch beside Sterling. "Just another fluid to me." He cocked an eyebrow, looking so much like their father used to. "Bet that just upped my importance in your eyes. 'Wow', he's thinking: 'Now I'll have my very own taste tester and shall never have to worry about ingesting a poison ever again. Gee, isn't that great.'" His voice had become sardonic, each word punctuated, accented with disdain. "Just so you know, brother mine, I work for myself. I didn't swallow all this shit just so I could find out how great your food is for you. I'm a trained assassin. I've had real world experience working on Jays' ship and I've been sent on missions by your twin." He crossed to the fireplace and threw his glass, still half full, into the flames. It flared up as he stalked across the room and pulled the door open. "I am my own man, brother. Don't think to use my services without a very heart-felt please and thank you."

It was perhaps a little melodramatic, but at least Sterling would know where he stood on the matter. He stormed out of the room, only to run right into a young lady.

"Milord Prince, excuse me."

"Don't worry about it," he muttered, trying to extricate himself from the situation. Damn women, always underfoot at the most ungodly times. He jerked his arm, hoping to have it easily come away from her, only to find one of the clasps on his sleeve to be caught on the lace at her bosom.

A soft blush crept over her cheeks. "Allow me." She quickly disentangled their clothing and stepped away with a low curtsy. "My apologies, Prince Aern."

He watched her go in bemusement. No one called him Prince Aern; granted, that's who he was, but still…few people seemed to actually know that he was one of the princes, let alone that he had a name. "Damn women," he muttered under his breath, storming off to his rooms.

Once there, he couldn't find a calm center within himself. He had over-reacted with Sterling; he knew that; he also knew he wouldn't apologize. He had over-reacted with several people in high positions over the years. The only apology they had gotten was a well-slit throat.

The problem was the girl, the woman. It didn't matter who she was, just that she was a woman. That smell, the softness, the femininity… "Damn women." He was doomed by them, he was sure of it. He hadn't been through everything just to become a simpering pup before some fool woman. He wouldn't degrade himself to that. Never again.

He made the mistake of looking out his window, only to see her sitting in the gardens, stitching amicably with other women. She was pretty, as far as he really looked at any women these days. Darker, certainly. Her skin was a warm sun-kissed brown, not as pale as most women he saw. Elven, too. Her eyes and ears had the upward tips of the Fae.

One of the ladies suddenly drew her hand back as if she had been pricked by her needle. Aern leaned closer to the window, trying to see clearer. It was one of Sterling's wife Meghan's waiting women, and she had just tumbled from her bench to the ground, apparently unconscious. The woman he had literally run into now unerringly looked directly up to his window and smiled a vicious smile. The others were so busy looking to the fallen girl, they completely missed the look.

He bounded down the stairs, directly to his brother. "Sterling, there's a girl…" He stopped short as Sterling's wife rose to look at him. "Princess Meghan." He gave a cursory bow.

"I was just telling my lord husband that there has been an unfortunate accident." Her eyes bore into his own. "I hear you may know something about it."

Aern looked to Sterling in astonishment. "You told her about me??? I didn't give you that information to just hand out!" Coming to Whitewind seemed to have been a mistake. He was more than angry that his secret was being spread; angrier still that he was thought to be behind this newest trouble. "And no, I don't know what's going on," he added. "I just saw this all happen from my rooms and thought you should…" Why was he explaining to either of them? They didn't issue the orders he acted on. And he certainly wasn't about to tell them about it. He'd go straight to the person who could settle this. "You know what – I'm just going to go talk to Silver about this." At least Silver had the sense to keep things quiet.

Chapter 27

"I'm so sick of this!" Kelly stormed into the solar, slamming the door behind her. Several of her sisters looked up. Her only brother, who shouldn't have been there, didn't look up from having his hair brushed. He loved his sisters and would have preferred spending time with most of them instead of his friends. Of course, their preening and coddling of him may have had some impact on the matter. He loved the attention.

Closest in age to him, Kelly felt a special kinship to him. She crossed to take the brush from her sister, plopping down and proceeding to pull the brush roughly through his hair.

Mayden yelped, putting a hand to the back of his head. "Lights, Kelly! What's wrong now?"

"Ooh!" She threw the brush across the room. "Father just won't listen! Pats me on the head and says 'good girl, go along now.' He didn't even hear me! He's going to marry me to Bricriu."

Her sisters flocked to her, murmuring and petting. She allowed it for a time, feeling better at their sympathy. Then the anger returned. She got to her feet, pacing. "Of all things… Bricriu! Even father doesn't like him!"

"I don't know anyone that does," Mayden muttered. He had been in the same Adept's home for training while Bricriu had been there. He had seen the idiot go up against that Adept. Stupid fool; he was obviously of the Fire element.

Mayden couldn't help a chuckle at that. He was a Fire, too,

but he didn't explode in anger anywhere near as often as Bricriu. He had learned early to rechannel the anger into passion. He loved women, even though as a mage still in training, he was supposed to stay away from them.

"He's nothing like his brother. Elizabeth got the decent one. Bricriu is just *mean*. All he wants is power."

Mayden nodded. "He's tried convincing a lot of us that the Keltori is wrong; that the old ways were better."

"Ooh!" She shook in her anger. "He's nothing but trouble. He shouldn't be allowed to … to…"

"Be a mage?" her brother offered.

"No! To breed."

"Sh! Sh!" The girls looked around in worry that someone might have heard while Mayden shushed her, hands up imploringly. "You know how badly fire mages are needed."

"But at what cost?" She beat a pretty little embroidered pillow against the chair. "Father sees us as nothing more than brood mares. Stupid sheep led to the slaughter. And we're not supposed to notice or complain? 'Good girl,' he says, 'marry and make more Fire Mages.' What about what *I* want?"

"Sis, come on." Mayden pushed her down in the chair. "I know its bad, but don't call attention to yourself. They can make it worse for you."

One of her sisters shuddered. "They could make you marry a farmer."

"You'd live in squalor," another whispered, horrified.

"No servants," added another.

"Nothing but work from sun up to sundown."

Another pet her hair. "Just be quiet, Kelly. Marry the mage. Better that than to lose everything."

They were all so worried for her and she appreciated it. Really, she did. But how could she shut up and just go along with this? It would be better to work hard all day than to sit and be pretty, to do nothing. She had some ability. She had used her father's grimoire. She had caused Luck to appear.

She sighed heavily, slumping back in the chair. "Better that than falling in love? Better that than having one special someone?" A faraway look came over her. "I want to be special to someone. I want to know I'm the world to him."

"Kelly," one of the sisters spoke, using a pacifying tone. "It doesn't work that way. Father…"

"May Kinthris take him!" she fumed, getting to her feet again. Kinthris was the embodiment of all things vile and dark. He was the creature everyone warned littles about, telling them to behave or Kinthris would find them and take them away.

She didn't really want her father taken by the creature, but… "If I can't have my dreams…" Tears welled up from somewhere and she angrily wiped them away. "I can't marry someone like Bricriu. I can't!"

Mayden put a hand on her arm. "I'll help you then, Kel. As long as I'm around, you won't have to marry him." His voice was quiet, resigned. "Even if means my death."

Chapter 28

He had gone back to his room, writing up the writ of execution. Assassinations were simple, but to be legal… he sighed. The woman had killed one of the queen's ladies-in-waiting. She would have to die. And only Silver knew the logistics that would be involved in a kill like this.

Scanning it one last time, he dressed and went to the ballroom. It was the eve before open court season. There were plenty more people present than he would have liked, but he figured that Silver would figure out what he wanted when he handed the paper over. It could still be managed discreetly.

He wore simple clothing with no ornamentation. Plain gray velvet, so deep as to appear black, was dressed up only in the pewter buckles that held it closed. Even within the court, moving among those dancing and drinking, Aern carried as many concealed weapons as he could. As he came within reach of his brother, visiting easily with the ladies and court gents, he brushed his brother's arm. Silver started slightly as Aern turned to him. "Silver!" He extended a hand to his brother in greeting, pressing the parchment into his brother's hand as they shook. "Good to see you again, looking well this eve!"

Silver looked briefly at the warrant in his hand, pressing the seal of his signet ring into the warm wax Aern dripped over it before passing it back to Aern. Within just a few minutes, Silver had signed the woman's official death warrant and Aern had tucked it into his belt. They exchanged pleasantries for a few moments more before Aern made his excuses, offering his greetings to his father, then escaping the ballroom.

Shuddering against the horrendous press of bodies he had come from, Aern happily went to the family quarters. He was good with people in small settings, could deal with death and murder when needed, but being used to open spaces, to cool shadows, alone most times…he felt exposed and in danger when put into a press of bodies. It took everything he possessed to move about, act and smile as if he belonged and was a natural when in the settings of the court. He hated large groups. Odd, thinking that he was third in line to the throne of Drikelldorn. It was certainly no occupation he aspired to. He was content to travel the world, doing the bidding of his uncle and his brothers.

A smile passed his lips as he met Captain Randulf in the halls. He would be leaving for the sea again come morning, Aern joining him on the ship Freedom. Randulf lived for the taste of salt air, the thrill of the chase and the danger of his piracy. Aern enjoyed the rock of the ship, the escape from most people and the ability to live according to his own rules.

Of course, his rules were held in check by the code of assassins. He didn't randomly pick and choose the way he lived. Honor was still honor. His father had instilled that in him as a child. Even today, he would respect that. He always honored his commitments, he always saw a job to completion, and he always did the best job he could while on assignment. His father, were he to know of it, would be proud, and he knew his mentor, Lord

Morenden held him in high regard.

Hells, seemed that everyone held him in high regard. To have been given a nickname, to have others speak of The Shadow in revered whispers…hell of a heady experience, considering that Aern was only 19.

Then there was the other side of things, the people that were finding out who he was after all the years he had spent disguising it. He was beyond upset. He had been home less than a month, had not even had a formal meal with the family. Someone knew his relation to the king. Someone would soon try for the king.

And they did. The Jakhil struck Whitewind less than a fortnight later. Members of his own family, people he had never really gotten a chance to know, would by that evening be dead or dying. Three days. Three days that took too long and too many lives.

Screams woke him; not nightmares, but true screams of terror throughout the building. Voices. Running in the corridors. It took only moments for him to orient himself. He was at Whitewind, his birth-home.

Hearing voices calling out the names of others, he hurriedly dressed, automatically fitting weapons and poisons about his person. As he fastened the last of the clasps on his tunic, his manservant gave a swift knock before entering the room. "M'lord, your family…"

He brushed past the man, and entered the hallway to see

reddish-orange flames from the children's wing. Kyle, his eldest half-brother, went running past with a large bucket of water.

Another scream sounded, stopping Kyle in his tracks for a moment. The bucket was tossed behind, forgotten as the water sloshed across the marbled floor. "Nairne!" He was off again at full speed.

Numbly, Aern remembered Nairne was a half-sister to him through his father. Kyle was a half-brother through their mother. Keno was also a half-brother through their mother. And Keno was married to Nairne. That was a complicated mess that made little more sense than all the commotion in the hallways as servants and others in the family ran past.

He saw a servant bolt up the stairs, going to Sterling's rooms. Several minutes passed before Sterling came out alone, racing towards Silver's room. Within moments, they both raced downstairs, disappearing from Aern's view as they turned a corner on the main floor.

Moments that took forever passed as Aern noted servants scurrying below stairs in a panic of some kind. Silver, usually dressed so pristine and perfectly, came quickly from his quarters, still dressing as he took the same path Sterling had taken towards the throne room… or their father's office.

Their father's… Aern's head shot up as the impact of everything slammed home in his mind. He was right in thinking his father would be first. That was all the time he had to register what might be happening before a rolling boom came from the other end of his floor, followed by smoke and flames. A fire was spreading from the nursery wing; a sister was in danger; the crown prince had obviously been summoned by the king; many others seemed to be in equal danger, due to their rooms' proximity to the fires.

It wasn't sentiment that moved him towards the inferno. Hells no! He had one very particular reason. Lights forbid: Sterling had a kid. That put Aern just a blink further from the throne. Not to mention that Aern had a soft spot for children he wasn't quite ready to admit to, despite his having volunteered to help Jays find his children. He had to make sure Sterling's son – and the other littles – were okay. Besides, Sterling had just been making strides in becoming a parent to the child.

Another scream split the air, shaking any last hesitancy from him. The twins had the king in hand, meaning Aern could find out more on what was happening below stairs later. He went to help with the children, running towards the nursery wing, no plan in mind. He never acted without a plan in place to keep himself safe. But this was different.

"Nairne!" Keno called to his wife from the hallway, shielding his now-blistered face with an arm, coughing against the smoke. "Where are you?"

"Keno!" He heard Nairne's voice call back from behind the nursery's wall of flames. "The children!"

"I've got'em. C'mon, Nairne, now!" Keno kept an arm up, trying to protect his face, and charged into the room, leaping through the flames to join his wife in the nursery.

"I'm here, brother!" A man similar to Keno but with darker hair was suddenly near Aern, startling him. He hadn't seen anyone coming from that side.

"Dylan!" Keno shouted back, coughing harder. "I need you in here!"

Between one blink and the next, Dylan had disappeared – literally popping out of existence. Aern could hear shouting and the voices of the three adults in the nursery, but with the flames and the smoke rolling, it kept Aern from seeing any of them.

Then Keno appeared with a tiny girl in his arms. A wild look around at the servants and family working feverishly to help, and Keno's gaze met Aern's. "My daughter. Here. I need to get Nairne out." And the little girl was thrust into his arms.

He had to fight the bile that rose in his throat. She was still breathing, but just barely. Worse, her skin was charred from the flames, and her tiny gown had started to stick to her where the burns were the worst.

"M'lord." A nursemaid had her arms out to him, waiting to take the babe. Gratefully, he handed the small bundle over and raced on to the next door.

"No!!!" One of his sisters stopped in the middle of the hall, her howl of anguish overwhelming her. Melantha crumpled to the floor, right in the middle of everything. "Nairne!!!" She clutched her arms around her stomach, rocking forward on her knees, her forehead to the floor.

Silver's young wife, still in her nightgown, brushed past

Aern to kneel beside Melantha, whispering soothing words while rubbing her back. He went to where they sat, right in the middle of everything in the middle of the hallway. "You need to get her out of here. Now."

Rebecca looked up in fury at his demanding tone. "Her twin just died! Go around us!"

Before he could process which was her twin, Kyle grabbed his arm. "C'mon. Crystal's in trouble."

Another of his sisters. There were too many to keep track of. Yet another sister came from the other side, blankets soaked in water filling her arms. She shoved several towards him. "Get Crystal out."

Kyle grabbed the remainder from the woman; Aern followed Kyle into a room that was nearly engulfed in flames. Sitting on the window ledge was a frail, petite form, huddled as close to the night air as she could without falling out. She stared at them over the orange glow in rising panic, her pale features looking haunted. "I can't cross it!" she cried.

"We're coming!" Kyle called back, nudging Aern. Throwing a wet blanket each over themselves, they raced through the flames. Kyle started wrapping the slight woman in the wet blankets. "Aern, her legs." His voice was brisk, cutting all unnecessary conversation. "She needs to be covered. Completely."

Not questioning it, he started wrapping the wet blankets around his sister. "Now." Kyle's voice was hoarse from the smoke, the tone strained, yet still in control. "Get her out of here. Go!" He picked the slight woman up, handing her to Aern as she tucked into as small a bundle as she could. Even though she was just under his own slight height, she was much, much lighter. She instinctively wrapped her arms around him as Kyle put a final wet blanket over her head and arms. Kyle gave Aern a shove back towards the flames, then shot past him to help others.

He stumbled out to the corridor, flames licking at his clothing where the now-smoking blanket didn't cover him. While not fireproof, his work clothes had been treated to handle at least a small measure of elemental damage before it would break through to him.

"This way!" the same sister that had handed him the blankets called. "We need to get her outside."

Aern followed her down the marble stairs, across the receiving hall, and out to the fresh air. The golden bark of the crystal trees that framed the entrance shimmered while the clear gems tinkled merrily overhead as he set the girl on the ground. Red and orange reflected from the crystal drops to surround them in an eerie glow.

The girl threw back the blanket that had covered her head and looked to him with her large eyes of liquid beauty. It was like looking into the depths of the ocean, drowning him. He shook his head to clear it as he set her on her feet.

He saw many others outside as well, but the ringing of steel sent him back inside the building. It wasn't likely the marble would fall, but any and all wood was engulfed in flames now, racing down the banisters; chandeliers fell, sconces fell from the walls, leaving shattered glass chimneys. And worst of all … the elves. Not the beautiful, regal elves that Silver had trained with. These, while good looking, were cold, calculating, and intent on causing death. They were so intent on felling the guards that they never noticed the assassin as he moved in to take a place alongside the defenders.

Poisoned dagger to the kidneys; acid laced dagger across the neck; others pushed into the blades of the king's defenders. A garrote to the neck of one and he was down in seconds, dead from lack of air. The guard that had been battling the now-fallen elf, spared a moment to rip her nightgown up to her thigh before kicking the now lifeless form. "Damned Jakhil," she muttered, spinning away to fight into the midst of more of the elves.

A cold frisson of reality traced down his spine. She had said Jakhil. Jakhil did this. They were real.

* * *

It had been a long night. King Grey Bradley, the father Aern barely knew, lay dead by poison. Two sisters had lost their lives in the fires, Nairne being one of them. Sterling's wife had also been laid low by poison. Luckily, the child had been saved.

Now Aern sat in the king's office with Sterling and Silver. The silence was so thick, the air seemed stifling. The only sound was the quiet rhythm of a water clock on the desk, despite the other siblings present. Aern wondered if the twins were going to fight over who had rights to the throne. Sterling seemed to have been favored somewhat; he had been married early and produced an heir. On the other hand, Silver was impeccable, spoke several languages, and had already forged bonds with outside people. *Either would do a much better job on the throne*, he thought, *than I.*

He didn't expect the words that came from the brother he'd only gotten to know as one grudgingly in line to take the throne. "I need to know the names now," Sterling said quietly, taking parchment from the desk.

One would never guess murder and mayhem had occurred this night; not the way these two behaved. They were both cool and professional as if it were normal occurrences they were discussing. They were probably in shock yet.

"Tell me where, first," Silver answered just as calmly.

"Hakon." Sterling set out the inkwell and quill.

Aern blinked, but stayed to the back of the room where he leaned against the wall, arms crossed. Hakon was the land Lord Morenden had sent Aern on for his first solo mission. "Their ways are little known or understood below the mountain range that separates us," he'd said.

Silver rose, taking the quill. "Just find me dad's file on the mages. I'll see to the letters… your majesty."

Aern watched wordlessly at the exchange between his brothers. There was more going on here than he could even guess at the moment. Somehow Silver was knowingly ceding kingship to

Sterling, desperately forcing his brother to acknowledge it.

Sterling seemed to only just be taking it in that he really was a king now. Just as Aern thought Sterling would pass out, having gone very pale at Silver's use of language.

Clearing his throat, Aern stepped into the circle of family. "I've been there. I know the land." Maybe he didn't know it well, but he apparently knew more of the land than any of the others present.

Looking up from the desk, Sterling gave Aern an imploring look. "Then I'm asking you to personally see our mother to this designated safe destination."

"I'll have things ready by dawn." Silver informed Aern. "I'll let you know then where to take her."

"You…" Aern stopped, stunned that such things were even in place. The mages of the north had been here over the years, of course, but everything Aern had ever heard of them stated them to be selfish, taciturn, and destructive… like the Jakhil. Yet this indicated a working relationship between them and his father. "How do you…?" he started again. He shook his head, trying to clear it, put his wild thoughts in order.

"How did we know to prepare for this?" Silver supplied. He seemed to generally be the smarter, quicker-thinking of the twins. "Dad did it. He knew he would die. Fate told him a long time ago that he…"

Sterling cut him off, looking to Aern. "Lord Bookworm here will tell you a novel if you let him. Let's keep it to bedtime story status: Dad once married the wrong woman. Had kids. Found out that by doing that, he had allowed the Lights-bedamned Jakhil into our lands." A cold smile graced his lips. "The bogeyman is real… and we're related to the half-bloods."

Silver must have seen the confusion on Aern's face. "I promise, I'll tell you all about the Jakhil and how they fit in our family, but not tonight. Okay?"

Aern could only nod numbly before excusing himself. When he found that sleep eluded him, he joined many other members of his family at work cleaning up from the fire. He helped for a short time in moving broken glass and burnt timbers but was drawn to the throne room where the children had been sent. They huddled together or cried, inconsolable no matter what the nursemaids tried.

They needed their parents; something that wouldn't happen soon. Not with all the matters that needed settling first. And nursemaids wanted to coddle and cuddle the children, only encouraging the wails. What the littles needed was a distraction.

Stepping into the middle of the room, Aern smiled as if he had a secret, pitching his voice just loud enough to get attention. "Has anyone ever fought a snipe?"

Several faces turned to him in curiosity. "I saw one just the other day." He nodded to encourage their belief. There was no such thing as a snipe, but they didn't need to know that. "It was bigger than me and had horrible breath!" He made a face and waved a hand in front of his face, eliciting giggles from a few of the kids. Others turned to find out what was funny.

He continued with a purely made up story of an adventure he had with the fictional snipe until all the children were yawning and starting to lie down. As the older ones settled down, the younger ones calmed as well. Soon enough the room was full of the soft sounds of children at sleep.

Accepting the thanks of the harried nursemaids, he made his way back to the main hall. Sterling and Silver were conspicuously absent from the dirty work, but Aern noticed that the men that had been closest to his father were all present, helping the family. On checking, Silver's wife was still on the steps outside the front door with Crystal and Melantha. He had been callous to her during the mess, especially since she had lost the bond with her twin at that time. "Hey," he said, sitting down on the other side of Melantha. "I'm… sorry. Would you like something to help you sleep?"

She shook her head, but Rebecca nodded to him. Without another word, he pulled a clean vial from his supplies, mixing a two liquids until there was a bright blue mix taking up no more space than his thumb would have. "Here," he kept his voice soft, as he would while talking to a mark that was possibly aware of his actions. "It's just enough to put you under. No harm to you. Promise." It wasn't much, but at least it would release her from the horror for a small time.

As she lay over, slumber overtaking her, he sat down and looked to the other one. Crystal. She was still sitting in soaked blankets, but seemed unbothered by the wet or the cold of the night air. She looked away before he could fall into the depths of her eyes again. "How do you do that?" he asked quietly.

Rebecca gave him a questioning look. "You really don't know much about your family, do you?" When he said nothing, she put her arm around Crystal's shoulders. "Most of the stories are true, prince. Crystal's mother was a water sprite. There really was one at court for a time. And a fairy."

"And a Jakhil," he added flatly.

"And a Jakhil," she answered with a nod.

Long moments stretched out. The only sound out here in the quiet was the rustling of trees, the tinkle of the two trees to either side of the door with odd crystal leaves on them, and the hushed soft sounds of life in the castle at their back mixed with the creaking and cracking timbers of wood still stressed from the fire.

"You have a good family," she said, just over a whisper, "worth loving." She turned a pretty smile towards him. "Even with Jakhil in the family. Even with the constant attacks. Even with the danger."

"We didn't ask to be different," Crystal added, finally speaking to him.

"Wait…" he interrupted. "Constant attacks?"

Both women nodded. Crystal, after looking to Rebecca, answered him. "The Jakhil really are as bad as you've probably heard. I was around when dad brought that woman here. It was bad. Really bad." She fell silent, obviously bothered more than she could say about the matter.

Looking now at the people in this room, those he'd never gotten to know… it was on him. They had started getting to know each other as adults; they had invited him in. It bothered him more than he wanted to admit that someone had hurt his family. He wasn't going to let it continue. Not anymore. *Lights*, he thought, his stomach sinking a little, *it was personal this time.*

And he realized, after all these years that his father hadn't sent him away for any of the reasons his childhood mind had imagined. His father had known there would be a chance for danger. The children had all been sent to different locations to be sure there would be a broad skill set, with coordinated measures to ensure their survival.

* * *

Three days of endless funerals followed. Not only his father and some of his siblings, but also for several children; nieces and nephews he hadn't had a chance to get to know. And servants. So many had given their lives in the fight with the fire to save the children. They were given the same treatment as the nobles in Whitewind; a place of honor in the throne room beside all the other caskets, and a blessing by either Sterling or Silver over the body before it was taken for burial.

By the third day, Aern knew the words as well as the twins. When he noticed them flagging, he debated only a moment before stepping up to put an arm on Sterling's shoulder. "I'll do it for a while. Go rest."

Sterling gave him a smile, but didn't go to rest. He squeezed Aern's arm in appreciation, then went to the office to continue with other work that needed to be done.

It took what was left of the week to assign different riders to the princesses and the dowager queen as guards for their emigration. Aern met with several others in the king's personal office towards the end of that week.

"I'm going to send each of you with one of the girls," Sterling said with a command to his voice that hadn't been there before. "It will be under cover of darkness for most of them." He consulted a list, matching guards and certain family members. "The ladies to go are as follows: Crystal, Melantha, Amethyst, Emerald, Sapphire, and our queen, Cassidy." At the last he turned to Aern. "Silver said you would ride escort with the queen." There was no apology to his tone, no question. It was a simple command. And although Aern rebelled at the idea of playing "babysitter," he had volunteered his knowledge of the land himself. He nodded once to his brother, letting all know he was accepting the direct order of the new king.

Two nights later, he rode out with only a full moon for light, riding escort to his mother. The thought first infuriated him; he had other matters that needed his attentions, things he could better help with at the castle. Worse, he had to ride a horse. Chirrit flew above, circling down every so often, not understanding why he didn't ride her.

He reluctantly understood Silver's request for him to do this, but still! He swore a silent oath under his breath. He still had trouble reconciling the thoughts of his youth that she had never been there for him. And as far as he knew, she had only lived the pampered court life, never seeing the hardships of living on the trail. Much to her credit, she hadn't complained once. In fact, she seemed wrapped up entirely in her own thoughts.

Silver had felt this would be a good opportunity for him to become reacquainted with their mother. And on some level, he wanted to get to know her. He wanted to find out what she was like and why she had never contacted him. But the more important question was: would his mother really want to know him? Not the "sweet" little boy she had sent away for training, but the hardened assassin he now was?

Chapter 29

The first night passed in silence. She was wrapped in her grief, and he didn't know her anymore. Several times he glanced at her, wanting to know what to say, how to help. But she was the mother. He had once wanted, badly, to have her be there for him. He remembered nights before he had left for training. There were times he had needed her there, and she had come. But not over all these last years. He had learned to rise on his own, to wait for his own sunrise.

Which was coming soon again. He looked to where she sat her horse, head bowed with the weight of all she had lost these last days. "We'll have to make camp soon," he said softly, not wanting to startle her from her reverie.

She sighed quietly, bringing her gaze up to start looking around. "There," she offered after several moments. Aern had thought she was just getting her bearings. Instead, she pointed out an overhang with decent protection. It would only need a little help to secure it as a place to let her rest.

Queen Cassidy surprised him again when they reached the spot. She didn't wait astride the horse for him to help her down. She efficiently dismounted, then set about removing the horse's tack. He stood in stunned shock as she rubbed down her mount, then saw to its comfort before moving to drop her pack near the back of the enclosure. "I wasn't always the queen, Aern," she offered quietly when he still stood silent. "I had a life before I met your father."

Curious, he followed her, woodenly taking her lead on preparing bedding, going through their travel supplies, gathering dry twigs. Where did a queen learn these things? He had learned in training but, generally, nobles didn't do such base tasks. "Here, let me," he offered when they had built a small pyre. Taking flint and steel, he drew a spark, fanning the small flame up just enough for their needs. "We don't want much of one," he offered in apology. "Safety. Can't have you seen."

She smiled, factoring more into his words than he had thought to mean. As hard as he tried to appear, she heard the underlying tone to his voice, letting her know that no matter how he had been shaped, he had turned out just as well as her other children had. Her youngest was stubborn, like her, but he meant well. And his actions marked him as kind, making her glad he had obviously been trained by good people.

Cassidy had hated letting her boys go off to be raised by other people. She had understood when Grey had said the kids would get better training than they could give. She had understood that the first generation of royals at Whitewind weren't as equipped in skills of sword or what have you as the other lands had become. Logically, she had understood, but she was still a mother, and it had broken something in her every time a child had been sent away.

She didn't know this strong young man before her. She should have been able to put her arms around him, to tell him she loved him, but she couldn't. There was something in his posture and his eyes that showed too much wariness to accept her as a mother after all these years.

Aern glanced at her several times as he finished preparing things for their rest. She had an odd look to her as she watched him, a funny little smile with such sadness in her eyes. When he couldn't take it anymore, he sat beside her with a heavy sigh. "Lady Mother…"

"You used to call me Mama," she interrupted softly.

"Uh…" he blinked, trying to reconcile what he'd been taught to call her with what she asked. "That's…"

"I know." Her voice was resigned, sad. "You aren't a little boy to use that now. Maybe…" she gave him a smile that was more peace offering than happiness, "how about just Mom?"

After only a moment's thought, he nodded agreement. It was a small thing to make her happy. "Mom." He gave her an answering smile of agreement.

There was nothing else to say. They found their respective bedrolls until the next nightfall.

The entire trip went in that manner. Fits and starts to conversations, awkward silences, and a few moments tucked in of jest and humor. She was a stronger woman than he would have thought at first, and he grudgingly gave over on the anger he'd carried about being abandoned. He let go enough so that, one night while both moons were high overhead, he broke the silence with one of the questions that had bothered him most of his life. "Why didn't you ever call me home?"

He buried his fingers in Chirrit's ruff, finding comfort in her warmth as he waited expectantly. Chirrit glanced back once, chrring her version of ease to him as she settled her wings more warmly about his legs. He didn't really care. At least, he kept telling himself that as the moments dragged on. It didn't matter if she didn't have a good reason.

"Lord Morenden sent us regular letters," she finally said into the silence. "He told us how well you were doing, but that you're training was more intensive than most." She fell silent again, remembering those letters; how he had said that her baby had a "soft spot that would destroy him." He had thought Aern needed to be cut off from the family if he was to be broken of his silly ideals.

Grey had picked out the "important" matters like Aern needing to focus on his training and how he was getting better at certain weapons, and how easily court etiquette seemed to come to such a young boy. But Cassidy had seen how the man had picked apart the things that made Aern special. She had wanted her boy home when she found out that the nobles where he was thought he was soft and wasteful. Could she tell him now that they had thought he was "silly" for having given his own possessions to better others? That they had thought he was "soft" for making sure none of the others went without? No.

She knew her silence had gone on too long when he bowed into his gryphon's neck, seeking solace from the animal. "Aern, I wanted you home. But look what you've developed into," she offered. "We couldn't have done that for you at Whitewind."

Yeah, look at me, he thought. He was a hardened killer, and his mother was proud of him.

She was proud of him. Despite whatever hardships he'd endured, he had remained a kind person, generous, like his father. "No matter what, Aern," she offered quietly, "you've become a fine man. You're father…" she stopped, choking on tears a moment as she mentioned her loss. Cassidy cleared her throat, trying again. "I'm proud of everything you've made of your life. No matter what." Even knowing he was an assassin.

Whether Aern knew it or not, she and Grey had been informed when his training had been completed. Only then had they been able to fully understand what they'd given their baby over to. Yet seeing him now, he wasn't the monster of the night that Kinthris was. There was no malice to the man sitting regally astride a gryphon. He was a good person. She was happy to call him her son. She only hoped her actions could tell him how glad she was of it.

Chapter 30

After a hard month of travel, he watched his mother escorted away by a member of the mage's council, the Keltori. Satisfied that at least his charge had arrived safely, he strode outdoors, whistling for Chirrit to land. She was still circling when a man cleared his throat from the doorway behind him.

Turning, Aern took in the visage of a tired-looking young man with fire-red hair. There was a certain aura of danger around him, but Aern was used to that feeling from those he associated with. The only difference was that this one had immense magical power at his disposal. Aern smiled his devil-may-care grin at him as Chirrit landed behind him. "Mage."

The man approached, offering a handshake. "I've heard much about you, Shadow."

Aern's surprise slid away quickly once their hands touched. A ring was passed to Aern in the touch: his brother Silver's ring. It was the same ring each member of the Bradley House had been given at their majority, with their individual initials inside. The outside was silver, with the raised design of a tree, bare of leaves, the trunk and branches delicately wrought in fine lines of turquoise.

His eyes narrowed towards the mage; he nodded once. His brother obviously felt there was reason to assist this man in an assassination. "Let's talk then." He dismissed Chirrit, following the man back inside.

The young mage poured them both a glass of golden brandy after closing the study door. "I was at your brother's wedding," he offered. "How's that going for him?" His voice was carefully neutral, being unsure of his own footing in the conversation. Speaking with an assassin was risky enough, but if the Shadow turned on him, told other mages about this proposition…

"She's dead," he stated flat and succinctly, shaking his head slightly to the offered glass. Everyone knew that Sterling's marriage had been THE wedding. For everyone but Sterling.

"I'm… sorry."

Aern crossed his arms. "What do you want?" He cut the mageling off before he could waste his breath. Silver obviously approved of this guy, so Aern wanted him to just get to the point. He didn't need platitudes, and he didn't make small talk with clients.

"My sister…" Mayden started lamely. He cleared his throat, trying again. "Look, there's a hell of a lot at stake. The Keltori is the Law here. If they find out I've even mentioned this to you…"

"Shadows don't speak, mage," Aern said, slightly annoyed. "Professional courtesy, hm? You don't know me, and I don't know you. Now what's the hit and what's the profit?"

The assassin was obviously younger than the mageling, but Mayden couldn't quite wrap his mind around how much older the young man seemed. He firmed his own spine in the face of this.

"My sister is promised to a man everyone would rather see dead."

A cold smirk graced the corners of Aern's mouth. "Sure it isn't the other way around?" He knew that the women were almost considered second class in this society, that the mages were everything, and that any non-mage "owed" their existence to the "beneficence" of the magic-wielders.

"Ah, no. Here's the thing: she's promised to someone with a really strong Fire gift. We can't officially afford to lose any more Fire mages, but he's a real piece of work. He's talked with other apprentices and journeymen about overthrowing our Keltori."

"So arrange an accident." The answer to this one seemed clear enough to Aern.

"It can't be traced back to anyone with the Gift of magic. It would condemn us to death for doing it."

Curious now, Aern really studied him. "Your sister means this much to you?"

Mayden looked down, embarrassed on some level. "Yes. She doesn't ask for much." He looked up at Aern. "She's smarter than a lot of the girls, and she looks out for the others."

"Others?"

"My sisters. There's…" Mayden tried to get a count in his head. "A lot of them. Father's had several wives and mistresses."

"I… see…" Aern said slowly. Why anyone would want more than one woman in their life was beyond him. One was too many. "And what payment are you offering?"

"I don't have much. I'm not a full mage yet." There was a

pause, pregnant with unspoken words. "I know the story surrounding your birth."

The only other time he had heard mention of anything about it had been from Jays in his first days on the ship. After that, nothing would convince Jays to speak of it again. And here was a mageling offering the information to him.

The full story was laid out for him, as pitiful as it was. A lot of confusion had almost destroyed relations between different lands, all because of the way he had looked when he was born.

He was still reeling with the strangeness of it when he left. He would look into the potential assassination further. It was the least he could do in exchange for the information.

The fact that he was still stunned may have been the reason he slipped and was nearly caught. He had half his mind on what he'd been told and the other focused on going through the desk and shelves in the office. He needed some sort of evidence to back up a job like this. Or something that said the family would stand behind it. He had hoped he'd find that something in the Adept's study.

There was nothing important in the desk, though. There was parchment, inkwells, a few odd personal trinkets like charms or jewelry chains. A large book stood in almost the center of the room on a wooden stand that tipped the book slightly upright. Bound in leather, his fingers easily slid over the page edges, but it somehow resisted any attempt to open it.

The books on the shelves were ledgers of accounts, records of students being trained… there! He found the name he was looking for. He couldn't believe the number of transgressions the man had acquired. It seemed Bricriu MacFurgal had been charged with several incidents against other apprentices and a few against the instructors. Twice he'd been sent back down to basic training due to serious transgressions. Seemed there were plenty of reasons to have this jerk eliminated. And if Silver was okay with it…

He put the book back, going to look over the desk one more time. He had just stood up from closing drawers to see the door open. Aern frowned. Hells. There wasn't supposed to be anyone here. He was well and truly caught in the study as the young woman walked in. But rather than act trapped, he scowled, leaning forward over the desk. "Explain yourself."

She certainly hadn't expected to run into someone here in this private office; especially not a handsome, dark-haired stranger. She had never seen the likes of anyone similar. The mages were all so full of themselves and the apprentices were either like those training them, or so unsure of themselves as to be worth no one's time. There were others, like the one she was betrothed to, but better not to think on that one.

She tried to gather her wits as she noted his looks, the dark clothing in a style that marked him as a visitor, and the easy manner in which he carried himself. He wasn't full of pride or arrogance, but he wasn't meek or timid, either. He simply, quietly, waited. That scowl indicated he thought he had a right to be there. "Explain *my*self? I think you'd better explain what *you're* doing here!"

Her voice was sultry, reminding him of the warm hum of voices around a campfire. It caught him off guard; to have such a beautiful voice come from the irate beauty before him was…

Wait. Beauty? He closed his eyes a moment, trying to clear his head. He slowly opened them to study her again. An almost ethereal complexion highlighted the light golden-brown eyes that seemed lit with an internal fire. Her hair hung to mid-back, straight and full, with lots of movement even as she stood there, quite still. It caught the firelight in its red and auburn colors, flashing sparks of color back. It would likely do the same beneath the moonlight just past the win…

He caught himself again, looking away with a scowl of irritation. Lights! She was just another woman; and one that was interrupting a mission, no less! He glanced back at her, trying to show her how irritated he was. What he got was a matching expression above a freckled nose. "You're in my house. Go away."

Giving her his most menacing expression, he leaned towards her. "I was hired to be here."

"Father would never hire you." She matched him again in tone and body language. "And neither would I."

He pulled back in surprise, a little-used laugh escaping him. Few were bold enough to stand against him these days. A woman from these northern lands was the last one he would have expected to have a backbone. He found he enjoyed this. "What's your name?"

"Names have power." Her eyes flashed in daring. "Give

yours first."

Chapter 31

"Shadow," he answered her, eyes narrowing slightly as he watched her body language.

There was no indication she knew of his reputation as she flipped her hair over her shoulder. "Kelly."

"You… you're the one I'm here about." He rolled his eyes, cursing himself for letting even that much slip out. What was it about her that seemed to disarm him?

Wary eyes studied him from a face set askance. She stepped further into the room. "If not by my father, then who?"

"Mayden."

She froze in place a moment. "He gave his true name?" Her own eyes narrowed slightly. "Who are you, really?"

There was something underlying her words that seemed to indicate it wasn't his occupation she was asking about. There was a Power of some kind that took interest in what the answer would be. It was almost as if the immortals listened with baited breath. "Aern," he answered succinctly.

Whatever the energy was, it felt like something settled as soon as he'd said his name, like someone releasing a held breath. Her smile seemed to warm the cool room. She came closer, passing the large book on the stand. Her fingers ran across it, almost a negligent caress. Aern had to blink, doing a double take. He could have sworn flames leapt up to touch her fingers, but on a second look there was nothing there. And Kelly didn't appear to have noticed anything odd.

Sitting in a chair across from the desk, she primly crossed her ankles, tucking her feet slightly underneath. "What are you looking for in my father's study?"

His suspicious nature snapped back into place in light of her feminine behavior. His court training came to the fore as he came around the desk to lean lightly against it, crossing arms and ankles. "Tell me why it matters." He kept his voice light, as if bantering or flirting with her.

Kelly sat forward, hands on the arms of the chair, brown eyes flashing almost to a garnet color. Her irritation raised her respiration, her cheeks flushing. "You're in the personal study of an adept! Isn't that 'matter' enough?"

Aern couldn't help a small laugh. "I could ask the same of you: what are you doing in an adept's study? I thought women weren't allowed."

She had the good grace to look ashamed, dropping her gaze. "We aren't." Despite her discomfort, she looked up again in the next moment, irritation in her voice and body language. "But we should! They aren't any better than us women!" Her voice lowered to grumbling, her arms crossing in annoyance. "Just because we're shorter and we don't do magic."

There was a long moment while she sat there, ruminating on the things that annoyed her, and Aern stood there trying not to laugh. He lost his battle. The whole thing was just too preposterous. She glared at him while he laughed. Finally gaining control again, he asked around his laughter, "What does your height have to do with anything?"

"Well, nothing." Her voice was just haughty enough, just irritated enough, and just baffled enough that it set Aern off again.

She intrigued him. For the first time in years, a woman fascinated him enough that he moved to the chair beside her, to sit and actually visit with her. He found her to be the same mix as her first impression: first full of vinegar, then fire, then a softly scented flower. Her moods were mercurial, but never in a violent, self-serving way. Not like what he'd been reading about the man she was intended to marry. Aern could see why her brother wanted to protect her. She was that rare combination that made her enjoyable to be around. Always just a little off center, anyone with her would be kept guessing as to how she would respond. He found he rather liked it. And he found that he wanted to take the assignment. Not for king or country, not for her brother, but for her.

As soon as the king was safe. The Llewellyns would need to wait just a little bit longer. War would come first.

* * *

Aern's hair was a shade of black so deep it carried blue highlights where the sun had framed him from behind, and his eyes had been such a unique shade of clear blue that they had leapt out at her from beneath a fringe of long black lashes. And the way he carried himself! She was used to the other men in her class; always so full of themselves and the way they seemed to puff themselves up to appear more than what they were. But this man was different. He didn't dress in "style" like others she knew. There was little of color or fashion about him. But what he wore was obviously something comfortable to him. Brushed velvet of some kind in dark colors contrasted her silken finery; fitted, knee-high boots against her dainty satin slippers; ribbons tied her clothing while his was done up with cold metal clasps.

Even his voice was beautiful to her. She couldn't get past the way it felt as his clothing likely did: velvet softness, with that dark undercurrent of something hidden. She thrilled to think of how they had talked, unbeknownst to her family. Her father would have punished her for speaking with a man unattended, which had only made the conversation that much more exciting to her.

And he hadn't been like other men in his exit either. Most would have kissed her hand, bowed, something…but Aern had simply smiled, then brushed past her, leaving her standing in the office alone. No goodbye, no formalities.

She really hoped she'd see him again.

Chapter 32

"Right then," Sterling said with little formality. "All but one of the girls made it north. Sapphire and her escort were cut down en route. It's time for war." His tone was professional, no hint of emotion; no hint that he might have gotten along with whichever sister had been killed. He looked around to each person in the room. "Let's get going on this."

They were all closeted in what had been their father's private office. All of his brothers were present, as well as most of what had been their father's most-trusted advisors. A few women, such as the current Captain of the Guard, were present as well. There were nowhere near enough chairs for them all to sit on, so they had been encouraged to take seats along the walls, on the floor. Even Sterling sat on the floor. Aern found it a bit odd to think this was the king now, sitting on the floor like a child would. He didn't sound much like a leader, either; not in the traditional sense, anyways.

Sterling glanced through a pile of papers in his lap. He pushed a hand through hair just a little too long around his face before looking to the rest of the room. "Now that my sisters are away, I want this to stop. My father let the attacks continue for too long. No more."

First listening to him, Aern heard a petulant child speaking, almost on the verge of a tantrum. But as Sterling went on, the training he had received over the years became apparent. He assigned different people tasks, set up a timeline and plan for going to war. He knew what weapons they had at their disposal, he knew what skills were best honed by those serving Whitewind, and he knew who their best allies were. Runners were sent with messages from Sterling's pile of pages to each of those peoples.

There was no hesitation to his voice, no compromise. For all his earlier tone of petulance, there was none of that by the end of the meeting. Everyone was jumping to do his bidding, even though he didn't exude that odd aura of power that usually went with rulership. He didn't raise his voice, either.

Watching the people, Aern realized that in part it was because Sterling was known here and that most genuinely cared for him. Whatever else they thought, they knew he was right for this job and they wanted him to succeed.

Through it all, Sterling saw none of this. He simply did as was needed. When only a few remained, he rose, looking to Aern. "You… and you," he looked to their cousin Brett, "will be needed once we make camp. Our troops aren't as ready as you two are. I need your help."

Aern nodded agreement. It wasn't a request from Sterling, as it might have sounded. Something lay under those words, some strength, some command that gave the order. Something that told Aern he would easily and willingly serve this brother.

* * *

He watched from halfway across the throne room. Across

the aisle, Brett stood in equal stance. Both were stiff, unaccustomed to the frippery and fluff that accompanied a court appointment. But this was a call to war. They had no choice but to be here.

Sterling, little more than a barely-known brother a few weeks ago, was now king. Aern noticed how Sterling sat easily on the throne, heedless of all the eyes upon him as he spoke quietly with several of his advisors. He doubted he could have done the same, not after so many years in the shadows. Granted, he had helped out during the funerals, but that was different. Everyone had been wrapped in their own grief, not really paying attention to who spoke the words of institution or offered the blessing.

The great doors behind him opened, admitting Sterling's twin. Silver moved with great purpose, his wife at his side, as they entered the king's presence. A curt bow and curtsy from them, and Sterling was on his feet. Removing the royal circlet from his brow, he stepped down from the dais. "Lady Rebecca," Sterling's voice carried easily over the hushed assembly. "Duchess of Whitewind, as my brother's wife, I ask if you willingly take the reins of my kingdom in hand until such time as I return. Should I not, hold it in trust for my child."

"Your Majesty," she dropped into a full curtsy. "I am honored to be entrusted with your people."

Sterling placed the circlet over her hair. "May you guard Her well." He turned to his twin, questions of fortitude and loyalty echoing between them. As he stepped forward, Silver fell in beside him. Rebecca assumed her place near the throne as the two men moved in sync, cool determination in features and movement. As they passed by, Prince Aern and Duke Brett Bradley stiffened formally before falling in slightly behind them. Two rulers in midnight blue with turquoise trim and two warriors in black with pewter trim; he knew with the swords and scabbards flashing at their hips they all cut a rather impressive figure. It only added to the image when several other brothers and cousins fell in behind them, enlarging the procession.

Despite it being a moment in the spotlight, Aern couldn't help the quirk of a smile at knowing how impressed most of the crowd was at the moment. The moment quickly faded though, once in the courtyard. The others mounted their horses; Aern went to Chirrit. He was settled comfortably on her back, watching the others say their goodbyes. It bothered him more than he liked that there was no one to see him off as well.

He looked to Sterling, seeing a man at a loss as well. His wife had died in all this, and he now left a very young son behind in the care of others. Sterling pointedly watched only the pommel of his saddle during these last moments at home.

Looking to Silver, Aern saw another story entirely. An elf, Silver's closest friend, sat easily a-horse beside him as Silver said his goodbyes to the temporary queen. Soft kisses, tender caresses, then simple hand-holding as Duchess Rebecca looked up at the elf, and at Sterling. "Take care of him."

The two exchanged a look before looking back to her.

Sterling simply smiled in understanding. Gavriel, the elf, reached down to take her hand. "Lady, I would give my life to see him returned safely. Trust in that."

He'd do *his* damnedest, too. So few had that kind of happiness as they did. Aern vowed to the Lights that he'd see those two reunited again.

Chapter 33

Aern sat near the crackling fire with his family. Silver seemed edgy, uncomfortable. Sterling absently poked at the orange flames with a stick. The steady scrape of Aern's blade against the sharpening block was the only constant sound against the backdrop of rising and falling conversations at other campfires.

His eldest half-brother, Kyle Erickson, moved around solemnly, making sure tents were set properly, that supplies were there and accounted for. Aern watched him for some time, amazed that he could be related to someone so different from himself. Kyle was more bulk and muscle compared to the rest of the Bradley clan.

There were a few other older half-brothers to Aern's name, but those he had seen so little as to likely not recognize them. This one acted with the quiet grace of a noble, yet did the simple job of a steward. The only difference Aern saw was that, unlike other stewards, Kyle didn't pamper Sterling. He fully expected Sterling to pull a fair share of work.

Then there was Kyle's half-brother, Adam Erickson. That man was so quiet with the adults, yet had spent the entire time traveling with one eye on Silver while keeping the young squires entertained with thoughts far from war. Even now, he wasn't despondent or worried as some of the others. He sat calmly at the next fire over, listening to the squires telling tales. Only his eyes gave away his alertness to something else. He often looked to

Silver and then scanned the perimeter of the camp.

Between Adam and the elf Gavriel, Aern had to admit that if one of the twins were to walk out of this war, it likely wouldn't be the king. Sterling may have the force of the army behind him and the respect of the kingdom, but Silver seemed to have at least two men that were willing to die for his safety.

Three, he reminded himself with a small smile. Rather he die himself than become the one on the throne. Even so, his reasons were selfish. The other two men were tight friends with Silver and demonstrated in their watchful manner that they truly would protect him at all costs.

Within a few nights, the men – and some women – had started to resolve themselves into a more settled routine. They weren't living with the overpowering fear hanging over them for that first battle. Battle tactics had been discussed, training in units had commenced, and most now seemed ready, excited rather than timid little mice.

Then true natures started to come out. No one was trying to "play nice" anymore. No one felt the need to act brave now, and it became easy to see which were used to hardship and which had been pampered. Aern found it wryly amusing that he easily could have been one of those needing assistance.

Some of the fools insisted on even having another help them dress. He fully expected those simpering idiots to fall within the first days of battle. There was always the chance they were acting, putting forth a false face, but even he couldn't behave so ridiculously. He couldn't help a small laugh as he shook his head, returning to sharpening his dagger.

Searching through his pack, Aern pulled forth several small vials, holding them up to the light. Choosing two, both a shade of brown, he dipped his smallest finger in one, touching it then to his tongue. Satisfied, he put one away. The other he shook lightly before applying a small amount to both his daggers and his arrows.

He smirked as some man squealed in outrage over something. Pulling out his finest rope, he began braiding a new garrote, listening to the fool screeching at his assistant; some ridiculous fit about how his precious fingernails weren't buffed to perfection. Aern pulled the braided strands tighter, chuckling. Fingernails were the least of his worries.

Tying off the ends, he struck a flint to burn and seal both ends of the work he'd just done. Snapping it taut to test the strength, he then twisted lengths around his hands, setting the center over his knee and pulling, testing again for durability. Satisfied in his work, the momentary thought crossed his mind to help the world by ridding it of the man so concerned with his looks.

Repacking his handiwork, Aern leaned back against a rock, surveying the camp before him. To their credit, his older brothers weren't counted as such fools. Sterling moved purposely through the men, often stopping to sit a moment near the different fires. Silver, on the other hand, still seemed a bit shell-shocked. Aern couldn't tell if that was because of the coming battles or the recent loss of family members. Either way, Aern was proud to say that at least Silver wasn't the fool the squealing man was.

None of his other siblings were, either. Several sisters had been lost in the attack, but the brothers were another matter. They all seemed to have different callings in life and had fit in perfectly to them.

All of them, plus his cousins, were here on the battlefield today. And not just the family he had met at the castle, either. When war had been declared, people were asked to report with certain numbers of troops. What had surprised everyone had been the Wild Ones that presented themselves for duty as well. Of those, he had a green-skinned sister, Mist, who brought the water sprites. She had been behind bringing most of those to the aid of Whitewind.

The other surprise had been a brother he hadn't even known about. He knew about his father's second wife, a fae named Kembrelei. He hadn't known there had been a child born of that union. And while the delicate, winged Rhys didn't have much to do with his "human" family, he, too, knew the stakes this war would have on the people he now ruled. All races seemed to have joined the battle on behalf of and for his family. He couldn't help feeling proud to be a Bradley.

This was especially true when he was able to see his cousin, Brett, at work. The man had more patience with recruits than Aern could hope to have. Aern, himself, was trying to explain to a small group of young men the method used for sneak attacks.

He continued to gain nothing but blank looks. Granted, it wasn't that he expected them to perfect a method of doing any kind of sneak attacking, but they should at least learn the methods used by others! They should understand that there were different ways to fight and to attack. In frustration, he left his group to watch the way his cousin handled his own green recruits, the ease with which he commanded and gave orders.

Aern doubted there was much hope of any of these dreamers walking off the battlefield. It was no wonder his father had never pushed for war. He must have known how inefficient his armies were.

"Watch your back!" Brett yelled as he attacked another in practice. "There won't be just me out there. The Jakhil won't wipe your ass for you."

He couldn't help a laugh at the image, even knowing what his cousin meant. A declaration of war was no play-time, and yet most of the ones here were treating this as a fancy outing.

The castle guard had learned over the years, but even they hadn't been able to stop the attacks. They hadn't stopped the death of the king. This is where he and his cousin came in. He had to consider what a sad state things were in when a kingdom relied on an assassin and a mercenary to save them.

But, as that *was* the case… He moved in behind the three currently trying to take Brett down. All were so focused on him that they had nothing left to watch their backs as they'd been told. Yet, Brett could use the help to reinforce what he was telling them, even if it was hardly worth it. He didn't even have to duck or dodge between people and shadows. He grabbed a staff from one of the men that idly stood waiting his own turn at Brett. Not waiting to see the reaction, he continued on with purpose.

He stopped behind the cluster, even giving them this extra moment to notice danger. Nothing. So.

The staff moved with lightning swiftness to crack the head of the one nearest. He turned with enough speed at that, but Aern ducked under the blade, his fist darting in to knock the wind from the man's midsection. The second finally noticed him, starting to turn too late. A garrote from behind quickly dropped him to the ground, gasping for air.

The third was a surprise. Firstly, the fighter was tiny, yet wielded two blades, darting and bouncing while managing to land a few blows against the seasoned warrior. Second, she was a girl. Unlike most girls he had met, she seemed to carry no qualms about this fighting matter. And third. Third… She knew he was there. Her focus stayed on Brett, but every move Aern made was sidestepped or blocked by her.

"Hold!" Brett finally bellowed.

She stopped immediately, yet didn't lower her weapons. Brett went on to tell the troop to follow her example. Every bit of it. Including her refusal to lower weapons.

"Because," Aern picked up, "it would be easy to step in. Prepared…" he closed the distance.

Her blades flashed, crossed, and came to rest at either side of his neck. In the next moment they were retracted and laid at his feet as she knelt. "Prepared, I walk away, your grace."

He waved away the formality, motioning her to rise in irritation. "Exactly." He looked over not only Brett's group, but on past to where his own now watched. "Learn this. Become a little jumpy; sneak up on each other until you anticipate it."

There was no doubt in his mind that most would fail abysmally at the task. It had taken him *years* of training to accomplish what he and Brett now demanded of the troops.

"You." Now that he really looked at the girl, he could tell she was the same one that had been in the family wing the night of the fires. She had been the guard fighting in her nightgown. "Who are you?"

She turned to him with arrogance in her stance, hands on hips. "Brady. Brady Randulf. Why?"

His shock bubbled over into laughter. "Related to Jays? The pirate?"

"Yes. Why?" She demanded again.

He shook his head, indicated the girl, then yelled over to Brett. "Promote her."

He smiled as he strode from the practice ground. He enjoyed seeing women with a little more strength and backbone. It was too bad more weren't like that; maybe they wouldn't annoy him quite so much.

Chapter 34

The first skirmish came at dusk the next night. Two of the Jakhil were caught spying nearby. A cry went up on both sides, bringing dozens to bear with blades before it was done.

The Jakhil disappeared back into the night, leaving their dead behind. It was the first opportunity Aern had been given to see what they really looked like.

Most of those on this, their own side, either helped other injured to their feet, or simply walked away from the dead bodies. Aern looked for his cousin Brett. A mercenary wouldn't leave a field like this. And he wasn't disappointed. Brett had a small group of men and women, some of them the green recruits Aern had seen just the other day, going through the belongings on the dead before moving them to a makeshift pyre that was put together.

Tucking his daggers back into his wrist sheaths, Aern bent to the work. The Jakhil were almost identical in looks to the Sithari. Sculpted bone structure, pointed ears… although their coloring was more like the Longredal. Their skin was the warmer wood colors of rich tans and browns, instead of the pale moonlight shade of the Sithari. But there too, their hair set them apart from the other two groups. Sithari were all light-haired and -skinned. Longredal were warm browns to match the forests. But Jakhil; Jakhil had dark to black hair, dark eyes and, even in death, their features were haughty and hateful.

Then there was the matter of what they had on them for

supplies. "Careful with the blades!" he called to the others as soon as he saw the sheen on them. Dry to the touch, but the gloss on them, when he touched a tongue to it, was poison.

From body to body he moved, each one the same. Poisoned blades, darts; some even had powders that, when they struck the ground, would raise a cloud to impede vision and breathing. Those he pocketed for himself.

He just couldn't get over that each one was set up as an assassin. He couldn't quite believe that an entire race would be made up like that. So, he took the assignments for reconnaissance missions to spy on them. Besides, he was one of the only ones trained for stealth.

Men and women alike moved in their camp, each with lethal skills they practiced against each other. There was plenty of talk about how they would take Drikelldorn for their own, as soon as the humans were out of the way. He found the campfire that seemed to house their "nobles," going as near as he dared to hear. What he found bothered him even more. The beautiful woman with the dark hair had a cold smile and a voice to freeze water. She joked and laughed about how she had already done her part by marriage and birthings. She knew the inner workings of the court and had relayed that information to the others. Best of all, according to her, was that she had been inside the king's personal space; that she was the one who had poisoned his last meal.

A cold settled over Aern as he realized he saw a woman that had been presumed dead; his father's second wife. She had tried to kill the two oldest children in the family. She had succeeded in killing one of her own. She had let murderers into the castle several times during her time there. And she had poisoned the King. The bitch had killed his father!

Arrogant in their security, she rose, excusing herself for a moment. As she slipped into the dark, Aern fell in behind her. She took a wandering path into a tree line to see to a "nature call."

Honor among thieves. Honorable death. Anger boiled through him as never before. She deserved no such honor. She had been behind Sterling's wife dying. She had killed their father. She had set this war in motion. He couldn't stop the war, but he could stop her. "Tawnadea." He struggled to say it clearly, calmly, with no trace of the hatred he was feeling.

She paused, her tunic up and her pants down at her knees. Aern saw only advantage. He knocked her to the ground before she could call out for help. Holding her arms down with his knees, he sat across her, keeping her legs still as well. Ripping a piece of fine satin from the hem of her tunic, he stuffed it in her mouth. His left hand quickly slipped between the clasps on his tunic, finding by memory a small vial in his concealed pockets. With the flick of a thumb, the cap was off the bottle. He removed the gag only long enough to pour the contents into her mouth, then stuffed the satin back in. A flick of his wrist and a dagger dropped to right hand. A subtle shift and the blade was driven into her heart.

Breathing hard, not from exertion but from adrenalin and anger, he stood over her, watching the convulsions start. Between the poison he had forced her to drink and what was on his dagger, she would be dead in moments.

Never kill in anger, he heard Morenden's voice in his mind. *It will only come back on you. Remain cool. Calm.*

He closed his eyes for a moment, breathing in the tang of blood and vomit. Opening them again, he watched her eyes roll back in her head, her body arching one last time before falling still. His tone was dispassionate as he spoke to the dead elf. "Never mess with my family."

Aern returned to camp, saying nothing of the dead woman or his part in it. There would be more death yet to come.

Chapter 35

That was a turning point for Aern. For the first time in all his years of training, he had let anger drive his actions. It had been justified, but it hadn't been done properly.

He needed help in scouting the Jakhil now. Two other times, he had found one of them alone. Two other times, he had assassinated… simply because of their race. It was time to show others how to scout, sneak, and observe.

With Brett's help, they picked a small group of the younger fighters. The seasoned ones were set in their ways and preferred to remain direct and in the front lines. The younger people weren't as set or, in some cases, had never even fought before. It was better to find them alternate paths, hopefully ensuring they lived through the war.

Attacks came more consistently, often striking even during the nights. Brett's unit pushed back, attacking directly into their camps. Sterling and Silver were relocated off-center of their own camp, in someone else's tent. The royal pavilion was left standing proudly – but empty – at the direct center. It was a ploy to make the Jakhil think the royals weren't afraid of them, while the king remained safely hidden among the others in the camp.

Aern's handpicked unit became just as hidden. One on one, he trained them by having them spy on others in the camp. It became a game to find the armbands that were given to each member. Their pride in wearing them the first weeks faded and changed to a pride in saying they still had theirs in their tents.

It was an even bigger sense of pride when one or another of them would present someone else's band back to Aern. It meant that they had successfully completed a reconnaissance into another's personal space, avoiding detection not only by one of their own unit, but by anyone else that happened to be in the area.

Only when every person was able to come with three separate bands did Aern feel like they were ready. Their games would become their lives from that moment. He sent them out, each alone, to cover different parts of the Jakhil camps, fully knowing some wouldn't come back.

He had to wonder if Lord Morenden had felt the way he did now, sending each of his students out into the world. He had to trust that he'd given them the best training he could in stealth. He had to trust that he had done all he could to show them how to handle hand to hand combat should it come up.

The hardest of all was trusting himself. He hadn't taught them anything about poisons, but he had passed on what he knew about stealth and spying. He had never tried teaching anyone before and worried that their deaths would be his fault.

All he could do was think what Lord Morenden might have done or thought on sending his young charges out of his care. Set aside emotion, trust his own judgment. *The sun would rise, it always did.* They would return, they always did… even if it was in death.

Chapter 36

Watching Silver with Gavriel made him laugh at times. Sterling had odd moments that humored him and Brett was serious all the time, but Silver…

The most fastidious and practical one in the family would revert to the playful behavior of a child when he and the elf were relaxing. They would wrestle, start mock battles, and posture between themselves over who was right or better. Hands on hips and chests puffed up, they would claim outrage and insult before falling into "fights" where name-calling and hard hits were offset by laughter. They didn't seem to take any of it seriously. Humor always laced these "battles," making them entertaining to anyone else around them.

Then there were other times he would see Silver almost broken in fear; never in front of the troops, of course, but around a "family" fire. Haunted eyes would stare into the flames, his hands locked together until the knuckles were white. It was at those times the elf would simply join Silver. No words; they seemed to understand each other just fine. Gavriel's mere presence would help Silver relax enough that they could talk the situation through. A sad poignancy filled Aern that he didn't have that kind of relationship with anyone.

Then there was Adam, a near-relation to Aern, whom was Silver's bodyguard. He would sit nearby, offering very few words, and no promises of "it's alright." He would only remind Silver that there was no point in borrowing worry from what hadn't happened yet. And it was never "if you fall" with Adam. He would state very quietly that "when we fall, we'll take care of the outcome then."

Aern liked him. He seemed well grounded and, while seeming to be carefree, was very aware of everything going on around him. This served during one of the next battles.

"Adam, to me!" Silver's voice carried quite clearly across the battlefield for his personal guard. Heads rose from nearly every campsite to look towards the young duke.

Aern was no different. "Shit, damn, hell…" The list went on in every language he knew as he gained speed, racing towards the trouble. The twins stood back to back, ringed by Jakhil at least three deep.

Faster than he could have imagined, Adam shot past Aern. The man carried no weapon and wore only the lightest of armor, but showed no caution as he raced into the situation. Aern had to admire the man's style, even in passing, as he raced to that same fight. With only fists and feet, Jakhil were falling around Adam.

Unfortunately, there were more approaching. He could see that Sterling was in bad shape, blood running down his face, although his blade continued to swing true. Silver's own blade moved so fast it was hard to see. There was an almost careless grace to the movements as Silver strovc to keep his back to Sterling. Had he been free to move in the true "dance" he did, it might have been more effective. All the same, the blade sang as it spun about Silver, slicing and cleaving almost effortlessly.

Adam went down, a blade cleaving into his temple. Another blade hit Silver's leg, earning a grunt of pain from the duke, his Elven weapon slowing, as blood poured from the wound. His knees buckled.

"Stay up, Silver," Sterling hollered, sparing a glance back. A mistake. The hilt of a sword landed at his temple, felling him quickly.

Better at sneak attacks, Aern didn't really care at the moment. He had to get to his brothers. They had to live, damn them! He refused to be king, and he refused to lose what he'd gained for family.

The mages had taken out a few of the Jakhil as well, but not enough. They'd never get to the men in time.

A small fox ran underfoot of the backmost soldiers, rolling, changing form to that of a man that quickly gained his feet. "Back up! Mages incoming!" the Hakon cried, changing course himself to clear free of the battle. As the mage ran from the immediate vicinity he shifted again, becoming the shape of the fox, scampering underfoot of those now trying to follow the order.

Aern looked up as a screech similar to Chirrit's broke the sky. Another gryphon, wings pumping furiously, came to the scene, now diving at the circle surrounding the king. Jakhil screamed, cursing in their own language as they tried to scatter. Other animals – large, predatory animals – herded them back to the spot. Mage spells erupted from everywhere. Chaos reigned as Aern stumbled back, away from the situation. He couldn't get in, damn it!

The gryphon swooped low, rising again without missing a wing stroke. Broken and unconscious, Sterling and Silver each hung limp from one of the gryphon's front claws. Before cheers could rise though, arrows rained upward, piercing the gryphon's beautiful wings. It tried; it really tried. Aern watched the creature working to get away from the scene.

His attention moved above the gryphon as he heard a victorious scream from another bird. The screech turned more to pain as arrows were aimed higher.

The gryphon lost its fight, plummeting to the earth with Aern's brothers. The bird that had screeched only grew brighter, a fire seeming to light it. Bright yellow, it had white heat shimmers, a little bit of a blue glow, and a tail of the brightest red crackling like flame behind it. Holy hells! A phoenix! Wings spread wide; it dove at the circling of Jakhil. All creatures and mages started running, yelling for everyone else to clear out.

The Jakhil milled in confusion, unable to effectively get away. A few others weren't far enough away yet when the bird landed amongst them with a deafening explosion. Men flew outwards from the blast, the ground shaking.

Several long moments of silence then reigned. A blackened crater still crackled with some small fires where a few dead Jakhil continued to burn. The fallen fighters couldn't be told from the charred remains of the enemy. All looked the same.

A large raven landed off to one side, shifting into a man

similar in looks to Aern. He knelt, a hand to something. As others moved closer, they saw the fallen Griffon. Mage… Griffon… had tried to save the king. Bloody and broken, all three lay too still. The mage, the king and the duke were either unconscious or dead.

In the ensuing chaos, he tried to get through the throngs of people milling around in stunned confusion. Before he could manage a handful of steps, a hard hit landed at the base of his skull. He damned himself as the world went black; damned his brothers for making him worry about them. He'd forgotten the first rule of warfare; he'd forgotten to watch his own back. He'd let himself be attacked. Stupid. Stupid, stupid, stupid.

* * *

Full night came again, as it had several times. Crickets, frogs and cicadas hummed in the still heaviness. The air was wet. Rain would likely fall, leaving the shit-hole he was in more of a mess.

He had no idea how long he'd been in the hole. By his reckoning, there had been at least five nights and days, but he didn't know how long before that. He knew he was missing days.

Voices above him, jumbled words in a language he still couldn't identify, couldn't make sense of. A jerk on the chains from above, his shoulders screaming in protest as his feet left the ground yet again.

Then he was in the fresh air, trying to ignore the pain in his body, taking deep breaths of air that didn't stink. He could barely register that it was himself that had begun to stink. The only thing he had had even close to a bath was his tormentors throwing water on him.

He stumbled, unable to get his bearings in the bright light, even as they pushed and prodded him. He fell against a large tree stump, groaning as he realized too late that he was *again* at the whipping block.

There was no pleasing them from this point. No matter if he stayed silent, screamed, or answered their questions, the whip would fly, tearing more of his back apart. All they wanted was to break him.

Too bad they had picked the wrong man. He fell back into a semi-conscious state as they continued, falling back on an old litany from his childhood. *He would recover; he always did. The sun would rise; it always did.* And he would pay these bastards back for each pain he now suffered. The Jakhil deserved to be eradicated. He would hunt them once he was out of this. He would…

Darkness claimed him, giving him a merciful respite from the pain.

* * *

Damned Jakhil. They were more insidious and twisted than any assassin he had ever trained with. And vicious. They did things just to do them; there was no sense or reason behind some of their actions.

And lucky me, he thought dryly, *here I am*. The pain was almost unbearable. He could barely muster the strength to stand in the small area he was chained in. He didn't know what the place was; wasn't sure he wanted to know. The smell was horrid; the walls were damp, and the floor hopefully just mud, although he strongly suspected some of it had come from him. He could hear his feet squish below him, and was glad there wasn't enough light to see below himself.

There had to be a way out. He just hadn't found it yet. Giving up wasn't an option; neither was giving them any information about the family. Even though each of those "interrogations" led to more pain, he wasn't going to bend on this. He'd die first. And the longer he stayed here, the more likely that became. He was becoming weaker from the "questioning" sessions, not to mention the inconsistent water and no food. It was taking a toll on him, though he was loath to admit it.

His hands were sticky with blood, as was much of his clothing. How long had he been here? Days and nights seemed twisted together, punctuated by the pain-wracked hours.

Into the stillness, soft voices floated. They weren't the cold tones of the Jakhil, but something kinder, gentler. "See?" One asked. "I knew he was here."

A second voice sounded from the darkness. "What should we do? He needs help." The pronouncement from this voice was one of almost despair.

"Release him, silly."

Two women stepped into his line of sight, one on either side of him. For the first time in weeks, the weight and restrictions of the shackles fell away. Without their restrictive support, Aern's legs gave way and he collapsed to the floor. *Thank the Lights*, he thought, *only mud.*

He was as good as dead and he knew it. He would die today and nothing, save the intervention of the Immortals, could save him now.

"Here, drink this, Aern." The voice was soft and encouraging, and yet somewhere in the back of his mind, it registered how odd it was she knew his name. When he didn't take the drink she offered, she sat on the floor next to him. "Please, Aern, you have to try. Here, let me help you." She slowly put the small vial to his lips, encouraging him. He wanted to refuse, to just die, but his body wouldn't allow it. Too long he had gone without food or water; his body reflexively craved what was now offered. The warmth of the liquid rapidly spiraled down to his stomach, spreading to his arms and legs. It was as if he drank from a well of Life.

"Quickly now," one of them said, "before the guards return…" The two women assisted him, with much pain on his part and struggle on theirs, to his feet. His body wasn't cooperating. Too beaten and broken, he could do little more than let them carry him. He wondered what kind of twisted game now awaited him at the hands of the damned Jakhil. There was also the question of how he was being removed from the hole without being pulled out, and by two slight women, no less.

For the first time in too long, he felt fresh air on his skin without the prodding hands leading him to more pain and, a few moments later, the kiss of warm sunshine on his skin. The brightness burned his eyes. With his energy spent, he now crumpled to the ground. He could hear the women talking to him, asking him questions but, before he could even try to answer them, his world went black, oblivion claiming him from the pain.

As he slowly swam back to consciousness, he was aware of many things. His body hurt in ways he hadn't known it could. His wrists burned where the skin had rubbed raw from the shackles; his shoulders throbbed from the release of being held over his head. Then there were the myriad broken bones and all the torture that had been done to him. Only as he fought past this, did he make out the voices of the women again.

"Give it to him, then. You wanted this for him."

"I didn't want *this* for him. I meant for the girl."

"All the same…" The woman smiled at Aern as he managed to open his eyes. "Hello, cousin."

He couldn't wrap his mind around this. She was dressed as a lady from Whitewind would, in fine silks of the current style, but completely untouched by the mud. Her hair was the same shade as his, and her features called to mind his cousin Brett, but he didn't know this woman; had never seen her before.

"I'm Brett's sister," she offered softly. "But know only that

I am Hope." Looking to the other woman, she demanded it again. "Give it to him, or he dies. He needs that and he needs his pet."

"She's…" He tried a second time, taking a painfully deep breath, "Chirrit's not a pet."

The second woman laughed in delight. "See? He'll be fine. Besides, it's not like he's going to remember this anyways. We're immortal." Her tone turned to one of pouting, as the other one must have given her a look. "Oh, fine. If you're going to be that way about it." Cheer returned again as she leaned over him, a shamrock broach on her drab dress sparkling in the light. "I have a gift for you, Aern."

He wasn't sure he wanted it, but was in no shape to deny her, let alone move. His head was raised and a corded chain laid about his neck with some sort of small amulet weighing heavy on his bruised skin. "For Luck," she said simply. In the next moments, between one blink and the next, both were gone. He might have dreamed the whole thing, but for the weight on his chest. He'd have to consider what had happened… right after he slept. He was so tired…

Chapter 37

He awoke to the scent of something simmering over a nearby fire. For the first time in he didn't know how long, he smelled something other than puss and shit. He shifted slightly, expecting overwhelming pain. It was a pleasant surprise to find that nothing was that bad. He still hurt in a bone-aching way, but that he could deal with.

Chirrit made some happy growls, beaking at his hair. He couldn't quite rouse himself from the pleasant lassitude he was in to stop her. She was loud enough, though, that it brought others to check on him.

Brett and Sterling were suddenly there on either side of him. Sterling held a hand around himself; likely nursing broken ribs. Brett looked tired, but whole, and smiling at Aern. "About time, lazy," Brett said in humor. "Thought you were giving up on us."

It took several tries before he could find his voice. And then it came in a rush as he realized Silver wasn't there. "Where's Silver?" He tried to sit up as hands moved to keep him down. No one said anything about his brother and he couldn't see him in the dim light of evening. "I'm gonna kill the bastards." His voice rose in panic over their protests. "They killed Silver! They'll pay for it; them and those half-breed sisters of ours! I'll get rid of every last one of the Jakhil!"

A blonde mage, with wavy hair hanging all the way down

his back, came from inside a nearby tent. His dark shirt seemed more suited to cooler climes, which would explain the rolled up sleeves. First wiping his hands on a towel he was using as an apron, he lightly touched his palm to Aern's forehead. A warm lassitude washed over Aern, making him fall silent as his limbs became sleep-heavy.

"As your healer," the man said, "I'm telling you, you need to stay calm, rest. Silver is fine." He took a small kettle from the fire, pouring a deliciously scented brew into a cup, holding it to Aern's lips. "Drink. Rest."

Chirrit lowered a wing protectively over him as the willow bark tea drew him down into a healing sleep again.

When he woke, it was to find his hand wrapped around the odd little amulet he had almost forgot receiving. And there was an odd sense of "otherness" with him. Maybe it was from the willow bark, but he couldn't quite shake the sense of someone else being near to him, although he rested alone now. He glanced at the amulet, noting the small sword flanked by wings emblazoned on it. Luck. It was the symbol used to represent luck. *Yeah*, he thought, *lucky bastard that I am…*

* * *

Aern sighed quietly to himself and stood up. He was tired and bone weary, and the events leading up to this point only compounded those facts. He found that neither of the twins had died. Sterling and Silver had both suffered injuries and narrowly escaped death. Had it not been for the Hakon apprentices breaking their reconnaissance orders, and literally swooping down to save them in the form of flying creatures, the Jakhil would have killed them. Mage Mayden Llewellyn had used his powers to ensure that they escaped to safety with Mages Griffin and Raven. Mayden hadn't survived, but by his act of selflessness, he had ensured the survival of the King and the Duke. He had turned into a fiery bird, plummeting down to explode in the center of the Jakhil, scattering them.

For all the circumstances and innuendos surrounding Aern's conception and birth, Mayden had been the first and only person to come forward with the information in truth. Granted, Aern had only been able to see red at first. It had been so stupid! Mayden's father, an Adept on the Hakon Keltori, had been accused of having an affair with Aern's mother. Jealousy had almost torn the court apart, had almost caused a permanent rift between Drikelldorn and the magic-users. But one only had to look at his cousin, Brett, to see the stupidity inherent in that thinking. He looked a great deal like Brett, color-wise. It obviously wasn't totally out of line to have a dark child after ones as fair as Sterling and Silver.

But to think that he had lived in that shadow for so long… when he'd chosen his secret identity, he had purposely chosen "shadow" when the servants at one of his first hits had said he had been a shadow that came to life. Now the name was also a reminder of the rumors about his birth. It was a shadow that had long hung over the family, explaining quite a bit as to why he had never been called home over the years.

His curiosity had been piqued by the information. The man offering it hadn't done it maliciously, or even with the full intent of something in return. Granted, Mayden wanted his sister's fiancé killed, but he understood that Aern didn't just kill indiscriminately.

They had even become fairly good friends during the war. The other mage apprentices in Mayden's group had quickly welcomed him into their company, as well. They were like a group of brothers, quick to jest, and just as quick to defend each other.

Yet they were just as quick to chastise their own. Several times he saw them dress down one of the other apprentices; a few times that person was Bricriu. They would quickly take charge of their own and head off away from the main war camp, informing Bricriu that his methods were stupid and dangerous. Raven and Griffin, two air mages, reminded the young fire mage that his ability was to be watched as a farmer would be when trying to clear out the underbrush where dry pine needles were near. Fire could just as easily take out allies as enemies. Bricriu obviously hated these "discussions," but he would appear to listen. They would all go on as if things were fine again for a time after that.

Their camaraderie was something not often found in Drikelldorn, but, as Aern was often reminded, they were simply older and had been through many trials and training together. Their study in magic gave many of them longer lives, granting longer apprenticeships while they never lost their youthfulness. That gave them a foundation of friendship that Aern almost envied.

He knew he was granted a privilege to be allowed in, and it was one he appreciated. He'd always been the black sheep, an outcast, whether he was a prince or not. This group, like his blood brothers, didn't care about that. They simply judged him for the man he was.

Aern paused before the flap to the royal tent, so noted only by a single turquoise pennant stuck in the ground before it. It was a battered old tent barely fit for travel let alone for a king to reside in, but both the king and the duke had insisted this be the place.

Before entering, he braced himself to see Silver, having heard he had been severely wounded, and to let Sterling know he needed to leave. Inside, he saw Healer Wyborn, the mage who had helped Aern, attending Silver. The damage from that fateful battle still had Silver out of commission. His leg was a mess, broken and infected, yet Silver offered no complaint. The paleness of his face, the press of his lips and the beads of sweat that dotted his brow gave proof to the pain he was in, but not a word of complaint passed his lips. Silver looked up at him as he entered the tent and offered a weak smile before tightly closing his eyes against the ministrations.

"I need to leave," he offered as he found the king. Sterling wasn't in good shape either, but at least he was upright. Bandaged and nursing his ribs, but upright. Both brothers were in disarray, as if they'd recently been in battle again, although Aern knew that Silver couldn't even put weight on his one leg. It seemed odd to see them as anything other than clean and proper.

"Aern, not now," Sterling's voice was weary, beyond exhausted, but still holding the authoritativeness of the King. "We just got you back. There's too many still missing."

A shiver raced down his spine. "What do you mean, missing? Who?"

"Gavriel may have been taken as well. Adam couldn't have survived the attack, but we can't find his body…" his voice faded, his eyes going contemplative.

Chapter 38

There would be no further information about Adam. The body was completely gone, along with anything he had been carrying.

Silver was out of the running for the time being, unable to move other than by horse. Several cousins Aern had never met, but who had obviously been close to Sterling, died in battles.

Most factions of the Jakhil were found and annihilated. There would likely always be a few, including the half-breeds he was related to, but most of them were destroyed.

Aern agreed to stay with the camp at least until they were able to start for home. He knew that any of the mages that had been there the day Mayden died could have taken the man's amulet home, but he felt a responsibility for it. He had gotten to know the man and had left Mayden's father on good terms as well.

In the mean time, he would look into the matter he had spoken to the younger Llewellyn about. Bricriu had survived the war. There had been an expressed interest in Aern taking care of the situation of the man's involvement in their lives and that of Kelly Llewellyn.

The case wasn't sanctioned by the royal family of Drikelldorn, but the very fact that an adept of the Keltori council found it a necessity made it intriguing to Aern. Kelly may have had something to do with it, as well. For her sake, he was interested.

He spent the time watching, noting the bad behavior and

mouthy attitude the man had. He had often been berated by others during the war for his actions, but since the end of the fighting, Bricriu was almost a pariah to the other mages. They ignored him when they could and stood as a group against him when they couldn't.

Very interesting.

It was a few weeks more before the elf would be returned. He was found in one of the small camps of the Jakhil, barely breathing. How he was alive absolutely baffled Aern. Gavriel had been nearly gutted, eviscerated. Almost every bone in his body had been broken. Infection coursed through the man's body and yet, he tenaciously hung on to life. Perhaps, though, if he could have smelled himself, he would have thought twice. The elf looked worse than Aern had after his time with the Jakhil, more resembling a mangled wreck than a man, but the smell was still more suited to something dead and rotting.

Mage Wyborn did what he could for the injured. As the facts settled for people that war was well and truly over now, some fell into old habits, wanting to be waited on. Others were in shock. For some, there was only so much horror that could be endured before the mind took them somewhere they couldn't come back from.

Finally the day came when the mages were going to start for home. It meant the main healer was leaving camp, but it also meant a few like Bricriu were leaving as well. It seemed to Aern that anytime trouble had come up in the tents, sooner or later that man's name wound up attached to it. And not just with fighting, but with those certain women that seemed to end up along with ventures of this sort. Several had ended up dead, with speculation aimed at the fire mage. Yet it was all quietly spoken of, not vented before the general masses. Even here, the mages kept to their own.

Aern wanted to thank Healer Wyborn for his help, finding him with mages Griffon and Raven. All three were amiable and good natured, the latter two trying to ignore Wyborn's ministrations which looked rather painful.

It was only now that Aern noted how their injuries coincided with the two creatures of like name that had saved his brothers. They seemed to know the moment he realized, too. They said nothing of it; just gave a smile and a slight nod of acknowledgement.

They joined the other mages and animals as they prepared for home. Aern watched them go, wondering at how many of the animals were mages themselves.

* * *

The Keltori watched their men return from the war, wondering how many had learned those lessons that no training could have provided, and how many had simply survived. The fact that more came in animal form attested to the improved skill and control of many.

Attaining the family totem could only come with mastery

of their base element. Some never managed.

The eyes of the four council members looked over those sitting horses. Was it inability or injury? Of course, too many of the young ones didn't know the old ways of war. They didn't know the pride the families would have felt to welcome back a newly totemed mage.

Chapter 39

None of them would ever be the same after what they'd survived. Even Aern and Brett, used to battles and wars, had suffered permanently from this. Torture and loss of family did something to a man. It was one thing to face a single opponent, but to never know where the next battle would come from, or what kind of pain was coming, Aern didn't want to even consider what he'd lived through. Daily torture, different instruments; he couldn't let his mind go there without tremors of fear riding through him.

He had been trained for death and torture. He could only imagine how much worse it was for those that had only served in the guard at the castle before this. Poor bastards.

Worse, there was no time to think on it. Camp was broken down and litters were made up for those too ill or broken to ride home. Within only a few weeks more they were on the road, heading for the castle.

Every morning found several needing help up into saddles, too proud to take the litters. Aern carefully noted which these were, including Silver. Those with the fortitude to make do without needing their valets, those he figured deserved some sort of recognition later on. Maybe they'd even do okay in the king's guard. It was something Aern planned to see about helping to rework, to make them better and more professionally trained.

Brett seemed to be thinking the same thing, riding alongside Aern to share comments about this or that person. Aern was pleased to find that Brett thought in terms of equality in the guards. It wasn't just a job for men, as had been proven throughout the war. The captain of the guard was elven, and female; the one who had fought in a nightgown… again, female. There were many that had earned the right to be called Drikelldorn's Finest.

He fell silent for a stretch during one of those conversations. His mind was on what had happened near the end of his torture. The women that had helped free him. The amulet he now wore. What was said.

"Aern?" Brett slipped a foot from his stirrup to lightly kick Aern's leg.

Chirrit reached around to snap, her wings mantling a little into Aern's way; that, more than his cousin's touch, brought him back to the moment. He noticed that he had the amulet out from under his tunic, his fingers running over it.

Brett reached over slowly, one eye on Chirrit, until he could lift the amulet himself. Surprised eyes looked up at Aern. "Where'd you get this?"

A moment of cold went through Aern, his heart dropping into his shoes. "You…recognize it?" His voice was hushed, his lungs tight.

Looking away, Brett rode silently beside Aern for quite a while. About the time Aern thought there would be no answer, Brett, face still towards the distance, said, "It's the symbol of Hope."

Aern looked down at the sword and wings emblem on the

amulet.

Brett glanced over the others riding nearby, then back to Aern. "One of the Immortals."

"I figured, but… isn't this Luck?"

He shook his head. "Hope takes wing despite adversity. That's what it means."

"So…" Aern's mind raced, trying to figure out how to ask what he wanted. Immortals were an abstract concept to him. There had been nothing in all his training to set him up for talking about the Immortals. Hells, he had never thought to have anything to do with them. "How do you know?" he finally got out.

"You mean, what it is? Or who it belongs to?" Brett watched Aern for a few moments, trying to determine what it was his younger cousin wanted. He offered a small smile at the other's confusion. "It's my sister's, okay?"

So there was a sister. No one in Whitewind had spoken of her. The dark-haired woman had spoken truth. Aern struggled to find a polite way to know more.

"She left a long time ago," he offered. "Talia joined to the Element Air and lives in Caer Sidi with the other Immortals." Brett focused on his horse's mane, running fingers through it. His voice was unemotional, flat, with his next words. "She took all Hope our family had with her."

The major part of the day went by in silence between them. Aern wasn't sure how to break it, and Brett seemed to be deep in thought. Brett finally broke the quiet as the sun started to set. "A blade with wings… means that no matter how bad it gets, something good will lift you up. Doubt I'll ever find my redemption, though." He put his heels to his horse and rode off, unwilling to discuss it further.

Rather than discuss it, Aern decided he'd been grounded long enough. He spoke to Sterling about leaving again, needing to return Mayden's magical amulet. Aern wanted to see the family again, to settle something about the girl, and see if the father felt the same way. It suited everyone's purposes that Sterling had given over the man's amulet and wanted Aern to now be the ambassador to return it home.

Chapter 40

Ayden Llewellyn sat quietly at the large dining table, watching both his mistresses and his daughters. The Dowager Queen of Drikelldorn was with them as well. She had been brought to his home, of all places, right before the war.

They all laughed and talked amongst themselves during the evening meal, unaware that anything was wrong. He hadn't told them yet that something had happened to Mayden. He knew – had known now for several weeks – that something terrible had happened to his only son, but he didn't have the Gift of Sight as some mages did. All he had was the ripple effect that had shimmered across his element, Fire to Fire, letting him know there had been a change. This kind of change usually came at a high price.

A servant at his elbow brought him back from his thoughts. "Adept Llewellyn, there's someone to see you in the Fire Parlor. He bears the royal crest of Drikelldorn."

The parlor was a vast expanse filled with the colors of his element: the deep wood of the polished desk was the color of embers just before dying, armchairs of white rested on burgundy rugs, while a few blankets and curtains held the subdued yellow that bordered on orange. Normally this room calmed him, centered him. But the idea of a message from Drikelldorn… He had once been given an accusation, and once been given charge of the Dowager Queen. Neither had made him happy.

He didn't expect this time to be any better as he strode into the room, feeling a rush of rage through his blood like a powerfully seductive drug. "What message do you bring me, messenger?" His voice was low and clipped, almost menacing, as he attempted to stay on top of his emotions; not easy for a Fire mage of any level.

The young man, dressed in smoky black from head to foot, turned to face him. His black hair was so dark it actually reflected the flames from the fireplace, and his eyes were an odd shade of blue. His voice was soft, yet firm, as he spoke. "I'm no page. I'm Aern Bradley of Drikelldorn."

Llewellyn stood in shock. This was the very boy he'd been accused of siring all those years ago. He had even offered to take the child, rather than have King Grey place any kind of stigma on the boy in his home court. Luckily, things had cooled within a year of the boy's birth, but the troubles that could have resulted… And now here stood the cause of all the upset. "What brings you to my keep, Prince Bradley?" His voice was measured in its response.

Momentarily taken aback by the use of his title, he needed to recollect his thoughts. There was something in the man's tone… and then he remembered; they'd told him during the war about the "stigma" around his own birth, and how it connected to this same man.

Clearing his throat, he took the moment by getting the amulet out of a pouch and unwrapping it. "I made a vow to Mayden that if anything happened to him, I would personally notify you." He extended the amulet and the silk cloth it rested in to the mage. "I'm afraid that Mayden, Griffin, and Raven disobeyed orders in the field in an attempt to save the King and the Duke."

The Hakon society held that names were a highly personal thing, capable of invoking magic against the person. They usually only went by their family name. It said much that the young man before Llewellyn had been given permission to call one, let alone three, by their given names. He slowly reached out to take the items that would confirm his son's death.

Aern waited for the mage to take the item before speaking again. "Thanks to them, my brothers are only wounded. Mayden sacrificed his own life to ensure their safety." He didn't wait for further words, didn't wait for a dismissal; just turned on his heel and went to the door. Once the door was pulled open, he paused, looking back at the man who now stood with his head bent in sorrow over the amulet. Aern wasn't used to dealing with emotional situations, but this man had lost his only son. Something should be said. "My brothers also offer their condolences. And I was honored to get to know him myself."

"Prince," Llewellyn called when Aern would have left the room, "I find it ironic that it's you that brings me news of my son's demise."

"I know," Aern answered quietly.

Llewellyn looked at the young man standing before him. There was a hardness to him that the father had never had and an acceptance of the fact that life wasn't always easy. "Stay the night,

Prince. We'll talk."

They met in the parlor again after a fairly quiet meal. It seemed all were on their best behavior for the visitor. Kelly glanced at him several times, a questioning look burning from her eyes, though she held her tongue in her father's presence.

Soon enough the women were sent back to their wing of the keep and Aern was again closeted with Llewellyn in the study. A small water clock ticked loudly in their silence until the mage finally spoke. "He was my only son." It wasn't as saddened as Aern would have expected. "Plenty of daughters, but that was my only son."

"About your daughters…" Aern offered hesitantly. "Your son spoke of his concern about Bricriu MacFurgal."

The mage stared into the fireplace for so long, Aern wondered if he hadn't said the wrong thing. "I can't go against the Keltori. Their word is the law," the mage calmly explained to Aern. "For all that I'm a member, I *do* see their reasoning. MacFurgal is the strongest line, next to mine. And with no son now…" Llewellyn sighed. "I must do what I can to produce more of the Fire line. But that doesn't mean I'm happy about this."

Sitting forward a little, Aern tried to read the body language of the man. These men were an enigma. His father had trusted them enough to send the princesses to them, but no one had really learned much of them. They had stayed fairly distant over the years, excluding short visits to Drikelldorn, and their part in the war.

He had to give the mages that much. If not for their aid, Sterling and Silver would be long dead at this point, placing Aern himself on the throne; something he definitely did *not* want. But this meeting wasn't about him. The adept seemed to be trying to say something.

"Mage Llewellyn," Aern finally stated into the silence that had opened between them.

"Ayden," he interrupted, "in private." As an adept, he couldn't have his first name used in public, but if his son had trusted this man enough, and considering the strange history that connected them, he could at least give him the privilege behind closed doors.

Aern's brows momentarily shot up at the honor. Being given use of a mage's given name was a rare gift. At least, that's what he'd been told by other young mages around the fires during the war. "Ayden, then." He offered a small smile in thanks. "I saw what the man was capable of during the war. There is no compassion I could see in him." He watched Ayden's expression carefully as he spoke the next. He didn't often speak of what he did to others, even in a hedged conversation. "Your son asked me to assist in the matter of Apprentice MacFurgal. In…getting rid of him."

The older mage looked around in shock, as if searching the shadows for something. "Shh!" he finally whispered, leaning quite close to Aern. "We can't do something like that… legally." He gave Aern a pointed look, as if asking, pleading that he do just that.

With a slow nod, Aern stood. "I understand, sir. I'll look into the options then." The situation wasn't as straightforward as most Aern had handled in the past. The longer he waited on this, the more complicated it became. There were whole layers to this society he was still unfamiliar with.

Thoughts of it were on his mind all night and stayed with him as he rode out the next day. He kept the thought of it as a potential hit along the way while he shopped for some of the odd items he used for poisons: datura, wolfsbane, rowan, and so many others hard to find in southern lands.

Thankful as ever that Chirrit flew the distance in a few days that would have taken a month of riding, he soon found himself back at the travelling war camp. Music played in the once silent rows of tents. He could see people relaxed and enjoying themselves as Chirrit flew lower, closer to a landing. Obviously none had been too far from camp since the fighting had ended. For all the happiness he saw, his nose told another story. The injured may be out of sight, but there were far too many to cover the smell. Death and illness had too distinct of a scent.

He frowned as he dismounted. Chirrit took the skies as soon after as she could, not wanting to be near the stench herself. They had to get packed and get moving. They were lucky wild animals hadn't yet started creeping into camp with the smell of injuries so strong on the winds.

Chapter 41

The Hakon boys returned as weary men. They had left excited for adventure, thrilled to be ranked as full members of their society, despite only being apprentices and journeymen. The Keltori looked at these young men now, seeing the playful childhoods now passed. Each of those returning had been sobered by events. They had not only used their magic, but had used it against others. They knew the true power behind what they were now capable of. For that, the Phelan felt they should be given their titles as mages.

"No!" Adept Shanahan fumed. "Maybe it was the old way to do that, but we aren't like that anymore! We don't war against each other."

"It will give them ideas that things can go back to the way it was," Llewellyn agreed. "That they could fight to be the strongest or the best of our society."

Shanahan nodded vehemently. "You've worked too hard, Phelan. We don't want to go back to untrained farmer's sons thinking they can overthrow trained magic users. Society will be nothing but bedlam again!"

Phelan sighed. "All the same, they passed their 'trial' by surviving. They aren't children anymore."

Quiet until now, Goldwin looked to the others. "I agree with Phelan. They've earned their ranks," the Air adept said. "Test them on the field. If they can control their element, give them the rank."

"Out of the question!" Llewellyn pounded a fist on the table. "You all know the rules we set: they need to control two elements to gain Mage status."

The standoff stood before the four council members. Two for; two against. Young Wyborn, who had acted as Healer during the war, knocked, entering with files. "I have the lists of injured and dead for you."

A calm settled over the angry men, one they couldn't quite define. Each looked to the other, trying to determine what was going on. The change had only happened once the young Journeyman mage had come into the room.

"Wyborn?" the Phelan finally asked. "Are you influencing our moods?" There was no hostility; simply an odd curiosity.

He gave an almost embarrassed smile. "Yes, Adept. It goes along with my healing abilities." He gave eye contact to each for the barest of moments. "I'm not one of the four elements, Adepts. I'm something else. It seemed everyone was getting too angry to think clearly here today."

For the first time, the Phelan questioned removing Remington so many years ago. Maybe the MacFurgals had been influenced. Maybe it was Remington they should have looked at. Maybe the man had been able to influence thoughts or emotions as Wyborn seemed capable of. And they had turned a very young Bricriu over into that man's care. It would explain quite a bit as to the extreme difference between Bricriu and Doran. Doran had already been settled into training with another mage. Bricriu… no one had wanted the untested child of a traitor; none but Remington.

If Remington could do what this young healer did… "Maybe they do each have two mastered." The other three looked to the Earth adept in surprise as he continued. "If Wyborn here can control emotions, maybe we've got some other element we haven't recognized." He got to his feet, indicating an end to the meeting and any discussion. "We will test them for their element alone. If they pass, they pass."

Then it was just organizing the tests. Apprentices were promoted at least one rank. Journeymen were made full mages. A few still didn't have the control or skill to handle most of the spells and were left as they were. But Bricriu, as they expected, had at least rudimentary control and easily passed the first round of tests. The second round was just as easy for the boy and the adepts began to worry.

There were only four rounds of tests, one for each element, to see how well the boys could work with each one. They were also tested on how well they could mix and merge the elements to get better results. This Bricriu was found to be lacking in somewhat. Unfortunately, he had strong control over Fire and had small, rudimentary skill with the other three.

With uneasiness from all members of the Keltori, Bricriu was granted his mage status; with great uneasiness and wariness, especially by Llewellyn. He stood to deal with the greatest issues that might arise with the boy in the future. Not to mention he had to house the new mage, as the Fire mentor, until MacFurgal could have his own home built. It also meant that one of his daughters would be given to him as a wife. Llewellyn was not happy.

Chapter 42

In the few weeks it took to break camp, Aern noticed a bond that had started to form with his brothers. It had probably started back in Whitewind, in the forging of the war. But whatever it was, there was a camaraderie between the boys that hadn't been there before. An ease to their traveling showed in the calm hours that passed between them. Hushed words were exchanged intermittently, quiet laughter as they found things to humor each other.

Aern found that he enjoyed it. He got along with his cousin Brett; that had almost been a given with their odd careers. But then there were the twins he had been compared against all his young life. On principle, before really getting to know them, he hadn't liked either.

But having seen what they had come through, how they had borne their injuries, and how they had rallied, he had to give them credit. That in mind, he leaned forward to tap Chirrit's beak, pointing towards Silver.

She chirred acknowledgement and moved up beside Silver's horse. The horse danced aside nervously, tossing its head, although Silver easily regained control in mere seconds, even with his badly wounded leg. He gave Aern a small, tight smile of acknowledgement of recognition, but said nothing.

Aern knew the look. Poor Silver was quite a trooper to say nothing about his injury, despite the pain he had to be in yet. So many others bitched about the lighter wounds that were healing well; the left thigh of Silver's white pants were stained deep red most nights when they dismounted. And that despite the wrappings and bandages.

Even now, Aern could see the tell-tale signs starting to spread. Having too much respect for him now, Aern said nothing. They travelled on in silence as Silver got control over the pain he had to be feeling.

"I miss Becky," Silver offered some time later. It might have been just to break the silence between them, or it could have been to distract himself from his pain.

There was only one person Aern could think that would be: Rebecca. "Your wife, right?"

Silver nodded, and they again fell into a companionable silence. Aern wasn't sure what Silver wanted to address with it, so kept his peace. Every so often, Silver would look to the litter that carried his elf friend. "I don't know if he'll make it."

Leaning back, Aern looked around at the extremely pale man, damp with fevered sweat. It was a wonder the elf was still alive, really. "Doubt it," he agreed. "He's pretty bad." He almost regretted saying it at the pitifully horrified look Silver gave him. Obviously Silver counted the man closer than family. He hadn't even looked that crushed the night their father had died.

The look in his eyes was one of a man looking for something to help hang on to some sort of hope. "Becky," he finally said, giving Aern a slight nod. The one word was almost a question, pleading for some sort of reassurance.

"Hey," Aern offered with a smile, trying to make up something quickly. "You two'll have years ahead of you. Lots of kids." He nodded as if reinforcing the last. He had no idea if it was even something Silver wanted.

It gained him a worried smile. Joking around wasn't his strong point, but he had seen that it worked when the elf had done it for Silver. He wracked his mind, trying to find something that might be funny. "You know," he finally offered, trying for a light tone (even though it didn't quite come out as jovial sounding as he'd have liked), "I'm going to need a reason to come back for visits. You having kids would let me spoil them…" he grinned, reaching over to nudge Silver's arm, "and annoy you in the process."

Silver blew out a hearty laugh, something unwinding in him with the relief. Aern would have to work on finding other humor that would keep this brother relaxed. That laugh was a good start. Things would be okay. Maybe not right away, but they would be okay. The sun would rise; it always did.

Chapter 43

People lined the road towards the castle. Even more cheered from the rebuilt ramparts. It seemed that everyone for miles around had heard the nobles were returning. Suddenly Sterling's order to have stopped some way back to freshen up didn't seem so stupid. They were all dressed in clean, if now somewhat worn, clothing.

He watched the spectators as they scanned the regiments behind the nobles. So many months had been taken from everyone, and so many lives had been lost as well. There were so many looking with worry and fear that they wouldn't find their loved ones returning. It was a little saddening to know there was no one looking for him.

Silver, on the other hand… he sat a little straighter as the castle came into view. Thirteen long months, eleven since the start of the war. It had been ages since that night their father had died; an eternity since Sterling had declared war; forever since his capture by Jakhil.

Aern had found out that Silver had only been married four months when the assassin struck. They had ridden out for battle on the eve of Silver's six month anniversary. Now they returned three months after Silver's first anniversary. There were a lot of important dates that had been stolen from Silver in the last year. No wonder his brother now perked up with the thought of seeing his wife again.

Silver threw his leg over and carefully slid to the ground. He was favoring his left leg yet, a tell-tale bloodstain already spreading. It felt as if they had all been in the saddle forever.

Sterling came up to his twin with a smile, one arm wrapped around his still-mending broken ribs, and clapped his twin on the shoulder. "Let's rejoin the living."

The others in their party were either dismounting to join the two men, or being carried in on litters before they fell in behind their king and followed him past bowing servants, into the throne room.

The reigning princess, Duchess Rebecca Kalinda Bradley, rose gracefully from the throne in her white dress, the turquoise trim catching the light as she dropped a curtsy before Sterling. "Your safe return is a welcome sight, your majesty." She stepped aside, motioning toward his seat. "Your throne awaits you."

As Sterling moved past her, she lifted her skirts in one hand, the other holding the coronet to her red curls, and ran to throw herself into Silver's arms. There was a grunt of pain as his arms came around her and they fell to the floor. As she rolled to his side, she noticed the dark red stain spreading across his white pants. His eyes sparkled at her even as he grimaced against the pain.

"Your husband has been grievously injured, milady," Sterling said as he carefully lowered himself into his rightful seat. "Perhaps you should make ready his quarters."

"I'll not find my bed until you do, brother." He was on his

feet again, but the entire pant leg had turned crimson. He gave his wife a wistful look before turning away from her. "We've much to do before we rest this night."

Chapter 44

The next few weeks went by quickly. The chaotic excitement of that first night was echoed over the first days, as people adjusted to the king being back, and further adjusted to it being their "new" king. Aern wasn't sure what the populace had been thinking most of the past year while King Sterling fought to protect them. Maybe they were just used to Rebecca, but now they had a tendency to first look at the throne, seem to not see him right away, then finally acknowledge who sat there.

Sterling seemed to take it in stride though, his young son often sitting on either his lap or playing at his feet. Aern vaguely remembered being allowed that same privilege when he had been small, too. He enjoyed seeing Sterling fill the role of father, and make it look easy right along with his duties to everyone else.

Even Silver had been given fatherhood. It had been a bitter pill for Aern to find that Silver, despite having been barely married before war, had come home to a new baby. Jealousy certainly was a factor, knowing he could never have one of his own, but there was something else, as well. Seeing Silver with the little girl was like seeing a room light up with sunshine.

Seeing that, and then adding Rebecca to the image, was amazing. Silver and his wife were one of those unions that gave Aern hope for the idea of relationships. They were an evenly matched pairing, complementing each other in both work and play. They took turns with the baby, rarely leaving her with the nursemaid.

Silver had found a woman that could easily hold her own; by the Lights, the woman had held the kingdom while they were away! And through it all, she carried a graceful smile and warm heart. Aern could see why Silver would have been taken with her.

Which brought him to thoughts of a woman in the north. Silver was taken with a strong red-head… and Aern found himself wondering about a fire-blazened beauty in Hakon. For her sake and her brother's, there was still a matter to settle with a Fire mage that had been disliked by his peers. Aern would deal with the trouble in the north in the near future. When the time was right, he'd again let Chirrit be the wings of an assassin, taking him where duty called. But family had to come first for him this time. He wanted to see them through the rebuilding and reforging of their rulership. He finally understood the importance of what he had in his brothers.

What he still didn't understand was the close bond Silver had with his elf friend. Months back home, and Silver still spent hours at the side of Gavriel. The man was recovering, but it was very slow going. Aern himself had checked in on Gavriel a few times; it wasn't good. The only thing keeping him going was sheer stubbornness to get well. The injuries had been so severe, Aern was surprised the elf had even made it this far.

While Aern had been tortured with broken bones, some burns, and lack of food, Gavriel had simply been beaten, then gutted. From just below the ribs, all the way down, the man had been cut open and eviscerated. Tenacity had gotten the man this far; his friendship with and for Silver seemed to be doing the rest.

That tenacity kept showing up elsewhere as well. There were those who had passed their trial of fire, and come through as hardened steel; men and women that had ridden their fear and come out on top, fists to the sky with exultant cries. These were the ones who realized that death was not the worst thing to face. They had dealt with pain, injury and loss of friends and family, yet they had come out. They still walked, and they held that badge with pride.

They weren't the only ones though. As he had noted on the long ride home, many others were not adapting to life after war. They were alive, but they had seen too much, looked too closely into the eyes of death. They were breathing, but with breath held for the next horrible thing to happen. They lived. They lived, but they saw nothing of what was in front of them; only what they had lived through.

Chapter 45

Since he could travel and return the fastest, Aern had been sent to check on the princesses, his half-sisters. It had only been six months since the end of the war. No one felt it to be truly safe yet for the princesses to return home, but King Sterling had asked Aern to check on them.

His first stop had found one of them deceased. She had been placed with a fire mage and his apprentices. Literally "playing with fire," she had accidentally been killed. The mage was apologetic and had already put together a package in recompense for his failure in protecting her.

Next was a stop at the Wyborn's to see Melantha. He didn't remember most of his sisters very well, but it seemed that he had heard almost nothing bad about this one. She was supposedly an even-tempered, kind woman, always sensible.

He saw a woman excited to see a long lost brother. She stood on one of the lower stair steps in the hall so she could give him a hug on more equal footing. Hugging: not his thing, but unique circumstances demanded unique handling.

Not for the first time, he wondered what it would have been like to have grown up in his parents' court. They all seemed overly affectionate and touchy-feely. Unlike himself, who had been taught to maintain a certain distance from others unless you were intending a killing blow of some kind.

He shook off those thoughts and smiled to her. He needed

information to return to his brother. "Tell me of your stay."

"Boring." She rolled her eyes. "I've done more stitching while the men played at war..."

At that moment, Apprentice Wyborn – not the healer, but his brother – came through the front door. He greeted Aern amiably, exchanging pleasantries, although neither touched the other. This was one of those courtesy things Aern had learned during the war: mages didn't like touching others unnecessarily. It was one of the few things he had in common with them, but for very different reasons. He didn't want others that close to him, period. They didn't want to pick up residue magic from another, nor offer their own persons to the other for counter-magic to be used against them.

Somewhere during their short conversation, Wyborn glanced at Melantha; so briefly most would never have noticed. Aern did. Unfortunately, he stood between them. That brief look charged the room. Aern felt like an intruder, like he should leave the room. Nothing in their tone or body posture changed; there was just an added "something" to the room.

Wyborn excused himself to speak with his father and Aern turned to Melantha. "If you love him..."

"Oh, Aern," she interrupted, "he's in training. Everyone knows they can't marry until they're a full mage."

That was the stupidest thing he'd ever heard! By the Lights, it wasn't as if the girl didn't have *some* pull! She just wasn't using her head. "Are you or are you not related to the king? Pull rank and get him if you love him."

"It's not my choice, Aern. We're good friends; nothing more."

He stared at her for long moments. "You do realize I'm not stupid? I saw it, Melantha. And either way, you get back to Drikelldorn, and Sterling will see to it that you marry *someone*. He wants the princesses protected in their own homes."

She sighed somewhat wistfully. "Home seems so far away. I miss Drikelldorn, I miss my twin, and I miss my room back at Whitewind."

Inwardly, Aern flinched at her words. He had forgotten that Melantha's twin had died the same night their father had. And he didn't know what to do with her. His training hadn't included consoling women. "Well," he finally said slowly, "I'll let Sterling know. I'm sure he'll come up with something." He handed her a small packets with funds, and quickly took his leave.

He was being a coward, but he didn't care. Give him a good situation rife with danger, and he could handle it. Torture; he understood that. Death, destruction; but women… he sighed, wondering how he got roped into these stupid assignments.

And he still had one more. He had to see to the sprite, Crystal, before going home. He had been to the homes where his remaining sisters had been sequestered, managing polite, short conversations to assure their health before giving them their "allowance" and moving on. They were the Jakhil half-breeds. As was Melantha. At least Crystal was something of more innocence.

Chapter 46

The visit with Crystal had been bizarre. She spoke little, her voice reminding him of a small, happy brook, although she didn't look overly happy. The girl herself was strange, pale, almost ethereal and, Lights forbid! She actually had a tinge of green to her pale hair and skin. This sister intrigued him because of her odd heritage. He really wanted to know what his father had been thinking in joining with sprites and fae and elves.

But he put that aside as he landed at Llewellyn's to visit with his mother next. She was still a pretty woman herself, even with the strain of the past years. As he approached, he noticed the small trace of silver starting to show in her hair. However, he said nothing as he formally dropped to one knee before her.

He was invited to walk the gardens with her, which suited him much better than sitting and having tea. She spoke of trivialities, things that didn't concern him; things that made him work at being focused on her conversation. She asked after his brothers, and how things fared back home, and then she got to asking about her keep. Aurora. It was the place Aern had been given to watch over in her absence.

More than anything, he thought perhaps Sterling had finally come to understand how much privacy meant to Aern. But he enjoyed watching over the estate. He enjoyed the tasks of daily life, the accounting, the management.

His mother watched him become more and more animated as he spoke about the small keep and the people and duties there.

She smiled, yet said nothing of it, merely letting him speak.

At long last, he fell silent, only then realizing how much he had talked. And it had felt good, having something that wasn't a secret, something that mattered to more than just a select few, to discuss.

"It seems in good hands then," his mother finally said quietly, giving him a small smile. "Thank you."

He knew the place was important to her. His brothers had all informed him of happy times there while they had been growing up. Both of his parents had used it as a "vacation" home to get away from the court at times. In truth, Aern was surprised Sterling hadn't kept it for that reason himself.

Giving his mother a slight bow, more a nodding of his head and shoulders, he pressed a pouch of coins into her hand, giving her the allotment until he could come north again. Then without another word, he went out to the courtyard alone.

Aern could have left at that point. He was standing beside Chirrit, ready to mount, when he decided to send her airborne again. It was crazy to consider, but he wanted to see Kelly.

Keeping to the wall, he crept around to the side with the women's quarters, then shimmied up the trellis, using the crenellations for support. Peeking in the window, he watched several of her sisters moving around the solar. Finally spotting her, he offered a quiet "psst!" when she passed near the window.

Her whole face lit up on seeing him. She pretended to straighten the curtains as she whispered out to him, "What are you doing up here?"

"Oh, you know…" he smiled. "Just hanging around."

Kelly rolled her eyes, having to cover her mouth with a hand to keep from laughing. "That was terrible!" she whispered.

"So come keep me from doing it again. Meet me in the garden."

"Fine!" She shooed him away from the window. "Go! Before you get caught up here!"

He winked, slipping from view and heading for the gardens.

Chapter 47

He went to the deepest part of the gardens where he knew a stone chess board sat. Several times he had been here this way, always meeting her for a match at the board. Unlike poker with his brothers, which could be analytical when they weren't goofing around, chess was a game of intrigue, strategy… things he excelled at. And to have an opponent like Kelly was a thrill for him. He couldn't quite get over the fact that she was such a quick thinker, often outsmarting his best moves at the table.

The rustling of her gown gave her away as she ran the last few turns to the center of the hedge maze. Her cheeks were flushed, laughter bubbling up as she extended her hands to him, palms down. "You could have been seen back there!"

Rising, he took her hands as expected, bowing over them. There was only mischief in his eyes and smile as he rose again. "But I wasn't, was I?"

She playfully slapped his shoulder, bouncing around him in a swish of skirts to take her place on the white side of the board. He smiled, noting that it had become "her" side, somehow. She had told him from the first game that his pieces should match his clothing… although she didn't match her side. She never wore white; always colors of fire.

With a practiced swivel of her hips, she sat in the wrought iron chair, her skirts billowing gracefully to one side. Aern was intrigued at the way she did it. Unlike most of the women he knew, who made it look like something to draw attention to their bodies, Kelly did it gently, carefully, as if any other movement would damage the dress itself. Everything about her was full of contained energy… like a small banked fire; pretty to look at, but there was so much more going on below the surface.

"Well, come on!" Her pretty smile turned to him as she waved her hand at "his" chair, wanting him to join her. "Let me beat you!"

Laughing, he sat, pulling the drawer out with the pieces and spilling them across the board. "You really think so?" He teased.

"What think?" she teased back. "I know I'm better than you!"

Both in a good mood, they set their pieces up for play, settling into a deep quiet as they contemplated their moves. Aern enjoyed these moments. There was no vying for position, no court games, no intrigue; just him and Kelly; just two people enjoying a pleasurable game.

They had shared moments about their lives over this board, information they'd never given to anyone else. She knew what he did, and why. He knew her dreams for a better life. And the more they visited, the more he wanted a good reason to help her find them.

Not marriage. That wasn't his thought. But, Bricriu. It all came back to that. He had seen in the war what kind of man Bricriu was. At the same time, he wasn't acting on anyone's orders now. Mayden had died. That meant the order had died with him.

Aern couldn't go in on a hit without just cause; especially if it was because of a personal issue.

"Oh, don't look so serious!" Kelly joked with a smile, her freckled nose wrinkling in merriment. "It's only a game! Besides," mischief lit her eyes, "You won't be alive much longer!"

His head jerked in surprise, even though he knew she didn't mean it the way it sounded. He tried to keep his tone light as he answered. "I'm alive because I'm smart enough to watch my opponents. Like this one." He moved his rook in line with her knight, planning to take it on his next move.

"But Aern, we can't *all* be opponents *all* the time." She watched his features warring with wanting to believe and total distrust of the idea, all the while not looking up from the chess board. "Look, I'm a fire child; my father is a fire mage. That doesn't mean I fight water. My father could tell you that sometimes water will temper fire. Maybe a best friend or…a woman…would temper your soul; not leave it so hardened."

He did look up at that, smiling warmly. "I'd not be as hardened as you think, Kel. I just protect my heart, or, as you said, my soul. I get attached to something and it could be used against me. I don't want to have a job jeopardized because I have a personal call to make on it; say, a wife or a child of mine instead of doing what I've been ordered to." He didn't even want to think about the stupidity he had shown in the war when he'd looked to his brothers rather than his own back.

"Sometimes," she moved her queen in front of the knight

that was threatened, "having another around helps protect you. Like this."

His rook slid forward, taking her queen. "Like this? The job – that castle – should be allowed to take my queen? To save my life?" He shook his head, eyes asking her to understand. "I wouldn't ask that of someone. I chose this life. I chose to forgo family. I highly doubt there's a woman willing to marry, knowing she may be asked to give her life for me." He couldn't quite hide the sorrow in his tone as he voiced a pain from so deep inside himself.

"I think you'd be surprised, Aern Bradley. I'm sure there are plenty of women that would love you as a husband, and…" she waved a pawn at him, "as a father."

He laughed lightly. "Play, Kel."

"Like so!" She said with a flourish, setting a pawn he hadn't noticed on the far side of the board, switching it back for her queen. "Through the child…the queen lives again!" She clapped her hands in delight.

A chill shook its way down Aern's spine as he stared at her. His voice dropped to a whisper. "What woman in her right mind would die for a man? Leave a child behind?"

She gave him a long, measured look before answering. "One in love. Without it," Kelly got to her feet, reaching out to purposely knock both kings over, "no one wins." She winked, blew him a kiss, and bounced away, leaving him in the maze, both the hedge maze and the muddled thoughts of his mind.

At least he would have the flight home to consider things.

Chapter 48

Sometime between Aern's flights north, and his missions for the throne, Sterling had met and fallen in love with a woman. So again, Aern found himself attending a wedding for Sterling. This time, though, he hadn't been ordered home. He wanted to see if this time for Sterling there would be the all-important blessing from the Immortals.

He joined the others in the gardens at Whitewind, sitting beside Silver and his wife, Rebecca. Their daughter had been given into Aern's keeping as they found their seats, the toddler resting peaceably in his arms. A pang of jealousy struck him that it would never be his own to hold. But he reminded himself that what he did was worth it; for the little ones like this tiny niece.

It surprised Aern that Serena, the woman Sterling was marrying, chose as her escort not a father or uncle, but little Raine, Sterling's son. Very proudly he walked at her side, holding her hand, looking around the room. He waved at some of his uncles as he saw them, including Aern.

Aern had to smile. He loved children, especially these nieces and nephews he had been getting to know.

The service was simple, presided over by their brother Keno. Keno had lost his wife – Melantha's twin – and some of his children to the fire before the war. But it wasn't for that reason he acted as officiant. He had some sort of connection to Life – to the immortal energies. He was acting on behalf of the Immortals.

The words were simple, compared to the last wedding. No elaborate speeches. "A bond like this," Keno said, "is not taken lightly. Your life is given into the safe-keeping of the other. Your heart to their own breast." He took a silken braid, twisted from the family colors of silver and turquoise, lightly wrapping it about their joined hands. "Love to Life, Life to Love." With his hands cupped beneath their joined ones, he looked up.

Slowly, everyone else tipped their own faces up. Silver and Rebecca shared a small smile, as did Kyle and his wife. On looking up, the afternoon sky had gone twilight dark. Shimmering lights danced and arced across the sky in a multitude of colors. This then was the Lights, the god they all believed in.

Several people made an "L" with their hand, pressing it to their foreheads in obeisance to the Lights above. A few others fell to their knees in humble gratitude. Sterling and Serena sealed their joining with a kiss, and the Lights slowly faded away, the sky returning to the regular late afternoon brightness. They had been given the blessing needed for the ruler's marriage.

Silver left to congratulate his twin while Aern got to his feet with the tiny girl in his arms. He shouldn't even show as much emotion that he liked the baby, but the truth was plain: he loved children, especially such a small innocent laying so trusting in his embrace. He hated to give her back over to Rebecca, even as his sister-in-law reached to take the child.

It was a heavy sigh on his lips as he passed the baby over.

"You should have one of your own," Rebecca offered,

settling her daughter in her arms. "You're good with them."

A sad smile touched him. "I can't. Even if I could, what kind of life could I give them?" He shook his head. "No, I'm meant to be alone. It works better that way."

"For who?" Becky gave him a warm smile. "Maybe you just need to look at things differently. Look at Silver and I. I'd never have dreamed of a match that would make me happy to get up, happy to move through my day, and happy to have that person join me in the evening. Sil's my everything, Aern. I love him more than life." She gently reached to touch his arm. "And having that, nothing else matters. I'd gladly walk any danger to keep him with me."

Long moments passed as Aern simply stared at her, trying to comprehend her reasoning. "Even death?" He finally asked.

"Even death," she stated firmly. "And he knows that he has my support at his back, like I have his. It makes everything more bearable." She watched the confusion flitting across Aern's features, watched him try to make sense of how simple love really could be. "You need to let your guard down a little, Aern. Enjoy being with someone first. When it comes to a point where you want their opinion, their smile, over anything else in the world…" she smiled, looking down at the sleeping baby.

Aern reached over and brushed his fingers over the baby's downy hair. "I'll think about it." And he would. It wouldn't change anything. He didn't want the guilt that could come if he were to be the cause of someone he cared for being killed. But then, he didn't want to be alone either. Not after seeing how happy Silver was. Or Kyle. Or any of the many others here at Whitewind that seemed so content with married life.

Chapter 49

The wedding celebrations were still in full swing, the castle full of guests. Several had been set as guards, even if they were dressed in finery, so the crowd would be monitored. Brett and Aern both needed to get away from the stuffy crowds.

"I have no idea how my brothers can stand living here with people watching their every move." He shrugged, as if shaking off a terrible feeling. "It makes my skin crawl." Irritation was evident in both his voice and pose. They left the confines of the Great Hall, heading for the courtyard.

"I've been thinking about the future." The tone in Brett's voice gave credence to the serious look on his face.

Aern glanced at him as they went out the back entrance, heading for the training salle on the far side of the bailey. When Brett said nothing else, Aern gave him a simple nod to continue.

"The men around here aren't exactly trained the best to defend the king. They need better training, and Sterling should have his own private guard, one responsible for the safety of him and his immediate family. Don't you agree?"

Aern was quiet as they crossed the outdoor training field, weighing the meaning of Brett's words before speaking. Brett had been trained as a warrior; had lived as a mercenary. He liked living by his own rules and having the power to change the things he didn't like. Here he was, thinking of changing his life from one free of anything but the next job, to one of duty, obligation, and honor. "You…wish to be a guard?" Aern couldn't hide the incredulous tone in his voice, nor did he try.

Not only was Brett not being realistic about what would come with a duty as a guard, but he wasn't looking at the other ramifications that would go with life here at the castle. In good conscience, Aern needed to remind him of that. "Come on, Brett. Like it or not, you're a damn duke and if you stay here you'll be expected to act as one. Kiss this kind of behavior goodbye. No more training sessions. You'll be expected to dress up and act like a court dandy." Brett was known for going around only half-dressed, looking like something from the fluff-novels he heard some of the girls liked. This kind of life change would bring a definite change to his cousin's wardrobe as well. He couldn't help nudging Brett in teasing. "Wouldn't your dad just love that?"

"Oh, what? And you aren't supposed to be a proper prince?" He laughed. "No. I have no intention of resuming my role as duke…or whatever the hell it is that I actually am. I need to be kept busy and I thought as long as I was here, I could at least help out."

Aern paused, really looking at his cousin. There was something else in his voice. Something he couldn't quite put his finger on. Even now, looking at him, there was something on his mind. His eyes had gone somewhat distant, one side of his mouth tipped up in a slight smile. Huh. Aern smiled to himself, moving on again. He'd almost bet there was a woman on Brett's mind.

"Thought I'd at least do something constructive with my

time." There was a pause before he looked to Aern. "Maybe you'd want to help out."

"Help do what? Run around pretending to be something I'm not? Look, people like you and me – we kill. We don't protect. Huge difference, you know: like as in the difference between me and Sterling. The same thing but very different."

Brett stopped and looked at his younger cousin. After all, Aern was right. They were trained to ferret out and kill the enemy, not stand and defend. The war had seen this talent exploited in both men. The reality was that the two of them had talents that others had never considered. They were both vital players in this court, but rarely active in it. This was a way they could finally belong in a place where they sorely stood out. And really, how hard could it be?

They'd managed to survive the war when so many others hadn't. Men that had been trained to defend had died; Brett's own brothers had died. "At least consider what I'm saying. Being we stay here at the moment, we might as well help the greener recruits."

There was a hesitation as Aern looked off into the distance at the very recruits Brett was speaking about. They were young; eager and loyal, but still needing the training. Training Aern knew he and Brett were capable of giving them. He'd have to think about it.

Chapter 50

The matter had been decided some time ago, but Llewellyn should have known to expect trouble from this child. It was time for her to start growing up and forgetting her fanciful ideas. "Kelly, I understand." Ayden sighed, sinking further back into his seat. He was tired and felt old before his time. So many children, so little time. He cursed the fact that he was one of the few fire masters; cursed the fact that he had been given little choice in his life. "Had your brother survived the war, things might have been different, but the way it is…"

"But why me? Jalisa's older, so is Kada." She hated sounding whiny, but she would rather swallow hot coals over having to marry Bricriu. This wasn't what she had meant to do the night she had called on the Elements.

Ayden had heard enough. He abruptly rose, slamming his hands down on the desk. Fire flared over his fingertips, the ends of his hair sparking licks of flame. "No more, young lady!"

Rarely did he raise his voice to the children. Kelly jerked back in surprise at the way his tone roared through his office.

"I am your father. You will do as I command." Each word was punctuated on its own, a testament to his control over his anger. He pointed towards the door, issuing one final order before turning away from this willful daughter. "Dismissed!"

She turned in a swish of skirts, furious at him. He could just go to the abyss for all she cared! She shouldn't have to marry just to have "strong fire males." It wasn't what she had asked for, it wasn't what she wanted, and Bricriu was the LAST thing she would ever want.

Chapter 51

Landing Chirrit in Llewellyn's courtyard, Aern swung his leg over, sliding easily down her side to land silently. She pranced a little, somewhat playful. Aern laughed, scratching deep in the ruff of feathers at her neck. "Take yourself off to scare some sheep or something." She chirred happily before launching into the sky. Aern watched her go before turning to the patio.

His mother stood there with the calm little smile she always managed to maintain. But then, being queen for so long, she'd likely had to perfect it. Another reason, he noted to himself, not to be the king.

Cassidy put her hands out to him. He approached, dropping to one knee and kissing her hands, as was expected. She promptly tugged him to his feet and into an embrace. If she felt the vials or the weapons he carried, she said nothing.

She promptly stepped away, motioning him to follow her inside. "You have reports on my manor?"

"Of course." He waited for his mother to settle into a chair in the parlor, and then taking a seat in the green crushed velvet chair opposite her. The room was surprisingly bright considering there was only one window and the fireplace. It was a comfortable room, done all in the tones of brown and green.

Only after she had poured the tea did he hand her the scroll case with all the reports. He skeptically looked at the teacup before him as she began scanning the reports.

He hated tea. His earliest poisons had been mixed into his tea, making them more palatable. Two years of that, and to this day, he couldn't stand the taste of tea. And he hated the dainty little cups. He'd much rather have something more filling, and from a mug that could handle more damage. These pretty little things would likely break with nothing more than a dark look.

"It seems to be doing well under your care."

He returned the smile she gave him. "I've enjoyed the work; even all this paperwork."

She laughed. "That's what you have a steward for. Ask Kyle for a recommendation on a good one. He'll help you."

"I thought you'd be coming home soon; that you'd want to pick for yourself."

A long pause followed. His mother calmly drank her tea, taking a few bites of the terrible little sandwiches most royals seemed to favor. He watched and waited, trying not to be irritated. Finally, "I've made some decisions."

He nodded to her, wanting her to just get to the point.

"I'm going to stay here. There are too many memories of your father there. I want you to take charge of Aurora, along with the titles that accompany it."

He sat stunned. "I…thank you?" He loved the country manor, but how to express that to her? 'Thank you' seemed rather… blasé, especially after his reticence to have stepped into the role of a noble, and how much he truly did enjoy the work.

"Grey didn't like people to dwell on what was. He was

quiet, yet commanded a room with that soft tone." Cassidy smiled to herself. "He would tell people to look forward when they came with an argument. To decide what was true and what was right."

She fell silent again, staring at her hands in her laps. Aern waited, not knowing how else to further the conversation. He could see his mother was grieving, that she missed her husband yet, but he had no words to say that would comfort her. He had never been that close to anyone.

Her words were soft when she finally looked up again. "Something your father said long ago stayed with me. 'Being human, elemental, mortal, immortal, or even dead… it's all a state of mind.' You see, to believe it, you become it. That simple. There is no cut and dry fact and truth. It's all imagined. You can't return to the past. Life is no longer what you expect it to be. It doesn't stand still, waiting for the return of one person. It moves on, growing and changing, becoming nothing but a memory. Move on, challenge the future… and jump into a new reality of living. It's what your father would have told you."

She put a hand out to a serving girl, who quickly stepped to his mother's side to hand her a rolled parchment. Holding it to her heart, both hands around it, she closed her eyes. Aern knew that look. It was someone saying goodbye to something.

There was a smile on her face when she opened her eyes again, extending the scroll to Aern. "Most Noble Prince Aern Hunter Bradley, Marquis of Aurora, I bequeath to you what your father had once given me." The expression on her face was one usually reserved for a small child; something of fondness, yet realizing they were doing something that would make that child face a grown up situation. "For me, Aern, jump into the new reality. Become the prince you were meant to be?"

Aern was still honored to find she could look at him as her baby, but he wasn't sure he could do what she was asking. When he unrolled the scroll, he found it was the deed to Aurora; his mother's keep. She was giving him all rights and titles associated with it. But he had been an assassin for so long now; it's what he was; what he knew. He stared at the words, wondering if he could take it. Did he deserve it? Did he want it? Could he stand being in court more often than what he needed to do now? What would happen to the work he loved? His mother believed in him and trusted him, so all he could do was try. Maybe it would only be a few less jobs for him, but he'd try. He rolled the scroll up, tucking it into a pouch to show that he was accepting her offer. Then he let her hug him; he was tense, and felt awkward about it, but he knew this was something else she needed. Awkwardly, he put his arms around her and accepted his mother's affection.

Chapter 52

The three months he spent with his mother at her – correction, *his* manor home – was more steady tediousness than he was used to. He was used to the wind rushing past his ears, to the thrill of skulking in the shadows, to the dark clothing that kept him concealed. More than once he found himself reaching to touch the garrote that should have been hanging at his hip or to roll his ankle to confirm the dagger that should have been in the hidden boot sheath.

Unable to stand it any longer (and with thoughts of Kelly tugging at the corners of his mind), he decided to take Chirrit north. The poor girl had been getting rambunctious at the inactivity and the lack of travel. So was he.

The open air was good. And as much as he missed the thrill of the hunt and kill at the end of most rides like this, he still found himself looking forward to visiting with the mage's daughter. Camping even had him looking at the stars and thinking of the sparkle in her eyes.

But when he landed atop the mage's keep, and saw her going out into the garden, it wasn't the joyful, feisty girl he'd seen before. She seemed tired, weighted down by heavy thoughts and worries.

He quickly made his way down the side of the building, using Bricriuks and window ledges as leverage points. He crossed stealthily to where she sat in a hedge mage, and popping out around a bend. "Boo!"

Wrong move. She was on her feet instantly and he felt the air knocked out of him as her knee made contact in places he'd rather it didn't. "Oh! Oh, by the flames, Aern; I'm so sorry!" Kelly moved to his side, patting his back. "I didn't expect…"

"'s okay," he managed to wheeze out from where he now kneeled. How had he managed to forget *that* part of her feistiness? There was more fire and kick to the girl than it seemed even he'd given credit for.

"Why are you even here?" she asked once he was well enough to move to the stone bench.

"Thought I'd come see you. Tell you what's going on south of the mountains."

She rolled her eyes even as she smiled. "Like it's that exciting."

"Oh, this is a good one." He went on to tell her about his visit home and his mother deeding her Aurora manor over to him. "So now I'm more than just the 'throw away' child in line to the throne. I've got this ridiculous title now," he rolled his eyes, his tone indicating how silly he found the whole thing. "The Most Noble Prince Aern Hunter Bradley, Marquess of Aurora. I'm not even sure I want it. It's only been official for a few months and I'm already missing my previous lifestyle. I just don't get to do as many jobs, considering all the regalia – did you know the family color is white and turquoise blue? And let's not forget all the stupid events that are going on for the king."

"You can't have everything the way you want it." Kelly said quietly after a comfortable time of silence had passed between them. "Lights know I've wished it enough." She scooted closer to Aern on the garden bench, twirling a flower in her delicate fingers.

His eyes slid to the side, noting her movements, her position. As if preparing for a job, his muscles involuntarily tensed unperceptively. It was a force of will not to move away from her.

Chapter 53

"But love isn't real… is it?"

"A person never truly forgets their first love." Kelly explained to her younger sister. "Even if that person doesn't love them back. Even if that significant person doesn't know they're loved." Her eyes wandered to the other room where Aern's laughter could be heard. "Sometimes, people do foolish things to keep the other." And she knew she was being foolish. She was going to get stuck with Bricriu. There was no place in her life for someone as wonderful as Aern. Even he had told her that. He was too worried that a wife of his would have to die for him.

But would it be better to die at the hands of a man that was *supposed* to love and cherish her? She shuddered as she thought about the evil way she would catch Bricriu watching her. She was terrified she'd die at his hands, despite all reassurances to the contrary.

Even if Aern didn't truly love her, she knew she could have made him happy. She could have given him a content life to come home to, no matter how simple it was. Kelly would happily have even traded in her lifestyle to become a farmer's wife, if Aern would have but asked. *He* was what she wanted. Not a fire mage; not any mage. She wanted away from this life. She wanted to find that one foolish thing that would let her keep Aern.

"Oh, Kel," Samantha sighed romantically, leaning against her sister. "I want what you say. I don't want to marry someone like you'll have to."

She smiled sadly, knowing she had no other options. But if there were anything she could do to save Sam… Sam was one of the younger Llewellyn girls, and Kelly's only full sibling. She wasn't yet jaded as much as the rest of them. Besides Kelly, she was the only one to hold onto dreams of something more than an arranged marriage. It wasn't right that those wishes should be taken away from every girl born to "privilege."

"I promise you, Sam, I won't let that happen to you. I'll find a way out for you. Mayden tried for us." She paused, a pang of loneliness for her dear brother washing over her. She missed him. She missed his pranks and his laughter. Mayden and Kelly had been only months apart from each other, he from their father's wife and she from a mistress. They had always been close.

She missed how he had tried to look out for all of the girls, especially Kelly. "And since he can't now, I'll do my best for you." She hugged her sister, each clinging to the other in silent hope. "I promise," she whispered, having no idea how she'd uphold that promise.

Chapter 54

Aern sipped at the brandy he held loosely in his hand. Silver Lightning it was called. It was supposed to have a nasty kick to it. Aern had never noticed. To him, it was a relaxing, soothing drink. It was also one of the few things that could still render him drunk. With all the toxins he'd ingested over the years, he was now immune to most things. This particular drink, though… it was a gift from the Elements to the Bradley family. It had a powerful drugging effect if taken in large doses, rendering even the heartiest fortitudes into a drunken state.

He drained the glass, refilled it, and sat staring into the metallic liquid. At twenty-something he was probably the only one in his family to remain unmarried or saddled with a child. He now took care of his mother's manor, alone but for the servants. Alone, it would seem, by choice.

The past years had seen him more often than not in the north to see Kelly Llewellyn; beautiful, smart, loving Kelly Llewellyn. He intentionally kept conversations steered away from love and marriage, but more often than not, he found her discussing it, or worse, himself thinking about turning husband, despite knowing she had been promised well before the war. Despite knowing he had formerly been hired by her now-deceased brother to off the mage she was promised to.

But with his duties to Aurora Manor and the throne, due to his obligation to do his job when directed by Silver's orders… how could he? He couldn't break the fragile truce that had been built during the war and through the exchange of his sisters living in those lands.

He was still in the wrong business for marriage, but the thought would occasionally cross his mind to leave his line of work, become a full time prince of the realm. Then the practical side of his mind would remind him that the realm certainly didn't need another prince; not with the king, the duke, the king's small son…by the gods, another prince was just another fop at court. This way, he was practical, useful. But…his last conversation with her had ended with her saying "without love, no one wins." Looking ahead, all he saw was either his own death while working or dying a lonely old man.

There was something missing in his life, and he worried that it might be the mage's daughter; worried for so many reasons. He couldn't marry. Not with this job, but more than that, Kelly was to marry some mage. Unless Aern killed him. He'd gotten to know Mayden a little during the war and knew the man hadn't done things simply for spite, which meant something was seriously wrong with the mage… if only Aern knew what it was.

He drained yet another glass, hardly tasting the flavor. He hadn't been able to find anything specific about the man that deserved death. It wasn't hurting his homeland, it wasn't that he seemed power-hungry. And Kelly rarely if ever said anything about the man. He sighed. He needed to make yet another trip north. He needed to know for sure what was going on.

A maid dropped a curtsy at the door. "Your pardon, sir, but there's a lady to see you."

He tipped his glass towards her, nodding slightly. This would be Heather. She had never married and was always finding reasons to stop by. And here it was, evening, and she probably, as usual, didn't have an escort.

"Lord Rory." She bobbed a curtsy to him.

That was the dumbest affectation of his title. Lord Aurora was bad enough. For her to assume the right to use something shorthand irritated him.

It was also obviously raining. Her honey-colored curls hung limp, her dress clung to her, and the ties of her soaked cape hung between the cleft in her breasts.

"May I find shelter here tonight?"

"Of course." He rose to his feet, letting the chalice miss the table and hit the floor as he set it down, giving the impression that he might be drunk. "We need to get you out of those clothes. You're wet."

As his hands reached the ties, her own came up to stop him. "You've been drinking," she said with a soft smile. "I'll borrow a servant to help me."

He had just poured himself another drink and dropped onto the couch when she reappeared. Barefoot, she pulled at the hem of one of his shirts. "You obviously don't plan for female company."

He had no need to. He never invited anyone. "Couldn't find the pants to go with that shirt?" This was a new one with her inappropriate behavior. And it irritated him.

She poured herself a glass and curled up on the opposite side of the couch, tucking her feet under herself as she ignored his question. She sipped daintily, then smiled again. "I can see why you like it." She swallowed half the glass and sighed dreamily. "This is wonderful." Her sultry smoke-blue eyes suddenly focused on him. "How drunk are you?"

Aern chuckled. "Why? Finding reason to worry?" He leaned towards her with the bottle. The first few drops intentionally missed her glass, raining down to her breasts. Aern quickly set the bottle down and brushed the brandy away with his fingers.

A soft gasp from her brought his eyes up to meet her own. Her hand gently covered his, pressing it closer to her breast. "What an amazing sensation. Does the brandy make you feel the same?" As she spoke, she had set her glass down and started to unlace the shirt he had untucked earlier, and pressed her hand to his chest.

It didn't. Not in the way she expected. He was so immune to things like this; he doubted he *could* get drunk on the family brand. But her touch… he was still a man and not immune. A groan escaped him before he could stop it.

"I know." When he opened his eyes, she was mere inches from his face. "Can it start fires?"

He pulled her to him, melding her body to his own. One hand traveled up her silky thigh and slipped under the shirt. Silver Lightning. A white-hot flash fire raced through him, driving sane thoughts far from his mind. Heather had always wanted to be close to him; had even tried to make him jealous as she would cling to other men.

Her warm breath came near his ear as her hands loosed his brays. "I want you to be my first, Aern."

His body demanded he continue, but the blood had begun to pound in his ears, pounding in time to his racing heartbeat; pounding as it did when something threatened him, threatened his life. Suddenly very clear-headed, he grabbed her hands. "No." He set her away from himself, every fiber of his being overly sensitive. "I will not." Heather was sweet, if somewhat empty-headed. He also knew that he was not to be her first. Heather had never married for a reason. She obviously didn't know that he knew her reasons. He wouldn't marry her just because she had succeeded in getting him to bed her. None of the other men had.

Anger flashed across her features; her hand flew even faster as it stung across Aern's cheek. "You are as cold as they all say. Bastard!" She turned and ran from the room in tears.

Aern sighed heavily. *The sun would rise; it always did. This would pass; it always did.* He refused to love. Refused. His was not a career for a married man. He would not misuse a woman's trust for a simple bedding; he wouldn't misuse his own emotions when it came to women. It was a simple rule, really: no bedding meant no falling in love, no love meant no marriage, no kids and no compromise to his profession.

However, that didn't help things now. He didn't even want

to bed Heather. It was Kelly that came to mind; her soft curves, her fiery temper. He had avoided bedding Kelly only to…not love her, surely not that. If only he could take his frustration out on Heather. Other men had. Others had even gotten her with child. He had heard that she had "done the right thing" about it and saved her father from disgrace. She was not what he wanted, not someone who could damage another person for no good reason.

He poured himself another glass, determined to slide into oblivion…right after he relieved himself of the throbbing pressure in his braes…

He threw himself into the lists over the next several weeks. When not out on "duty" with his talents and when not practicing with his own weapons, he was helping with the training of the others, especially the younger men. The older men just wanted someone faster or stronger to practice against, but the boys…he saw himself at ten or so, struggling with weapons that were too large for their young frames. The captain of the guard saw him as a valuable resource, using him until he was ready to drop. If nothing else, he was too exhausted to deal with guests or women or thoughts of the future.

Hells, he hadn't even been able to finish the job for Kelly's father. He wasn't sure of his reasons anymore. Did he want to do it just because Silver had okayed it? Or did he want to do it for Kelly now? Was there a real reason for *him* to have to do it?

Chapter 55

Cooling down with Brett in the salle from a practice with swords, he thought back to a conversation they had had a few weeks before. Becoming a guard really seemed a step down from the lives the two of them had lived before the war. Even if no one had known specifically who he was, he had enjoyed a certain notoriety. He had enjoyed learning, enjoyed the chase, the hunt, and had thrilled at each successful kill. Not that he loved death, but that he hated those who worked against the greater good.

But then, maybe he could help out in that same way here. His father had died by poison. He could train others how to watch for others like himself.

He looked to the very recruits they had been talking about. They were young; eager and loyal, but still needing the training. Training that he wasn't sure he could give them.

Brett responded as if he had read his cousin's mind, "I know we can't train them to defend this place. Not well, anyway, but we could teach them how we operate. Then they'd know how to defend against people like us. Jocasta could add that to her regular training schedule. What better way to learn how to defend against attack than by training with the aggressors?"

Turning his attention fully back to his cousin, Aern held his gaze several seconds before grabbing a pair of staffs off the rack by the wall. Tossing one over to his cousin, he twirled his effortlessly, deep in thought. "I'll agree to help," he finally answered, "but let's make one thing clear – I'm not giving out any of my poison secrets. Even a tiny bit of knowledge is deadly in this art. That's my only condition."

Somewhat taken back by Aern's quick agreement, Brett stood motionless holding his staff. After a few seconds and an inquisitive look from Aern he began to warm up, twirling the staff and flexing his wrists. Soon the air was filled with the sounds of the staffs whirring through the air.

Without warning, Aern struck first, his staff connecting with Brett's exposed calf. A low grunt was the only audible sound other than the humming of Aern's staff as it twirled about.

Brett quickly retaliated, his blow knocking the wind from Aern's lungs as his staff found an opening. Ignoring the injury to his side, Aern artfully dodged a couple of lightning fast strikes as he retreated back across the yard.

Brett ruthlessly followed Aern, his calf still smarting and probably even turning a lovely shade of purple. After this exercise he was certain he'd be sporting several bruises and welts. Aern had always been better with a staff. Everything about Aern appeared simple and non-threatening. A simple walking stick could often end in a deadly confrontation with this man.

Another sharp pain shot up his leg as Aern again struck low. It was a common and effective attack move and one that Brett had yet to properly guard against. A slight shift in Aern's body posture gave away his next move. Suddenly jumping, Brett avoided a third painful blow to the calf and delivered one of his own.

Surprised, Aern looked up at Brett to see a smug look of triumph on his face. Well, that just wouldn't do, Aern thought to himself. It was bad enough he'd lost his sword to Brett, but no way in *hell* was he going to lose a second time to Brett today. After all what would people think?

Watching as Brett adjusted his grip, Aern moved out of striking range, watching and waiting. With a sword Brett was a perfect tactician but the wonderful simplicity of wielding a staff sometimes got the better of him.

Aern watched him advance, slowly moving in a sweeping circle around Brett, just out of range from his staff. Quickly Brett lunged and swung but his staff only met air.

At the first sign of his intention, Aern quickly ducked and rolled sideways, swinging his staff in an arc inched just above the ground. Catching Brett from behind, his feet were again swept out from under him for the second time that day. Landing with a solid thump on his back Brett blinked as he tried to regain the breath that had been knocked from his lungs. Looking up he saw that Aern stood over him in victory, a wry smile on his face.

The sound of applause attracted both their attention. Gavriel and Silver walked towards them, giving a polite round of applause, obviously entertained by their demonstration.

"I'm surprised to see that Silver is not the only Bradley that knows how to wield a staff, even if it was less than graceful."

Both Brett and Aern would have taken offense at such a

stinging insult had it come from any other source but Gavriel. He was a lethal opponent; one that they both respected and he the same of them.

Wordlessly both Aern and Brett relinquished their staffs to the blonde elf. It was not very often that he and Silver trained in full view of everyone, often times preferring to practice in the early morning hours or late twilight. Their thinking was that one should always be prepared, regardless of the time or conditions, and what they did was not a spectator sport; they played for real.

The two men were ruthless and harder on each other than anyone else in the training grounds. By the time Aern decided to check in on some of the other squires, both men were already carrying bruised cheeks and bloodied knuckles. There was no telling how many other minor injuries were blooming hidden beneath their clothing.

Chapter 56

It shouldn't have taken him by surprise when Sterling pulled him from the lists shortly after that session, requesting a "walk."

Aern pursed his lips slightly, wondering what Sterling could want. It had been five years since the war. He had been using his singular talents less and less since then, spending more time watching his brothers, learning to be the prince he was. And when it wasn't that, it was travelling north to check on the women of the family.

Every time he did go out now, he held a little bit of nervousness. It wasn't that he worried about whether he could do the job; he knew he could. His problem was knowing that there was always the chance he wouldn't come home. If he didn't come home, there was a certain lady that would never know what had happened to him.

That certain lady was also out of his league. He wasn't a mage, and the job he did – the assassin work – certainly wasn't secure. No father in his right mind would marry a daughter to him, prince or no.

"Would you object if I didn't send you out anymore?" Sterling finally asked. "I'm thinking I need your talents here."

Aern clasped his hands behind his back as they continued to walk. He was curious at the turn of events, but wasn't about to tell the king that. "What've you got in mind?"

"Well…I've been thinking. Have you given any thought to settling down?"

"Mm." Aern said noncommittally, smiling. "Some."

"Marriage? Lots of fat babies?"

Aern laughed. "Marriage has crossed my mind, yes. But I'm not as hell-bent on sex as the rest of the family seems to have been." Most of them had married young, or otherwise ended up on the wrong side of the sheets. "Besides," A heavy sigh followed the sad look in his eyes. "My life is too screwed up to bring anyone into it. Children? Mm-mm." He shook his head. "I have Chirrit. She's enough. I'm not really the type of material to turn husband or father."

"I wasn't either."

He shot his brother a concerned look. "You're not happy with Serena?"

"Never said that." He gave a wicked smile as he arched his brows. "But…you: If you had a different lifestyle?"

Aern sighed. There was no point getting into the specifics of his life. Nothing could be changed now. A different lifestyle didn't automatically mean wife and children for him. Even if he didn't have those that would love to see him dead, his seed would forever fall barren. No woman would want a life without children. "This is who I am, Sterling. I serve my purpose. I'm good at it."

"I didn't ask about that." He hadn't forgotten a kitchen conversation he'd had with Aern years ago, when he'd found out that his brother would never be able to father children. Best get to the point. He shifted the direction of the conversation. "Jocasta's leaving at years end. I'll be needing a new Captain of the Guard."

Already thinking of possible candidates that would fill the position nicely, he was surprised when Sterling stopped to face him. "Would you consider becoming the next Captain?"

"Me?"

"Why not? You have a talent for it, you know more about weapons than any other human alive, and as close as you are to the throne, I wouldn't worry about you turning traitor on me."

They both laughed as they started walking again.

"Let me think on it." Aern answered at last.

He retreated to their mother's manor, his home, needing to think things through. He didn't know what his life should be anymore. He enjoyed the adrenaline rush just before he struck, just before the dart or the knife would find its home. But he also enjoyed the rush he felt when Kelly smiled at him, laughed at his jokes, flared in anger when she disagreed with him.

Chapter 57

He dreamt of wild, adrenaline-filled days. He hadn't much cared for his time on the actual high seas, but serving the king on a "merchant" ship had been a heady experience. Even then, his father had thought him in Lord Morenden's court, training to be just like his older brothers. Instead, his orders had come to his foster brother, the captain of the ship, from his father's court.

His uncle, the Grand Duke, had usually been behind the orders; sometimes his father was. At the end, even is brothers had sent requests. They only sent their orders to the best. Captain Jays attained a reputation through Aern's profession.

Only the best at sea had requests for service coming from the high court. At fifteen, he was considered the best. At fifteen, he should have been done training and home a year past. Rather, he had still been listed as still "in training," while he was making a living by working for his father, all unknown. He preferred it that way. No need to have let his father in on what he did. It would probably have upset the old man that his youngest had no comparison when it came to providing a clean death…or a just death.

His reputation had started among the crew when he had accepted a bet to swallow some vile concoction, earning him a pocket of coins when he remained hale and healthy rather than dead. It was reputed that he could drink anything, that he couldn't be killed, and that his blades moved so fast one would never see them. He highly doubted that last, but wasn't about to disabuse anyone of that rumor. As to the others, he knew his time was marked. Every move he took was probably nothing more than a roll of the dice for Death.

Now, at 24, he woke to other dreams. A woman. He sat up, running fingers through his hair, away from his eyes. He blew a deep breath out as he looked around the room. A stable home. His mother's manor, but still, not a ship, not on the move, not worried about someone stabbing him in the back… Granted, he still did the occasional job, but it wasn't night after night like before, always wondering if he would be fast enough, silent enough. More often than not, he was assisting in the lists.

Maybe taking the position, becoming Captain, would be a good change for him.

He threw his clothes on, heading down to the kitchens. The masons were making great progress on the remodeling project he had initiated. He'd ordered the stables repaired along with the small section of wall that had been razed during fires. He'd been concerned that the repairs would not be completed when his mother was scheduled to visit home.

He paused momentarily. He'd need to see her again soon, let her know the status of things. He started moving again, determined to find his breakfast.

* * *

His mother was thrilled with the repairs and the way things

were going. His sisters seemed to be settling in to new lives in the north, with little interest in coming back to Whitewind.

The visits, while short, boded well for alliances and future agreements. Sterling would be happy to find that several of the girls had fallen in love and wished to marry. Or rather, he thought with a laugh, they had told him they were going to. Seemed he hadn't realized how strong the women in his family actually were. They were more like Kelly's personality than the average female he'd met.

And with her on his mind, that would be his final stop. He landed, moving into the Llewellyn gardens, and let Chirrit soar the skies where she'd see the gryphon from the windows.

It was only minutes until she came running, out of breath, into the hedge maze. "Aern! What are you doing back here?" She leaned against him in a quick hug, then moved to take her regular seat at the chess table.

"Checking on family." He took his accustomed seat, opening the granite drawer to pull out the small marble pieces. "Figured I'd get a tongue lashing from you if I didn't make an appearance here as well." His voice was laced with humor as he dumped the pieces to the board.

"And how would I have known?" She started setting up the pieces, taking the white for herself. "It's not like father would tell me, a lowly girl, about such lofty affairs as a prince moving through the lands."

Aern laughed at the way she made fun of herself. She was

such a bright spark every time he visited. There seemed to be more to this "moth to flame" analogy than he would have thought; her family being fire, and he flighted by Chirrit… too close to home. Too close. Yet he couldn't resist the breath of fresh air she had become to him.

The game passed mostly in silence, rarely speaking to each other about anything but a missed move. But near the end of the game, she slid her bishop in to take his rook. "Aern," her voice was sad, quiet, making him look up from his next move. She held the rook gently in her hand, staring at it as if some answer would be found in the pale marble. "I'll have to marry before long."

His features settled into the calm blankness he wore while on a job. He didn't like this conversation. It had only come up a few times in the past, but she had hinted quite strongly at her feelings for him. "I'm sure it won't be that soon," he offered in pacification. "Didn't you say you're to marry a fire mage? And there aren't that many, right?" He smiled at her small nod. "There, then. See? No worries yet."

"But Aern, if it's Bricriu…"

"It won't be Bricriu." He spoke a little harsher than needed.

"But if it is, promise me you'll still come see me." Kelly's voice was soft, gentle, not holding any of the panic and fear lurking in her eyes.

"There's nothing saying you'll marry him yet," he tried to console her. "The man can't seem to finish his training. Maybe your father will still find you someone else." Aern deliberately looked away as he said this, knowing that she wanted him to be that someone else, knowing that he couldn't. He should have stopped these visits, should never have allowed themselves to become friends. Now she wanted more from him.

"You know he won't." Now she looked away, out the window, anywhere but at the man she truly wanted. "This has been arranged for years. It's been signed and sealed in all but the act." Kelly covered his scarred, calloused hand with her petal-soft one. "I don't want to be with him, Aern. I love you."

Covering her hand with his other, he gazed into her eyes. It killed him to be in this position. He didn't want to have feelings for her, didn't want to hurt her. "I can't marry, Kelly. I can't. There are other things that prevent that life for me."

Wanting to run from the room, from his cryptic messages, she forced herself to a calm she didn't possess. Were she to run, he would never return, would never be her strength or support. She needed him in her life. She needed to know that he would be there no matter how terrible Bricriu would be during her upcoming marriage. "Then promise you will still see me. As a friend."

He smiled as he raised her hand to his lips. "Always, Kel. I'll always be there if you need me." At least, he tried to believe that. In truth, he knew he would likely need to bow out of the picture once she married. Definitely once she had children. Most men he knew tended to jealously guard their wives, and to see any kind of friendship with a man as something more. Especially with someone as pretty as Kelly.

Watching her, he could see there was something more she wanted to say. Considering how stubborn and opinionated she could be, he was well aware she'd find a way to say it if he gave her the chance. He didn't want her to. He didn't want to lose the moment to more talk of promises and love.

A loud whistle from Aern made irritation flash across Kelly's face. He gave her his most playful smile as he waited for Chirrit to come into view overhead. He glanced up at Chirrit's call to him, then back to Kelly.

Her eyes had gone all soft again. Aern damned himself in that second, not wanting to cause the look to leave her. No one had ever looked at him that way. He should have left or said something callous, but instead he leaned over and placed a soft kiss on her mouth. Hoping she would have the sense to pull back or slap him, he was surprised when she tentatively returned the kiss. Her touch was soft and yielding, forgiving him for being what he was even while healing his heart, knowing he'd have this memory for a lifetime.

Breaking the kiss, he quickly stood, going to where Chirrit danced in place for him. Only after mounting up did he dare look back to Kelly. She stood with her back straight and proud while a soft smile of bemusement touched her lips and eyes.

She'd be able to take care of herself, find a way to be happy with someone that could be there every night for her. She'd have all the things at her disposal she could want, without the worry of someone like him.

Besides, she wouldn't need him. Not really.

Chapter 58

He had come a long way from the naïve child of yesteryear. No longer did he accept gifts or treats – especially treats – from others. *Hells*, he thought, *I don't accept anything anymore.* At twenty-seven, he'd become as hardened as a man of forty.

The firelight flickered warmly, reflecting through his glass as he raised it, inspecting the rich silver wine within. Sinking back into the thick leather chair, he let his arms rest over the sides, his glass hanging loosely from his fingers as he watched the flames dance merrily.

So much he had given up. So much he had chosen to let go of and lose. He closed his eyes, letting his dark countenance relax, falling back against the chair with a sigh.

A soft footfall pulled him back to the present. All senses immediately alert, he opened his eyes but didn't move. He focused his hearing more towards the sound behind him. To any other, he would still seem relaxed, asleep.

When the sound was just to the right behind the chair, he went to his feet in a fluid move, letting the left-hand dagger drop from its wrist sheath to settle in his hand as he brought it up to the intruder's throat. A startled young lady stood there, eyes wide in fright. With trembling hands she raised a shaky tray in her hands higher, letting him see the meal he had forgotten he had asked be brought to him.

"My apologies," he muttered, taking the tray. It could as

well have been said to the wind. The servant had fled the moment the tray left her hands. He would need to do something about that. He loved this house. The servants had been nothing but good since he'd taken over. He didn't want them to live in fear of him.

He had seen both methods. Morenden led by fear and forced respect. Whitewind was a force unto itself. The people served there because they *wanted* to, no matter the station they had been born to. He wanted that here; people that would serve him because they could, not because they had to.

Taking his own dishes back towards the kitchens, he noted how many changes had occurred here already. Aurora looked more like a home, less like a place waiting for someone to live in it. And he wanted to share the accomplishment with Kelly; tell her what he'd done to improve one small thing in life.

With a whistle on his lips, he went in search of Chirrit. He'd fly north and see her now. Maybe even convince her to come see the place.

* * *

Landing in the gardens, he pat Chirrit on the neck and bounced silently down the steps to the lower garden. There had been so much going on; he was actually looking forward to telling her about it. But as he rounded the corner, he froze. His eyes took in the image of Kelly in the arms of Bricriu. She wasn't fighting. She wasn't pulling away.

She was actually letting the ass kiss her!

His world shifted upside down on him. He had actually let himself care for her. A tide of misery swept over him as he watched Bricriu kiss her again. That could have been him. He had turned her away though, and she had gone straight to the mage.

Turning on his heel, he made his way back up to Chirrit. The melancholy slowly changed to loathing what he had allowed in himself. He had weakened. The loathing became anger. He had known better and he had gotten close anyways.

"Chrr?" Worry laced her voice.

Aern closed his eyes a moment, hands balled in fists at his sides.

* * *

Kelly couldn't imagine things much worse. Bricriu had found her in the gardens and pulled her in for a kiss. She was stunned, shocked that he would dare to touch her without a formal betrothal. He had told her that he was going to marry soon, and he had been told it would be to her. He had taken the initiative to find her and let her know that he was going to ask for it to be sooner rather than later.

Then he had pulled her to him, warned her not to pull away with a cold tone and a hard look in his eyes. In shock and some fear, she stood still, letting him kiss her.

* * *

Trying to take a steadying breath, he opened his eyes again, only to see Chirrit's golden eyes looking at him as she had every time he had gotten sick on a new poison. Only this was worse. The hardened assassin crumbled under that gaze, leaving only the fragile boy he had once been. With tears glistening unshed, he wrapped his arms about her neck for comfort. "It's okay, girl. No big deal." Although it was. Although it mattered more to him than it should have. Although he had fallen in love, despite everything.

But that still left a large question for Aern. He wanted what was best for Kelly. He wanted her to be happy. And if that meant Bricriu… how could he kill the ass if Kelly loved him?

Easy. He wouldn't. And he wouldn't come north again.

Chapter 59

Adept Llewellyn gave his daughter a sad smile. He carried a beautiful red dress trimmed in silver, which he laid over the back of a chair in the women's solar. He couldn't bear the look of haunted horror on her face. Inside, he felt the same.

Kelly knew what the dress was for. The look on her father's face said it all. "Daddy, no…" She half-rose from her chair by the window, one arm stretched imploringly towards him as he simply turned away, quietly closing the door behind him as he left.

Her sisters sat silently, looking to her. Samantha, the youngest, leaned over to pick up Kelly's embroidery, which had fallen forgotten from her lap.

The dreaded day had come. There was no discussion of it, no warning. Her mind spun in a hundred directions, trying to figure out a last minute escape. Aern had said he was supposed to save her. He had *said.*

Bricriu wasn't supposed to be her husband. Lady Luck had promised her something good. She was supposed to get true love; someone that cared about her.

Her sisters said nothing as they started to move around the room. One went for the box of hair ribbons, another for a brush. Still another went to the dress, lifting it and turning to Kelly. They had helped other sisters on their wedding days. They would prepare Kelly now. Even though they all felt more like they were preparing for a funeral. Not one of them was happy about the situation.

In shock, feeling wooden inside, she let her sisters dress her, lacing her tightly into the fitted gown. Tiny straps went over the shoulder, shimmering a silver that reflected the red of the dress. The material had a soft sheen to it, the light chasing shadows across the faBricriu as she moved, making it look like a warm fire chased over her.

Her father claimed her, giving her a pat on the hand, as if that would make everything all right. Not a hug, not a word; just a pathetic pat on the hand. Then he took her to the Phelan's home.

The landscape outside was cold and bleak. There was nothing but slick ice and bare trees as far as she looked…until they reached the Phelan's holdings. The land's lay in the shadow of the ragged black mountain his home was built into. It was like going into the jaws of Kinthris.

Then again, maybe that would have been easier; to be taken by the world's soul-eater, consumed until she was nothing more than an empty husk.

She didn't want this. Tears fell unchecked as she entered the Keltori Chambers. She just knew in her heart that married to Bricriu she'd end up as empty inside as if Kinthris had eaten her.

Her father left her just inside the door as he moved up past Bricriu to join the other Adepts. As he passed by the bridegroom, Bricriu risked a glance at the assembled adepts, noting that their eyes were now on the girl. A firey look scathed over her from head to feet, noting the way the dress showed off her curves. Even the yellow ribbons twisted into her reddish hair were reminiscent of fire and flames. She appeared meek, timid almost, which was all the more to his advantage. She'd be easier to break to his will.

Balling her hands into fists at her side, she took a deep breath and moved forward. She was not weak and she certainly wasn't going to make her father look bad. Not now. If there was no helping it, then there was no helping it. But she couldn't help the shivers that chased up and down her spine at the lascivious look in his eyes and the leering smile he gave her. He was a terrible man; she knew from everything she'd heard and seen over the years.

Kelly forced her eyes to her father. She'd stay focused on him through this. Through the negotiations, she remained quiet, as a "good" daughter should; not really hearing what was being said. She knew her father would bargain the best he could for her. The question was, would it be good enough?

When her father moved to sign the contract, she shifted slightly so she could look at it. She was able to see something about "no child nulls" and "failure to support" before Bricriu noticed her looking. He stepped into her way, blocking her view as he gave her a sneer over his shoulder. "You won't need to worry about the details, wife."

And it was done. Bricriu and her father had signed before the full Keltori. She was now a MacFurgal. Feeling a chill inside that had nothing to do with the weather, she looked to the men she had looked to for protection all her life, wondering how they could do this to her. Like property, they had signed her over to him. She had been given no say in it. Her signature wasn't even on the contracts, like she didn't really matter.

"Come, wife." There was no emotion in his voice as he took her arm just over the elbow in a grip almost vice-tight.

She looked back to her father one last time, beseeching him with a look to stop this from happening. Her heart sank as she watched him let a breath out, his head drooping a little, and closing his eyes to keep from seeing her.

She was taken to the village below the keep. They were given a pretty little cabin for their marital consummation. It had a large fireplace that was unlit, a small kitchen area, and a large feather bed. There was nothing of affection though. There were no candles – for romance or lighting, no wedding gift to her, not even a bouquet of flowers.

Her cloak was pulled roughly from her shoulders. "Well, strip." His tone was cold, impatient.

All she could do was stare at him. He couldn't mean to be this…methodical about things. Surely he wanted at least a little romance; at least for their first encounter.

Darkness flashed across his features, anger brought his fist up to crack hard against her cheek. "When I give you an order, you'll listen, woman!"

A hard slap followed from the other side, driving her off balance and to the floor. His fingers twisted into her hair, pulling her back to her feet as her hands went up, trying to pry him away while a scream ripped from her throat. She found herself face to face with him, his hand still in her hair, pulling too tight. There was nothing loving in that face.

His free hand went in the neckline of her dress, pulling away roughly, ripping the material, strands of hair ripping from her head. Shocked, terrified, she let her mind slip away from the horror. This wasn't marriage. This wasn't love.

She curled on her side, trying not to cry when it was over. He had told her she would say nothing of it to the Keltori; not if she wanted to live. He had said her life would be her choice; if she behaved and did as he said, she'd get what she wanted. If she didn't… she could hardly believe he'd be so cruel.

Her only consolation was that she'd be at her father's keep. As a newly appointed Mage, Bricriu hadn't yet acquired his own keep or lands. That meant she'd at least have her sisters for comfort yet. For a little while.

* * *

A woman from the village tapped at the door, entering timidly. Kelly still lay on the bed in shock. The woman pulled a quilt over Kelly, built the fire back up, directed a few others to bring in water, which was warmed over the fire, then dumped into a large copper tub. When it was just Kelly and the woman again, she came over and carefully touched Kelly's shoulder.

"Miss, ye'd be a right mess. Bathe. Please." She gently helped Kelly out of bed and into the tub. "Some men ain't got the right of it, honey, but they figure it out." Her voice wasn't totally convincing. "They figure it out," she repeated quietly, almost as if trying to convince herself.

She was given a simple homespun dress by the kind women of the village. She had nothing else to wear home but that. The one she'd worn, the one she knew had cost her father good coin for, was nothing but rags now, ripped in several places. Even her cloak, which he'd pulled off of her; the clasp was now broken. She had to hold it closed on the carriage ride home.

Bricriu didn't even come to join her on the ride home. She sat alone in the cold carriage, every bump jarring her, causing further pain in her battered body. But he was there at the front door, coming to help her down from the carriage as if he were a proper, doting husband to her.

Chapter 60

Moving as a wraith through her own home, Kelly was little more than a shell of her former self. She had wanted so little from life. She had called upon the Immortals, asking for aid in finding only one thing: a happy life with a good husband. Bricriu provided neither.

She was always sore, or bruised, or bleeding from a hundred places that would never show in public. There was nothing but Fire in her husband; fire, and anger. He always looked sullen, no matter the circumstances, but once he had her behind closed doors, any attempt at civility was gone. He had nothing even remotely nice to say about her family, but there was no reason given why he hated them so much. Or why he had even agreed to marry her, other than the fact she was the daughter of a Fire Adept.

Even then, he hadn't given any indication that he wanted to get her with child. It seemed the only thing that gave him any pleasure was her pain. Had it just been words, she might have been able to handle it, but it was the beatings, the rapes…

Her only solace in those first months had been her sisters. And the only reason she still had that was because Bricriu was only a newly appointed mage. He hadn't yet been able to get a home of his own built. It was tradition that the magelings train under a master of each Element, ending with their strongest heritage. The final one to train them continued to house them after passing their final test; at least until they had been given time to find or build a home of their own. Until then, a student simply lived in the keep of the Adept he studied under.

So, Bricriu had stayed in her home, training under her father. He had leered at her, said things in passing when others wouldn't hear, but he had never once hinted at how awful he could be. And then he passed. He tested, becoming a full mage. By dark the next night, her life had become hell. She had learned the true meaning of brutality and pain. All she had were her sisters, and the solace of knowing none of them were going through this. But as time went on, she noticed even they were pulling away from her. Bricriu was probably threatening them as well.

She needed to know she could survive this. With Bricriu gone Lights-knew-where for a short time, she had managed to dress moderately well, leaving the rooms she was supposed to be happy in. Wearing anything close fitting was out of the question, since it rubbed in a hundred places over her sores and abrasions. Not sure she could manage to not limp or hold her ribs, she stayed to the servants hallways.

Several of them gave her sympathetic looks, knowing full well what the man was doing to her. She hated them in that moment, wishing they would do something to help her. In the next, she amended her thinking. If they were to even look directly at Bricriu, he had been terrible to them. Even before marrying into the family, it hadn't been beneath him to hit them if they dared to look right at him, or Lights forbid, speak to him.

At least she didn't see her sisters. She made it to her father's study, glancing around quickly before ducking inside. She had risked a visit here before. She had to try once more. Better death by her father's hand for disobeying the Laws of Mages and touching a mage's grimoire, than to slowly be destroyed by a man that hated everything she was.

Opening it carefully, she marveled again at her father's beautiful scrolled handwriting. Each book was carefully written by each mage and protected just as carefully. She had always heard that none but that mage could even look at it. But somehow, she could. She wasn't sure what all the words meant, but she had guessed before and gotten Luck. Carefully flipping the pages, she ran fingers over the words, figuring out what she could as she went.

Slowly enunciating the words of the Immortals, she sounded out the spell she had chosen. The room remained quiet as she looked up, turning slowly to see if there was anything different about the room. As she turned again to look at the book, she jumped back a step. A gorgeous woman stood leaning on the podium, arms draped languidly over the book. Red hair shimmered like fire flames down past her butt. Her dress was provocative, clinging and barely there. "Darling," the sultry voice from her was more suited to a bedroom, "calling Fire is deadly."

Recovering quickly, Kelly stepped forward, laying her hands on the woman's arms. "Then please! Kill me! I can't live like this."

Sliding her arms free of Kelly with some disdain for being touched, she paced away from her. "Never touch an Immortal without permission."

Her heart dropped in surprise. "They truly call you?" she whispered. On some level she had known, but to KNOW…

An amorous laugh escaped the woman. "Who do you think came before? Our messenger?" She closed the grimoire, making even that seem sensual. "You've been chosen for a task, my baby blaze. You'll need to see this through." She walked towards the windows, her hips swaying seductively, the cut of her dress letting a leg or hip peek out at times. As she neared the windows, she glanced over her shoulder. "You don't need your father's book. The words are within you. All you need is to say them." In the next few steps forward, she was gone, leaving Kelly staring at an empty room again.

So there was something to save her from this hell! She just needed to discover the words! Hope welled up in her, despite the odds. She would find the words, no matter how long it took.

Chapter 61

Thoughts of the coming trip were driving him insane. Not because of his mother, but the woman. He was used to having an iron grip on his thoughts and feelings; this woman was driving him nuts. Sitting in the breakfast nook, he waited for the servants to bring him something to eat, absently cracking his finger joints as he looked out the window, trying to squelch thoughts of Kelly from his mind. She wasn't even attainable to him. She was betrothed to a man of her own kind; had been for years now.

Watching the trees sway in the wind, he thought of her hips as they gently swayed to the rhythm of her walk, the sound of her sweet laughter filling his mind. Over the last five years, he had had many reasons to visit the northern lands, his mother and sisters included. But the thing that continued to draw him was the elusive daughter of one of the mages.

He swore an oath as he slammed back the rest of the White Lightning he'd been drinking. He was weak. He had allowed a soft spot to ferment the very fiber of his being. The silver liquid cooled, coated his throat as it slid down easily. Unbidden, his thoughts returned to Kelly. Satin skin that would be so easy to slide against…

Paralyzing fear gripped him for a brief moment. He took a deep breath and shook his head to clear the oddness away. He found this happening more and more often since the end of the war. Just as odd were the moments of pure elation that enveloped him. Either feeling would strike at a moment unbeknownst to him, leaving him unsure why it came, but completely caught within it. Only lately, these moments left him with a distinct impression of "Kelly." It was as if the feeling came straight from her.

Probably crazy. That's what it had to be. He had put so much garbage into his system in the last fourteen years that it had probably messed with his head. All the same, he intended to see her again.

He knew she was betrothed to one of the men soon to become a mage. He also knew that both she and her father disliked the arrangement, but were unable to stop the arrangement should the man pass his test.

Bricriu. The man's mere name gave Aern pause to shudder. He knew him well; too well, in fact. Aern had never considered himself to be a compassionate type of person, but he actually felt pity for any woman who made the unwise decision to share Bricriu's bed. Bricriu was violent, that he knew. He'd witnessed it firsthand on the battlefield and during excursions with the looser women. Bricriu had a nasty case of bloodlust and a nasty temper to go with it; a volatile combination at best. He'd heard stories of Bricriu wanting to "spice up" his sexual relations with willing women and had heard others telling of women ending up so badly beaten they were never the same. To think of Kelly with a monster like Bricriu made his blood boil. Just knowing he was training under Kelly's father was enough to make him furious.

He had been trying to figure out the best way to assassinate a Hakon. Nothing he had been able to find out over the years had been of help, although he hadn't given up. He didn't want her to marry such an asshole, but was he furious enough to take matters into his own hands? Did he actually…love her? It was the last thing he wanted; the gods only knew, he didn't want to be vulnerable, laid open for someone to hurt him, use him again, but…

A shudder coursed through him. It wasn't him. Fear, disgust… all in one morning. He had no reason to go north, no reason whatsoever to justify visiting Mage Llewellyn's home, but something was wrong. Kelly was scared to death; he knew it more solidly than he knew his own heartbeat. But that was impossible… wasn't it?

Chapter 62

Rising from the floor, she had had enough. His crazy rantings, his accusations… no more. If the immortals wouldn't help her, she was going to do it herself. She was *not* going to die for someone like this. Limping on her badly bruised leg, she moved for the door to their chambers.

"I'm not through with you yet!" Bricriu was enraged. It took so little to set off his quick temper that Kelly normally walked on eggshells around him.

Normally… but not today. "Well, I'm through talking to you. I'm through taking your abuse." Kelly's voice rose a notch higher in her own anger.

In a flash Bricriu was standing in front of her, a towering menace that stood between her and the door. A menace that was very real and very angry.

"Let me pass. I have no desire to share the same room – the same air – as you." The disdain in Kelly's voice only stoked Bricriu's anger to burn hotter and more volatile.

As she moved to pass him, he reached out and grabbed a handful of hair, grabbing it with such force it snapped her head back, nearly throwing her to the floor in their chambers. "I said I wasn't through with you, *dearest.* Accommodate me. Your wifely duties, or do I give you a refresher of the other night?"

The malevolence in his gaze gave Kelly an involuntary shudder of fear. He liked inflicting pain; that was a lesson she'd learned immediately after the papers had consigned her to this hell. She forced her voice to remain calm and steady. "Bricriu, if you continue this behavior, I could very well lose the child I'm carrying." Maybe that truth would help stay his hand. "Surely that means something to you."

"What, you?" he sneered. "With child? How unfortunate." The derision in his voice was only slightly less dangerous than the look on his face. "The last thing I want is a child of mine to be tainted with Llewellyn blood. I have bigger plans that don't involve my children, my dynasty, having *anything* whatsoever to do with the Llewellyn family." As if to underscore his point, Bricriu twisted her hair around his hand, almost ripping some of her luscious fiery locks out by their roots. "You are as disposable as horse manure to me. You'd do well to remember that or you'll suffer the same fate as your *beloved* brother."

Kelly's eyes widened at the mention of Mayden's demise. "What about Mayden? His death was honorable; everyone knows that."

A sadistic grin twisted the mage's features and his eyes narrowed to small slits, "Honorable? Of course." He sounded so smug, so full of himself, actually believing what he was saying. "Exactly as I had planned. Funny how even your illustrious father believed in that 'honorable' nonsense, when the spell I threw at him was one they had supposedly practiced since Mayden was a child."

With joy, he remembered that day in vivid detail. He was

more caught up in his version of war events than he was in the actuality of a baby in the here and now. "There was fighting everywhere and the King and his brother were alone, all but defeated." Glee filled his voice. "Do you have any idea how fortunate that was for me? Mayden disobeyed orders with those idiot friends of his and tried to save them alone. I caught him completely off-guard!" Sadistic joy filled his voice. "It was almost too easy!"

Kelly watched in confusion as his expression went from joyful to almost imaginative. It was almost as if he were making up the scene in his mind as he spoke it.

"I can still smell the burning of his flesh, his screams of agony." Bricriu's free hand moved up to caress her jaw and the delicate column of her neck. "This is all nothing, compared to what your father took from me; how he let my parents die for going against the Keltori; leaving me an orphan, dependent on the will of an ancient order. I vowed then to destroy Llewellyn. You're part of that." Moving his mouth a breath away from hers he continued, "So you see *darling*, it is in your best interest to keep me well satisfied… in all matters." As if to emphasize his point, his free hand moved slowly down her neck before reaching the neckline of her gown and tearing the material, exposing her breast. Gazing down at her with a smoldering look in his eyes, Bricriu engulfed the whole breast in his hand and gave it a rough squeeze.

Releasing her from his grip, he crossed his arms and stood in front of her, his face a mask of pure malevolence. "Now *dear wife*, beg me for your forgiveness. Maybe I'll let you live to birth that Llewellyn spawn you seem to want so badly."

Kelly took an involuntary step backwards, knowing what the tone of his voice meant for her. There was more wrong with him than just his anger. He was crazy.

"Disobey me, and you *will* suffer the consequences. Now bow to me! Beg for your life!" He jerked hard on her hair again. "I will have it before I leave our chambers for this farcical on-going training. Either of your own submission or I will take my due. You know I like a little fight, but then," he ran a finger along her jaw line in a loverly fashion, at odds with his manner, "it's your choice," he twisted her hair painfully as he gently kissed her cheek. "Willingly, or broken and bleeding."

Knowing how perilous the situation was for both her and her unborn child, Kelly did as he commanded. She'd long ago learned that he was not a man to expect kindness or compassion from. There was not a single shred of emotion in him. He enjoyed the suffering of others.

Closing her eyes against the sight of him, and her mind to the physical onslaught that ensued, Kelly focused her mind on happier times. All the while, silent tears wet her cheeks.

As a child, she'd imagined being married; not a romantic marriage, but one of respect and understanding like her father had with his wives. Now she knew men such as her father were a rarity. This man simply saw her as a warm body to use and abuse as he saw fit.

She wondered about the magic. So long ago, it seemed a lifetime ago, she had used her father's book. Had it been a trick? A terrible joke? She had been told she'd marry for love. Why this? This wasn't anything she would have wished for. It wasn't what she'd been promised. And she hadn't found the words that would save her.

Upon leaving their chambers that morning he had informed her she'd "done a fair enough job," atoning for her disrespect, and he'd decided that she would be allowed to continue to carry the child. He had already warned her that regardless how heavy she got with child, he still expected her to accommodate his needs.

When she'd dared to ask why he couldn't have a mistress service him, his response had been a hard crack across the mouth. The impact had split her lip and the sight of the blood flowing down her chin only served to entice his lust to brutal proportions. He had grabbed her and thrown her upon the bed, his lust and anger leaving her bloodied and bruised.

After hours of his ministrations, it had taken her almost another full hour to regain her composure and manage to get out of bed. Kelly stood in front of her mirror looking at the fresh bruises that he had left during their argument and resulting coupling that morning. He was always careful to almost never leave marks where anyone would see while she was dressed. However, he did take an almost perverse glee in reviewing his handiwork. Often times he made her undress so he could view his latest "marks of possession." She didn't carry the man's mark, and he seemed to think bites and bruises were a good secondary option. She was a possession to him, plain and simple, and he used her as such.

Aern would never have treated her in this manner. Had the choice been hers, she would have taken Aern to husband. A good friend, he would have seen to her comfort and protection. She hadn't even seen him since her marriage a few months past. He wouldn't know that she was married now, or that she carried a child of fire and hatred.

Kelly's hand absently traced over the fresh bruises on her breasts and hips before settling possessively over her womb. MacFurgal may not want this child, but she did. She'd always dreamed of having her own children and she'd do whatever it took to ensure this child made it into the world.

It was at that point in time she'd dared to ask aloud to be delivered from her hellish marriage. She'd met, but never quite believed, in Luck before. But what, other than hope and luck, did she have left to believe in? She dropped to her knees and begged for Hope or Fate, or with any luck, Lady Fire, to strike her husband down before he could bring further harm to her family. As tears of pain, anguish and frustration flowed down her cheeks she begged Luck to deliver her from her misery and grant her the life she so desperately wanted in her heart.

What had happened? Had she really caused this horrible life by messing with her father's book? Had her one wish, her one request to the gods, caused this misery she now had to call a life? "You promised me something good!" she yelled into the empty room, sobs then overtaking her. "Please…" she whispered around her tears, "stop this madness…"

Little did Kelly know that at that precise time both Hope and Luck were listening, all too eager to grant her the most secret desires of her heart. "Oh, Aern," she whispered to the freedom beyond her windows, "I wish…gods, I wish…" Tears slipped unchecked, pooling on the cool stone floor. "I wish you could save me from this. Become real and deliver me from the nightmare that is my life."

The words had finally been said.

* * *

A strange sensation caused Aern to drop the staff he'd been using to train with Brett. The first time had been midmorning, and it felt as if Fate had settled around him in some way. This time, it was followed by pain. He staggered back as if he'd been hit across the face. He shouted at what felt like a blow to his side.

"Aern!" Brett was at his cousin's side instantly. "What's going on, cuz?"

"K… Kelly." He accepted the arm to steady him.

"…Who?"

"Mage Llewellyn's daughter," he got out around another bout of pain, feeling like he was being beaten. He'd felt worse. He's lived through worse. Breathe through it. Even though his muscles continued to flinch against the ghost sensations, he used every bit of his training to think through it. "She's in trouble. I have to go north."

"Whoa, wait a second," Brett caught his arm before he could head out to call Chirrit. "You need to do this right, if that's true." He pushed him towards the castle. "Wash and dress to meet the mage. Go."

He staggered inside, taking time only to dress in his formal uniform of brushed gray velvet and black suede boots before he ran out the front doors, whistling for his gryphon. In moments he was in the air. The compulsion was driving him. He needed to reach her. Thanks to flight, it would only be a few hours and he would be on Llewellyn's doorstep.

Thank the Lights; his gryphon could keep him astride. He was struck again by overpowering fear, sharp pain in his back, knocking the wind from him. He pushed her harder, needing to be there. Ungodly pain and pressure, as if a vice gripped his left knee. And to think, there were hours of flight left to him yet.

Anything could happen to Kelly in a few hours…

* * *

He stormed through the front doors, calling for her father, for Ayden. Llewellyn came running, knowing Aern would not use a mage's first name lightly. Aern headed for the stairs, unerringly moving towards Kelly's room. "Your daughter," he threw over his shoulder at Llewellyn, "is in trouble." He stopped abruptly before a door that, he knew not how, was hers. With a sharp motion, he waved her father towards the door. "You go in or I will."

"You bitch!" Bricriu's voice was clear and strong, even through the thick oak door. A sound of something crashing to the floor gave evidence to the struggle that was taking place behind the door. "I'll kill you!" They heard from the other side. "And your beloved father," the words were snide, low, "let's just say he's in for a rude awakening. He deserves to die a slow, painful death." Bricriu sneered at Kelly, enjoying the look of terror as it distorted her features. "This keep will be mine! I'll be Adept here."

Without hesitation Ayden threw open the door of the chamber. The sight before him stopped him dead in his tracks. Bricriu was holding his daughter a good foot off the ground, one hand wrapped tightly around her throat, shaking her as if she were no more than a mere rag doll.

"I want you to watch," the young mage went on, "while I kill your father; Him and the man that left that mark on you. Try to hide the name of that man from me and I swear to the Lights you'll beg to allow me the pleasure of ending your life."

"Bricriu! Release her at once!" Ayden's voice was full of authority; Authority and absolute anger.

"Oh, now look at this: *Daddy* is coming to stick his nose into matters that don't involve him." His tone was cold, spiteful and full of malice. "How convenient for me." Casting his wife aside like a piece of discarded garbage, Bricriu turned and faced his father-in-law. Something inside him had finally snapped, driving him past the brink of sanity.

"What's the matter Llewellyn?" Bricriu sneered, "Don't

care for how I operate? How I teach my wife to know her place? Oh…" he crossed his arms in irritation, "that's right: you're not that type of man are you? No," he continued to rant, "you're not a man at all; just a puppet for The Phelan, a token Fire Adept… and a poor one at that. No wonder Mayden died so easily. He didn't stand a chance against true power and talent."

Ayden watched his son-in-law from the doorway, his body keyed, ready to act. His eyes narrowed, watching and waiting. This man was nothing like his elder brother. Doran MacFurgal was also married to one of Llewellyn's daughters. Yet he was a refined and reasonable soft spoken man, angered only when those he cared about were threatened.

And contrary to what all the adepts had thought, Bricriu was not among those Doran held close. He had turned against everyone, including Doran, over the years. And now, watching the wild lack of sanity, Llewellyn knew the fire mageling was trying to bait him into acting as irrationally as MacFurgal did. Little did Bricriu know that better men had tried and failed. An Adept should be able to handle himself no matter the circumstance. Llewellyn hadn't burned out as a young man on such stupidity; he wouldn't now.

He took a soothing breath before addressing him, offering insult in the use of a first name, a name of power. "So what are you trying to prove today, Bricriu? That a true man needs to beat his woman senseless? You're right in that respect; it's something I've never done." The calmness of Ayden's voice was in direct contrast to the physical changes taking place. His eyes twinkled brightly, golden sparks flickering from beneath his dark lashes. The air around him shimmered with the heat that radiated off of him; his hair took on a bluish cast as his element grew within him, awaiting his command.

"If you wish to settle this like men, outside on the training field. Now." Llewellyn cocked a single eyebrow in challenge before he continued, his face a perfect mask of disregard. "Unless, of course, you'd be afraid? I'd expect as much from the son of a coward. I'd be happy to report that to the Keltori: a genuine lack of character and honor."

"I'm no coward! I'm a MacFurgal and I'll never be afraid of a stinking Llewellyn!" Bricriu's outburst and denial simply brought a cool smile to Ayden's face, giving him a sadistically serene look.

"Well, we'll soon see won't we? We'll find out if you're as brave and powerful as you claim to be. You'll either win or die. My bet is on the latter of the two." Ayden's gaze traveled to the crumpled form of his daughter on the floor. Her breathing ragged, blood from a gash on her temple forming a small puddle on the chamber floor. Kelly's fearful gaze met the stoic look on her father's face. She'd witnessed that look once before and the person that had invoked it had died slow and painfully.

Turning on his heels Ayden left the chamber without another word, the ends of his hair glowing brighter in the darkness of the hallway. Today two of the remaining sons of the only Fire families would face-off. Only one of them would survive, ending years of hostility.

Ayden hoped it would be him standing at the end of the ordeal; he had much to live for, too many people depending on him. He had ultimate faith that Lady Fire would not desert him in this, his hour of need. His life would not come down to anything more than this one meeting of power. Today would be a day of reckoning. Yes, a day of reckoning all the way around.

Chapter 63

Sobbing uncontrollably, Kelly was gathered into Aern's arms. He knelt at her side, lightly rocking her, making soothing noises, his chin resting on the top of her head.

As she calmed, Aern pulled her to her feet and handed her into her maid's care. In the hallway, his weary, pain-darkened eyes met his mother's. He gave her arm a light squeeze and stepped past her, going to sit at the bottom of the stairs. He put his elbows to his knees and dropped his head into his hands as a fireball exploded outside, lighting up the yard, and then quickly subsiding.

He didn't know how long he sat there. Shadows crept towards him when he finally ran his hands through his hair and pulled himself to his feet, stopping short of running right into his mother.

"Let's walk."

"I…was kind of…I have…" His shoulders slumped. "Okay."

They were in the gardens before she spoke. "So. Kelly Llewellyn. Everyone has been wondering about the mystery woman you've been coming to see all these years."

He flushed slightly. "I just bring updates on your manor, your reports…"

"Your manor, Aern. Which you do," She stated matter-of-factly. "But then you disappear."

"It's not…I've never…" He gave her a cornered look. He

had been here for official business. He had reason to come. "Has someone said something?" he asked in a small voice.

Cassidy laughed, linking her arm through his. "Just that whoever it is, the father would be lucky and honored to have you even ask for her."

"Ask?" His voice remained small, much as a child cornered in trouble. "As in… marriage?" He took a deep breath, getting his bearings straight – finding his backbone again. "Lady Mother, I will admit to visiting a certain woman within these lands, but I have never planned to marry. We're good friends, nothing more."

For a long moment, Cassidy said nothing. "Good." She lightly squeezed her son's hand, turning to go. "Then you won't care to know that she bears a mark."

Aern went cold inside. A mark? They only received those in these lands when they truly loved their man. His stomach turned as he considered that maybe she had wanted Bricriu; maybe she had loved him.

His mother went on. "You know that having a mark means…" She paused a moment, giving him a small smile. "Then again, perhaps you don't. It seems these marks are a purely northern affectation."

"I know. I've studied enough over the years." He winced at himself with how harsh his voice had sounded. She had no way of knowing what he knew.

"Well," she smiled. "Then you know how rare it is. And how unlikely it is to be her husband's."

He gave his mother a confused look. The last time he had seen Kelly, she had been in the mage's arms. It had looked comfortable enough to his eyes that he chose to stay away from her after that. Yet now his mother spoke of them not getting along… Was it wrong to have a moment of hope climb in his chest?

He had enjoyed her company. She wasn't like the other women he had known. She had enjoyed his visits, their debates and discussions. There had never been bargaining for things he couldn't or wouldn't deliver.

There was that little issue with his heart giving a funny lurch every time he thought of her so far away. But that could be that he had no one else to really discuss things with. There had been no one he could sit with like he did with her; no one made him so comfortable, or could make him laugh like she did.

So what of the anger that had just gripped him? He wondered that it should have made him happy to hear her want to marry; instead, it was anger – anger of the kind that itched for the use of his blades. He wanted to know who this other man was.

A shiver ran through him as he realized that he carried a possessiveness of her. How had he fallen so low and become so weak that he…*needed* her?

By the gods, he *was* in love. He had never thought to lay himself so open or to threaten his way of life, but he found that he would happily give up everything if he could but have her at his side.

That left only one option. He had been offered the position

as Captain of the Guard. He would take that; he had already settled into his mother's manor permanently, so… he just needed to talk to Mage Llewellyn.

He needed that night to gather his thoughts. Staying in the Llewellyn's guest quarters, he was given the quiet he desperately needed. Over and over, the thoughts circled in his mind.

Could he keep her safe? What if someone tried to use her against him? What if she wanted children? What if she didn't like being away from all the magic users? And the changing seasons? It never snowed in Drikelldorn. She might miss that.

There was little sleep for him that night. He had no way of knowing, but at the other end of the hall was another left sleepless. After almost a year of missing Aern, not seeing him, he had appeared from no where, saving her life. A moment of comfort, and he was gone again. She didn't know he was still in the same building with her. Her tears and her grief held her locked in fear that he was gone again. Her safety was gone.

Her safety was gone, he thought, if he were to take her back with him. He thought he'd die if he had to leave her here, never knowing she was alright. But the alternative was to worry every time he went out on a job. Unless he strictly worked as the Captain of the Guard. He could train the guards at Aurora to specifically watch out for her.

That decided, he finally settled down as the soft dawn light crept in the window. A few hours of rest, and he'd speak to her father.

Chapter 64

He went out to the practice field, not looking back. Only when he stood just off center in the circle did he turn to see Bricriu coming at a leisurely amble. The young man's lack of control showed though. Despite trying to look in control of his abilities, flames burned about his head and shoulders. The land lay scorched as he lifted his feet.

Llewellyn wished this day had come much earlier. If the boy had only lost his control before the test, or at the least, during the test! All the same, the day had finally come to settle the matter of this wayward mage. Too long this had gone on. Other mages had dealt with the boy's insolence, his anger, yet not once had it been directed towards Llewellyn himself. The boy had been careful, always doing as he was told, always following instructions to the exact letter he was given. Yet there had always been something there, something held back. The look in MacFurgal's face should have warned him worse was coming.

And to know his daughter had kept this all a secret! She had kept anyone from knowing how truly rotten the man was to her. That alone raised Llewellyn's ire to a killing edge. He would have trouble containing his own temper at this rate. Yet, he needed to. He needed to be aware and remember everything he did to the boy this day, knowing the Keltori would want a full account of it.

Bricriu didn't wait to reach the protected circle. He pulled his right hand back as if to pitch a ball, letting fly with a ball of flame twice the size of his palm.

Immediately calling a shield of his own fire into place, Bricriu's flame was simply absorbed into it. With a loud whoosh, the shield came down by the will of Llewellyn's left hand as his right readied a blast of flame. His hand glowed white hot with the intensity, yet he felt none of it as the gout of fire sprayed outwards towards the boy.

The younger man wasn't as quick in raising a shield, the flames licking against him before he could fight them back. Bricriu shouted in a mix of pain and anger. His shield slowly came into being, pushing back Llewellyn's attack inch by painful inch.

"You can't hold it, boy!" Ayden taunted. "You never mastered more than just the fire!"

A look of pure hatred glared at the Fire Adept from across the field. Bricriu muttered a few words, raising his hands as he spoke, then dropped them in a quick, harsh movement. Sheets of roaring flame slammed down around the training ground.

Llewellyn watched the random walls drop from nowhere, strike the ground and roar up impressively in a maze pattern. An advanced fire storm, granted, but it didn't damage the land, and would only damage an opponent if they got in the way of it; which Ayden didn't plan on doing. Besides, they were poorly constructed. With a blast of fire aided in being pushed out with gouts of air, it quickly collapsed Bricriu's walls of flame.

Small red salamanders crawled from beneath Bricriu's clothing, scurrying across the ground towards Ayden. Tiny trails of smoke and flame were left in their wakes as they came ever nearer, twisting and climbing over each other. Again, they were easily stopped by the Adept. With a flick of a wrist, the fire creatures created by Bricriu turned to the will of the Adept. They twisted back around and scurried to the other mage.

There was a moment of panic in Bricriu as he was swarmed, but he quickly regained his thoughts, refocusing and dispelling the fire creatures. He glared at Llewellyn as he called forth Brimstone. A foul, acrid smelling burst of fire enveloped the older mage, engulfing him in the strong smell of sulfur.

The response was not what Bricriu wanted. Ayden laughed. He laughed! "Boy, you really don't know my power at all if you think that will work!"

Bricriu's rage only increased, his control decreasing as his fury grew. What looked like two foot spheres of fire burst from his hands, shooting towards Llewellyn. A roaring filled the air as the balls of flame rushed at and around the Adept.

Calling a combination of air and fire to his summoning, it swept over Ayden in a half shield to protect him as the orbs exploded all over the training field. As the last of the bursts went off, Ayden dismissed his shield, picking up several pebbles. Casting words of magic on the handful, he tossed each one individually. Bricriu threw up his hands for protection, turning partly away from each small explosion as the impact of the flames splashed up and out as easily as water. His distraction gave Llewellyn the extra time he needed to build a bigger event, the coup de grace.

MacFurgal may have been granted the privilege of the title of mage, but he hadn't truly earned it. Too many of the boys back from war had been cheated by "earning" titles for their help. This one was a prime example. He only had true control over his own element. To be made a full mage, he should have had complete skill with at least one other. He didn't.

But Ayden did. He called on Fire, Water and Air now to bring in a roiling mass of thundering clouds. With one hand to the sky, and one stretched out towards Bricriu, he called. Words of incantation and power slipped easily from him, with little thought. Punishing winds rose as the clouds became darker and darker.

Before Bricriu could fully drop his arms, before he could think to cast another spell, Ayden threw the last of the pebbles. Bricriu's arms went up over his face, he turned away again, trying to protect himself. Without losing concentration, Ayden still had his other hand lifted to the sky, the words still coming to maintain the storm he was building. The wind currents were moving and twisting around each other, buffeting Bricriu where he stood. His footing was becoming unsure, dirt rising in the winds, stinging his eyes. No matter which way the mage turned, the winds and the dust conspired against him now. His movement slowed, pulled in by the contrary currents of air, his vision became more limited for the dark clouds forming around them.

None of it affected Ayden, as he held complete control over his element. This was why he was an adept. This is what he had spent years upon years studying for. He had earned what this upstart hadn't. And for a surety, the worm had *not* earned Ayden's daughter. For all he had heard and for all he could only speculate on, he had had enough of the boy.

Leaving his right hand with a palm to the sky, controlling the swirling winds, he spoke other words, words of earth, and lightly touched his knee with his left hand. Then he fell silent. He let Bricriu realize his voice had fallen quiet, despite the other noise surrounding them.

With his right arm slightly above his eyes, Bricriu squinted, looking under his arm towards the man that had finished his training. Llewellyn stood extremely still, his right hand to the sky, his left knee raised, and the winds whipping his white-laced red hair. He looked like a flame-touched statue… until the smile spread across his features. He knew what was coming. He knew something Bricriu didn't. And for the first time, Bricriu worried that he wouldn't be able to overcome the old man.

Then there wasn't time for worry. Ayden closed his right hand into a fist and slammed his foot downward, driving it hard to the ground. Lightning flashed, slicing through the odd darkness, ozone crackling and the ground trembled. He raised his leg again, and again it came down, this time with the ground responding. Lightning danced around Bricriu. A sonic boom echoed through the area as the ground rippled, raising more dust, fingers of flames dancing along the swells of dirt that undulated in waves in ever widening circles out away from the Adept.

A combination of the sonic boom, the flaming surges of

land and the lightning all touched Bricriu in the same moment Ayden released all that power, shifting both hands forward, pressing the advantage of Bricriu's pain. One last spell, one only given to adepts; he spoke the words as the winds and the clouds began to disperse. MacFurgal's blood began to boil, his skin growing darker and redder. A last strike of lightning hit the mage. The added heat and the spark of electricity pushed the blood past the level of maintenance. With a scream, MacFurgal's body exploded, blood spraying across the training field, bits of gore flying with it. The skeleton stood that extra second, unaware the body was gone, then it too crumpled. It rattled in a tiny mockery of the thunder that was now fading away.

It was over. Bricriu would never hurt his family again. Even if it meant his own death now.

Chapter 65

"Got a few minutes?" Aern asked from the open door.

Ayden's harried face rose from behind mounds of papers on his desk. This had not been a good day for him. His daughter's life threatened, killing one of his son-in-laws, not to mention one of the few Fire Mages, for it, now needing to continue sorting through the mounds of offers for his daughters. It needed to be decided quickly, considering what could happen in the next few hours. But a short break would be welcome. "Definitely. If I have to look at one more suitor's bid…"

Aern laughed nervously. "So…which of your daughters will it be this year?"

He sighed, sinking back in his chair. "There aren't enough good matches left allowed to my family. I'll be looking at lesser sons at this point."

Trying to sound nonchalant, he asked, "What about Kelly?"

"Kelly? She can't marry again. As I said…"

"And what if someone were interested? Would they have to approach you about one you're trying to match this year?"

Ayden rolled his eyes. "Gods, no. I'd like them to have…something…to speak for the suitor. I'm certainly not going to send my daughters to a sheep farm or anything."

"But you did say that lesser sons of noble homes are fine?"

Ayden suddenly came to full alertness, leaning forward. He had so many daughters that needed to be married off. "Please tell me you know of a few men."

"Uh…" He massaged the back of his neck. "Just one, really." He resettled himself, unexpectedly nervous. "I'm…I'd like to…" he cleared his throat. "I haven't submitted a formal proposal or anything, but it's…I'm interested in Kelly's hand."

Laughter roared from Llewellyn as he put his head into his hands. "More the fool am I. All this time…it's been *my own* daughter." He took a deep breath, regaining his composure as he wiped his eyes. "Do you know: I asked the Keltori about your visits. I said that with five years of your visiting, someone should know *something*, especially if it was their own daughter." He gave Aern a warm smile. "Any one of us would have been honored to have you approach us. A Prince of the Chosen Lands, intelligent, more than capable of protecting her, and a good head on your shoulders." Llewellyn got to his feet, extending a hand to Aern as he decided to break yet another law of the lands. He'd just add this to the list of things he had to face the Keltori with. "And with everything else that's happened now, I'm more than honored to welcome you to my family. She couldn't get a better protector."

Relief flooded through him as he stood, taking the offered hand. He hadn't realized how badly he truly wanted Kelly. Not until this morning. Not until her safety was threatened, until now when her father could have turned him out. "You won't regret it, Adept Llewellyn."

"I know, Aern. You're a solid man; don't know that I've ever heard you've made a rash decision."

Giving him a half smile, Aern raised his eyebrows. "This is about the rashest thing I've ever done."

Both men laughed, knowing that five years was anything but rash. In the next moment, Ayden was deathly serious again. "I'd ask a favor of you, Aern." Not waiting for a response, he pushed on. "I'm trying to settle this…" he indicated the paperwork before him, "before the other mages get here." Worry creased his features, making him appear infinitely older than he was. "I killed a mage, my former apprentice, the one I was still helping to fine-tune. With full rights," he added, "but still, I've violated one of our basic laws. I should have turned him over to the Keltori for trial."

"You were protecting your family." Aern tried to justify. "I'd have done the same. Truthfully, if you wouldn't have survived, I'd have gone after him myself."

Ayden smiled at that. "Like I said, I'm honored to have you join my family. That's why the favor. If I'm taken into custody, or Lights forbid, condemned to death, would you see to my family?" He placed his hands on top of the folders covering his desk. "I'm trying to arrange marriages or placements for all my girls, but…"

Aern leaned forward. "Don't." He stopped the man's worried words. "I'll see to it if the time comes." He really shouldn't promise something like this, but if it meant taking Kelly home with him… "My brothers will help find them good matches." He got to his feet, Ayden doing the same. "I'll do my best for you. *If* the need arises." With a clasp of hands, Aern went to find his love.

"Kel," Aern tapped lightly at her door, waiting for her to give him leave to enter. "Kelly?" He gently pushed it open, stepping just inside to see her face down across the bed, heaving sobs shaking her slight frame. He carefully set his palm against the small of her back, hoping not to scare her further.

She didn't hear the door open or her name called, but when the hesitant, gentle touch warmed her back, she knew Aern had come to her. She turned, throwing herself into his arms, holding on for dear life. His strong arms came around her, his chin atop her head. Safely cocooned, she breathed in the scent of him, her own arms wrapped just as tightly about him. His was not the scent of ash, of blazing fires; Aern carried the night about him: the cool scent of dew in the air, moonflowers, the damp of the shadows. These were her comfort, the scents that lulled her, gave her peace.

With a heavy sigh, she let go of the fear. Aern was here. He would make things right again. He had come; as if he had heard her heart crying for him, he had come, saving her and her unborn child.

Chapter 66

Theirs was a simple hand-fasting ceremony. A fire red braided rope was twined around their joined hands by her father and his mother. Simple words from her father, binding them together, as the braid was bound, intricately woven. There were no rings, no fancy clothes, no elaborate written agreements, yet the bride beamed in happiness. She could have been in rags, for all Aern cared. He was going to take her home to safety. She'd never be hurt again. Not on his watch.

She was so frail yet, her pale skin made the dark purple shadows under her eyes seem even darker to Aern's worried gaze, but he didn't tell her that.

"I'm sorry," Ayden apologized to Aern, "that it wasn't a wedding fit for a prince." He offered a chagrined look. "This was simple; something the farmers might have done."

"I really don't care, sir." Aern responded with a smile. "I'm a simple man myself. I like the way things are done outside of our pampered lifestyles."

Wariness crept into the Adept's eyes. "She's not used to living other than she has," he warned.

Aern couldn't help a moment of angered irritation. The man had let her sink lower than anyone had a right to. She hadn't been used to abuse; did that mean she should be now? Pushing his anger aside at the thought, he offered a pleasant, if forced smile. "I'm a prince, sir. And a duke. With my own home."

He watched the wince cross Llewellyn's face, knowing he'd struck a small blow. It was expected here that a newly appointed mage wouldn't have his own keep yet, but still… Aern was very proud of how hard he had worked at renovating Aurora. It was defensible now, and she wouldn't be lacking for amenities. He'd be sure of that. "I'll keep her in fine clothes, sir." He offered with a slightly more friendly tone. "And if I may, I'd like her to bring one of her sisters along; for company. And I'll see about arranging a marriage for whichever one as well."

That seemed to be the appropriate way to allay the near insult about the home. Llewellyn was more than happy to let Kelly choose one of the girls to go with. Then it was just a matter of getting things packed and the girls saying goodbye.

The next morning, Kelly and Chirrit eyed each other warily outside the stables. Samantha, Kelly's youngest sister, was just as nervous, but stayed quietly focused on readying her own gear. The servants had done all the packing, but fussing was a good excuse to stay far from the anxious gryphon. At least she wouldn't have to ride on it, like Kelly intended.

Aern stretched a foot forward to lightly tap Chirrit's front leg. In response, she lay down. He tapped a wing; she spread it up and away from them. With a smile, he turned to Kelly, setting hands lightly at her waist. "Ready?"

She shook her head no. "Yes."

With a laugh, he lifted her easily to Chirrit's back, then mounted up behind her, a strong solid arm about Kelly's waist.

With Samantha's horse a few paces behind them, Chirrit's wings folded back warm and comforting over their legs as she led them out and away from the Hakon holdings.

He pressed hard that first day, despite the girls' complaints. He wanted through the mountain pass before dark, knowing the dangers that could lurk there. Wild creatures, probably rogue Jakhil, and possibly even Kinthris, if the fear from the girls became to strong.

The sun was long gone by the time they made it down into the foothills. Both women were exhausted and Samantha's horse looked ready to drop. Aern's nerves were frayed from watching not only for potential danger, but from making sure Samantha didn't take a wrong path with her horse. Chirrit was irritated from the required grounding, with only brief forays into the air when Aern had the girls ride together. It was with relief they all dismounted.

Aern set up a makeshift camp, then walked a small distance away to give them both some small measure of privacy. By the time he came back, Kelly was sitting next to where Samantha was already sound asleep. She smiled to Aern, rising to come to his arms.

In all the years of visiting, they had only ever touched the day he had stopped Bricriu. He had held her to calm her fears, and then turned her over to the care of her maid. The touch had been necessary, but didn't really count to either of them. Neither did the brief hold the morning after Bricriu's death, when she had found out she would go with Aern.

For the first time, they were alone, and together. They folded into each other's arms as if they had done it a hundred times, a soft slide of touches bringing them chest to chest with no awkwardness, their arms encircling each other, warm hands touching each other's backs. Despite the grime and the dirt from the day, they held each other, inhaling the scent of each other, and knew they were home.

This was what the promise of forever was supposed to feel like; safe, warm, and held close. With no other contact for the entire trip, this was the one thing they came to count on. Simply sitting before the fire, held in each other's arms, they were home.

Chapter 67

Kelly shivered before the night's fire, wrapping her arms about herself. Sitting this close, she should have been quite warm, but there was so much that had happened in the last while, the shock kept her feeling cold inside. She watched Aern moving about the camp, making sure things were safe, knowing, without knowing how, that Aern would keep her safe.

He smiled over at her as he finished his check of the perimeter. It was harder to watch over three than just him, but he didn't really mind. Neither had been too much trouble, despite the stress and trauma the trip surely caused on them. He frowned as he noticed Kelly's shivering, scooping up his cloak from his bedroll as he crossed to her. "Here," he offered softly, settling it around her.

As he leaned down over her, the amulet about his neck slipped loose of his tunic, flashing in the firelight as it swung brightly against the dark gray of his clothing. Kelly's eyes widened as she stared at it. Hesitantly, she reached up to cup the small disc in one hand. "This…" Her eyes went to his in wonderment. "How did you know?" Confusion in his look was enough for her to continue. "I have that mark." Her other hand came up to trace over the image. "The same sword; the same wings. It should have been something fire related, something related to what Bricriu was. But it wasn't. I asked the Lights to help me; I guess I finally found the right words. It showed up that next morning." Tears sparkled in her eyes. "He saw it on my hip… I… He would have killed me that day."

"Shh," he offered, dropping to sit beside her, pulling her into his arms. "He couldn't kill you." He smiled against her hair, his voice soft and soothing. "I knew. I knew you were in danger. I came, didn't I? You're safe now."

"Aern?" Her voice was soft, hesitant in a way he wasn't used to. From the circle of his arms, she looked up at him, watching his expression. "It wasn't just me you saved." She let one hand slip down over her stomach, her eyes following her hand for a moment before looking back up at him with a nervous smile.

"You're…?" He moved one hand to cover hers. He smiled at her hesitant nod. He could see she was terrified of what he'd think. She thought he would be angry she carried another's child.

He was angry, but not for the reason she would be thinking. He had seen what Bricriu had been doing to her, how beaten she'd been. Even now, she carried the bruises from that day. He was furious that Bricriu had to have known and had intentionally tried to destroy Kelly *and* their baby.

It took everything in him to quell that anger enough to give her an honestly happy smile. "Kel… I can't ever sire children." He couldn't quite keep the wonder out of his voice. "You have no idea what this means to me. A family. Of our own."

* * *

Weeks passed. Samantha grew grumpy. Aern understood;

this would have been a few hours by air. He'd had to do this trip once before, with his mother; it hadn't gotten any better.

At least he was used to camping and harsh conditions. Samantha had never been outside the walls of her father's home. She tried starting arguments at times by sniping about the weather, their travelling, or, Lights help her! about the baby Kelly carried. She seemed to enjoy trying to rile them up with thoughts on what would happen if the baby were a boy.

A girl would be forgotten in moments. But a boy; a boy would be watched closely to see if the Mage Gift appeared. If it did, the child would be called back to the Hakon.

Aern did his best to calm Kelly that he wouldn't let it happen. He was pretty sure he would have the backing of his family, but then again… he didn't tell her that there was a small chance Sterling would ask them to send the child, just to keep peace between the lands. Better to just keep that little piece of information quiet for now. She was already worried.

And her sister… Aern sighed. It was hard enough to be getting used to Kelly with him. Samantha's sarcasm drove him crazy at times.

"She's just scared," Kelly would apologize. "She's never been away from home before. And here I'm taking her to a whole new land." She squeezed Aern's hand, leaning against his shoulder. "She'll adjust though." She smiled up at him warmly, content to merely be with Aern anywhere. "She just needs to know you like I do."

* * *

Neither was used to roughing it, so when Aurora finally came into view, it seemed even more stunning than the small manor should have. Both women were delighted with the simple furnishings, with the rugs and tapestries. They loved the lands with the bright colors, so at odds with their homeland where there were mostly only tall pine trees.

But even better, the staff loved the two women. Where they were still wary of Aern's stand-offish ways, they warmed to the women right away. They loved having a woman to cheer the place and share her passionate joy. Within days, Kelly had taken complete charge of the manor and the servants.

Samantha settled into being a teenage girl, interested in finding out about those living nearby and fussing over her appearance. Aern found he liked her a lot better than he thought he would. She had the same strange illogical arguments Kelly had, making him laugh when he least expected it.

The one thing Aern found most amazing though, was the ease in which he adjusted to life at the manor. He wasn't taking assignments anymore, instead focusing entirely on the training of the guards. He loved the work, but it was the coming home every night that he looked forward to. Knowing that Kelly would be there, that she would have the servants happily harried into doing some odd project, that she smiled again, that she lit up with enthusiasm when he appeared.

No one had ever done that for him. And slowly, as the weeks and months started to creep by, he realized that it wasn't the manor that was home. It was her. Kelly had managed to do what no other woman had; she had made him into a friend, and she had given him a home.

EPILOGUE

Exhausted, Kelly fell back into her pillows. With a tender touch, Aern brushed damp hair from her face.

"A daughter," she whispered in relief. "Praise be, a girl." In relief, she drifted off to sleep.

Only then, after looking to where Chirrit danced on the balcony, did Aern go to the bassinet, lifting the tiny babe free of the blankets. Not his daughter by blood, but the most treasured gift his wife could have given him. He ran a battle-scarred finger across her tiny palm as she reflexively closed around it.

Overwhelmed, he held her close as tears ran unchecked, quiet sobs shaking his shoulders. His wife had survived this nerve-wracking ordeal and given him this beautiful little girl. He was a father; the one thing he had never thought to be.

For years he had been told that the toxins he had filled his body with would take away any chance to sire a child. But, thanks to a horrid man, he had this child.

Other toxins had nearly destroyed Kelly, but that too was past. Doran MacFurgal, the only one remaining of that line, waited patiently for word of the child's gender. The midwife let him in as she left.

"I'm sorry," he offered to Aern. "For everything. I never knew…"

Aern stopped him. "Don't. We've got nothing to worry over now. It's a girl…"

"And my brother is gone." Doran gave a small smile. There was no malice or anger to his tone, just an expression of wishing things could have been different. He inclined his head to Aern in respect. "I'll let Adept Llewellyn know it's a granddaughter. And prince…Our mother's name was Tiffany," he offered as a parting gift before leaving to take the news back to the Keltori.

Well then. Tiffany would want for nothing. He vowed in that moment that she would be spoiled, given everything and every advantage at his disposal. Placing her back in the bassinet, tucking blankets warmly about her, he stepped out onto the balcony. Leaning against Chirrit, his oldest friend, as she curled a wing around him, he looked to the early dawn sky, whispering a thank you to Lady Luck. This was his life; it had been his choice. Dawn had come, as he'd told himself so many times it would. With a safe position as Captain of the Guard, a wife, and now a child; his life was complete. "May yours," he whispered to Luck, and to Hope, wherever they were, "be as happy as mine has been made."

Appendix

Bradley Family (in order of birth)

King Grey Bradley was with, in order, a sprite, a fae, and an elf before finally marrying Cassidy Atheron, the one the Lights had ordained for him. Between his and Cassidy's, there were a total of fifteen children.

- Crystal and Mist Bradley – half water sprite twins, daughters of Reflection and Grey. Crystal has need of being around water, yet lives indoors. Mist is one of the Wild Ones, preferring to live in nature. Very different with little connection between them.
- Rhys– half fae, son of Kembrelei and Grey. Lives in the fae lands of Wisteria with his mother.
- Keno and Dylan Cairne – half immortal twins, sons of Bryan Cairne and Cassidy.
- Melantha and Nairne Bradley – half Jakhil twins, daughters of Tawnadea and Grey. Tight bonded connection.
- Kyle Erickson – human son of Blaine Erickson and Cassidy. Kind and friendly, he loses his older half-brother Adam Erickson (human son of Blaine Erickson and K'Tira) during the war.
- Emerald, Amethyst, Diamond, Sapphire Bradley – half Jakhil quadruplets, daughters of Tawnadea and Grey.
- Sterling and Silver – full human twins, sons of Cassidy and Grey. The "heir and the spare" to the throne. Silver was sent to the Sithari elves to train in diplomacy, where he met his best friend Gavriel.
- Aern Bradley – the "baby" of the family. Trained in Pathicos to be an assassin.
- Jays was a fosterling of the Bradley family for some time, but is

not one of them.

Duke Gunner Bradley

Grey's twin brother, older by a few minutes. He was more of a realist to Grey's dreaming big. He married Beth when her daughter Talia was still an infant. Together they had one son.

- Brett Bradley – Aern's cousin. Son of Gunner and Beth Bradley. Preferring physical work over court duties, he was one of the lead men in the palace armaments.
- Talia Bradley – Aern's cousin. Daughter of Beth Bradley. Was elevated to Immortal status as the aspect of Hope. Aern never found out how that worked.

Mages

Located in Hakon, north of Drikelldorn past a dangerous mountain range. Mages rarely provide or use their first names, as names have power.

- Keltori Council: Group of well-established mages who have reached Adept level of skill that operate as the "government" of their lands. Established by The Phelan, with 5 members, each representing an element.
- The Phelan: Leader of the Keltori. Earth Mage. He believed that might wasn't always right, that justice could be found through a trial by the Adepts that sat on the council, thus providing a peace the northern lands had never seen before.
- Trevor Phelan: Younger brother of The Phelan. Earth Mage.
- Aiden Llewellyn: Fire Mage, Adept on the Keltori. Father of one son and fourteen daughters, including Kelly. Gets stuck with Bricriu.

- Bricriu MacFurgal: fire apprentice that saw his parents destroyed for treason. He developed a hatred for the Keltori. His brother Doran was older and saw the truth, choosing to study with the mages of the Keltori.
- Remington: rogue mage that wanted pre-Keltori ways re-established. Encouraged Bricriu's hatred.
- Goldwin: Air Mage, Adept on the Keltori. Knew the importance of getting fire mages trained as they usually burn out. Took on the training Bricriu
- Beagan: Spirit Mage, Adept on the Keltori.
- Shanahan: Water Mage, Adept on the Keltori.

Theology

Deity presents as the Aurora Borealis, only appearing rarely, such as events that will have major impact in some way down the road (like blessing Sterling's wedding). They are more of a watcher than an active part of the world. Instead, general guidance is provided by a team of Immortals, some of which are introduced in this book. The mages each seem tied to the Elemental Immortals, but there are many others. Those mentioned are below:

- **Hope**: Talia Bradley. Assumed the mantle as a teenager.
- **Luck**: Not introduced by name, other than to say it is a woman. An unreliable aspect that works by her own whims, usually to the benefit of others.
- **Fire**: Roan. Kelly calls her under the guise of Love, one of the aspects of fire.
- **Earth**: Bryan Cairne. Father of Dylan and Keno Cairne. He is the twin brother of Air, who is not introduced at this time.

- **Kinthris**: While not described, this creature of nightmare is long of limb and very thin. It feeds off negative emotions such as fear, jealousy and hatred. It is very active in the world and moves where it wishes. Small children are threatened with this to make them behave.

Races

- **Humans**: Until Drikelldorn was settled in the center of the continent, most were smaller groups that stayed nearer shorelines.
- **Elves**: Hair, eyes and personalities specific to each group
    - **Jakhil**: Most muscular builds of the elven races. Darker hair and eyes, skin-tones more golden or sun-bronzed, suiting the more desert-like terrain they live in. They tend to dislike other humanoid races, prone to either attacking or infiltrating to destroy. Due to their long lifespans, they have no problem with plans that can sometimes take years.
        - Tawnadea is half human. Red hair, green eyes.
    - **Sithari**: Taller with lean, well-toned bodies. Pale skin and hair that is either more silver-blond or sunlight-blond. They live in white stone cities near the eastern shores with pale to white sands. They favor the arts of all kinds, including the **Ansavru** (ahn-sha-VROO), their "dance of death."
    - **Longredal:** Forest dwelling elves that hold to their privacy very tightly. Unlike the other two, these prefer minimal clothes and simplistic lives. They are most

likely to kill outsiders before asking questions.

- **Fae**: Living in the central south of the continent, their wooded areas are hard to enter. Even if access is granted, finding them is nearly impossible unless they wish it. They range in height from five to six feet. Part energy, their true forms and colors are hard to determine as they adapt to either their surroundings or their whims. Many have wings ranging from butterfly appearance to crystalline clear membranes.
    - Kembrelei is a full fae, enamored of Grey for a time.
        - Son Rhys fought in the war with the Bradleys.
- **Elementals**: Living in nature, they inhabit all areas and have a wide variety.
    - **Sprites**: Tend to be associated with lakes, rivers and ponds. Greenish skin, delicate features, never taller than 5 ½ feet.
        - Reflection is a full water sprite that could not stand being away from the water, even choosing to leave her twin daughters behind to return to it.

Rulers

Lord Hennin – Ruler of Pathicos

- Lord Morenden works for him

Adept Phelan – Ruler of Hakon

- Leads the Keltori. The keltorin is a collective of all full ranked mages. The Keltori is comprised of the best Adepts in each element.

King Grey Bradley – Ruler of Drikelldorn

- Appointed by The Lights

Made in the USA
Columbia, SC
23 September 2019